ADAM IN TAOLAND

Dreaming Dreams I

Jack Tymann

&

Ayesha Abdul Ghaffar

Copyright © 2022 Jack Tymann

All rights reserved. This book or any portion thereof may not be reproduced or used in any manner whatsoever without the express written permission of the publisher except for the use of brief quotations in a book review.

To my Luciana – you are the love of my life, my best friend, my soulmate forever.

To my children and grandchildren – I love you. You make my life complete.

To the Angels who enter my life when least expected – you are my blessings.

To my writing coaches, editors, and beta readers – thank you for bringing "Adam" to life.

May each of you dream dreams that never were – and then make them happen.

CHAPTER 1

GRADUATION DAY: MOLEG UNIVERSITY, 3266

Novana – where advanced robots provided for every material need.
But where their accommodations had horrific consequences.
In Novana, our souls lacked basic sustenance.
There was no gratitude – only entitlement and enslavement.
There was no joy.
No shame meant no pride.
There was no hatred, which sadly meant no love.
No one strived to succeed.
Human emotions had ceased to exist – except in my case, despair.
Unlike other Novanians I felt something, if only profound emptiness.

A sea of emotionless faces stared at the Plakerol mindlessly calling out names. They could have at least summoned a Grand Master to Moleg to grant us our diplomas – the single greatest achievement of our numbed existences in Novana. The ritual of it all was ironic – programmed bots announcing the achievements of their enslaved humans.

"Adam 35110432460645. Graduating with Top Honors in Pseudo Thought Creation," creaked the officiating Plakerol. I fell into the actions expected of me. Standing up in one rigid motion, my arms tight by my side, face blank, I marched to the stage as my fellow students had done. I couldn't look into the eyes of the doltish blob who presented my certificate because it didn't have eyes. Plakerol faces were like fluid crystal gyroscopes, constantly shifting as if trying to jumble some sense of expression.

As I accepted my honors, a deep yearning grew within me, a hunger for something more – perhaps a simple 'congratulations'. But that was impossible from a soulless machine. I returned to my place in the auditorium and glared at my pointless diploma. Behind it rested another piece of paper that I shifted to the front as I sat. It was my job assignment. Everyone was given a job when they graduated from Moleg, but it was never related to their studies. The Plakerols needed slaves not thinkers. The document stated I was being commissioned to duty at a security outpost near Novana's southern border.

At that moment something inside me cracked.

How dare these witless clots do this to me?

Do I matter? Or am I just matter?

Vomit rose in my throat as I anticipated my likely lifetime assignment, alone, at some desolate fortress – where I would use nothing of what I'd studied at Moleg. I needed to escape – or perhaps end it all. So, I ran. I darted out from the Graduation Hall – with no destination in mind – except anyplace other than the Sentry Post I was directed to command. I tore across the university's cheerless gray lawn, leapt over a fence, and thundered into a darkened woodland – where I released a primal emotion-filled scream.

If I took up residence at my Sentry Post, I knew I'd be provided for. Plakerols would deliver my food, all gray and tasteless. They would provide the water I would drink. I would avoid the wine they offered, believing it to be laced with mind-numbing drugs. Plakerols would provide my clothing, gray and shapeless, like every human wore. They even showered and brushed the teeth of some Novanians, but I resisted that. I wondered why the Plakerols made human life so effortless. I concluded caring for us was their sole mission, even if that meant our enslavement. After all, these machines could not possibly be concerned that slavery always destroys human purpose.

Sitting on a slab of stone in that bleak forest, I decided I would never surrender my life to them. Unlike my fellow students, my miracle had made me different. A decade ago, when I was only ten, Adriella had arrived, sent by a higher power to save me from nothingness. She appeared as a face inside a three-inch glowing translucent sphere. Silver hair flowed from her circular head framing her rosy countenance. Her emotion-filled eyes immediately became a window into my soul. She showed no other features other than two dots that looked like tiny nostrils and a slit for a mouth, arched slightly upward as if starting a grin.

That day Adriella planted in my chest a glowing seed that she called the *Key to the Wind* – a guide to human knowledge accumulated over the past 10,000 years. The *Key* provided awareness to countless past realities that were hidden from other Novanians. Reading and watching recordings over Novananet via the *Key*, I discovered countless masterpieces of ancient literature, music, film, and art – compilations of holographic printed, audio and video messages. I learned about love and grief, triumph and defeat, loss, pain, and pleasure – about emotions and how humans once expressed them – about human achievements and human failings.

After that first day Adriella appeared sporadically. But not yet on Graduation Day.

Where are you today, Adriella? I need you!

We never communicated in words but in thoughts exchanged telepathically. She let me know I must keep the *Key* a secret. She informed me that no other being on the planet of Talus could see her, nor had any other received the precious gift of all prior human thought and experience.

I rose from my cold frosty seat and meandered aimlessly amongst the trees. I thought about all I had learned afar from the walls of Moleg. In the years before university, using the *Key to the Wind*, I came to understand past cultures. Great artists, writers and film-makers gifted me with lessons, insights, and inspirations. I explored eras when individualism reigned. Of times when one could dream, achieve, and own the fruits of one's labors. I discovered that humans of past millennia had purpose and were self-reliant. I wanted this. I wanted to be liberated from dependency on free stuff from mindless robots – the most insidious form of servitude. Even though I understood that freedom demands responsibility.

I want to dream dreams that never were – and then make them happen.

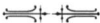

With hopeless thoughts spiraling toward utter rejection, I wandered out of that dreary forest into a clearing, hoping to escape despondency. *Adriella!! Where are you?* An unexpected roar summoned me, but it did not come from Adriella. I turned just as a large pilotless flying machine, a Novadrone, dove and swept me in its claws into the bleak, gray sky. It hoisted me above the southern border, then turned to the west.

Fierce winds of a winter storm thrashed against Novana's Great Barrier, gusting with no result against the gargantuan structure. Towering waves collided violently with rocks and spindly trees at the base of the massive concrete barricade, but they were similarly rejected. Beyond the Barrier, in the skies beyond the Great Canopy that diminished any light above Novana, lightning flashed violently across the heavens, ripping open the firmament above the ocean.

I looked down as the Novadrone approached the Sentry Post. I was at my wit's end, tormented by the idea of a monotonous life as a guard where no enemy would ever appear. It was time to end it all. Using all of my strength, I wrestled free from the Novadrone's grasp and plummeted toward the rocky lands below.

Apparently, my own time for death was not my choice to make. When I fell toward the base of the Sentry Post where I'd been assigned, a huge Plakerol, clearly a Grand Master from posters I'd seen at Moleg, held up its metallic arms to manipulate gravity, and I plopped gently to the earth in front of this creepy machine. It was more humanoid than the other bots, displaying vague facial expressions as it spoke in a tinny voice with a buzz in the background.

"Adam, we need you to accept your assignment. It is critical." Its voice was stern but not angry. Even Grand Masters were void of emotions.

Still on the ground and stunned, I responded, "I can't believe I'm speaking with a Plakerol."

"It is more difficult for me to accept that I am conversing with a human. I have never done so before." The Grand Master's voice seemed to lift as if intrigued.

My inquisitive spirit longed to know more about it. "Do you have a name?"

"You can call me Rossum."

This could not be happening! I was chatting with a nonhuman pile of junk. I scrambled to my feet and dusted off my uniform. "You say my sentry duty is important. That's ridiculous. Nobody will ever penetrate Novana's borders."

"The human race was almost extinguished five hundred years ago by the Great Pandemic that originated elsewhere on Talus. It took the lives of 80 percent of all humans across the entire planet. We need your help in preventing that from ever happening again."

"I know all about the Great Pandemic."

Whoops. I immediately regretted revealing something I should not have known.

What looked like a feeble attempt at shock crossed Rossum's otherwise vacant face. There was suddenly something quite different about him; something almost sentient.

Adriella appeared behind but the Plakerol didn't seem to notice. She flinched, whined, and protested telepathically, urging me to avoid blowing my cover. I was never to expose my access to the *Key*.

Rossum blinked its eyes furiously. "You cannot possibly know about it. If you do, how were you informed?"

I scratched my head and quickly regrouped. "It came to me in a dream. I saw billions of diseased bats leaving their caves, swarming, spreading death in their paths."

Rossum appeared perplexed if a robot could appear so. It was briefly speechless, perhaps processing my assertion.

"What else did you dream about?" it asked.

"I saw humans in hazmat suits everywhere." That wasn't a lie. I did actually see that, not in a dream but over Novananet.

Rossum pressed. "Did you learn the nature of the disease?"

I shuffled my feet and lied. "No. Could you tell me? If I'm to help protect Novana I should know what almost ended human life here."

"We have never spoken to a human about this. But since you display an uncommon inquisitive nature, and you are to assist us, I will instruct you."

"Please do." I spread my arms out, gesturing to the pile of lonesome rocks surrounding the citadel. "There's no other human around I could share the info with anyway."

We moved across a dusty granite surface to the tower entrance where Rossum continued, "It was the deadliest ever strain of what was called the Ebola Virus. It began in 2666. That's when diseased bats fled their caves with EBVID2666. The killer virus spread across Talus. The Pandemic resulted in shortages of everything, the worst deficits being food and drinkable water. Nations decoupled from others. This ultimately led to the Final War of 2724–2734."

The landscape was barren, gray, dismal in every regard. The cheerless tower rose above, eighty feet to the top. To call the scene gloomy would be minimizing the appalling desolation. We stood, not entering the tower.

"So, what happened next, Rossum?"

Rossum's response was without eye contact. But it blinked mechanically with each word. "The Final War wiped out half of the remaining population of Talus. That's when we Plakerols arrived."

"Where did you come from?"

"That is not for you to know." Its stoic rigidity told me it was hiding something. "We were sent to provide much-needed technological miracles to save Novana."

"Sent by who?"

"That is not for you to know."

"Was there anything that survived the Final War here?"

The Plakerol blinked wildly, its brows shifting a bit. Perhaps it was wondering – could it wonder? – if I knew something more than I was telling.

"Novana's computers and AI networks were preserved in hardened sites, most more than 1,000 feet below the surface. We destroyed the Novatrons that Novanians relied on throughout the war."

I was aware of those earlier bots morphed from twenty-second-century mechanical robots. But I kept my silence, feigning interest while remaining emotionless.

"We launched a new Agricultural Revolution. And to protect all from outside invasion we constructed the Great Barrier and the Great Canopy, employing humans for all labor."

This too I knew. I'd studied all I could find about the first seven decades following the War, when the Plakerols ordered human thralls to construct the Great Barrier – the gargantuan wall around the entire 6000-mile perimeter of Novana that prevented access to and from the seas. I'd learned too about the Great Canopy, an arched cloud-like mass – an impenetrable force field that blocked access or escape via the skies. They'd made Novanians construct the very barriers that kept them enslaved.

I pushed harder, asking questions yet unanswered throughout my hours of studies via the *Key*. "What you call employment I call slavery. Surely the surviving humans of Novana did not willingly surrender their freedoms; nor did they knowingly agree to isolation from the rest of the planet."

Rossum bristled, shaking its head back and forth. "Novana's depleted populace fell into complete dependency on us. Everything we did was in their best interests."

"You're making an excuse for destroying human purpose – for sending human individuality and dreams to the dustbins of history."

Of course, a Plakerol couldn't understand human needs and emotions. Yet as Rossum stood to depart, its squeaky voice thickened. "Except for you, Adam. Apparently, you can dream." Rossum actually squirmed. "Stay here and serve what is now your purpose." The machine stood, turning its 'face' from mine, and departed. That was the last I saw of Grand Master Rossum.

As I climbed the tower each step brought ever-darkening thoughts about my plight – the crappy job assigned by the Plakerols. Adriella flittered by my side. Ten feet from the very top, I pushed open a creaky rusted door to a scantily furnished room with a metal bed and blanket, all gray of course. A table with two chairs sat at the center. The rest of the space was barren.

Every night for the next month I tried to avoid sleep, dreading the thought of waking to face nothingness anew. I longed for something, anything, that might provide even a crumb of purpose to my inconsequential existence. I rarely changed or washed the gray pants, shirt, underwear, boots, cap, and coat provided. Why bother?

There was no one with whom I could share what I'd learned via the *Key to the Wind* or commiserate about the complete void in my soul. In my entire life, I'd never had a meaningful conversation with anyone, not a single human being. The unit of people once called family had ceased to exist a half a millennia ago. I had no friends.

I had learned using the *Key* that all new life in Novana was consummated by AI^2 – artificial insemination programmed by artificial intelligence. All actions, including procreation, were overseen by the Plakerols. But Adriella informed me I was different. I was the result of an experiment spawned by outside forces – her 'bosses' she called them. My embryo was created by a special donor sperm from elsewhere in the Universe that penetrated a carefully selected Novanian donor egg. That's why I looked different from the others: a bit taller, with darker skin, finer features, lighter sandy-brown hair, and most notably – awakened green eyes. But I was the only one who seemed to notice the differences.

Here I was, a month after Graduation Day, and a half millennium since dominance by the Plakerols, with a worthless degree presented by one of these obtuse pieces of garbage, and a shitty job. I was condemned forever to the culture our captives had imposed, an empty existence where human interactions were rare, impersonal, non-confrontational, and pointless. I heated some slop for dinner and slumped at my cold metal table.

The knowledge delivered by way of the *Key* bore bitter consequences. I would never use any of what I'd secretly learned. If you don't know what's out there you never yearn for it. I knew I'd never make any dreams come true. A mind exposed to unreachable dreams is a dangerous thing.

The more I learned, the deeper became my despair. I wanted to learn nothing more of the liberty I longed for but could never have. So I stopped using the *Key*. I'd exhausted my curiosity about human knowledge and Adriella knew this. She stopped appearing, as if surrendering to my impending doom. It would be a gross understatement to call my existence in Novana painful and intolerable.

I slapped away the disgusting food, sending it flying across the floor. Then I kicked over the table. Nothingness bore down on me like a drill and I could bear it no longer. I shoved open the exit door nearly tearing it from its rusty hinges and pounded up the steps to the platform encircling the very top of the tower. The wind howled and whipped my hair into my tearing eyes, further infuriating me.

CHAPTER 2

AN INVITATION

Alone atop the tower, I swallowed a silent scream. Escape was the only option, but I had no idea where to go or how to get there. Living each tomorrow was the worst of all tortures, being aware that I would hate not only that day but every second of every minute of the rest of my life. With no way to extricate myself, I had lost all will to live.

The bitter-cold, salty air attacked my face and lips without mercy. With numbed gloveless hands I gripped the top of the metal railing and raised my leg to climb over, fixated on the menacing rocks looming eighty feet below.

It's time to end this.

Then, just as I surrendered myself to leap, a blazing light pierced the shadowy sky, interrupting my plan. A huge scintillating cloud slowly descended – constantly changing shape – its dazzling glow forcing my mouth and eyes wide open. The diaphanous mass paused but continued altering form – above the plateau on which my fortress stood.

The strange formation in the sky called to something deep within, causing me to reflect on how I got to this place and why I found myself in such utter despair. Shaking with uncertainty, I withdrew my leg from the railing. For the second time in a month, my attempt to end my life was disrupted – this time by the pendulous form that resumed its slow descent from above. I stiffened in place as the huge mass came to rest vertically but continued swirling – a hundred yards from my fortress. My death mission averted, at least temporarily, I stumbled down the dark spiraling stairs and moved cautiously onto the naked plateau. The night air ripped through me.

My heart pounded as if it might explode. I crept to a spot some forty feet from where the massive gossamer substance bounced ever so gently on the bleak mesa. The form bobbed up and down like a buoy on calm seas, a weightless jelly. My body froze in alarm.

Am I dead? Did I actually jump?

A deafening silence filled the air. The proportions of the cloud were constantly shifting, wider than my fixed field of view and rising at least twice as high as the tower I'd just left. Its glowing interior pulsated mysteriously and emitted a strange humming noise. Subtle bluish and silver tints flared across its surface, yet it remained translucent. I was able to see through it to observe stars I'd never seen – way out over the sea beyond the coastline.

Radiant light from the ever-changing accumulation revealed the landscape I'd come to hate, a desolate place with granular gray soil void of vegetation. Then, unexpectedly, a wave of whispering warmth pushed away the icy evening air, caressed my face, warmed my hands, and calmed my trembling body – a comforting vibe at a time of despair.

I spun in stunned disbelief and looked straight up into the heavens. The entry hole where the strange cloud had punched through Novana's impenetrable Great Canopy was expanding in an oval shape, pushing away the gray artificial curtain above the land. The breach grew to half the visible sky, unveiling celestial bodies not seen since Novana's umbrella was completed. Mystical music broke the stillness, evoking peace as soothing tones from the cloud spoke in harmony with the Universe.

I marveled at countless intertwined solar systems and masses of ionized gasses lighting the otherwise blackness of the Ahmetus Galaxy. Endless flurries of stars blended with enormous nebulae of snow-like swirls featuring twirling hues of colors. I'd witnessed similar panoramas over *Novananet*, but never dreamt of seeing such beauty for real.

My gaze returned to the surface and I dared to take a few steps closer. The slowly increasing brilliance of the pulsating, translucent form illuminated a section of Novana's Great Barrier, the gargantuan bastion now visible a half mile away at the ocean's edge. A new relaxing tone, complementing the mellow music, called my attention toward the center of the strange mass.

An ethereal, winged figure appeared, exiting the remarkable cloud some twenty feet up in the air. Floating, she waved her right arm, and the entire area erupted in unimaginable splendor. An unending meadow of fresh green grasses and a startling sea of sweet-smelling flowers burst onto the scene. Unfamiliar bushes paraded full blossoms of many colors, though winter was not yet ebbing. The temperature rose to a comfortable level and the scent of vanilla wrapped me in warmth.

I couldn't imagine who she was or where she'd come from. She was clearly not human, but she was not one of the Plakerols. She drifted down to the earth.

Her lithe body was wrapped in a golden neck-to-toe body suit. Pure white feathered wings rested gently upon the back of her shoulders. A physical force touched me when her oversized eyes fixated on my own. A sublime sensation cradled my entire body. She moved toward me slowly, stopping several times to gather flora in her path. She stopped about ten feet away. In a soft voice, fitting her uncommon beauty, she introduced herself.

"Greetings, Adam. I am Malaika."

I looked into her eyes and saw infinity, the vast knowledge of space and things that I couldn't even begin to imagine, let alone understand. The pleasant breeze lifted her golden hair revealing long slender ears disproportionally large for her exotic face. Her six-foot height matched my own. Awestruck and frightened, I somehow found words to respond, "H-how do you know my n-name?"

As I welcomed the magical emergence of springtime in the middle of winter colorful insects I'd never seen darted about, each bearing four gold-and-black striped wings with brilliant blue dots – adding to the moment's ecstasy.

"Oh, I know far more than your name, Adam." She stopped several yards away. Her honey-colored countenance, a shade or two lighter than mine, featured nostrils but no nose and puffy pink lips.

She was surely not from this world. Yet, she spoke my language.

I backed off. "What is that blob you just emerged from?"

"Please do not refer to *Wanderer* as a blob. It is the Fifth Dimension, a force of renewal which I pray you will enter with me."

"It's not a spaceship?"

"No, it's a dimension beyond the physics you understand. A dimension where magic replaces scientific realities. Where facts give way to fantasy. A place where space, time, velocity, and distance no longer matter."

Blown away by her curious response, I simplified my next question. "Where have you come from? And why?"

She took another step closer, forcing me to retreat a bit. "Never mind where I come from. I am here to offer you a game-changing proposition, a life-altering idea."

A different life? Hardly possible. The Plakerols totally controlled the game here, including every aspect of my life. There would be no life-changing option in this dull, demoralizing place where human existence was purposeless.

She blinked. "Are you interested?"

Everything within me screamed 'beware.' She didn't even know me. She'd arrived uninvited and interrupted my plan to end it all, and now she was offering me a different life. If that were even possible, I thought she must have some motive – probably evil.

I hid my suspicions by gazing directly into her emerald-green eyes. "What makes you think I'm looking for a different life?"

A puff of air brushed my face when Adriella issued a startling squeal and soared toward Malaika. This stranger from above swept my friend up in cupped hands and pressed Adriella's orb to her cheek. *Apparently they're acquainted.* I'd never heard a sound from Adriella before, but I swore she was giggling.

Malaika released Adriella to dart off and enter *Wanderer*. She then returned her attention to me, displaying a knowing grin. "Oh, please, Adam. We both know you want out of Novana. I am here to help you discover a new life."

I'm certainly done with the old one. "How can you know what I want in my life?"

"Well, you were about to end it before my arrival."

"You've taken Adriella."

"She's traveling with us."

I scratched my head. "How come you speak my language?"

"I speak the language of the Universe, as will you, if you travel with me."

None of this made any sense. This had to be an absurd dream. I stiffened when she took yet another few steps toward me, invading my space.

What could she possibly gain by giving me a new life?

"Shall I share my idea, Adam?

Attempting to resist her magic, I shoved my hands into my pockets, shuffled my feet, and looked away, shrugging to fake aloofness. "Malaika, I'm not the slightest bit interested – but I'll humor you. What's your offer?"

She opened her wings ever so slowly. "Pretty simple. Enter the Fifth Dimension that is *Wanderer* and travel with me to Taoland."

"What's in it for you?"

"For me? Rescuing others is my calling. It is what I do, and I love it. There is no greater reward than the satisfaction of helping others." Joy spilled from her eyes.

Too good to be true means probably not true. "You're suggesting I cross over with you into some unknown dimension and travel to some unknown world. You must be joking."

"No joke, Adam. Just a simple invitation for a once-in-a-lifetime opportunity." She motioned toward the heavens.

I threw my hands into the air. Raising my voice in frustration, I said, "I have no idea who you are. We met only a moment ago. I'm quite sure you're not human. I've never heard of Taoland. And you . . . you call your idea a simple invitation?"

A mysterious grin spread across her pretty face. "Yes. Pretty straightforward."

Absurd. I focused on the beautiful scenery to avoid her eyes. "Are you bonkers? I've got a new job here. And no problems."

She is evil – masquerading as an ethereal, magical, and utterly beautiful being.

She took a few more steps, and again slowly pulsed her wings open and close, recapturing my attention. "No problems? Is that why you were about to leap to your death?"

Her wings now fluttered, stirring up luscious scents from the strange flowering trees and bushes. Additional colorful insects darted back and forth, making enjoyable buzzing sounds. Small unfamiliar animals scampered about. The scene and her presence were pleasantly intoxicating.

"Malaika, I'm clueless to whatever it is you're talking about." I crossed my arms and tried to ignore the scene, her alluring presence, and whatever strange force kept drawing me toward her and the blob.

"I am offering you a chance to discover who you are and what you are looking for."

In mock outrage I again raised my voice. "I know exactly who I am. And I don't need advice from some nonhuman from who knows where."

She stared, this time more intensely, and squinted. "If you decide to remain alive, will you be content in solitude at this remote outpost?"

"Maybe." *Of course not.*

"Did you go to school to learn some specific skills to secure your job here?"

I hated sarcasm. I pushed back. "For your info, I recently graduated at the top of my class from Moleg University, with an advanced degree in Pseudo Thought Creation. I seriously doubt you know the first thing about that."

"How impressive, Adam." She fluttered her eyelashes.

More sarcasm. This time she raised her wings skyward. They were more than half her height. In freshly green treetops, songbirds danced, their melodies filling the air in perfect harmony with the mellifluous sounds from *Wanderer*.

None of this makes any sense.

"And your reward is assignment to senseless guard duty, without any human contact? Kind of bizarre."

The truth hurt. I had to deflect it. I pointed to *Wanderer*. "More bizarre would be for me to enter whatever it is that transported you here."

"Where is your trust? Your sense of adventure?" All nature around us responded to her slightest movement, continuing to explode with new life. Countless colorful trees, bushes, and flowers burgeoned everywhere, bending in the gentle breeze.

"Trust? Why would I trust you, a complete stranger? And I don't need any adventure. I've got all I need here." I gestured to my desolate tower. "I can do my work without breaking a sweat. You want me to surrender this – to head off to where?"

Malaika pressed her hands to her cheeks. "Adam, again, please do not insult me by suggesting your existence here is OK with you."

I bent down to brush some flower dust off my right shoe, hoping this might somehow extract me from an uncomfortable conversation – and help me avoid sharing with her the truth of my pointless existence. "It's not perfect. But I'm safe here."

"Safe? Then why were you about to leap to your death before I arrived?"

Now she's really annoying me. I turned and stepped toward the tower, thinking I might finalize the act of desperation I'd started before Malaika invaded my privacy.

She asked from behind me, "Do you have a lover stashed up there?"

Lover? There was no female friend or any human at this outpost, or anywhere in this dismal land. I ignored her query.

She continued to badger, "Please, Adam. Let me in on your secret. What have you been doing atop your grotesque citadel?"

Shut up! Damn it.

I turned to her. Instead of simply saying: 'nothing,' I smirked and fabricated a purpose. "I wait."

"You wait? For what or for whom?"

"For unexpected and unwanted visitors." I crossed my arms and bore my eyes into her own.

She arched her brows, scowling. I suspected in jest. "Like me?"

"Well, I wasn't expecting you and *Wanderer.*" I grinned. "But I didn't say you're not wanted."

She chuckled teasingly. "Now I am finally sensing some love here."

"I also read atop my tower."

"I know you read."

"How do you know?"

"Adriella is part of my team. Via the *Key to the Wind* we have exposed you to countless books and 'stories' and the history that preceded your current nightmarish existence."

"Adriella?" On discovering Malaika's role in my one saving light, I looked at her differently. "Thank you."

"You must have yearned to live one of those stories. To live like they did and experience the adventures found in ancient writings."

"Many times." *Who wouldn't want such a life, something meaningful and adventurous?*

"Why?" She continued to engage while a gorgeous butterfly flapped its wings against her delicate fingers.

"Because my life here is without purpose. I'd love to do something, anything, that matters." I released a tear that reflected the total void in my existence.

"What if you could live such a life? Just as the butterfly emerges from darkness, you can also. What if I could take you to a place where that is possible."

"It's not possible." I hung my head and looked away.

"I want to take you to where you can write your own story."

"Write my own story?"

"Yes. Because without it you do not exist. I want you to travel with me to Taoland, where you can dream dreams that never were and then make them happen."

The weight of her words crashed into me. Before I could respond, she changed the subject. "How old are you?"

She must have surely known the answer and only asked to set up a follow-on query.

"I . . . just turned twenty."

"Will you sit up there in that citadel until you are thirty? Or older? Until it is too late to try something utterly amazing? You must know your life will only waste away here."

I was tempted to admit she was right, but I was too scared and reluctant to yield, so I feigned outrage. "Listen, Malaika. You've told me absolutely nothing about this place Taoland. It would be absurd for me to surrender my security without any knowledge of where you might take me. Give me one good reason why I should take the risk?"

"Why? You have absolutely nothing to lose. And I say lots to gain."

I turned away from her infectious smile. "Can you please tell me something about Taoland. Where is it? What is it like there?"

"I will not tell you anything about Taoland. It must be experienced. But it is a safe bet your life there would be more fulfilling than what you are facing here."

This was beyond ridiculous! But I couldn't deny her suggestion. I had no dreams, no refuge, no aspirations. I was condemned to utter insignificance. In all but the physical sense, except for my reading projects, I was dead. But I was safe here and couldn't risk my security. Then again, I'd been seconds away from ending it all when *Wanderer* arrived. Taoland could not possibly be worse than Novana. I was torn between risking Malaika taking my life or ending it myself.

"I still don't understand your game."

She rolled her eyes. "Please do not call what I do a game. As I have said, I am simply here to guide you, if you will but trust me."

The risk of entering the Fifth Dimension was overwhelming. Yet, without a clue as to what I might find in Taoland, or if I'd ever arrive there, I still couldn't come up with a single reason to stay in Novana. *I'm so confused.*

"Part of me wants to trust you, to enter *Wanderer* and never look back. Another part of me wants to stay here in my comfort zone. All I know is here in Novana – miserable as this place is. I don't have a clue about life in Taoland – and I'm terrified by you and your offer."

She tilted her head. "You are not frightened by me or *Wanderer*. You are terrified not by concerns about Taoland – but by what you know about Novana. The notion of eternal nothingness petrifies you. That is why you were preparing to leap to your death."

The reality of her words struck home. *She knows exactly how I feel, even if I don't.*

She again approached. Her delightful fragrance filled the now tiny space between us. "Come with me, Adam. I promise you a journey of discovery not remotely possible here. The *Spring of Truth*, flowing from *Wanderer*, will scatter the darkness of your servitude with a light unknown in Novana."

She pointed to *Wanderer* and continued, "A new dimension is open, like a door to the future, for you alone. Why not enter? Doors open all too infrequently. And doors close all too quickly."

Startled by a low-pitched hum, reminiscent of a harpsichord's pleasant tones, I turned to discover a brilliant white horse-like creature standing at the edge of a newly created lavender woodland. A long, multicolored spiraling horn rose proudly from its forehead. I gasped.

"Malaika . . . is t-t-that a unicorn?" Recordings of ancient mythologies reported of their magical gifts, told that sightings were rare, and some argued against their existence.

She replied, "It's a qilin."

"A qilin? Is it real?"

She waved at the animal, and it bowed. "Well, neither of us is hallucinating, so yes, it is real. Qilins always signify amazing adventures ahead. Without fail, sightings bring good luck."

The qilin reared, locked eyes with me, and boomed, "Do it, Adam." Then it disappeared.

As I reeled from the shock of not only seeing the creature, but hearing it speak, Malaika continued, "A future in Taoland may raise doubts and pose new risks. But, Adam, you know with absolute certainty what staying here means – either death at your own hand or long joyless years of life without meaning."

The oscillating light, the intoxicating music, the soothing purring from *Wanderer* and the qilin – it all elicited a complex mixture of hope and doubt.

Can there be something marvelous out there – beyond my fears?
Or is she trying to abduct me with evil motives?
Does it really matter?

CHAPTER 3

INTO OUTER SPACE

I froze when Malaika turned toward *Wanderer*, gathering more seeds, blossoms, and stems from flowers and bushes. She stopped and gestured, offering me samples of unfamiliar aromatic herbs. I approached to accept.

Delish! How have I missed these all these years?

"Malaika, why are you collecting these things? You must have brought them here. They're not from Novana."

"Adam, these are from Novana. Sometimes seeds, like ideas, are buried or otherwise hidden from view. I will share them with the people of Taoland."

When she turned again toward the Fifth Dimension, fear consumed me anew. I had to decide. Would I go with her or say goodbye? Should I choose death here, or death at her hands? I'd never made a real choice before. My instinct to flee was overwhelming.

"Are you coming, Adam?"

I dragged my trembling fingers through my hair. "Sorry. I can't enter *Wanderer*."

She stopped moving forward. In a firm voice, she spoke. "I believe you mean *won't*. Thus it is perhaps best that you return to your fortress."

I wanted her to force me into *Wanderer*, to make this decision for me. I looked into her expressionless eyes and pleaded, "Aren't you going to try to convince me?"

"Adam, I only advise. I do not cajole, nor make your decisions. But I will ask one final question. What are you really afraid of?"

I laid out the truth. "Putting my life in your hands."

"You told me your life is meaningless."

"Yes . . . b-but . . . I still can't grasp why you're here."

She offered no response but moved again toward the Fifth Dimension. Of course, it really didn't matter why she was here or what harm she might inflict. Nothing could be worse than my empty existence. Still, I froze in some primal fear even the Plakerols couldn't remove. Staying in Novana would be the safe bet – unless I took my own life as I'd decided. *I'm so raddled.*

"Stop, Malaika." I raised a question I'd failed to ask earlier. "How long would I be in Taoland?"

She turned. "Totally up to you, Adam. A few days. A few years. The rest of your life. Your call."

An excited jolt shot through me. "This isn't final? I can return to Novana when I want?"

"I never said otherwise."

Immediately my fears yielded to a sigh of relief. "OK. I'm OK now. I'm OK. I want to go with you. Let's do this. I'm sorry for wavering."

She shook her head, feigning annoyance, but smiled, opening her palms to the skies.

Whatever happens now will be my destiny. So be it.

She came to me and lifted me in her wings as if I were weightless. We floated up toward the center of *Wanderer*. Two small deer, a pair of squirrels, and a couple of wild rabbits, some animals I'd only seen using the *Key*, scampered with us. Colorful insects, tiny birds, and various rodents scurried alongside. My heart pounded as we entered the Fifth Dimension. Malaika held my trembling hand and guided me to a virtual opaque bench suspended in

Wanderer's core. There I perched, weightless, gently held down by some sort of gravity inside the cloud.

Magic? I believe in it now.

Malaika raised her hands, summoning a hologram of a heads-up display. When she issued commands in an unfamiliar language, *Wanderer* lifted. Slowly at first, then quickly. Novana's Great Canopy and its force fields restored themselves as we ascended through them.

We exploded into space at awesome speed. There was no motion, no bumps, no exertion on my body. Within seconds, Novana and Talus grew smaller, then disappeared from sight. I felt relieved as my planet faded. There was nothing there that made it home.

Spectacular vistas of the Ahmetus Galaxy gave way to awe-inspiring panoramas of other galaxies. The translucent *Wanderer* was surrounded in every direction by the beauty of the Universe. Intoxicated by it all, I found a few questions. "How far will we be traveling? How long will it take us to get to Taoland?"

Malaika considered a measured response. "In your science, Adam, the answer might be some trillions of light years. But we are not restricted by the time domain, nor by the speed of light. Distance, as you comprehend it, is not meaningful here in the Fifth Dimension. Nor is time itself."

I decided for the moment to simply accept her strange answer. The temperature inside *Wanderer* was perfect, so I shed my coat, which floated away. I'd made the most difficult choice of my life, yet I felt oddly at ease – knowing a return was possible.

"Adam. How does all this make you feel?"

I hesitated. "Trivial . . . Unimportant . . . Insignificant."

She cradled my hands in her soft slender ones. "You are anything but trivial, as you will discover in Taoland. You are important. And significant."

"But why did you choose me? Among all of the humans on Talus, why are you taking *me* to Taoland?"

"In all of the Universe you alone are Adam of Novana – created not by the Plakerols but by outside forces. You have been given an imprint unlike any other. Now, we are about to unleash your untapped potential, which is meant to benefit countless others. You will leave an imprint as no other can do."

"We?"

"My umm . . . my big boss and me. And the rest of the team."

I scratched my head. "I don't understand."

"We will discuss this some other time."

Some other time? I wanted answers *now*. I struggled to understand why she and her 'boss' considered me special. But my inclination to debate was softened as I gazed out at galaxies of all shapes, sizes, and colors interrupting the blackness of space – each new panorama more astonishing than the prior.

Malaika followed my gaze and asked, "How many galaxies do you think are out there?"

"I've read there are trillions."

"And how many stars?"

"Likely trillions times trillions."

"And how many planets, like Talus?"

I placed my fingers on my chin. "Well, probably more than trillions times trillions, though most suns are without planets."

She grinned, one long ear lobe to the other. "Your estimates are quite a bit low. But at least you know the numbers are beyond human comprehension." Malaika moved a few yards to a more obtuse area of *Wanderer*. She reached into the cloudy wall, retrieved a gilded cup, and offered it to me.

Now she will poison me! But at that point I no longer cared. I'd surrendered to fate. So I accepted the cup and drank the aromatic deep-red elixir, finding it delightfully sweet – more delicious than anything I'd ever tasted.

A sweet grogginess swept over me. My eyelids fell heavy and shut. When I opened them, I assumed sometime later, I was no longer seated. I was floating. Malaika sat below, still on the virtual bench. She reached out her hand and gently pulled me back to her.

"Did I fall asleep, Malaika?"

"Yes. You had a lovely nap."

"For how long?"

"I told you, time is not relevant in the Fifth Dimension."

Wanderer was speeding toward a golden ball, likely a planet. Taoland? Three moons circled it, their orbits evidenced by rings of dust painted in the skies. One moon was green, another reddish orange, the third silver in color.

"Is that Taoland?"

She responded, "Yes," as *Wanderer* headed toward the green moon.

"You said I was going to Taoland, not one of its moons."

"The golden planet is Tao. The three moons orbiting it comprise Taoland. Humans cannot live on Tao's surface – it is too hot and mostly gas. It is an orphaned planet, without a sun – a wandering, rogue planet."

"A rogue planet?"

"It defies all you believe about science."

"So, will I be staying on that green moon?"

"Yes, for the immediate future. You will likely later spend time on one or both of the other moons if you stay around here long enough."

What is long enough?

Wanderer descended. It continued swirling as it hovered near the edge of the green moon's currently dark side. "Welcome, Adam, to the Moon of New Beginnings."

Nervous tremors shook my frame. "Will you be staying here with me?"

She stood on air, inviting me to do likewise. "I am not departing here. I have others to gather. My friend, Roshi, will meet you below."

"Roshi?"

"He is a guru. A really huge guy. Unusual in lots of ways. You cannot possibly miss him. I know you will like him."

Malaika was my ride back to Novana. "How will I let you know when I want to return home?"

"Just call my name and I will come. But you might decide home is here in Taoland." She gently kissed my cheek. "Now go and start becoming the man you are meant to be." She handed me a purse with the stuff gathered in Novana. "Please give these to Roshi." She slipped a piece of paper into my shirt pocket.

Just who is this strange, enchanting creature?

With renewed doubts I descended gently to the surface. The animals and insects we'd gathered in Novana departed *Wanderer* with me. Adriella comforted me, hovering by my side, silently listening to my every thought. After taking my first steps on the moon, I looked back to the opening where Malaika had stood. She was gone. *Wanderer* lifted into the heavens.

I found myself alone, in the dark, once again.

Terrified anew.

CHAPTER 4

FIRST FRIENDS IN TAOLAND

Fright rooted me to the spot. *What have I done?*
Wanderer had disappeared into a hint of light appearing across the morning sky. A tremor besieged my body; the finality of my situation consumed me. I'd never been more uncertain throughout my dismal years in Novana.

When a tiny sliver of Tao breached the horizon my lips parted in astonishment over the sights, sounds, and aromas all about. The hilltop beneath my feet was full of sumptuous grasses, plush bushes, and unfamiliar trees. A dozen shades of green burst forth at the dawn of a new day. When I bent to touch some multicolored flowers, several giant blooms actually smiled.

Flowers can't smile.

The birds and insects from Novana darted back and forth, lifting my spirits. I was half-tempted to join them as they frolicked with Adriella in the plush green carpeting the moon's surface. I unfolded the note Malaika had placed in my pocket.

"My dearest Adam,
Thank you for trusting me.
Enjoy constant springtime on this Moon of New Beginnings.
May hope fill your every moment.
May dreams of happy tomorrows sustain you and end your nightmare of despair.
May you find peace in each new day and joy in loving relationships.
Rejoice in song as you shed fear and doubt.
Dance as if no one is watching.
Come to trust others, as they will you.
Be selfless in all endeavors.
Envy not the talents nor the possessions of others.
Be kind to everybody and to all creatures.
Honor and respect those with whom you interface – especially those with whom you disagree.
Have no expectations, but abundant expectancy. Just let it all unfold.
Avoid the need to understand. Just believe.
Know I am here for you, holding your hand, even when I am not seen.
Love, Malaika
PS: This is the beginning. Why are you here?"

Startled by the clamor of heavy footsteps, I turned to see an enormous creature approaching. "Hi, Adam. Welcome to the Moon of New Beginnings, which we simply call the First Moon."

"You must be Roshi?"

"None other!"

He was way older than me. And colossal. His bizarre costume dovetailed with his ridiculous features. A small third eye with a bright green pupil rested above the bridge of his massive nose. His long tail draped to the moon's surface.

Definitely not human.

Roshi continued in a bellowing voice consistent with his overwhelming size, "I pray your stay here will be enjoyable."

I tried to mask my shock at his appearance. "You speak my language."

"Not exactly. Folks arrive here from all over the Universe. We speak in our native tongues. But we understand each other as if we were speaking a common language." He scratched his large head. "Please don't ask me to explain – it's simply part of the magic here."

I accepted his bizarre assertion. *Why argue anyway?*

Roshi was at least eighteen inches taller than me and more robust than any of the behemoths I'd met in fantasy novels over *Novananet*.

I nodded. "Magic is okay by me."

His unkempt bushy hair hid any ears he might have. The color of the mop on his head matched the white of his long beard and hairy leather-like tail. Bushy white eyebrows sat atop his reddish face and oval violet eyes. Parted orange lips revealed a mouthful of perfectly shaped glistening yellow teeth. His large girth was firm and not at all flabby. Then there was that weird middle eye blinking out of sync with the normal two.

"Nice to meet you, Roshi. Malaika told me to turn myself over to you. That's fine with me because I've absolutely no idea what I'm supposed to do." I handed Roshi the purse with what Malaika had gathered in Novana.

The mammoth gloved hand he reached out startled me. "Thanks. I will happily add these to my gardens."

"So, here I am. What's next?"

"I say we begin by heading off this hill. I want you to meet a couple of super-nice folks who are on their way here."

I hid a grin as I observed Roshi's loose-fitting long-sleeved green shirt with orange polka dots. His bright red suspenders held up blue-and-yellow striped baggy jeans, oversized and in disarray. To call his garb and color combinations awkward would be way too kind. While amused by Roshi's bizarre appearance, I took an immediate liking to my massive new friend.

With surprising agility, Roshi led me down a winding trail. I followed him without hesitation, gingerly jogging to keep up with his super long strides. I chuckled silently at his long hairy tail – exiting a hole in the rear of his pants and bouncing on the moon's surface. Brightly colored wildflowers reflected in Roshi's shiny black boots.

I touched the soft-flowing greenery on either side and delighted in the pleasant aroma of the mulch. We reached the bottom, pausing between clumps of trees blossoming in whites and pinks.

"We made it, Adam. I'm not even winded. How about you?"

With a dismissive wave of my hand, I fibbed, "I'm good."

As we proceeded, I moved to avoid a litter of cute chubby-cheeked striped rodents tumbling in the wood chips. Several larger rodents popped their heads out of nearby holes, observing us. I swore I detected grins on their oversized bucktoothed faces.

Soon we found ourselves at the edge of the luscious green fields I'd observed from atop the hill. A variety of playful unfamiliar animals scurried about. A pair of bandit-masked mammals appeared, resembling Novanian raccoons but twice the size. The squirrels, rabbits, and deer we brought from Novana and Adriella were already playing with the other critters. It was as if the animals had no fear from each other nor from us. Detecting my awe, Roshi grinned. "You've not seen anything yet!"

Variants of hoofed animals grazed as equals in the fields. A dozen dusty-pink animals, with large heads, pointy ears, and long snouts, grunted in a mud pit off to my left. Near to them, three-foot tall greenish fowls clucked and splashed in a pond. A group of enormous animals with bright green antlers appeared at the edge of a graceful woodland.

I gasped when I saw a beautiful white stallion approaching – with green mane and tail and a long, spiraling neon horn. A qilin! I fell back when this amazing specimen raised high upon its rear legs and bellowed, "Greetings, Adam," before it galloped away.

Another qilin speaks to me!

Roshi placed his herculean right arm around my shoulders.

"Time to meet a couple of your new neighbors." A man and a woman entered the scene from the direction of some buildings, perhaps a village. The approaching twosome skipped in laughter and song. A pair of happy, barking dogs, somewhat like Novanian sheep dogs except for their forest green fur, danced playfully alongside, their lively movements blending perfectly with the dazzling scenery.

When they drew close, the couple and their dogs came to a halt. "Hi, Adam. I'm Randahl," announced the dark-haired, oddly handsome man. "Welcome to Green Valleys."

I shook the dark-skinned hand he offered. "Green Valleys?"

"Our neighborhood, where you'll live and work. I'm the President of the Green Valleys Civic Association. The best part of my duties is greeting newcomers."

His pale-faced partner interrupted. "I'm Lorelai. I'm the GVCA Social Director. My husband might welcome newcomers, but I make them feel like family." She swept her curly purple hair over a slender shoulder.

Randahl knelt to settle one of their dogs. "When Roshi alerted us to your arrival, we rushed to welcome you to the Moon of New Beginnings, which we assert is the best of Tao's three moons." Randahl was a good six inches shorter than me, with an oval head seated atop a boxy build. He and Lorelai wore lightweight spring clothing, considerably more sedate than Roshi's glitzy garb.

Lorelai spoke. "Roshi will help you settle in at his place. But don't take too long. You're invited to our annual GVCA Picnic today. It begins at noon. Come around eleven and help us set up." She winked. "We won't take no for an answer."

We turned and headed toward the village, with Roshi's ridiculous oversized boots squeaking loudly all the way. When we reached a fork in the road, a majestic stone-faced building, four stories high and probably five hundred feet wide, appeared through some trees.

"What's that?"

"Oh, that's where you will be working. The headquarters and engineering facilities of Tezhouse First Moon," Lorelai answered.

Randahl chuckled, with a wink. "And an additional bit of news – I'll be one of your bosses."

I welcomed the notion of working for such a friendly character instead of being enslaved to a bunch of mindless machines.

At that fork in the road, one path led to the left, the other turned to the right.

"Which way do we turn?" I asked.

"Depends," Roshi responded, "on where you are going."

"I don't have the slightest idea."

"Well then, it doesn't matter which fork you take," roared Roshi. His friends laughed as well. I didn't get the joke if there was one. Randahl and Lorelai, still amused, turned to the left, waving. "See you later."

Roshi clapped me on my shoulder and gestured to the right. "My cottage is down this road."

I couldn't go to the picnic dressed like I'd just stepped out of a workhouse in winter. "Roshi, these are the only clothes I have. They are dark gray – and heavy, winter weight. I can't go to a springtime event looking like this."

"Don't fret. Back in my cottage, where you'll be staying for a few weeks, I've got everything you'll need." I winced, assuming I'd be dressing as a clown, just like him.

Roshi seemed anxious and began tucking his shirt in and securing his bootlaces. "But we must hurry. Grab hold of my shoulders."

"Why?"

"It's faster if we fly there. Hop aboard. We'll be at my place in minutes."

Fly? This guy is as batty as he looks.

Before landing on this moon, I'd have scoffed at Roshi's invitation. He bore no wings, and he must have weighed a quarter of a ton. But I was already getting used to preposterous happenings, so I grabbed hold of his broad shoulders. He flapped his gigantic arms. We lifted off, flying to the left at maybe eighty feet above the surface. It was pure magic. Unreal. And thrilling.

But I was petrified about what might lie ahead.

CHAPTER 5

ROSHI'S COTTAGE

Everything I'd experienced in my first hour was too good to be true, which could only mean what was happening was not reality.

Smiling flowers and talking qilins? Flying on the shoulders of a giant?

Exhilaration mixed with apprehension as we hovered above a property Roshi proudly announced as his home. He waved his enormous right arm, inviting me to view hundreds of acres of fields, farmlands, forests, creeks, and small bridges. A cottage stood near the center. A strange sense of nostalgia overwhelmed me. The quaint lure of the pathway heading to the small house hinted of a favorite memory. This made no sense as I'd never been to Taoland.

And I couldn't shake my fears and the premonition of darkness ahead.

Roshi landed on a meandering walkway of irregular blue-gray steppingstones leading to a rippling stream. He puffed out his chest and pointed to a small arched stone bridge inviting access to the cottage beyond. Flowers, blossoming trees, and bushes dotted the landscape in every imaginable color, with pink the most predominant.

"This has been my lifetime work, Adam."

"You created all of this?"

He beamed as if observing his place for the first time. "With my own two gigantic hands."

I've accomplished nothing, and Roshi's done all this.

When we reached the bridge I drew in a long breath, mesmerized by the painted landscape. Clear waters rippled noisily over rocks in the lively stream below. Colorful fish jumped out, seeming to greet us. Large, mostly pink birds squawked cheerfully. Again I was startled by impossible smiles. Blossoming trees, flowering bushes, and tall wispy green grasses danced in the early morning breeze. I could have stayed in this moment forever, though I couldn't settle my nerves.

I'm intoxicated. That's it. Must've been that drink Malaika gave me.

We restarted our short trek to the cottage. To keep up with the long-legged giant, I jogged on the steppingstones, brushing lush plantings on either side. Large pink boulders lay on a carpet of green blanketing a gentle hill down to a valley where the stream pooled up behind a small rock dam.

My new friend's two-story log creation featured four shuttered windows, an emerald-green front door, and a brick chimney looming above. Roshi, pride obvious across his round face, said, "I assure you my cottage is as strong as it is beautiful."

"Did you create the gardens too?"

"Mostly by myself." He pointed to the left. "We'll make a new patch there with the seeds and cuttings you brought. 'Novana Nook' – that's what we'll call it. You can help me."

Help him? All I knew how to do was stand atop a stupid tower.

"You can better understand life when you get down and dirty in the mud. We'll also plant an apple tree sapling and name it the 'Adam Tree.' To establish a new life is to believe in tomorrow, just as ideas are the seeds of invention."

Roshi had something to do, something to live for, something he loved. *I want a purpose like his.*

"I'll show you my farmlands and ranch tomorrow." He slowed to caress some plants and prune others.

I couldn't help but ponder the differences between Taoland and my homeland. I should have left Novana behind, along with recollections of its dull sadness, but it hung over me like a dark cloud. "Roshi, we don't have gardens in Novana."

Roshi popped up from inspecting a blossom-filled bush. "No gardens?"

"Nope. And we don't have private farms."

He raised his eyebrows. "Don't you eat fruits and vegetables there?"

"Of course. They are provided, all we need, lots of varieties."

"Where does the produce come from?"

"From automated farms operated by very advanced robots."

He frowned, twirling a twig in his fingers. "How boring."

Although he was right, I defended Novana. "It's efficient – and productive."

Roshi squinted, scrunching his forehead. "Humans play no role?"

"Of course, we do. We're the consumers."

"Yes, Adam. But depending on machines is enslavement."

I lied. "We love the system. We are well fed, healthy. And we don't have to do anything – except pick up the goodies the robots provide for free."

He grimaced and led me to another patch of flowers. "Nothing is ever for free. Seems you Novanians surrendered essential liberties to get things you say are 'free' – a very dear price indeed. Tomorrow, I'll show you a better way – reliance on self. Production not by machines, but by ingenuity and arduous work, resulting not only in needed produce, but in self-satisfaction and pride."

"But I don't have your skills."

After a brief silence Roshi grasped my shoulders. "You've got buried talents, different from mine, Adam. You'll discover them here in Taoland."

To create all this, Roshi had to be free, unencumbered by rules established by mindless bots. He had to decide his every action; then follow through. I longed to be free enough to have such dreams and bring them to fruition. "Roshi, your cottage and gardens are so colorful. In Novana, everything is the same color – gray."

He winced as if injured by the thought. "How horrible."

"You can't begin to imagine the place I come from."

Roshi folded his arms. "I'm sure I don't want to."

Everything said 'welcome' as we approached his shiny green front door. There was a rustle in a patch of bushes and out poured five tiny, furry puppies. Their little tails wagged nonstop as they squeaked gleefully at Roshi's return. When he knelt down the litter smothered his right hand.

I'd love to have my own puppy.

Seemingly reading my mind, Roshi grinned and said, "You can choose one for yourself."

I hesitated, not knowing how to care for a dog, but then responded, "Thank you so much. Can I have the little white one with brown ears?"

Roshi pressed the pup to me. "He's yours now. It's a boy. We'll train him together."

We didn't have pets in Novana. I held the little ball of fur to my chest. His dark, inquisitive eyes melted my heart. "I'm going to call you Apollo." The dog smiled when I announced his name.

A smiling puppy. Perfect!

"I detect a mutual love fest beginning. Your Apollo is a Taonese, a hybrid of small dogs from throughout the Universe. You'll take him with you in a few weeks when you move into your own place."

My own place? I set Apollo down with the other puppies.

"Tomorrow, we'll tour my properties. I want you to understand something up front. With all the amazing magic and beauty you'll discover here, you need to know evil finds its way in. You must never let down your guard."

"We don't have evil in Novana."

"Oh, Adam. There is no greater evil than lack of purpose. We'll discuss this some other time. Right now, you need to get dressed for the picnic." He turned and opened the front door.

A small living room led to a dining area with a table and six chairs. The kitchen was in the left rear. A large, pane-less window looked out into the backyard. I ran my hand across the beautiful, smooth wood of the table. "I'll bet you made this furniture too."

"Yup. All my own designs."

"Can you teach me?"

"I could – but I won't. Your role is not my role. Your talents and your mission are unique. While you might admire, never envy the accomplishments of another. Hone your own skills, as you discover your special purpose."

Malaika wrote something like this.

"Roshi, finding the reason for my existence is why I've come here."

"You'll discover that in Taoland. Let's have a quick cup of tea with biscuits before we head out."

My stomach was rumbling – I had no idea when I'd last eaten. Roshi rambled in the kitchen while I sat on a couch. It was my first private moment since meeting Malaika back at my Sentry Post. While I'd found nothing to dislike so far, I was troubled by Roshi's warning about evil in this peaceful place.

Every drop of his delish tea warmed my soul, and I enjoyed every last morsel of the buttered biscuits. "Roshi, why are you taking me in? What's in this for you?" I asked, mouth still full.

"My life's purpose is not building cottages or gardens. It's guiding newcomers like you. I'm considerably older than you – eleven times your twenty years. My mission is to share with you the wisdom of an elderly man."

220 years old! Give me a break.

I was taken aback but ignored his delusional comment. I was far more interested in getting to the picnic. Roshi stood up and carried the dishes to the kitchen. "Enough talk for now."

He led me up a wooden staircase to two nicely outfitted bedrooms, both doors open, one to the front and one to the rear of the cottage – with a shared bathroom between. "My bedroom is forward, Adam. Yours looks into my backyard. You'll find everything you need. There's a private sink in your room, and I've arranged some clothes for you. I suggest we burn what you're wearing. Gray simply doesn't work here. Clean up and choose something to wear. I'll be downstairs."

I braced myself for what kind of clothes I would find, considering his tastes. Surprisingly, everything was simple and modest. And fit me perfectly. After a quick wash up, I was back downstairs in fifteen minutes, wearing lightweight tan slacks and a dark green short-sleeved shirt.

"I'm good to go, Roshi."

"You look great, my friend. Help me finish packing the food." I followed him to the kitchen where we placed dishes of food into a large picnic basket. "Are you gonna fly me into town?"

"Yes. But not on my back. I've got my noli ready in the back gardens."

"Noli?"

"Yes. My nolidrone. Named after its inventor, Noliander, from the Pretoria Galaxy. You'll get your own noli soon – as a signing bonus for joining Tezhouse."

Bonus?

Roshi pulled the rear door behind us. He did not secure it.

"Don't you lock your door? You told me evil exists here."

"Evil here is far more insidious than the crimes of a simple burglar."

CHAPTER 6

ON A PICNIC MORNING

As we departed for the picnic, I was filled with abundant expectancy.

Roshi's backyard was equal in splendor to the front, but even more colorful. Perfumed blooms captured my senses. A tiny pink bird lit on a branch for a few seconds, flickered its wings, and grinned.

Another smiling bird. Why not?

We approached Roshi's noli, a bright-green, egg-shaped craft about ten feet long, sitting at the rear of the yard. When he said, "Enter," the full length of both sides popped open with a hiss, easing up like the wings of a colossal bug. We loaded our baskets and settled into two front bucket seats. Roshi commanded, "TowneCentre." The noli lifted silently and soared through the surrounding countryside.

"How does your noli fly? It makes no sound and has no wings."

"Beats me. I gave up asking that question many decades ago." Like Roshi, I too was starting to accept the magic of Taoland.

A spring shower had forced the picnic indoors to the Green Acres TowneHall. We arrived early and began working with Lorelai's team, setting up tables and chairs. After we finished, I meandered to the entrance where a green canvas canopy rejected the rain. A cool mist from the morning shower brushed my cheeks as I breathed in the intoxicating scent of ozone. A shiny black noli landed, twenty feet forward and down a sloping lawn from where I stood. The passenger side popped open.

She stepped out.

Soft drizzle dampened her burgundy, shoulder-length hair, intensifying her ravishing appearance. Beneath curved bangs, her pretty face featured high cheekbones resting aside a perfect nose. Her golden skin glistened. With a long, graceful neck and poppy-red lips curved slightly upward, she was absolutely gorgeous. Her pleasing smile touched my heart . . . no . . . my soul.

I'd never looked at a female this way before. A pleasant ache tingled my chest.

That's her.

She was average height for a female, maybe five foot six. A breeze pushed open her lightweight silver raincoat, revealing her slender body, bathed in a multicolored vertically striped velvet blouse and an emerald-green knee-length flowing skirt. Her long legs were slightly exposed as she splashed shiny black leather shoes into a puddle at the bottom of the steps.

She looked up, met my gaze, and smiled. Hers was an easy smile sending a warm 'hello' without a word being spoken. She wore no makeup and didn't need any. I couldn't take my eyes off this beauty. I silently repeated: *That's her.*

When she arrived under the covering, I quieted the butterflies fluttering in my stomach. "I'm Adam. Sorry, but I couldn't find an umbrella."

The deal was sealed when I stared into her dreamy electric-blue eyes, framed perfectly by brown lashes and inviting brows. At the moment, there was simply nothing more I needed to know about this creature. On a picnic morning, without a warning, I looked at her, and somehow I knew.

My future – it's in her eyes.

The blue of her eyes surpassed the tones of the most beautiful of skies, the most spectacular of oceans, and the most exquisite of sapphires.

She will become a special part of my life.

I would never be able to describe the unfamiliar excitement of this magical moment when I first set eyes on this woman. To attempt to explain to another this never-hoped-for miracle would be futile. A rumble of thunder shook me as if I'd been transformed by the preceding lightning bolt. I was lost in sudden euphoria by this stunning apparition just a few feet away.

"I'm Tariana. I haven't seen you in Green Valleys before." That voice! Delicate, yet deep in tone. Raspy. Teasing me unintentionally. Dripping with intelligence, though few words had been spoken. A voice I could probably listen to forever. Captured before she'd spoken, I was now far more so.

I wrung my shaky hands and responded, doing my best not to stammer. "I . . . arrived in Taoland this m-m-morning."

"Oh my. I've been here for sixty days. So, I'm an old-timer compared to you." An easy chuckle escaped her lips. "Maybe we'll get together so I can share what I've discovered about this enchanting moon." Before I could add another word she brushed my hand, giving me chills. "I've got to find the lady's room. A towel is my immediate goal. Maybe I'll see you later."

You bet you'll see me later.

Staggered by the encounter, I moved to a table near the entrance, joining Randahl, Lorelai, and a handful of others. Randahl examined my face and lifted a sly grin from the corner of his mouth. Before he could tease he looked over my shoulder. His countenance darkened. "Danger incoming. Bogart is headed our way. He's got his chief goon, Hannibal, with him. Both look more than mildly angry."

The man stomped toward me, stopping within a foot of my face. Offering no greeting to the others, he barked, "Who the fuck are you?"

My breath quickened. "Are you . . . talking to me?"

"Who do ya think I'm talking to, Asshole?" His face reddened more deeply.

Stunned, I responded, "I'm Adam." Adriella blinked furiously.

His black eyes pierced me. "And who do you *think* you are?"

"Err . . . Adam. I'm Adam from Novana. I arrived here this morning."

"Well, I'll call you Adam with No Manners. Asshole Novana who just arrived but doesn't know his fucking place."

I backed away from the nastiness of his breath and wiped his spittle from my cheek with the back of my hand. "Are you angry with me? This is no way to greet a newcomer."

He was forty pounds heavier than me with greasy black hair matching his personality – as did his tight-fitting all-black clothing. He was plain ugly.

"It's exactly how I greet a newcomer who tries to steal my date. My guys tell me you hit on her as soon as she entered."

"Tariana? Are you the one who drove Tariana here?"

He inched closer, his stench now overwhelming. His slobbery lips revealed sharp, yellow teeth below a distorted nose and black slicked-down mustache. "Stay away from her!"

He must be part of the evil Roshi mentioned.

"Or you'll wish you had," growled the scowling, unshaven Hannibal, in a manner even more threatening than Bogart's. He thrust his middle finger in my face.

With only emotionless humans in Novana, I'd never been treated like this, never experienced someone else's anger. Fortunately, Bogart and Hannibal whirled and crossed to the other side of the room. "What was that all about?" I asked my new friends, open-mouthed.

Randahl huffed. "Bogart is the big boss, the President at Tezhouse First Moon. He's my direct boss. You'll be in his organization as well. Not the greatest of intros for you. Avoid him, at all costs."

Lorelai laid a hand on my shoulder. "You'd best heed Randahl's warning and try to become invisible to Bogart. He is the worst of the worst of bullies."

I grabbed a napkin and wiped my face. "Is being a bully the way to succeed here?"

Randahl waved off my concerns "You'll find mostly good people, team players, at Tezhouse."

"So how did Bogart become the big boss?"

Randahl sighed. "Bottom line, he gathers ugly secrets about others and threatens to reveal what he knows. Shouldn't work, but it does."

Tariana came toward us and greeted my friends. When she smiled at me, I blushed.

Was that a wink?

"Bogart came looking for you, Tariana," Randahl announced.

"Oh, he drove me here. I live two miles away."

"Isn't he your date?" Lorelai asked.

"Certainly not. Bogart called me when the rain started and offered me a ride. I accepted. I normally enjoy walking, but not so much in the rain. But he's not my date. Did he say he was my date? No way. He's hardly my type."

Lorelai quickly ended the topic. "Maybe we assumed wrong."

While I didn't talk much, I enjoyed the friendly chit-chat and joking – something nonexistent in Novana. They seemed to genuinely enjoy each other's company, which pleased me.

"Food is ready. Let's eat," Lorelai announced. She led us to the buffet tables. Savory aromas wafted from uncovered dishes, begging, 'try me.' The offerings were not totally unfamiliar. I'd witnessed picnics from hundreds of years ago over *Novananet*, and Roshi had told me human foods eaten throughout the Universe were remarkably similar. But the floral centerpieces! Wow! It was impossible to convey their beauty over a cyber network.

Aromas of sliced veggies and grilled meats and fish mingled into an enticing aroma. Sandwiches, salads, soups, and sweet desserts had my mouth watering. Randahl warned of the alcoholic contents of pitchers of flavored waters and teas, sodas, and several drinks. I chose a liquid called rewski.

"Be careful, Adam. Limit yourself to one or two cups an hour."

After cleaning our first plates, we returned to the buffet for refills. It was easily the best meal of my life. And this was my very first day in this new land.

Musicians took up their instruments in the center of the hall, and couples left their seats to dance. I'd always enjoyed videos of dancing over *Novananet*, but, of course, I'd never participated. Tariana stood next to me, extending her right hand to mine. "Would you like to dance, Adam?"

My body tremored. "I don't know how."

"Don't be silly. Let me teach you." She pulled me to my feet.

Her delicious scent destroyed any resistance. She took my left hand high in her right, placed my right hand on her hip, and laid her other hand delicately on my shoulder, brushing my neck. Our bodies were not touching, but I instantly wished they were. I flushed.

"Just slide your feet, lifting them slightly back and forth as you sway. It's easy. I'll lead you to begin. Feel the music."

We danced to a beautiful slow song. I sort of got it, but far from perfectly. Then her presence became so intoxicating I forgot I was dancing.

"This is my first attempt at this, Tariana." I didn't tell her about the countless hours I'd observed dances using the *Key*.

She responded with a luscious smile. "Seems like you've been at this forever."

Talking with her was easy, as if we'd been friends forever. I felt exhilaration as her hand held mine. The band switched it up and began playing more lively songs. I froze, before someone tapped my left shoulder. It was Lorelai. "I'll take it from here, Tariana. I'd love to teach Adam the lunady."

Over my mild protestations, Lorelai taught me several varieties of fast dances. The Hot-Peppers, the Doggie, the Fountain Trot, the Froggy Leap, the Green Valley Hop, and the Tezhouse Tumble. Embarrassed at first, I struggled but caught on quickly. Each new step learned boosted my confidence. As I watched other guys bumbling and stumbling across the dance floor, my ego swelled.

I'm rather good at this.

"You're a natural, Adam."

When the music slowed down again, Lorelai paused. "I only do slow dances with Randahl."

I returned to our table and asked Tariana if she'd like to dance again. As we reached the floor she drew closer, resting her head against my chest. When her cheek brushed my own, I trembled. When fast music played again, I didn't hesitate to display my newfound Lunady skills, to her delight.

Between songs I awkwardly admitted, "I'm really enjoying this, Tariana."

"Please, call me Tari."

Out of nowhere, Bogart invaded our space, his noxious smell announcing his presence. He pushed me. Hard.

"My turn to dance with you, Tariana," he insisted.

"Sorry, Bogart. Adam has danced my feet off, and I need to rest." She turned and hurried rudely back toward our table.

Bogart cast his gaze on me, his sallow color once again turning crimson. His disgusting breath filled the space between us. His black eyes expressed unrestrained fury as he snarled, "You're an asshole, Novana. A nothing. A lowly insect. If you ever again crawl in front of me, I will crush you. Squash you. Destroy you."

What is wrong with this guy? The thought that I'd be working for him made me cringe!

His overreaction hit me like a hammer, and my hands trembled. He was the big boss at Tezhouse, and I had innocently pissed him off. Not the best way to begin my new life. When he stormed off I returned to our table, deeply concerned.

Roshi came over to announce he had to leave early.

"No problem," Randahl said. "I'll get Adam back to your place later."

An announcement boomed over the intercom: "The rain is finished. Let's head to the park."

We exited to Omphalos Park, a beautiful space in the heart of TowneCentre. Less than a third of Tao remained above the horizon. The delicious smell of ozone lingered in the air. An immense rainbow arched from one of the corner fountains to the other. Another more massive fountain surged a hundred yards away in the center. All were illuminated with brilliant green spotlights.

Lorelai stood beside me. "Every evening dozens of surging fountains are lit throughout our community – a spectacle you'll never tire of." She pointed to the one in the middle of the park. "That big one is simply called 'Green Fountain.'"

Everybody, including Tari, wandered off to participate in a variety of sports. Having no clue how to play, I observed from a stone bench. There were games involving running, jumping, and throwing balls and other strange items – so much going on I couldn't begin to figure out the rules or objectives. I promised myself I'd soon learn to participate.

Two hours later, with Tao now set, Randahl came over. "Let's head to my noli. I'll drop Lorelai and Tariana off at my home and deliver you to Roshi's."

"Tariana will be staying with you guys?"

"Yes. She and Lorelai have become good friends."

Tari and I hopped into the back of his dark green nolivan, a craft considerably larger than Roshi's noli. She took my hand with a gentle touch that sent shivers down my spine. After a short flight, I walked her to the front door, while Randahl remained in his nolivan, discussing something with Lorelai.

I stood there trying to find the right words. "I loved spending time with you, Tari. I'd like to see you again."

She stood with her head down; her silence in response rekindled my nerves. Thunder cracked loudly as the first drops of evening rain fell upon us. After a pause, Tari flinched and looked up. "Well, I guess I better go. It was nice meeting you, Adam." She stepped inside, lingered for a moment without looking back, then closed the door.

CHAPTER 7

LIFE IS LIKE FARMING

I couldn't recall a more refreshing sleep.
I leapt from my comfortable bed, awakened by melodies from songbirds and buzzing insects wafting through my opened window. Drawing in the sweetness of the predawn air, I explored the still-darkened heavens. An enormous spiral of stars and nebulae – a galaxy through which Tao was passing – painted the sky.

My closet door squeaked when I pulled it open to choose some clothing. I dressed and headed downstairs, propelled by the rich aroma of freshly brewed coffee. Roshi was nowhere to be found. Tao began peeking over the horizon, adding early light to everything in view. I filled a mug, added cream, buttered a biscuit, and headed out the door.

The treetops whispered as I ambled down the front lawn to the pond I'd noticed the day before. I headed for a large pagoda protecting four colorfully cushioned armchairs. I stepped onto the bluish-gray flagstone patio and brushed my fingers over the top of a green mosaic metal-framed table. Fire crackled in a grill to the right side releasing a delightful aroma from logs Roshi had apparently lit earlier.

He built all of this, and I've never built anything.

My coffee finished, I moved to the pond's edge and sat on a smooth green stone. The top of the golden sphere of Tao now took up a sliver of the horizon. *Plash!* An unfamiliar animal popped its weird-looking head out of the water ten feet away. I couldn't tell if it was a mammal, huge bird, amphibian, or a mix.

"Who are you?" the creature asked abruptly in a squeaky tone.

A strange opening line from this strange specimen.

"I'm Adam."

In a voice too high-pitched for its size, it said, "I'm Abraham – the Greeter."

A musky scent filled the air. Abraham's scaly skin was mostly pink. White, fluffy fur tightly covered the bottom-half of his circular face, which was twice the size of mine. The same fur covered his chest. His oversized powder-blue eyes were perfect circles, spread six inches apart on his large forehead, at least two inches in diameter and dominated by pupils. The lower half of his body was submerged, but if proportionate, he would be about my height.

Through a toothless bright red mouth, Abraham asked, "Why are you here?"

"I came to Taoland to answer that question."

Cackling, he danced and splashed noisily, revealing folded pellucid wings tucked at his back. "You are the seventh visitor in a row to admit you don't know why you are here. By the way, those who've claimed otherwise didn't have a clue either."

I flinched, but only for an instant. When he raised his body on bony legs, I confirmed he was in fact my height. He exited the pond and sat beside me. Something propelled me to reach out and touch his leather-like skin, gently so as not to hurt him. He obliged, his white, furry tail twirling like that of a pleased cat. Little surprised me in this strange land, but he was quite the sight.

"Welcome to Roshi's. You must eventually discover for yourself why you are here. But I know in part it's because you've accepted a challenging opportunity. How about you ask some other questions."

My ears perked up, eager to find someone willing to entertain my curiosity. "Well, Abraham, you might tell me a little about Tao and this moon. I don't get this orphan planet thing. Morning light and warmth is entering our space, but Tao is a planet, not a sun."

"Tao is not a part of any solar system, nor any galaxy. It's a self-fueled, gaseous, wandering planet providing what is needed by each of its three moons. We call this time our Taorise, though it's our moon that's rotating."

"OK – I guess." I would have to ponder his answer later.

"Something else. Everybody here speaks his/her native language, yet we understand each other. Roshi simply says its magic. But I can't grasp that."

"Our words are miraculously translated to a common language as they leave our lips and enter the ears of others. Common dialect as well. Roshi is correct. It's part of a mystery that makes Taoland special."

"B-but . . ."

"Just accept any and all Taoland magic you will encounter here. There's lots of it. Delete the need to understand. Just enjoy it all."

Another of Malaika's suggestions.

"Another question. Roshi told me he's human. Is he?"

Abraham arched his hairy brows. "Yes. Of course. Why would you doubt he's human?"

"Well, for starters, he's way larger than any human. He has a tail. Plus, he has a third green eye on the bridge of his nose."

"There are thousands of species of humans in the Universe. Roshi came here from the planet Excelsior in the Pandora Galaxy. They all look more or less like him there. What makes one human is not the appearance of the flesh but the spirit that dwells within."

Hmmmm. I never learned such stuff over Novananet.

"Next you'll try to convince me you're also human."

He belly-laughed. "That would be a stretch."

I giggled as well. "Another question." I wanted to ask all I could about this place while I had the chance. "Roshi told me he's 220 years old. Now that must be a fib."

"It's the truth. He arrived in Taoland 200 years ago, at the age of twenty. Folks from Excelsior can live to be 300. Over their many years, Excelsiorians gain great wisdom. That third eye of wisdom you mentioned emerges at around the age of 175 – then grows larger with every passing year."

While confounded by his answers, I was finding my new friend, with his squeaky voice and musky scent, more likable by the moment.

"Well . . . why was Roshi chosen to come to Taoland?"

"He was trained as a farmer on Excelsior. His know-how was needed in Green Fountains. Plus he came to serve as a guru to share his knowledge with others, like you, who might value his sageness."

I do want to learn from the friendly giant.

"You'll meet lots of humans here in Taoland, Adam. Many will look somewhat like yourself. Similar appearances are part but not all of the criteria used in selecting candidates. Varied species of humans who would look even more bizarre to you than Roshi populate other special places like Taoland throughout the Universe."

"But I still don't understand what makes them human."

Abraham looked at me, gathering his thoughts. "All humans, highly intelligent beings regardless of appearance, are capable of similar emotions, desires, and accomplishments – in varying degrees, of course. Plus, they have souls. We relish what is common to all, while accepting and respecting the differences."

Souls? I'd read about souls but didn't understand them. A remarkable calmness came over me as we sat together. I posed a question to lighten up the conversation. "OK. Help me with this one. Why does Roshi dress the way he does?" It was hard to hold back the smile threatening to appear.

"He must want to be noticed." We cracked up in unison.

We turned when alerted by Roshi's squeaky boots. "Good morning, Adam. I see you've met Abraham." Roshi was outfitted in wilder colors and stripes than the day before, even more outrageous. "Sleep well?"

"Like one of the logs you placed on the fire this morning."

Roshi pulled up a chair and sat a thermos and basket on the table. "Hope you enjoyed the coffee. I always add fresh goat's cream and sweet fruit leaves. Want a refill?"

I happily accepted a second cup.

Roshi removed several items wrapped in cloth from the basket. "I brought breakfast. Abraham, can you stay?"

"No. I've got to head out. This new guy is wearing me out with tough questions." He winked at me. Abraham's long legs creaked as he ambled to the left, charged forward loudly, flapped his wings, climbed into the sky, and disappeared.

The morning splendor was intoxicating. The blending fragrances of brightly colored flowers and greenery made for a truly delightful moment. I turned to watch Roshi cooking at the grill. The aromas of grilled meat, eggs, and fresh bread gladdened my nostrils. Gentle breezes rustled through blossoming trees and bushes. The first bite of breakfast exploded my taste buds.

As we cleared the table Roshi asked, "Did you make your bed?"

"No, not yet."

"I always make mine as soon as my feet hit the floor – accomplishing something right out of the starting gate – every day. Good habit, I say."

I accepted his advice gratefully. He was teaching, not lecturing. When he moved to the edge of the water I followed.

"Well," – he propped his humongous hands on his hips – "it's time for the grand tour. By understanding my farm, my ranch, and my teammates, you'll learn about all you'll ever need to know."

We crossed a small dam serving as a walking bridge and headed toward the farmlands. The sounds of the rippling waters relaxed me as we climbed a hill overlooking dozens of acres. "This is one of my favorite views," boasted Roshi.

I admired the panorama. "How did you do all of this?"

"It all began with opportunity – as everything in life does. Soon after I arrived in Taoland, the community leaders of Green Valleys accepted my vision for a new enterprise that promised jobs and abundant foods."

"And then?"

"They approved my detailed plans and provided start-up resources. From there it took many years of arduous work."

There was nothing like this in Novana, at least not since the Plakerols took over.

He waved his right arm and pointed out different fields of vegetables and fruit trees. "Actually, it's taken 200 years for all of this to materialize."

"You live alone, Roshi. How do you work and maintain the farms?"

He shook in laughter. "Certainly not by myself. I hire folks, pay them, and give each a piece of the action. They do the work. I'm too old, in case you hadn't noticed."

I'm young, but I've never worked.

I pointed to the left. "What's that section of bright yellow over there?"

"It's a farm of seed-bearing plants called brylio – a fantastic source of vegetable oil and surprisingly a major source of protein for our animals."

"And those buildings?" I queried, looking at several barns.

"We breed the animals there – most for the markets where meats are harvested. Other livestock provide muscle to help with our chores. We have fish farms behind those barns."

Roshi chatted cheerfully with the workers we passed on our tour. A bulky man with a neat beard announced, "We've got a seriously broken fence. A herd got spooked by a nearby explosion and went wild. Pretty extensive damage. We've got to redesign and make the barrier stronger."

"Do whatever is necessary," Roshi coaxed, smiling broadly and placing a reassuring arm around the worker's shoulder.

When the man departed, Roshi went on, "Delegation. The most important of all management practices. You've gotta trust and respect your people and delegate responsibilities. But always retain personal accountability. Never play the blame game when things go bad."

"So, now that guy will deal with repairing the fence?"

"Totally. He'll assemble a team, gather what he needs, and I'm certain he'll make it stronger than it was before. I never micromanage any projects. But I make sure to thank and congratulate them once done."

I admired this giant man greatly. "You have great camaraderie with your workers."

Roshi smiled. "They are like family and my most important assets. They're not just employees; more like teammates. In the early years, we all worked with no pay. Our only compensation was the food we produced. We struggled for decades to get by."

"And now?"

"When we became profitable, I compensated each of my employees based on their efforts. Here we are, 200 years later, after many turnovers in personnel, generational in some cases, prospering more every year." He twirled a blade of grass and tossed it aside.

"I hope I can do something like this someday."

Roshi waved a finger. "Your achievements won't involve farming. Each of us is blessed with unique talents. We've gotta use them to the fullest. Meanwhile we must never envy the skills of others. Adam, you'll accomplish wonderful things in life by honing your own special gifts. Do what you do well. Trust and leave the rest to others."

As we continued, I learned much, not only about farming, but about life where humans worked for themselves instead of machines tending to their every need. About folks working with each other toward common goals. Back in Novana, I'd read about this in ancient books. Now I was learning about it firsthand through newly opened eyes and ears.

We meandered side by side. Roshi shared how they'd chosen the land and crops, how they'd broken up the soil and tilled and seeded it, how frequent spring showers provided the right amounts of water, and how Tao provided the perfect light and warmth.

"Roshi, how did you know the people would buy your products?"

"My plans were based on what the market demanded – folks buy what they need. Never start anything without understanding what your customers are looking for. Offer what people need at a fair price. This requires that you know your competition as well."

A row of buildings covered with transparent plastic-like materials flanked the edge of a field. "What are they for?"

"Those are hothouses – where we initially plant seeds we get from all over the Universe and develop new products, including hybrids."

We moved on to where large green pods grew a top ten-foot-high stalks. Roshi reached up and extracted one of the foot-long products. He peeled away its casing, revealing a bundle of hundreds of individual yellowish-orange seeds, each about a quarter of an inch around, fused into a single mass.

"We call this mazzor. Some of this is used to feed the animals. But we humans eat the sweetest of this amazing vegetable."

He does call himself human!

"I'd love to taste it."

"We've got some ready to eat – snacks for the workers." He led me to a long wooden table. "Everybody loves mazzor. You will too." He placed a hot foot-long cooked and buttered pod into a paper and handed it to me. I held it with both hands and followed his lead in devouring the treat.

"Oh my. Talk about delicious." Butter dripped onto my arm, but I didn't care. I ate until the last of the large, sweet seeds reached my stomach. Then I asked for and gobbled down another pod. We enjoyed sandwiches and tea as well.

This day was better than any I'd ever spent in Novana.

"Adam, like farming, all businesses come with lots of surprises.

Always expect the unexpected. It took decades before we figured out how to grow this delicious mazzor. We failed several dozen times until we got it right."

Somehow, Roshi and his team had pushed through their setbacks. "So, you persisted." I had to know where he found the strength to carry on. "How did you not despair?"

"Never defeated by the roadblocks you'll most certainly encounter. Have hope. Take measured risks and be patient. A tree never bears its precious fruit until it receives ample light and rain over several years. Right, Jared?" Roshi nudged a worker who nodded in agreement. "It's unwise to ever try to speed up a process. The more patient you are, the quicker you'll achieve your goals."

We finished lunch and approached the barns. Moos, braying, cheeps, clucking, and cackles coming from the corrals accompanied some rather unpleasant odors. I stroked every animal I could. Most purred and grinned at me.

More smiling animals.

"Do you uh . . . slaughter the animals here, Roshi?"

He cringed. "No. Just not in my heart to do that part. I understand it's their purpose to provide humans with protein. But we sell the animals alive and let others do the dirty deed."

We moved on. In a field nearby, workers dragged tools over the earth, preparing it for new plantings. Roshi invited me to join them, tending the soil on our knees. "It's helpful in understanding any business to get your hands dirty. Scrape here, Adam. Plant a few seedlings. I'll show you how. Then we'll let nature take its course."

Tao had passed its zenith and was on a lazy journey to the horizon. "Time to head back and wash up for dinner. You should probably get to bed early. Tomorrow will be your first day at Tezhouse. You'll want to make a good impression."

Not wanting this day to end, I continued to prod information from him as we headed home. I needed a pep talk for my first day at Tezhouse. "Roshi. Can you share some tips that helped make you successful?"

"You've gotta have a vision; that's where it all begins. I saw things that weren't yet reality and made them happen. I applied my given skills; then brought teammates on board to fill any voids."

Do I have the talents I need?

"What else?"

"Always be honest."

Not the answer I was expecting. "Anything more?"

"Oh yes. Be flexible – and aways be open to new ideas and technologies. Never stop improving."

"You've taught me more about the real world in the last four hours than I learned in four years at university."

"Adam, life is like farming. The requirements to be a successful farmer are the same required in anything else. Be diligent. Persevere. Stay focused. Never stop learning. Ask questions. And most important of all, you've gotta respect and value others."

"I will never forget today." Having someone guide me was priceless. The Plakerols never taught us Roshi's lessons because they didn't want us to succeed.

Roshi paused and leaned down with his hands on his knees. "Let's go eat. Hop on my back." I climbed up, and we flew swiftly back to his cottage. The flight now felt normal.

As we approached his front door I said, "Your farm provides for I'm sure thousands of folks in this area. They are fortunate to have you and your team. And you're lucky to have found your purpose."

"My farm is not my purpose. It's what I do to earn a living. Never confuse the two."

"Then what exactly is your purpose?

Roshi looked at me and smiled. "At this moment, Adam, you are my purpose."

CHAPTER 8

ORIENTATION

Randahl's noli settled on the dew-covered lawn. When the door hissed open he invited me in.

"Ready for this, Adam?"

I hid my nervousness with a forced smile as I settled into my seat. Swallowing my fears and crossing my arms to hide my shaky hands, I answered, "Absolutely." In truth I was terrified – afraid of failure on my first day in my new job.

I had no clue what would be expected of me nor if I would fit in at Tezhouse. For twenty years, I'd submitted to governance by and accepted handouts from the Plakerols. Now I had to provide for myself. My stomach churned noisily, though filled with a sumptuous breakfast.

We lifted off. "Randahl, how do the nolis work? They are wingless, make no sounds, and send out no smell. What powers them? Roshi says it's magic."

"Nobody knows for sure. Some believe it's etheric power, part of the astral realm of the Tao. I prefer Roshi's notion of magic – like with lots of stuff here."

I'd only raised the question as a distraction. Concerns about what lay ahead consumed me. "Will I be running into Bogart?"

Randahl responded with a warning, "Not if you can avoid him, which I certainly hope you do."

"Why was he so nasty with me?"

He sighed. "The man's extremely insecure. All bullies are. Both you and Tariana tapped into his self-doubts. He brought her to the Picnic hoping to claim her as a conquest who might make him feel temporarily powerful. Tariana rejected him and chose to spend time with you instead."

Tari chose me? Or did I choose Tari?

I grimaced. "She's not Bogart's girlfriend. And I did nothing wrong. He overreacted."

"Bogart cannot accept failure. His rule is 'bow to me or die.' Rejection by Tariana kicked his insecurities into high gear. You ignored his demand to stay away from her and, instead, danced with her. A no-no."

"So, what do I do?"

"Whatever you do, never let him intimidate you. If you fear him, he wins. All bullies are cowards. You need not worry about Bogart if you stand up to him."

But I did fear Bogart. I'd never been threatened before. I didn't know how to respond.

Randahl changed the subject. "So, Adam, what are your expectations as you start at Tezhouse?"

"I have no idea what's on the agenda. I don't even know what my job will be."

Our brief noli flight traversed the same path Roshi and I took to his cottage two days earlier.

"Orientation will take five days. It will begin with badging, a medical exam, and a brief interview. Then you'll tour our facilities and meet tons of people. Each day there will be schooling in Tezhouse's history, culture, policies, leadership, technologies, products, and services and the markets we serve. There will be case studies, with you and fellow newbies in role play."

I couldn't stop doubting my value. *What if I screw this up?*

Randahl continued, "In your case, there will be interchanges with our best experts in robotics, AI, cyber telecommunications, and cyber security. Tezhouse hopes to benefit from your expertise – a key reason you were selected for Taoland."

"I hope I do okay," I said, hoping he wouldn't detect the quivers in my voice. Being singled out and selected based on my skills was foreign to me.

"You'll shine here. You bring a great attitude and a likable personality. You've got valuable talents."

I have nothing to offer. They'd likely decide they didn't need me after my first day.

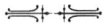

―――

We landed in a large lot filled with nolis of varying sizes, shapes, and colors. Randahl walked me to the front entrance and quickly departed after introducing me to Safari, a smartly-dressed, friendly, svelte woman with blue hair. The sun shone in through the door revealing a slight iridescence on her pearly skin.

"Good morning, Adam. I'll be your guide and assistant for the week. I'll manage schedules, get you and other newcomers from place to place, and answer any questions."

"Great. Thanks in advance, Safari."

When she smiled her slitted eyes flickered from green to a bright blue. Yet another variant to the standard human form I knew. "Let's begin by getting you signed-in and through a health check."

Health check? I would pass easily. All Novanians enjoyed perfect health. Safari moved to the front desk and spoke the words: "Check-in." To my left a virtual display appeared and prompted me to insert my information for registration. A photo-badge was immediately produced.

The health check was well orchestrated and efficiently done. A nurse drew blood and worked up a detailed analysis and DNA recording. Machines whirled around me conducting total body scans. When results were delivered ten minutes later I sat face-to-face with Dr. Santiago, a pleasant older dark-skinned woman with excellent manners.

"Adam, your results are the best for a twenty-year-old I've ever reviewed. You must have been doing something right back home."

"Our DNAs are carefully chosen by Plakerols in Novana. All food and drink are provided throughout life – healthy and in precise amounts. We have daily monitored exercise routines. Most diseases have been completely eradicated."

The doctor scrunched her brows. "Plakerols?"

"Highly advanced robots."

"Hmmm. Well, I've been told your DNA was selected from somewhere beyond Novana. If you don't mind, I'm going to inject a vaccine we give to all new arrivals. There are a variety of plagues throughout the Universe – against which we provide lifetime protection." She turned and prepared a syringe on the table behind her. I rolled up my sleeve and gladly accepted the serum in my arm.

After applying a tiny bandage, she patted my shoulder. "All done, Adam."

"Thank you, Doctor. Any follow-up?"

"Well, you can opt to take an annual physical. Your choice."

After Dr. Santiago shook my hand, Safari guided me out. "Next on your agenda – we'll get your *swish* device." She explained, "A *swish* is worn on the left wrist and is unremovable except by a magic tool. *Swish* provides, via voice commands, all personal information and business files over *Taonet*. All data is DNA protected."

Unremovable? Will I be like a prisoner again?

I'd seen these bracelets on Roshi and others at the Picnic. Something didn't sit right with me, but I didn't want to voice my concerns.

"Can I use it immediately?"

"Yes. You'll use *swish* for all communications and research, usually in hologram fashion. We've already loaded contacts into your file, and you'll add more in the days and years ahead."

Can I swish Tari?

"We don't have anything like *swish* in Novana. But then again, we never connect with others."

"How sad," she murmured.

We entered a door marked SWISH. Once again, the procedure was efficient.

"Ahh, Adam, just the guy I've been waiting for," said the technician, hopping up from his chair. "I'm Gary." I shook his hand, and we exchanged pleasantries.

Gary placed a quarter-inch golden hoop over my left hand. He knelt down, looked over his glasses and commanded in a coaxing voice, "Install." For a moment there was only silence, as if the hoop were deciding whether or not to obey. Then it shrunk gently upon my wrist until it form-fitted perfectly, flattening to about a half-inch width.

"Done," Gary announced. He grabbed a piece of paper from his desk. "Please read to her this list of words, phrases, and sentences so your bracelet will learn your voice and respond to you alone. It 'hears' in your native language and automatically translates so other *swishers* 'hear' you in the language of Tao."

I read every word and phrase from the list. My device beeped after each. Then Gary announced, "Your *swish* is now ready for use. Let me know if it gives you any problems."

Safari led me again into the main corridor. "Next, Adam, it's time for your interview – a short walk from here."

Don't screw this up.

A nervous rattle swept through me as I broke into a mild sweat. Adriella smiled, offering comfort.

Safari opened a door to an empty, white conference room where sat a large table with only a single chair. "To begin your interview, Adam, simply say 'embark.' I'll pick you up when you're finished."

I walked into the sterile-looking room, took a seat, and spoke the word 'embark.' Immediately a bobbling figure appeared across from me. It didn't need a chair. It was just a head. Cube-shaped, with an awkward grin on its blue face. It bounced in the air as if on an invisible spring. A suspended hologram.

"I'm Millie. Just a few questions. Your name?"

"Adam."

"Full name?"

"Adam 35110432460645."

The head flickered. "What?"

"That's my ID. I was born in the thirty-fifth province of Novana on the eleventh day of the fourth month of the year 3246 at 06:45 in the morning."

"How dehumanizing. We never use numbers to ID people. OK if we register you as Adam Novana?"

"Sure."

"Your birth date tells us you recently turned 20."

"Yes." *The dates here are the same?*

I had begun this interview filled with anxiety, but so far this was easy.

"So why are you here? In Taoland?"

That question, once again!

"I came to Taoland for adventure. To do something useful. So, I'm excited to begin work at Tezhouse."

True, but seeing Tari again was the main thing on my mind.

"What is your greatest strength?" Millie asked with a straight face.

"I finished at the top of my class at Moleg University and received an Advanced Degree in Pseudo Thought Creation. So, I'm pretty smart."

"And not overly humble. Where do you think you can most improve?"

"Well, I've never held a job before, except for a brief assignment as a sentry. I know nothing about working in a corporation, and nothing about interfacing with others."

"We've never had that response! Anyway, this interview is over."

Did I blow it? "That's all?" It was over so quickly I thought I'd blundered.

"We only needed a few basics. Thank you, Adam Novana."

Poof. She disappeared.

I spent the rest of the day getting to know the other apparently human newbies. We all looked different but got along famously. I was relieved to fit in easily. Suddenly Safari appeared, out of nowhere, making us all jump. "Next will be presentations about Tezhouse – in the auditorium."

We learned the enterprise began over a thousand years ago. We were taught about the founders and past and present leaders. Different presenters spoke on the history of Tezhouse innovations and inventions and current product offerings. Happily – no quiz. But there was homework. Lots more to study via *swish*.

"Same time tomorrow," the instructor concluded.

Each day featured tours of different facilities and introductions to folks throughout Tezhouse First Moon. Managers briefed us on the roles and missions of each department. The final introduction was to the Senior Management areas – where to my great relief Bogart was nowhere about.

Every day ended with a homework assignment which consumed my free time back at Roshi's. Tari held a frequent presence in my thoughts, but I barely had time to breathe. That said, I found satisfaction in being swamped with studies. I'd always feasted on reading. With the Tezhouse materials, I was finally studying with real purpose.

On the fifth day of orientation the morning was chock-full of additional presentations that got down into technology discriminators that distinguished our offerings from those of our competitors. While lunching with my fellow newbies, menacing clouds suddenly invaded a clear blue sky, dimming the Taolight that brightened the glass enclosed cafeteria. Rumbling thunder outside gave way to the sounds of stomping boots. It was Bogart and his goons. As soon as he entered his black eyes stared menacingly in my direction.

He approached, an ugly sneer across his face. "I warned you, Asshole, to never cross my path again. And yet here you are."

I was speechless. And embarrassed. My knees shuttered uncontrollably.

"You've been placed here, but not by me. You'd better tread carefully. Because I'll be watching you, you fucking lowlife. Obey me or you are finished. The first time you screw up – you're out of here. Got it?" When he moved on all I could do was tremble. He was the big boss and Randahl said not to fear him. But I did.

My new friends, mouths wide open, gasped in confusion. A skinny black-faced guy leaned forward. "Do you know who he is? He's Bogart, the President."

"I do know that."

Another exclaimed, "I've heard he jumps on people, but never a newbie."

I shared my dismal start with Bogart at the picnic. Each showed compassion mixed with concern.

"Be careful, Adam. He is known to be vindictive, hateful. You don't want to be on his bad side."

I'm already on his bad side!

After lunch, Safari took us to the parking lot where Randahl hosted a 'Graduation Ceremony.' Each of us had been assigned to his group. After congratulations, he concluded, "Welcome to your new world. The work will be challenging. You'll be rewarded according to your contributions. Dedication will reap personal benefits. And now a surprise. Look over there."

A dozen bright and shiny nolis, the smallest of the varieties, were parked facing us. "There's one for each of you. Just swipe your *swish* bracelet on the vehicle of your choice. Welcome to Tezhouse."

I darted to a cobalt blue vehicle, pinching myself all the way. I *swish'd* to claim it as my own.

It's mine! The first really special thing I've ever owned. I couldn't wait to show my noli to Tari.

Plakerols provided material things on Taoland – the bare essentials. But never anything like this. I became consumed by euphoria. I was loving Taoland, loving my noli, and I wanted more.

We newbies boarded our vehicles. A team of technicians helped us learn the fundamentals of noli-flying – a simple task of sitting inside, issuing verbal commands, and trusting in the magic.

We began in a semi-manual mode, where our nolis never rose more than a foot above the ground. Each of us meandered throughout the Tezhouse properties, controlling the speed and steering with the words 'start' – 'stop' – 'faster' – 'slower' – 'right' – 'left.' There were miniature cameras embedded all around our vehicles. Speed and collision avoidance made travel simple and safe.

This is amazing!

When we returned to the parking area a technician advised, "Time for your virgin high-flight. Command your noli to take you home and then return to this spot."

Excitedly I commanded, "Roundtrip, Roshi's Cottage and back." The noli flew as directed. The whole thing reminded me of a 'magic carpet' I'd read about in a novel written, I thought, back in the Second Millennium.

Magic. I love it. Talk about fun!

After circling Roshi's place, my noli and I returned to the parking area without a hitch. I still had another appointment – with Dr. Garvens, Director of the Advanced Technology Department.

Safari guided me to the 'Tomorrow Today Café' – the name Garvens had proudly chosen for his department's dining room. Director Garvens stood tall, dark-skinned, with fine features, sporting a nicely trimmed gray beard as he introduced me warmly to a dozen members of his team. "Let's greet the newbie, Adam Novana." All immediately welcomed me with applause. I'd never received any acclaim, not for anything. Heck, I'd never been invited to be in a group before. With a flushed face and fluttering heart, I managed to respond, "Thank you."

Garvens squared his shoulders and continued, "Adam comes from a place where highly advanced robots took over after safeguards were lifted by government leadership, something we will never permit here. We will continue to employ technology judiciously but will never allow it to replace human innovation."

Lunch was served buffet style. Several additional members of the Advanced Technology team joined us via *swish*. After some small talk, Garvens began again. "Technology will never become our master. Adam will be sharing his firsthand experiences with the unintended consequences of uncontrolled AI. He has excelled in related studies at university."

The next two hours were awesome for me. Employees briefed me on Tezhouse's most advanced designs. We exchanged knowledge about computers, robots, software, and AI – in Novana and in Taoland. They were especially interested in my expertise in cybersecurity protocols.

They know about my education. They respect me.

Dr. Garvens put a reassuring arm around my shoulder. "You bring critical know-how to us. We're delighted you are joining us."

Others explained the precautions they took to prevent runaway technology and takeover by nonhuman forces. They wanted to understand how Plakerols had seized control. And why leadership in my homeland had allowed this. I shared the history and demise of Talus and Novana.

"Thank you, Adam," said Dr. Garvens. "We are aware that the destruction of human purpose that you've experienced has happened elsewhere in the Universe. You are the first human we've met who actually suffered such dominance. We want you to suggest improvements to what we believe are foolproof safeguards. Help us prevent what happened in Novana."

A sense of pride swelled in my chest. "I'll be honored to be part of this work."

"In the process, we hope you'll be helping to develop new products for our portfolio. We are really looking forward to your contributions. You'll be busy indeed."

It had been like going to a half day of graduate school, but in this case, I was contributing, along with my 'professors.' I was respected here. And needed. With my orientation over, I was far more confident than when it started. I headed to Roshi's, proudly flying my own noli.

I'd put Tari on a back burner for too long. It was time to reconnect.

CHAPTER 9

FIRST DATE

My noli self-landed in the lush rear lawn of Roshi's property. Instead of going inside, I headed 'round to the front to find Apollo, who welcomed me with his adorable smile. I scooped up my furry friend and rubbed his brown ears. He welcomed my affection and licked my face. We headed to the pond, drawn there by the scrumptious aromas and sizzling sounds of our dinner-to-be.

Roshi, dressed as ridiculously as ever, greeted me, "How was your final day?"

Sweat glistened on his face in the glow of red-hot coals burning below the cast iron grill. Utensils, pots, and pans hung from wooden beams of the pergola, away from the heat. Juicy slabs of steak begged me to stay, but I first had a mission to accomplish.

"Can't talk right now Roshi. Gotta *swish* Tariana."

"Oh, you mean the young woman you flipped out over at the picnic then totally ignored once you fell in love with Tezhouse?"

I ignored his jab, an unwelcome slap in my face, and headed to my boulder at the edge of the water. Freed up from Tezhouse obligations, it was time for me to ask Tari out on a date. I needed to know more about her and wanted her to know everything about me, dismal as my story was. Randahl had provided her contact information. My heart fluttered as the time finally arrived for me to *swish* her.

A splash broke the surface of the pond. Abraham rose on his spindly legs and sat beside me. "You're contacting Tariana?"

My hands shook. "Yes, but I don't know what to say to her. I'm new to this girl–boy thing." I'd never spoken with a female in all my years in Novana. "Please help me."

"Just breathe, slowly, in and out. Relax." He raised and lowered his hands in tune with exaggerated breaths.

"But what do I say?"

A smile tugged at the corner of his toothless mouth. "I suggest you begin with 'Hi.' Then let nature take over."

"Will you sit here while I *swish*?"

"Not so good if she spots me here, looking like I'm coaching you. I'll drop back into the pond and eavesdrop."

I whispered 'Tari' nervously. My gold *swish* band flushed to more of a rose gold, almost as if it knew Tari was a love interest. A brief beep signaled that Tari was with me – virtually. Appearing as a hologram maybe six feet in front of me, seated at a glass table, she leaned toward me, her burgundy hair falling over one shoulder. *Wow.* The light glow of the evening served as an enchanting backdrop. Tari's beauty exceeded the view, but I didn't want to stare, so I shifted my gaze nervously out over the pond.

"Hi . . . It's Adam."

"Adam who?" she teased with a smile, feigning confusion.

This relaxed me. I returned the banter. "You know, the nicest, best-looking guy you've met since you arrived in Taoland."

"That must have been a long time ago because I have no recollection of ever meeting you." She scrunched her eyes and put two fingers to her chin as if trying to remember.

My heart leapt. Her razzing forced a huge smile on my face and a pleasant ache in my heart.

"Seriously, Tari, I don't have a great excuse for not contacting you before this. Please forgive me. I've been swamped with orientation at Tezhouse and lengthy reading assignments every night."

"A pretty lame excuse, indeed." She winked. "Especially if you want to impress me – and maybe woo me."

Her clever smirk increased the fluttering in my heart. "Tari, I'd love to see you again."

She batted her eyelids. "Oh my. I had given up on you, thinking you and I would never happen. Now I don't know if I can fit you into my busy schedule."

Her witty remarks continued to ease tensions and grant me confidence – and had me dreaming about what it would be like to spend my life with such a spirited woman.

"I've got my first assignment at Tezhouse. And I've got my own noli. It's cobalt blue. And guess what – I even got my first salary – my own lunies. I'd love to share what's happened this past week." Caught in an unfamiliar giddy euphoria, I blurted out, "Would you like to go to the theater with me?"

Tari leaned forward and propped her head in her beautiful hands. "Hmmm. Give me a minute. Oh well, I guess I should stop taunting you. I've been thinking of you lots since we said goodbye after the picnic. You did make a great first impression, Mr. Adam of Novana." She toyed with a strand of her hair.

"How about tomorrow night? I know where you live. Randahl told me. I hope that's OK. I could pick you up at around five."

She was beaming. Glowing. "I'm working tomorrow and don't get home until six. Can we make it six thirty?"

"Perfect." I was shaking when we ended the *swish*. Abraham popped his peculiar head out of the water. "Congrats, my bold infatuated friend. You've nabbed your first date. Skillfully, I might add."

Roshi called out from the patio, "Steaks are ready."

The food was amazing once again. I gobbled down my entire hunk of meat in just a few minutes. Roshi, eating far more slowly, sat his fork down and looked at me with concern. "Slow down,

Adam. You can't taste my incredible cooking if you don't take a breath between bites."

Abraham joked, "I think Tariana took his breath away."

I was barely able to converse. My head swam in a light stupor as I anticipated seeing Tari again. I offered a few tidbits about my final day at Tezhouse, and the good news I'd be joining Dr. Garvens' team. But most of all I just grinned.

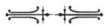

What seemed like a decade passed before the next evening rolled around and I stood at Tari's front door. She answered wearing a flowing organdy dress, scoop neck, sleeveless, down to just above her knees. She took my hand as we walked. I gulped when she sat beside me in my small noli, exposing a bit of her legs. We smiled but barely spoke on the trip into TowneCentre.

Maybe she's as nervous as me.

We landed on a lovely carpet of grass in front of the Green Acres Concert Hall, immediately across from the center of Omphalos Park. Waters from the 'Green Fountain' splashed and gurgled a hundred yards away. My first month's pay had been deposited in advance into my new account, accessible via my bracelet. I puffed my chest out as I went to purchase tickets.

My own money – and the freedom to use it as I want.

"The two best seats you have, please."

"For what day?"

"This evening, of course."

"We've been sold out for over a month. The next tickets available are in another three weeks, or thereafter." Adriella fluttered by with a grimace.

No. I gulped air, dropped my head to my chest, and returned to where Tari stood, a frown across my face. "Sold out."

She shrieked in delight. "Fantastic! We can walk in the park instead and get to know each other."

She took my trembling hand in hers. *Or is that her hand shuddering?* We strolled through the elaborate gardens, chatting with ease once we'd broken the ice. We talked about our jobs – hers as a nurse, mine at Tezhouse – and just a bit about our homelands. We shared our first impressions about Taoland.

The sweet-smelling evening air blended perfectly with the beauty of the Taoset. The reddish Second Moon was rising off to the left, tugging at our emotions. The silver Third Moon was falling to the right, like a flower in the heavens smiling on the night. We soon found ourselves in front of the *Tavern on the Green*, near the dancing 'Green Fountain' alit in varying shades of the color whose name it bore. Romantic music filled the air.

"Shall we have dinner, Tari?"

"As long as you can get tickets. Hope it's not sold out," she teased. *This girl is awesome.*

The restaurant greeter seated us at a great table with a view of the sweeping lawns and a small lake. Dinner was perfect. The conversation was far better. Tari's grilled fowl sizzled on her plate. The exotic aromas of my savory seafood mix pleasured the space. We delighted in tasting each other's choices, and the delectable flavor of a mahogany brown soda blended with a mild tasting liquor. Her selection. We each had a second drink – lightening our heads considerably.

"I'm loving this, Adam."

Flickering candles added to an ambrosial mood. The Fountain, visible fifty yards away through the glass enclosure, added the perfect touch. After dinner, we strolled to the nearby lake, once again her soft hand in mine. The now full Second Moon created streaks of red rippling across the waters in a soft breeze. When we sat on a bench where she gently rested her head on my shoulder.

A first date to remember – forever.

We flew back to Tari's place, where I walked her to her front door.

"Don't be a stranger again, Adam."

Hoping for a second date I asked, "Can we get together again, same time, next week?"

"Sure. But *swish* me in the meantime to chat, if you can tear yourself away from your work."

She kissed me softly on my cheek, her hair brushing my face, and went inside.

Tingles traveled up and down my spine.

CHAPTER 10

LOVE AND MARRIAGE

Every date, or at least most of them, was better than the last. The only challenges involved my Tezhouse duties, which often interfered with our planned times together. One evening, three weeks into our courtship, after a forgettable film at the Green Fountains Cinema, we meandered into the park, reluctant as always to let the evening end. We soon found ourselves on 'our bench' at the lake.

We turned toward each other, bodies touching gloriously through our clothing. I brushed a stray strand of soft hair behind Tari's ear. Our lips met softly – for a brief moment – then lingered. The first kiss was gentle, warm, chaste. Our second kiss was firmer. She stiffened, then fell limp into my arms. I held her waist. Our lips opened. Our bodies melted as we pressed against each other. We continued kissing. Passionate kisses, tender and gentle at the same time. Our heavy breathing and rising heartbeats freed us of all concerns.

Oh, those first kisses. My first ever. Promises of what we would become.

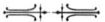

⸺

Two months into our courtship, I first spoke the words, "I love you" – words foreign to me back in Novana. She responded, "I love you more." This was right. Without a doubt. During this magical time, we shared hopes, dreams, and things previously never voiced to anyone.

Whatever was happening could only be described as 'love.' First love, beyond infatuation. I was alive in a way I didn't recognize, nor had ever imagined. Our newfound love was, of course, not a mature one, but the intense, passionate love of two young adults – a period of awakened sexuality, a time for exploring what it meant to have someone special in one's life.

On our next date, while strolling in the park, I asked for the first time, "Do you miss anyone back home, Tari?" Neither of us had yet spoken in any depth about our origins.

She dropped her eyes and fidgeted. "I miss my family, especially my mother, my sisters, and a few dear friends."

"And your father?"

"He died when I was eight. We were close." She paused, continuing to look down. "He was my daddy. I loved him so much. But he took his own life. I was there in the room, but he didn't even notice me when he put a bullet in his head."

I raised her chin to find tears filling her beautiful eyes. No one had ever revealed themselves to me like this. Nor had I to anyone. *I love her, with all of my being.*

After a pause, she began shaking and melted into uncontrollable sobs. "I hate him. How could he do that to me?"

I pulled her head to my chest until she recovered her composure a bit. Not wanting to prod, but knowing it would help for her to talk through this, I asked, "Why do you think he did it?"

She raised her head and dabbed her eyes with her handkerchief. "He lost his right hand in a work accident. It was his fault. He'd been drinking. After surgery, he could no longer work. To compound things, they took away his driver's license."

She took a big breath and blew it out, but her expression remained tense. "He became depressed. He turned completely to alcohol, which had long been his weakness. He was drunk all the time and terribly mean to my mother."

"Tari, when your dad died you were old enough for that horrible moment to be forever implanted – but too young to understand why he despaired and gave up."

Tari paused before delving deeper into the trauma of her past. "Killing himself was selfish. I want to vomit when I talk about this."

While I'd never lost anyone, I felt her pain and heartache.

"Your dad probably decided he had no reason to live." I could relate to this and shared with Tari my reasons for leaving Novana. How I was without purpose there. I revealed I too had contemplated suicide because my own life was meaningless.

"So, I can understand why your dad took his life. He had no purpose."

Tari grimaced with unfamiliar eyes. She snapped in anger. "What about me! Why didn't he make me his purpose? He was a selfish coward."

I squirmed but dared to continue, "You left your mom and siblings and friends. Was it selfish for you to come to Taoland?"

She scowled, not expecting this. "Yes. And I suffer guilt every day."

"You must have had a good reason to leave."

She turned away, appearing shamed. "We were extremely poor. My Mom, my two sisters, and I slept four to a bed. She tried her best, but we never had enough food to eat. So, she sold me. My Mom signed a contract with this creep, and we were soon to get married. Can you fathom that? She sold me!"

"No chance it might have worked?"

She stood and backed away. "He was despicable. There was none of the magic you and I share. There was no conversation. All he wanted was to maul me. He forced me into slobbering kisses, thrusting his slimy tongue into my throat. I can still smell his foul breath. He tried to have sex with me every time we were together."

I teared up in protective jealousy. "I'm so sorry."

"He was ugly. And obnoxious. His body stank worse than his

breath. I was without hope. I contemplated taking my life, like you did. And my dad. Except my dad went through with it."

Learning about Tari's past helped me understand and love her even more deeply. "What happened? How did you get here to Taoland?"

"I was rescued. A handsome winged creature named Gabriel descended from the heavens in a cloud. He offered me this opportunity – Taoland. I took it on the spot. Without telling anyone."

"That's sorta how I got here, except it was another being like Gabriel named Malaika. But I left nobody behind. They must miss you – your family and friends."

"Even worse, I'm sure they still suffer, not knowing what happened. They likely constantly search for me. And there is no way to contact them. It was selfish of me. I am utterly ashamed."

We stopped speaking for maybe five minutes, then sat on a grassy spot where Tari asked, "Adam, don't you miss anybody back home?"

I squirmed. "Nobody." My answer was cold but genuine.

"How about your father and mother?"

"I have no father. No mother. Most Novanians are produced by AI^2 – artificial insemination by artificial intelligence. But Malaika told me I was created by forces outside Novana, as an experiment. She told me that makes me special, but I don't understand."

"Do you miss your friends?"

"You are my first-ever friend. We don't make friends in Novana."

She stared at me, wide-eyed, but said nothing.

She looks horrified. I don't wanna scare her off.

We flew home in silence. At her front door, we held each other for a long time before parting. Something had changed in our relationship. We had discovered a deeper understanding of each other.

Our conversations continued to intensify as we spent time together physically or over *swish*. But my work priorities frequently created tensions. Several times I missed or canceled dates at the last minute. Once, while I was buried in a project, Bogart, through one of his minions, piled on more work than I could manage, and I neglected Tari for an entire week.

It seemed Bogart was intentionally trying to destroy my relationship with Tari, but I couldn't figure out why. When I apologized to Tari about missing dates she harshly expressed not only displeasure but anger. Six months into our relationship, on a night when Tari managed to pin me down for a date, she voiced distress as we strolled.

"Adam, I'm worried about us. Your priorities are with Tezhouse, not with me. And this is happening – more and more – while you're still new to your job and we're only dating. I'm concerned it'll get worse."

The force of her admonition stunned me. Yes, she'd complained at times. But the sternness on her face and in her voice were different and quite disturbing. I squeezed her hand, stopped walking, and turned her to me. "Tari, it's not because my work comes first and you second. I have to do my job. I have no choice. Do you think we can make our date times more flexible?"

She glared. "Adam Novana, can you hear yourself? Do you know what you just said? You just admitted your work takes priority over me and our relationship. I've begun doubting we have a long-term future."

"Tari, they need me. I'm the only one who can do what I do. We have deadlines. If we're behind schedule, we have to pick up the slack."

Her glare turned to a pout. "You don't get it. Do you ever think I need you?"

It was unfair to ask her to accept my misplaced priorities. She needed my attention, but I was unable to give it. I had no clue how to divide my time properly between Tari and Tezhouse. I had dreams and career goals to achieve, and it would take constant focus to get there.

"I repeat, Adam. Have you considered how much I need you? I *need* you. We date only once a week. Your *swish* calls in between are too often rushed. I have a job too, you know. But I've never missed one of our dates or *swish* connections."

"I'm sorry, Tari." *Dumb.* I knew a half-hearted 'sorry' never solved anything.

She raised her voice. "*Don't apologize.* I can't stand that. You make your choices, not me. I'm trying to understand, but I don't. Set boundaries at Tezhouse, or they will swallow you up and end us."

We'd never come close to arguing before. Seeing the hurt on her face was deeply unsettling. "You are the most important person in my life, Tari. You know that. I promise, I'll do better."

She shook her head. "I'm not going anywhere, my love, at least not yet. But I'm deeply troubled. And I've remained silent too long. I know I'm the only one you love as a person. But you have a second love affair going on with Tezhouse – and I have no way of competing. We both have to communicate openly about this. We mustn't allow your duties at Tezhouse destroy what we have."

<hr />

My honest effort to 'do better' for the next couple of months worked. I planned more carefully, *swish'd* daily, and showed up on time for our dates. Things got better, though I often found difficulty tearing myself away from work. I was passionate about my job.

If only Tari could only come to understand this!

Of course Bogart remained on his war path. He must have accessed my personal schedule because he frequently had others, outside Dr. Garvens' Department, assigning me work on date nights. This couldn't have been only because of what had happened at the picnic. There had to be a deeper reason. *Why does he hate me?*

Separating at the end of our dates became more difficult for Tari and me. Our kisses lingered longer, with more touching, nibbling, and deepening arousals. Everything about her thrilled me. Her scent, her soft moans, and the taste of her. We both longed for more, but we agreed not to engage in sexual intercourse unless and until we married.

<hr>

On our eight-month anniversary we returned to 'our bench' at the lake. With shaky hands I knelt on one knee and presented Tari with a jeweled ring – nothing ostentatious, but brilliant and gorgeous, like my bride-to-be. Meeting her loving eyes I asked, "Will you be my wife, Tari, for the rest of our lives?"

She sobbed as I slipped the ring onto her finger. "Of course, I will."

We held each other and kissed. "I will love you forever" was the promise we made to each other at that special moment. We made the wedding preparations ourselves. We booked the venue for a ceremony to take place four months after our engagement. We signed up a band and caterer, chose the décor, our attire, flowers, food, and wines. Most importantly, we each took time to write our vows.

Three weeks before our wedding, as I walked down a hall one afternoon at Tezhouse reviewing our wedding invitation, Bogart blocked my path. He snarled, "Getting married I heard, Asshole."

I responded, showing courage I'd earlier lacked, hoping to infuriate him, "Yes. To Tariana. Do you remember her?"

His black eyes sunk deep into their sockets. "Yeah. The bitch whose taste for men really sucks."

I snapped back, sarcastically, "Thank you for your kind words and best wishes."

His face turned beet red. "What are you holding?"

"Our wedding invitation."

"Want my address, so you can send me one?" he barked, venom dripping from his ugly lips.

What a great opening! "Not necessary. We're only inviting friends," I chuckled, aware this would further piss him off. He clenched his fists and snorted, "You really don't understand who you're dealing with." He huffed, whirled, and slithered away like a snake.

I will never cave to this bully.

Our plans proved flawless. The wedding took place in the TowneHall, one year after that life-altering picnic when we'd first met. Roshi officiated in a black tuxedo, looking way more normal than usual. Abraham, shockingly similarly dressed, and Lorelai, in lime green, served as our best man and maid of honor. Adriella danced joyfully in the air throughout the ceremony.

I gazed into Tari's breathtaking eyes as I spoke my vows. "You are the 'Love of My Life.' I promise to be the best husband I can be. I can't promise perfection, but that'll be my goal. I promise you will be my only-ever lover, and we'll always be best friends. I promise to be a good father and provider for the children to be born from our love. I promise to fill your heart with joy, every day. I promise to love you forever."

She squeezed my hand, tears falling to her soft cheeks. "Adam, I promise to be a good and faithful wife, for as long as we both shall live. I promise to love you with my entire being. I promise to be your best friend, your confidant, your soulmate, and your sidekick throughout the journey ahead. I promise to hold and comfort you in times of distress – and to be your caregiver whenever you need me. I promise to be a loving mother to our children. I too promise to love you forever."

Everything, including a three-tiered cake compliments of Randahl and Lorelai, spelled perfection. The décor was exceeded only by the loving wishes and congratulations from magnificent friends, neighbors, and coworkers. After hours of dancing and merriment, we snuck off to change our garb, then hurried furtively toward the exit.

We'd fooled no one. Our guests were at the door, bubbling with excitement. Celebratory music filled the air. The whole group sang. Some danced. It was time to leave, but nobody wanted the celebration to end. The tip of Tao dropped to the horizon, giving the skies a gorgeous glow. Everyone tossed flower petals as we headed for a large silver noli, devilishly decorated to announce our union.

Without warning a rawness filled the air. I turned to detect a dark figure emerging from a corner of the building with hate evident across his monstrous being. His uninvited presence cast a long ominous shadow blocking Tao's remaining light. His intense black eyes pierced my joy-filled heart, dampening my exuberance and all but evaporating my glee.

It was Bogart.

He just stood there, arms crossed, fury distorting his already grotesque face. I could actually smell evil in the air. I flinched, pondering whether to confront him on the spot and defend my right to live out from under his oppressive thumb – or let it go.

A comforting hand landed on my shoulder, pulling me out of my rigid stance. Randahl was there reminding me to stay grounded. I turned and met his ever-friendly smile.

"Come on, Adam. Ignore him. Take that gorgeous bride and be away with you." With a knowing nod I shook my friend's hand. Tari – visibly shaken by Bogart's disruptive appearance – wrapped her hand in the crook of my arm.

We headed to the outrageously adorned noli – as we took the first steps of the rest of our lives.

CHAPTER 11

BUILDING A CAREER

Throughout my early days at Tezhouse, my life was torn in two. One life with Tari and later with our children. The other at Tezhouse.

My career was launched when Dr. Garvens assigned me to Dr. Marlong, whose team was working on next-generation cybersecurity solutions. When we first met she'd said, "It'll take some time to get you up to speed, Adam. But your credentials and academic achievements in Novana suggest you'll be a full contributor very soon."

Her confidence boosted my own. "I will, Dr. Marlong."

Head high, I immersed myself in my assignments, working longer hours than most others on the team. Early on, Dr. Marlong gave me the lead role in design efforts to leapfrog competitors by making all Tezhouse devices 100 percent impenetrable from outside hacking. I was shocked by the assignment. This had never been accomplished after centuries of trying. The 'bad guys' were always able to defeat any designs thought to be foolproof.

We altered access codes in real time for every user, employing DNA. But every time we invited cyber experts to challenge our latest designs they broke us in days, if not hours. "I'm really frustrated, Dr. Marlong. It feels like we're going nowhere. And so many say we'll never achieve the goal."

"Adam, never let the noise from naysayers drown out your own inner voice. Maintain courage and fortitude. Follow your convictions. You might fail ninety-nine times, but if you succeed on the hundredth attempt you will be altering the course of cybersecurity forever." She pulled me to observe a hologram behind her desk. It was the face of a nice-looking man with dark hair. Scripted words at the bottom spoke to me.

When something is important, just do it – even if the odds are stacked against you.

Then a signature. *Noliander.* The inventor of the noli. "Adam, these words inspire me, and I hope they will inspire you. Of course there will *always* be those who argue that what we are attempting is impossible. I say only impossible until we do it."

She squeezed my hand in both of hers as we locked eyes. "I believe in you, my pupil. You will produce the protocols that will finally solve the challenge. You will lead Tezhouse in creating a whole new family of products."

Adriella's eyes beamed in a knowing smile. In times like this she would always show up to remind me of all I'd accomplished and to encourage me to persevere. I got her message – and Dr. Marlong's – and resolved to never again be distressed over failed attempts but to instead look forward to ultimate success. I knew I was on the right track. But we were constantly up against the clock to show progress to the R&D Committee and secure new funds. Each failed attempt made this increasingly difficult.

Of course, my long hours never sat well with Tari. But we worked through the conflicts, and our love deepened with each passing month. Then I discovered a third love. Six months after marrying Tari, with our first baby on the way, Randahl introduced me to the game of *clubbing*. "It's important you learn to play, Adam. It's the best way to socialize with top management and customer folks."

Tari agreed it might be a good way for me to 'chill.'

Randahl took me to a grassy practice area and showed me how to use a four-foot-long metal rod, an adjustable hitter called a *wacker*, with a shapeable head at the bottom. Without Randahl's awareness, I engaged Adriella to help me with her magical powers.

Whenever I prepared to hit a small ball and have it land at another location – some as far as 300 yards away – I worked telepathically with Adriella who figured out the *wacker* setup, length, and shape according to the demands of each shot. She also guided me in silence about swing speeds based on distance and wind conditions. Of course there was one major problem. Adriella had never played the game. And once I felt more comfortable, I dismissed her – deciding it would be cheating to use her help.

The goal of the game was simple – take as few hits as possible to reach ten targets spread out over an eighty-acre course. My first round with Randahl was fun, but I played less than poorly due to my lack of skill and inexperience. Randahl offered encouragement, as was his nature. "Not bad for your first time, Adam. Now get yourself some lessons, and practice, practice, practice. You'll be as good as me in no time."

I took Randahl's advice and scheduled a weekly training session. I improved rapidly by hitting balls after work at lighted training ranges. The only problem? Clubbing placed an additional strain on our marriage. With our first baby on the way, and Tari working hard as a nurse, she complained about me spending too much time clubbing, especially when I left her alone on weekends. I told her, "Excelling in clubbing is necessary for my career advancement."

She didn't buy it. Her angry response was, "Nonsense."

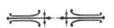

Ten months into our marriage, with Tari approaching the end of her pregnancy, my team and I at Tezhouse produced a cybersecurity breakthrough that even the 'best of the best' couldn't defeat.

We dubbed my invention *SuperCyberX*. I was granted my first patent. Shortly thereafter, Dr. Garvens chose me to represent Tezhouse at a Conference of the Taoland Society of Young Engineers on the Second Moon. He warned, "Don't provide any details about your designs. The patent filing tells them little. Keep them in the dark. Let them waste their time trying to figure it out."

This led to my first major blunder as a husband. I was away at the TSYE Conference when Tari's water broke. Lorelai took her to the hospital for the birth of our son, Tojo. I was not informed until the difficult delivery was over. The birth was two weeks early, but there was no excuse for my leaving Tari so close to her due date. In fact, she had begged me not to go to that conference.

I *swish'd* when I learned the news. Tari held up our new baby boy at what should have been a joyful moment. But she was not smiling. She barely looked at me through teary eyes. Adriella scowled.

Consumed with guilt, I struggled for words. "I'm so sorry I was away." Hardly adequate.

Eyes still downcast, she responded, "I'm exhausted, Adam. I need some sleep."

I hung my head in shame. I sobbed, consumed with an overwhelming sadness instead of the elation I should have felt.

I would never forgive myself for not being there. *Nor will Tari.*

Tari quit her job to care for Tojo. For me, finding a balance between work demands and helping care for our son was challenging. Despite my best efforts, I was less than successful. And our marriage became further strained at a time we should have been delighting in our baby boy.

Fortunately, I was there when our second child, Kaleeva, was born sixteen months after Tojo. I held Tari's hand in the delivery room, supporting her as she bravely dealt with pain. Her labor continued for five long hours, the most severe part lasting a full hour. Tari was clingy like I'd never experienced. Wet with sweat, she cried out in anguish as she squeezed my hand more firmly with each push. She grunted and groaned, looking to me for strength.

She'd insisted on natural childbirth; thus the doctors administered no pain-blocking medications. Her agony was way beyond what I'd anticipated.

I remained calm as I comforted Tari, repeating over and over, "I love you." She blew out deep and rapid breaths between pushes. With the last bit of her strength, Tari delivered our daughter.

Witnessing Kaleeva's birth was exhilarating beyond the ability of words to explain. But in the midst of it I silently berated myself for missing Tojo's birth. I was consumed in shame that she had given birth to our son without me by her side.

After letting me cut our baby's umbilical cord the nurse passed her to Tari, who held Kaleeva to her bosom. I softly caressed them. In stunned amazement, intoxicated by a fresh, sweet smell, I rejoiced at our baby girl's first beautiful cry.

When Tari handed Kaleeva to me again, I wept touching the cheek of our warm and soft little miracle. An unexpected avalanche of love, a rush of utter joy, lifted my heart from my chest. Holding her in my arms, her tiny fingers clutching one of my own, I was hooked for life.

What a tragic loss for humans in Novana to never experience the creation of new life – to never know the joy of family, of holding your own child in your arms. Parental pride never captured Novanian hearts. They never dreamed of, with, or for their own children. How terribly sad.

Whatever forces had brought me here to Taoland had truly saved me from a dismally lonely existence. As we shared our private moment with Kaleeva, I felt a presence descend into the room. It was Adriella. She appeared in a corner, glowing softly, waiting for me to beckon. I nodded, and she glided over and stroked our baby's precious face with a pure light – an extension of her being. Adriella's glow pulsed brightly, encompassing Tari and me, along with our precious creation.

When a magic energy passed through us, Tari asked, "What is that I feel, Adam?" I didn't respond. My precious bride became visibly refreshed, serenity on her face. Adriella congratulated me telepathically and disappeared.

After we brought Kaleeva home I took a week off, resolved to begin spending more time with my family. But after that brief respite, work demands only intensified. I became increasingly driven to be my best, earn more money, and provide for my growing family's wants and needs. The constant thought of whether I was doing this for them or myself tugged at my being.

<hr>

As mentioned, my work at Tezhouse was frequently plagued with failures, but Dr. Marlong always coached me through. "Adam, you're authoring the story of your career. Never give up because a few bad chapters or a few antagonists creep into the scenes. Be doggedly tenacious. Always remain confident." I would not have made it without her ever-supportive presence.

Two years after *X1*, I was granted my second patent for *X2*. The patent for *X3* came another year later. My star was rising. I received two promotions and three salary increases. Significant ones. Lead Senior Engineer at the age of only twenty-seven, with triple my starting salary.

Tari did sort of congratulate me occasionally, but without sincerity and void of enthusiasm. In fact she became increasingly disinterested in my achievements. "I know you're adored at Tezhouse," she'd say, "but I need you to spend more time helping me with the children. You need to ask your bosses to cut back on your work hours."

Nag! Nag! Nag!

I tried but failed. Instead I hurried to the lab most days soon after waking. I rarely sat at the breakfast table. Instead, I'd kiss Tari and the kids and head for the front door with toast and jam in my hand. This always annoyed my wife. She was jealous of my zeal for my work and now she hated my passion for clubbing as well.

I was lured by money and position. I took pride in my talents and was thrilled when my achievements were generously recognized. Career success – and the power and glory it brought – was the reason I'd come to Taoland. My fear of failure gradually faded.

I need the accolades. I never get them at home.

When Tojo and Kaleeva reached the ages of seven and five-and-a-half, we took a vacation at a lake. For a week – the longest I'd ever spent away from Tezhouse. On our first night, Tari seized the opportunity to vent some pent-up frustrations. After the kids went to bed, she poured two glasses of wine and invited me to our balcony. A qilin skirted away in the sand below without even looking at me. The silver moon, full in the sky, provided no comfort. Adriella was nowhere to be seen.

"Adam, we're drifting apart. I told you, before we became engaged, I was concerned about your work obsession. My worst nightmares have been exceeded. It's time for you to pause and reflect on what you're doing, and how your false purpose is threatening our marriage and our family."

False purpose?

I was not expecting this. Not just as we started our vacation. I usually kicked conflict down the road to avoid unpleasant arguments – always changing the subject whenever Tari mentioned my screwed-up priorities. This time, I decided it was time to get our problems out on the table.

"OK. Let's talk."

"Adam, if you continue to be 'all work' our marriage will end. I need you to spend more time with me and the kids. I want you to pursue interests outside Tezhouse, and I don't mean clubbing. Success at work is not your true purpose. It's merely a stepping-stone toward becoming the person you are meant to be."

I genuinely wanted things to change. Letting down my wife and children was not my idea of success. But I couldn't risk losing my edge as a rising star at Tezhouse. "Tari, you know advancing in my career and making more money is good for our family. Everything I do is for you and the kids."

Ooops. Why did I say that again? I knew this argument would piss her off.

She scowled and growled. "Don't ever say that again. *Never again!* If you believe that you're delusional. It's a lie. You're consumed with blind ambition. You're driven by fear of failure."

Fear was what drove me toward over-achievement, and I readily admitted that. "Yes. I'm terrified about the possibility of failure at work. All the time."

Red-faced, she barked, "Well, where's your fear about failure as a husband and father? You came here from a dark place, where family didn't exist, and where individual accomplishments didn't exist. As a result, you've adopted a false purpose – always putting your career first. You've got responsibilities to me and the children as well. I'm asking you, begging you, start saying 'no' to Tezhouse."

I went silent, reflecting on her selfless sacrifice in retiring from nursing, which she loved, to raise our children. She was the one who changed their diapers, fed them, played with them while I went off to work, admonished them, and took them to school. She was the 'stay-at-home mom.' I was the far-too-absent dad and husband. I grasped her hands. "Tari, I never thank you for being a perfect wife and selfless mother while letting me pursue my goals. It's really not fair. I get that."

She gazed somberly. "I cherish my role as a mother, though my job is way tougher than yours."

"I know that."

"I need you to change your ways. Consider this an ultimatum."

That was enough. I'd had enough. I tuned her out. Her face darkened.

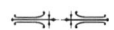

As the kids grew, Tari volunteered for a nonprofit – Tao Services for the Underprivileged. She repeatedly urged me to set aside some time to volunteer with her at TSU, but I ignored such suggestions, always shifting the conversation. "Tari, even after years here I struggle constantly. I hide my insecurities at work by always going above and beyond. It's the only way I know to succeed at Tezhouse. But I do want to be a great husband and father at the same time. You've gotta believe me."

Her countenance turned forlorn. "Enough! Drop the excuses. Today you are further away from striking a balance than ever. There are only so many hours in a day. If you don't change your ways, our fall into a perilous place will intensify."

CHAPTER 12

A BOMBED PRESENTATION

One day I received a surprise *swish*. "Yours is a meteoric ride, young man. I say, let's fasten our seat belts as we ride into the future with the Inventor from Novana."

A shock wave darn near pushed me over. A hologram of Komourin, the Tezhouse CEO, unfolded before me. I'd never spoken with him before. He congratulated me for being named "Entrepreneur of the Decade" by TSAE. In my career I'd already received five recognitions – the first when Tezhouse named me 'Rookie of the Year' after my initial patent. After that I'd received other accolades from advanced engineering societies, one every year or two.

And now this. From TSAE. Recognized by Komourin!

"Well done, Adam. Your contributions to Tezhouse are greatly appreciated."

I only mouthed, "Thank you," before we disconnected.

This award was mind-boggling – and Komourin's response was unexpected. I was chosen after receiving my third patent. With the help of my team, I repurposed the software architecture from *SuperCyberX1* and *X2* and applied it to medical engineering with my latest invention – the *X3*. The bad news – Bogart publicly seethed.

He was quoted as saying to his staff, "Asshole Novana must be stopped. And I am the one who will do that."

Soon after receiving the TSAE recognition I accepted an invitation from the Taoland Institute of Higher Learning to address their 'Conference on the Future.' I was to present *SuperCyberX3*, now in promising Beta testing. My knees buckled when I learned 500 plus of my peers would fill the room where I'd speak. For weeks, I carefully prepared my speech, in solitude. The day before the event, I shared my presentation with Roshi and Abraham.

"What do you think, guys?"

After an uncomfortable silence Roshi tugged at his beard, a pained look on his face. "Boring. Too much information. I'm afraid you'll stink up the place."

I wrinkled my forehead. "Your thoughts, Abraham?"

Abraham held his nose shut. "Roshi is being kind. I say you should call in sick. This is not repairable overnight. You should have sought professional reviewers much earlier."

It was too late. There was no way out. I worked through the night trying to make last-minute repairs. The next day, midafternoon, I found myself exhausted and fidgeting nervously while waiting to be called to the podium. My friends' critiques fueled my pessimism as I waited my turn. My heart thudded against my rib cage when the emcee introduced me.

Randahl and Bogart sat in chairs in the front row, my nemesis with an ugly smirk across his hideous face. Shockingly, next to them sat the man I'd *swish'd* with but never met in person – Komourin. He'd come all the way from the Third Moon. The knot inside twisted tighter.

I gulped and began anxiously. The joke I opened with was received in silence except for the loud groan coming from Bogart, a boisterous insult throwing me further off-balance. My hands shook causing the high-intensity laser pointer to dance wildly on each visual. I turned to speak to the virtual display, losing eye contact with the audience. Laughter from Bogart ensued.

This is a disaster.

After fumbling the opening, with repeated grunts from Bogart messing with me, I moved to the second portion of my presentation. Showing 3-D depictions of new *X3* medical devices was sure to hook the audience. I had preloaded exciting holograms, being careful to withhold proprietary information. I cleared my throat and directed, "Display Image A."

I let out a torturous sigh when Image A was displayed – upside down. Bogart shrieked in delight for the entire room to hear. Bile rose in my throat as I managed to rasp out, "Rotate image 180 degrees." My *swish* device decided to cooperate this time, but the crowd was already murmuring amongst themselves, and the emcee had to quiet them down. It all went from bad to worse as I made blunders at every step.

When the thirty-minute horror show was over, Bogart unnerving me throughout, I opened the floor for questions. Not a single hand raised. The only sound was a loud rude yawn, again from Bogart, before the emcee declared the session ended. The audience scurried to the exit.

Within a few minutes, the room was empty – except for Komourin, Randahl, and Bogart.

"So, how do you think that went?' asked Randahl.

I hung my defeated head in shame. "It sucked. I sucked."

"What a gross understatement," offered Bogart. The first smile I'd ever seen on him stretched across his face. "To call today a complete bomb would be beyond generous. That was two horrible presentations at the same time."

"Two presentations?"

Bogart snorted. "Yeah, Asshole, your first and your last for Tezhouse." His loathsome laughter filled the room.

Komourin interrupted in anger. "Shut the fuck up, Bogart. This is not a time for insults. Come with me, Adam. We're going to dinner." He put his arm around my shoulders, waving away Bogart and Randahl who froze with mouths open.

Komourin and I bonded over a delicious meal. He advised me he'd been watching me, and that he'd help me going forward. He coached on how to improve my presentation skills and said he'd be sending me to a special school for this. He offered to serve as my mentor. Instead of destroying my career with a ghastly presentation, my career had just been kicked up a notch or two.

A month later, I attended and found terrific value in a seminar on presentations. With practice, I soon became highly skilled. The bad news? I wound up making pitches all over Taoland. My assignments dragged me away from my family, further disrupting the balance I sought and sorely needed. Sales based on my inventions grew to one-fourth of all Tezhouse business. My star kept rising. Bogart reaped the benefits in sales and profits, but openly hated the acclaim I received.

For the milestone delivery of our 100th *SuperCyberX* system, I invited Komourin to join us at Tezhouse First Moon. "What's the agenda, Adam?" he asked, stepping out of his corporate noli.

"I'd like you to thank those who made this happen. The engineers, model shop workers, production team, testing personnel, quality folks, publications team, those who package and ship, and the field service personnel. The least of these we too often forget."

"Perfect. Let's go."

We spent a half day in Tezhouse engineering, manufacturing, and test facilities. Then an hour with those in publications and services sections. Komourin was a natural at 'working the room.' He looked every employee in the eye as he touched their hearts with thanks and congratulations. His generous and sincere words uplifted everyone.

We ended up in Bogart's main executive conference room where top management, all Bogart cronies, gathered to seize the moment and make presentations. Komourin excused himself to freshen up, and I took a chair against the wall, not being senior enough to sit at the table.

Attacks against me started flying as soon as Komourin departed. The Controller, a balding plump gray-skinned man, crossed his arms and huffed, "Well, there was a day of productive work thrown down the toilet. You pissed away thousands today, Novana." The Director of Budgets added his two lunies worth. "Yeah, what a total waste. Plain dumb."

I glanced over to the entrance of the room. Komourin stood there, hands in his pockets, barely detectable in the shadows. He didn't need the restroom. He just wanted to eavesdrop on the jabber from those believing he was out of earshot.

Bogart, oblivious to Komourin's presence, snarled, "Just what we expect from Novana – kissing the ass of the CEO. The asshole knows Komourin likes to rub shoulders with the troops, so he set this up to score brownie points."

"A total waste of time and money," added the prudish Chief Accountant with an upturned nose.

Another attendee, the Marketing Director, couldn't resist adding his criticism. "We could have far better used this time updating Komourin on our business plans. You're a worthless jerk, Novana."

Without warning, Komourin thrust himself noisily out of the shadows, his presence filling the room. He passed his seat at the head of the table and moved to where I was seated against the wall. He knelt beneath me on his right knee, his back now to the others. He knelt!

Is this happening?

No senior executive, certainly not the CEO, had ever bowed before an employee.

"Adam, what else can I do? I can skip these inane briefings if there are other folks we've missed. There is nothing more important than thanking those too often overlooked."

"Thanks, Mr. Komourin. We're good. Everything went perfectly today. I assure you those you touched are most appreciative."

A dozen boring financial briefings followed. Komourin's yawns and failure to ask questions proved he found them useless. With full certainty, I knew what had just happened would ramp up Bogart's self-proclaimed war against me. Sure enough, as the meeting ended, Bogart slumped in his chair, his hair wet and steepled in front of a face even a mother would find revolting; his rage-filled eyes locked on to mine.

CHAPTER 13

UP IN SMOKE

A dozen important officials, prospective customers in medical technologies, gathered in our Advanced Engineering Lab. I never grew tired of meeting new folks from throughout the Universe. They were each different, they were each the same. I was especially pleased to see two Neflarians – a species highly skilled in healing and the early detection of lesions. Inputs from these pale-skinned monomorphic humanoids would be valuable.

All were eager to learn about *SuperCyberX3*, which had finished Beta testing and promised to be a game-changer in medical engineering. Of course, whenever we briefed top management on this Bogart would scoff. "Waste of our research funds. Let's focus on markets where we already make good profits."

The demo was to be the decisive step in a major competition against Huggles, the front-runner. The winner would immediately seize market leadership. The loser would be left outside looking in.

The *X3*, building on the successes of the *X1* and *X2*, employed other advanced Tezhouse technologies in early detection of incurable diseases, and applied AI to aid in pharmaceutical cures. I was confident we'd win, launching us into an exploding market. My *X3* team was buoyed by the idea of sparing suffering and saving lives. Such an altruistic goal was unfamiliar to me.

Tari and I had friends whose elderly relatives had suffered and died from neurological abnormalities and brain deterioration. End of life in these cases was lengthy and torturous – for patient, caregivers, and family. But my focus with the *X3* was making money for Tezhouse, thereby advancing my career. Yet I had to admit, I felt mildly inspired by the good we might do. Tiny sparks of servitude bloomed within me. I thought of Tari's volunteer work with new appreciation. I thought if we can help others, while making profits, why not?

Whoops. Let's not get too soft here.

When I took center stage, I was surprised to see Bogart present in the room.

Was he hoping the demo would go poorly?

I still couldn't figure out why he hated me so much.

I began with a virtual display presentation, overviewing the various diseases we were targeting. It went well. I took a few questions before launching the actual demo. One guest raised his pen. "We understand *X3*'s use of AI to analyze complex data will expedite the development of medicines and vaccines for unconquered diseases. Correct?"

"Absolutely. AI implementation will assist in developing pathogenic agents and therapeutics, some hand-tailored for individual patients."

One of the Neflarians, pale skin shimmering, asked, "Is there hope for early detection or even cures for totally unknown neurological diseases arriving from outside Taoland?"

"Yes. We're exploring electrical neurostimulators, similar to traditional heart pacemakers, to be implanted in patients we find suffering from such diseases."

An overweight Maykinian looked over the top of his glasses and queried, "You've also mentioned incurable cancers. Can you expand on this?"

"*X3* with AI will analyze data to expedite the detection of ever-emerging cancer variants, at earliest onset, via simple blood tests. Patients will swallow our tiny *X3* cameras and transmit digital images of the digestive and intestinal tracts, identifying early precancerous polyps and sources of microscopic bleeding. These cameras will also be steered to various organs, helping in early detection and throughout needed surgeries.

Another potential huge profit-maker. That's what matters.

"Wonderful," said another, nodding as he scribbled notes.

"We will help doctors analyze biological markers via breath analysis to identify the seeds of dangerous viruses. In partnership with the medical community, we will custom design pharmaceuticals to trick viruses into self-destruction, while boosting the auto-immune system. We look forward to collaborating with all of you on these breakthroughs."

The Director of the Tao Scientific Research Institute stood and led the others in applause. "Well done, Adam! Enough talk. Let's have the demo."

I spoke the words 'Begin Demo' with full confidence.

Boom!

Everything moved in slow motion as loud ringing filled my ears. Racks of computers exploded simultaneously. The room shook. The virtual display went eerily blank. Testing equipment blazed and spewed out smoke. Everyone covered their noses and mouths to reject a stomach-wrenching stench. Dreadful crackling sounds echoed from the equipment. Everyone pushed to the rear of the room. A deafening hush settled over the attendees.

My invention is in flames – my dreams are up in smoke.

Raucous laughter emerged from the shadows of the drifting smoke. It was Bogart, unable to hide his delight.

How could he take pleasure in such a disaster? Maybe the prick caused this!

Bogart's snickering rose even above the sounds of the smoldering flames. His hateful beady eyes met mine. I returned his sneer.

Randahl rushed in, alerted by the blaring alarms. "What happened?"

Holding back tears, I answered, "I have no idea."

To those now cowering in the corners I said, "Please, let's move calmly to the exit, so my guys can figure out what happened. We'll keep you informed."

I gave my team directions, *swish'd* Tari with the bad news, and headed home.

My head hung low as I dragged myself to the kitchen sink, where I vomited. I entered the living room and slumped into the couch. Tari sat alongside. "I'm here for you, my love." Without asking for details, she pulled my head to her lap and held me for a long time before we even spoke a word.

She's here for me, in spite of my failings as her husband.

I couldn't eat or sleep. While my team worked through the night, I stayed in contact via *swish*. Early the next morning, we gathered in my conference room for a somber meeting. I began. "Bottom line – have you figured out what went wrong?"

Noel, my Chief Engineer, responded, "We're flabbergasted. We'd rehearsed the demo a dozen times, without a hiccup. The damage is extensive – a total wipeout. No way this could have happened without external interference."

"Any thoughts as to the cause?" *I know who caused it.*

"Sabotage is the only possible answer, but the fire destroyed any clues. There had to be serious rewiring of the power structure, explosives that left no trace, and some triggering mechanism. But we can't figure out how or when or by whom. We were there all day every day. The lab has been totally secured, in lockdown, for months."

"The damages?"

"We estimate 5 million lunies. We'll need to start the build over – from scratch. Making matters worse, it'll take six months to get back to where we were yesterday."

A dozen medical associations, universities, and hospitals had collaborated on the request for proposals. The award, a 50-million-luni development contract with ten times more in sole-source follow-ons was to be announced within weeks. Huggles would certainly be chosen now, even though our technology was far superior. They would capture leadership in a vast emerging market. I had no inspiration to offer. "Keep searching for clues. Try to figure out – if it was sabotage, what triggered it?"

This literal 'crash and burn' in front of key customers topped with falling behind Huggles in a new market would likely end my skyrocketing career. *I'll be severely punished. It's over.* Remaining in the stench-filled lab was unbearable. I ended the meeting and once again dragged myself home.

The next morning, the second since the disaster, began early with a ray of hope – a *swish* text message – from Dr. Nouvelle, Director of Parismo Medical Technologies, a highly influential group. She wasn't present at the demo. We'd never met. Her text read, "Adam, we are saddened. Have you unraveled the cause?"

I texted back, "Dr. Nouvelle, every trial run of the demo was flawless. The explosion and fire destroyed any clues. The only thing that makes sense is sabotage, but we can't figure out how or by whom or why. Please don't repeat these suspicions. We don't want to publicly assert something we can't prove."

She texted, "And the impact?"

"Five mil and six months."

"On no! Our team favors the Tezhouse solution, but I don't see how we can postpone awarding the contract for that long. Let's put our heads together."

"I'd like that."

"Meet me at the Tavern on the Green, in the park, at noon."

CHAPTER 14

BOGART: DOUBLING DOWN

"I need your help, Trafica."

"Name it, Bogart." Ugliness oozed from the gangster's wrinkled orange face.

It was 7:00 a.m. the second morning after the 'accident.' I'd *swish'd* Trafica from my home. I'd totally fucked up Asshole Adam's demo. Now I'd use this thug to end Novana's career once and for all.

Trafica ran a brothel, in the foothills, forty miles from our facilities. Law enforcement knew about his illicit enterprise, but he knew how to placate them. He frequently provided me with prostitutes whenever I needed to bring some senior manager, politician, or customer around to my way of thinking.

I was still applauding the success in blowing up Novana's demonstration. One of the happiest accomplishments of my life was about to get even better. I was about to hammer the final nails in the asshole's coffin. "Trafica, I need your most voluptuous slut to be at the Tavern on the Green today. I need her to help me take down an enemy."

Stomping on Asshole Adam while he was down and watching him piss in his pants would be the ultimate delight. Destroying his reputation and marriage in the process would be icing on the cake.

"Sure, Bogart. Give me the details."

He's too dumb for any details.

"I need a full-bodied hooker. Ultra-sexy. Nice tits and great ass. Aggressive, when needed. Dressed scantily, in fake business attire, one or two sizes too small. Tight silk blouse she can hardly button, barely holding everything in. A short loose skirt – easily lifted. Intelligent enough to listen to a technical conversation and appear interested."

Trafica placed his right hand on his chin. "I've got just the whore you need. I get a hard-on just thinking 'bout her. She's Marinese. You know how curvy those femes are. Goes by Destiny." He was practically drooling while speaking about her.

Hmmmmmm. I might wanna taste this delight myself.

"Today she'll be Dr. Nouvelle, Director of Parismo Medical Technologies, on the Second Moon."

"She don't look like no director of nothing."

What a meathead. But a useful one.

"Put a pair of dowdy glasses on her. Hannibal will prep her for the mission. Can she bluff interest in technology? At least for a few minutes?"

"Don't worry. She's multitalented." He choked out a dirty laugh. "Slutty, but smart. Plus, your mark won't be able to take his eyes offa' her."

"Have someone drop her off at the rear of the parking lot to meet Hannibal at 11:00 a.m. He'll check her appearance, fill her in on the plan, and rehearse her. He'll pay Destiny and give her an envelope for you. Don't let me down."

"Got it man." We disconnected.

I rose from my desk and stretched. No one in all of Taoland could pull off what I was about to do, without leaving fingerprints.

I wished I could return to my homeland for a moment, resurrect my fucking father from his grave, and make him eat all the insults he vomited on me. Good thing I got away with offing him long ago. My hatred for that prick was topped only by my loathing of my mother and the siblings she cowered over. They all treated me like I was infected shit.

Thirty minutes later, Hannibal entered with coffees, into which I splashed some booze. "You've done it, Bogart. Novana is finished." We grinned menacingly as we swigged our spiked java.

I returned to my chair and crossed my arms behind my head. "Hannibal, I'll never forget the look on the asshole's face when everything blew up and his guests ran into the corners. One of the greatest moments of my life." We belly-laughed as I retrieved a baggie from my drawer. I dropped two lines of white powder on my desk and offered Hannibal a snort through a 100-luni note. He jumped at the chance.

"We're not finished. I've got more in store for him this afternoon. He's gonna attack a hooker in public. I need your help pulling it off."

Hannibal perked up, an evil sneer across his disfigured kisser. The dude loved doing evil deeds for me. "I'm all ears, Boss. Whatchathinkin'?"

"The Medical Engineering Delegation is still in town. I've directed Randahl to host them for lunch at the Tavern on the Green. Novana will be at the restaurant – separately. We're gonna humiliate him in front of everyone."

One of my girls, a busty, Sequet female – not exactly human but a great fuck – entered the room with snacks. She bent over and placed a tray on the table, wiggling her round ass in our faces. I winked. "Later, Babe."

"When and how do we mess with the asshole?" Hannibal asked, unable to peel his eyes from my sexy Sequet.

"Novana will arrive at the Tavern just before noon. He won't know about Randahl's luncheon. The corporate noli with Randahl and his guests will depart headquarters at noon sharp and arrive at the restaurant ten minutes later."

"Why the Tavern?"

"That's where Novana had his first date with his bitch, Tariana. He proposed to her nearby. I relish the idea of ending his career there."

"You really hate this guy."

"I do."

"Why? It can't be because he stole your date at a picnic years ago."

"My hatred of the asshole has nothing to do with Tariana. Of course, I was hoping to get in her pants that day. But I found a much better lay. My focus on this guy has nothing to do with her."

"Then why?"

"Novana's been in the spotlight from the moment he arrived in Taoland. He's an ass-kissing Goody-Goody-Two-Shoes who's got the CEO mentoring him. He's the only one standing in my way to replace Komourin, who, along with half the Board, thinks he's special. He's a *fucking know-it-all*. I don't give a shit about the technology he's so expert at. I leave the engineering to the geeks. My expertise is hiding the fact I don't understand a fucking word they're saying."

"Got it. So, what do you need?"

"I want you to meet a whore named Destiny in the back of the parking lot at 11:00 a.m. From the way Trafica describes her she'll be easy to spot. She's gonna be impersonating Dr. Nouvelle, Director of Parismo Medical Technologies, a member of the delegation who was absent from the demo. You'll have an hour to prep the bitch. And don't taste the goods."

"What's the plot?"

I stood up and poured more booze. "Make sure Destiny, now Dr. Nouvelle, meets the asshole at the Reception at noon sharp. He'll be standing there; he's always early. The Greeter, Kathleen, is on board. She'll escort Novana and the hooker to the leather loveseat behind her post. She'll apologize for the delay and leave a bottle of sweet red wine for them."

Hannibal squirmed and grinned, displaying his crooked brown teeth. "Then what?"

"Destiny should engage the jerk by offering condolences for the mishap two days ago. She should say her team would love to get Tezhouse an extension for the bid. This will capture his attention. Then she should ask Novana about his invention. He can't possibly resist this request."

"Seriously, a prostitute as a scientist?"

"Trafica says she's bright. Prep her as best you can. Make sure she wears geeky eyeglasses. Tone down her lipstick if it's too much. Run through the scenario several times with her. Put a badge on her, with name and title, and give her a burner *swish* device."

"I hope she can pull it off." He knitted his brows with concern.

"Walk behind her to the restaurant. When Kathleen leads her and Novana to the couch, hide yourself in the vines and arbor at the top of the deck, to the left of the entrance. You'll have a perfect view through the foliage for recording everything. You've gotta buzz Destiny on her burner the moment you observe Randahl and the customers entering the restaurant."

Hannibal's face lit up. "I love it. I'll record everything."

I twirled my mustache. "Timing is critical. When Randahl arrives and Kathleen escorts him and his guests into the restaurant, at that exact moment, the phony Dr. Nouvelle has to launch the dirty deed – splash red wine all over the asshole, pop her blouse buttons and let her boobs fall out, and raise her skirt to her waist, exposing her ass for all to see."

"What next?"

"Tell her to wrap her naked legs around him and plant a slobbering kiss on his mouth. Kathleen will shriek, to alarm everybody in the restaurant. Destiny will scream, 'Pervert!' and pull away. In the confusion she'll rush outside, half naked. You've gotta then quickly whisk her around the side of the building, put her in a wig and a full coat, and stealthily make your way arm in arm to your noli."

"Budget?"

"You decide what to pay Destiny and also give her an envelope for Trafica. I've already taken care of Kathleen."

"Consider it done." He rubbed his hands together as he drooled.

When Hannibal departed, I *swish'd* my cohorts on the Tezhouse Board. They were seated in the main conference room at headquarters. They'd heard about the explosion but not about today's plan.

Dragoon rested his head on his fist. "So, is Novana finished?"

"For certain. No way he'll be granted the 5 million needed to rebuild. He'll be fired."

Schmohun fidgeted. "Well, it'd be great to get into the medical engineering space. But destroying your nemesis takes precedence."

Rimoltz downed a shot of something dark. "We'll get into that market as soon as Novana's gone. We own his patent and his team. We'll get the customer to reopen the door. They know our solution is far superior to Huggles' proposal."

"What about Komourin?" asked Swaltman. "Has he rang in on the disaster?"

I answered, "Not yet. But there's nothing he can do."

Dragoon stirred in delight. "Well then, it's 100 percent certain you'll be our next CEO. There's still Randahl, but he'll resign once pressured."

"Of course, Komourin remains close to three of the Board members plus the Chairman," advised Rimoltz. "They all hate you, Bogart. Hard to imagine, with your warm, fuzzy personality."

We roared in unison.

How wonderful to be detestable.

Schmohun raised his hand and offered advice. "Bogart, you need to kiss up to the newcomers, Figaro and Rigsby. They remain uncommitted. To get to five votes, we need one of them with us, by whatever means."

I appealed to the four with a quizzical look. "I'd love to find a way to get Komourin out early."

"Not gonna happen." Swaltman concluded with a stern look. "Not as long as he keeps indulging his senior managers with bonuses, gifts, and handwritten notes every time they manage to achieve anything."

"We'll find a way to get rid of Komourin once we've secured five votes," offered Dragoon. "I'm getting tired of knowing he has something on each of us. Especially on you, Bogart."

"That's the only reason it's taken me so long to get rid of Asshole Novana."

An inquisitive grin tugged at the corner of Rimoltz's mouth. "Bogart, how did you pull off the explosion? Novana's team wouldn't have let him launch the demo unless they knew it would go perfectly."

"Well, you know me. I'm shy. I don't like to brag." I couldn't disguise my proud grin.

Raucous laughter again filled the *swish* space.

I continued, "Months ago, when the prototype construction began, we smeared hi-tech explosive paste at every power node – where max damage would result. We hid tiny receivers to trigger explosions throughout the demo and lab equipment."

"How come the paste was never detected?" asked Dragoon.

"It's an advanced invention. Undetectable. The patent is held secret by its inventor, which by the way is Huggles. Don't ask how I got it."

Dragoon stirred in his seat. "We don't need to know. How were the explosions activated?"

"This is the best part. Novana himself triggered it all when he said, 'Begin Demo.' He destroyed his own masterpiece."

Rimholtz looked puzzled. "I don't get it."

"We programmed the triggers to respond to Novana's voice and native language, using recordings from his Tezhouse entry interview. We only needed to know the words he would speak. They chose 'Begin Demo' weeks ago."

Swaltman leaned back in his chair. "Brilliant, Bogart . . . absolutely brilliant."

I bet my old man's vomiting in his grave right now.

"Others conducted dry runs in their own languages. But the embedded triggering devices only recognized Novana's voice and language."

"What if they'd changed the command at the last moment?"

"We had eyes and ears in the lab. We were prepared to remotely adjust the trigger, again using bits from Novana's earlier recordings."

Rimoltz chuckled, "You're not as dumb as you look, Bogart. We'll talk again soon."

"OK, guys. Stay tuned. We're doubling down and getting Novana deeper in trouble today. I'll call when it's done." I disconnected.

I stayed at home to await Hannibal's *swish* informing me of success at the Tavern. I went to the kitchen for a snack but heard my wife's nagging and immediately escaped to my home-office. I slammed the door behind me. The walls shook. She could always rile my temper. But I needed to stay focused on destroying Adam Novana.

Hannibal *swish'd* shortly after noon, head down, unwilling to meet my gaze.

"What happened?"

"It went bust. I did all you asked. But Randahl screwed everything up."

"What?" I shouted, ready to wring his neck. *I'm surrounded by incompetence.*

Hannibal squirmed. "Everything was on plan until the delegation arrived. Destiny was perfect. She met Novana at noon, and Kathleen took them to the love seat. I took position, out of sight, with recorder focused. The Tezhouse noli landed. I watched

Randahl and several of his staff leading the delegation toward the Tavern. When they reached the steps, I signaled Destiny's burner. That's when everything went wrong. The delegation never entered."

"You fucking idiot." My face burned in rage. "You screwed it up!"

"Fuck you, Bogart. I already told you it was Randahl. Somehow, he knew our plan. Right after I signaled Destiny, Randahl turned and told the others, 'You all head down to a private table they've set up by the lake. I'm going inside to confirm the menu.' When staffers swiftly led the delegation away Randahl turned and glared at exactly where I was hiding – and smirked."

"Fucker. He had 'ears' in my office this morning. We were the only ones who knew."

Hannibal was visibly shaking as he tried to absolve himself of all guilt. "Yes. Yes. Randahl knew. *He knew.* He barged past Kathleen and yelled at the whore who had spun into action and declared he had called the police. Some minor good news, I was still able to get condemning recordings."

"Fucking Randahl."

"Destiny ran out, and I took her away as planned. When I looked back, Randahl was ushering Novana away."

I slapped violently at dead air to disconnect the *swish*. I smashed my fist violently into my desk. My knuckles bled.

Fucking Randahl will pay for this.

CHAPTER 15

STUNNING SURPRISE

My *swish* bracelet buzzed with a text message from Komourin. "Adam, I need you to fly to the Third Moon and meet me at headquarters. *Chieftain* will pick you up at 8:00 p.m. tonight."

This is the end of my career.

When I sunk into the sofa Tari put a comforting arm around me. "Are you scared, Adam?"

"Petrified, honey. After the demo disaster, the cost and schedule impacts, Huggles will be chosen. I'm sure my days at Tezhouse are over."

"Do you think Komourin also knows about the scene in the Tavern?"

"He knows everything. Randahl told me a video was sent to the Board."

She rested her head on my shoulder. "But why would he fly you all the way to the Third Moon? He could have just ended it by *swish*."

"Probably wants to tell me in person."

She kissed me softly. "No matter what, my husband, I'm here for you. I love you. I'll be waiting with open arms when you return. We can live a simpler life. We'll be fine."

My purpose is corporate success. I can't start over.

Komourin's interlunar craft arrived after Taoset. Tari and I embraced. The kids hugged me as well. When Apollo scampered by my side I scooped up my ball of fluff for one more needed snuggle. I boarded *Chieftain*. Soon the green moon faded behind and the larger silver moon came into view ahead.

The craft covered the distance in a few hours before plopping into the snow-covered front lawn of Tezhouse corporate headquarters. It was my first trip to the Moon of Blissful Snow. Midday light glittered on the surface. A cold wind emerged, biting my face. I shivered, despite my coat, not accustomed to the temperature.

I couldn't resist bending down and scooping a handful of the fluffy white stuff. And tasting the snow – the first I'd ever experienced. The crunching sounds of my own footsteps eased my tensions as I headed briskly toward the entrance. The landscape was bathed in white, as were enormous snowcapped mountains, puffy clouds, and a silvery lake reflecting Tao's light. Even the tall evergreens and six-foot holly bushes held fat piles of snow on their branches.

Contemplating what lay ahead returned me to reality. I trembled in response to both the winter chill and apprehension. The magical scene faded from my focus when I reached the mammoth front door. Surprisingly Komourin was there to greet me, his welcoming smile momentarily easing concerns.

"Welcome, Adam."

We headed to his office. The pleasant aroma of walnut-scented polish greeted me as we entered. "Welcome to my digs." It was hardly a humble abode. Yet dozens of well-placed artwork, photos, trophies, plaques, awards, carpets, and other trinkets made the room somewhat inviting.

"Your office is like a museum."

He laughed. "Are you calling me old?"

An uneasy grin spread across my face. "Whoops. I wanted to get off to a good start."

"Souvenirs. Feeding my nostalgic cravings. Memories of the life I've lived, the many roads traveled. At least the good parts. I'm twenty years older than you. I suggest you and Tariana begin collecting your own stuff."

Is he suggesting I'm staying on?

We sat facing each other on chestnut brown leather couches – an exotic, carved table in between. He uncovered a plate of cookies and poured tea. A large, maybe four feet by two feet, piece of what looked like petrified wood, worn around the edges, hung behind Komourin's desk. The beautifully scripted words seized my attention.

"Some see things as they are and ask why?
I dream dreams that never were and ask why not?"

Komourin followed my line of sight. "Does that resonate, Adam? Inspire you?"

"Yes."

"That maxim has inspired me throughout my life. The plaque itself is almost 1500 years old. In the lower right you can see RFK, the initials of the gentleman who spoke those words when he was here in Taoland. My ancestors burned the quote into petrified wood, as best they could recall. I treasure this priceless piece." He paused, staring at the piece of art as if in reflection. "I guess you're wondering why I summoned you today."

"Of course." I nearly choked on a cookie.

"Why do you think?"

"I assume it's because of the explosion that will cost Tezhouse 5 million, and worse, a six-month delay in the *X3* rollout. And because, the contract will likely go to Huggles."

"What do you think caused the explosion?"

"My team is still investigating. It doesn't make sense. We suspect sabotage."

He leaned back, interlaced his fingers, and laid them across his middle. "I also received a revealing recording of you with a half-naked woman at the Tavern, two days later. What do you expect me to do now?"

"You're gonna fire me."

He roared. "No way."

My sigh of relief was uncontrollable – and clearly audible.

"My advice, Adam? Forget the explosion and the Tavern incident. Neither was your fault. Bogart arranged both."

"Bogart?" *I knew it!*

Bending forward, Komourin passed me a plate of nuts. "He orchestrated the destruction of your prototype, and he arranged the Tavern event."

"How do you know? We couldn't find anything."

Komourin placed his hands behind his head. "I have spies, human and sophisticated devices, everywhere. I've got tons of evidence on Bogart's deeds over the years. I've shared it all with my friends on the Board. In this latest case, I leveraged the dirt I have on Bogart to force him to destroy all his fake 'evidence' from the Tavern fiasco. Of course we cannot undo the demo explosion."

I blinked in a speechless stupor. ". . . OK . . . I guess."

"My files on Bogart's past are my arsenal against him, to use when needed. Sadly, he's got files on me, so we exist in a kind of a stalemate."

"I don't understand."

"More later. I first wanna impress on you that Bogart will continue to do everything to destroy you. You must wake up and fight back."

"Why does Bogart hate me? I don't get it. I've never done anything to the man. Yet he's hated me from the moment we met."

Komourin leaned forward, his hands again upon the table. "It's impossible to hate someone you don't know. He hates the idea of you. Someone younger, more talented, far better liked and highly respected, and dedicated to Tezhouse. He's jealous of your natural leadership qualities. And he fears you will steal what he desperately needs – becoming CEO."

"I'm only thirty. How could Bogart see me as a threat?"

Komourin called out "Service." The door immediately opened and two pale-faced Aborgees entered to clear the table.

"Well, Adam, I'm a long way from leaving, so your age is sort of a plus." He leaned back again, grabbing the arms of his chair. "You are a real threat to Bogart. When I retire in about fifteen years, you'll be forty-five. My mission is to get you ready by then – to replace me as CEO."

What? I sat at a loss for words for what felt like minutes. "You . . . you've gotta be kidding."

Komourin chuckled, got up, and ambled to his bar. "Let's switch to something a bit stronger." He poured drinks, and we moved to two plush chairs flanking a large bay window with a bookshelf in between serving as a table. Outside, the vast wintery landscape gleamed. A small herd of muric as white as a bleached cotton blanket picked their way across a field, their black antlers like dark cracks in the canvas. They looked up with glowing, blue eyes, startled by something, then continued their search for food. I gazed out the window, transfixed on the scene.

"Adam, you've got special talents. You're imaginative, flexible, and enthusiastic. Nothing great was ever accomplished without enthusiasm. You have an open mind and positive outlook. You're a creative thinker – a natural innovator. Importantly, you're a good person, a man of integrity, and a born leader." He glanced at me with a reassuring nod. "You'll make an enormous difference at Tezhouse when you take over. Trust me – and dream dreams that never were."

I focused on objects around me, struggling to get my bearings. Words etched in a glass plaque sitting atop the bookshelf caught my attention.

> *"Few will have the greatness to bend history itself.*
> *But each of us can change a portion of events where we play a role.*
> *In the totality of these acts will be written the history of our generation."*

The initials RFK again appeared in the lower right corner. I swallowed and gathered my words. "I'm dumbfounded. I wasn't expecting any of this. I was certain my career was over."

"Not over, just beginning. Next, we're moving you out of engineering. You and your family, along with Randall's family, will move to the Moon of Abundant Harvest, where most of our key customers are headquartered."

Tari leaving Green Fountains? Not gonna happen.

"What? Out of engineering? Did I do something wrong?"

"Of course not. You've excelled. Inventions, patents, recognitions, and all the new products you've added to our Tezhouse portfolio. This gives you credibility, as we reach out and expand our customer base."

I was stunned, with no clue what it would mean to relocate on the Second Moon. I calmed my nerves and asked, "What will my assignment be?"

"You and Randahl will be named Co-Presidents of Tezhouse Second Moon. Also, you'll replace Vester as Corporate President of Business Development and Customer Relations. He's retiring."

"I know nothing about business development."

"You've been involved in business development as an engineer. You've led dozens of important proposals, briefings, and competitions. That's business development. Now you'll become our lead marketeer. You've got all the qualities needed. Great with the customer. Intuitive, off the scales. Glib, in a good sense."

I glared at him. "Glib? That infers lack of depth. Shallowness."

"You're anything but shallow. You're glib in a positive way. You don't care about and never get bogged down in details. You know enough to explain the big picture while leaving the specifics to others. You simplify the complex, as few engineers can."

I struggled to understand his compliment. "T-t-thank you . . . I guess."

"Some might mistakenly call you lazy, never willing to get down and dirty. They misunderstand. You're not lazy – you're a born delegator. Most can't delegate. But you have no qualms about handing off work to others, while you focus on the big picture. And on to the next idea. It's in your DNA."

Roshi taught me about delegation.

"Yes. I do leave the details to others. They are better at that than I am. But I never blame them if things go wrong."

"That's why everybody likes working for and with you. In delegating, you show trust and empower your team. That's what leadership is all about."

"Again . . . t-t-thank you."

The clouds outside gradually swelled with redness from the rising Second Moon, painting a brilliant multicolored display that shone upon the whiteness.

"Most engineers share unnecessary details that make our customers' eyes glaze over, as they pray for the bar to open. You understand advanced technologies at a 10,000-foot level. You speak to nontechnical folks top-down. You focus on concepts and big pictures. When you're asked questions and don't know the answers, you inform the customer you'll have your experts get back to them. Perfect traits in business development."

His praise was slowly inflating my otherwise slack level of confidence. "To say your faith in me is appreciated is a massive understatement."

"We're getting you and Randahl away from Bogart, on a different moon. Randahl will replace Weaver as Director of Tezhouse Services. You'll both report directly to me. Bogart will remain President of Tezhouse First Moon and corporate COO."

I took a swig of brandy, trying to figure out how to express the concerns swirling in my head. "But Tariana . . . she loves her life and friends in Green Fountains."

"When she learns of the perks, she'll come around. I'll *swish* her if you'd like."

"Yes. Please do."

He's wrong. She'll hate this. Tari doesn't need perks.

"I'll explain to her that your kids will go to the best schools with full scholarships. Both are bright and personable. They'll thrive in their new environs."

"When will this be announced?"

"Tomorrow. And steer clear of Bogart when the announcement is made. He might literally explode." He chuckled and swirled the brandy in his glass. "You don't want his brain matter all over you. Be prepared for his ramped-up jealous attacks. It will not be a pleasant war – and there will only be one winner."

A robotic minibar rolled over, and we refilled our drinks.

"Calling it a war – isn't that a bit of an exaggeration?"

"The most devastating of wars are those where no bomb is dropped, nor missile fired. Interpersonal wars. Wars of envy, jealousy, vindictiveness. No rules. No fairness. Just an obsession to win by destroying the other guy."

I asked a burning question, "There's something I can't understand. You said we'd get back to this. Why haven't you exposed Bogart or fired him for his behavior?"

Komourin hung his head. And paused. "It's complicated. He 'owns' me. The garbage he has on me would destroy my marriage, my family, and my legacy."

"But you're a good man."

"Let me shock your virgin ears. I've led a secret life. I've been a womanizer. When I was young, I lost tons of money gambling, ran with the wrong crowd, skimmed money from Tezhouse contracts to pay debts. I'm an alcoholic and a sloppy drunk. I've used illegal drugs. Bogart has proof of everything. Fortunately, he's a far worse character than me. I've got tons of worse stuff on him. So, we coexist in deadlock."

I shook my head, unable to accept this Komourin self-description. "You're way too smart to have behaved recklessly."

He took another gulp of his booze. "I'm weak and stupid in ways most never see. Bogart knows I won't allow my wife and others know all the bad I've done."

"I'm so sorry . . . I . . ."

"I was blinded by a false notion that my commitment to Malee shouldn't constrain me. What she didn't know couldn't hurt her. I was stealthy, so both she and Tezhouse officials remained unaware. I thought I'd never get caught, never have to surrender my marriage, or my position in the corporation."

"So where does Bogart fit in?"

"Turns out he orchestrated everything, like he's doing with you. He set traps and found ways to parade temptations to my weak flesh and weaker mind. He supplied the women, booze, drugs, thugs, and unhealthy habits that consumed me for five years. I entered therapy a decade ago and grew up."

Despite the bad he'd done, I admired the man for acknowledging his vulnerabilities and moving beyond them. "So, it's all in the past?"

"Totally. I resist temptations now. But Bogart retains evidence of my past. He's evil, Adam. He's got four Board members in the same position. He 'owns' others at Tezhouse, and even some in the customer community." Komourin looked away. "Enough for now. Let's head to my home for dinner. Malee will love you, as you will her."

We left our seats, moved toward the door, and donned coats before strolling out into the snow. "So four Board members are in bed with Bogart. Would the other five favor Randahl?"

"Chairman Westin and two others would. The two newbies are neutral. They're all watching you. They know I'm grooming you to replace me."

"Why not Randahl as your replacement?"

"He'd be an excellent choice. But he's not you. He'd never make the impact you will someday. Besides, Bogart is confident he can extort Randahl with materials he would simply fabricate. Randahl would choose his family over the CEO role in a heartbeat, if he were ever threatened."

We boarded Komourin's noli. He'd given me a huge promotion. And I could now dream that I might replace him. Finally, I knew my purpose – to become Tezhouse CEO.

But what about Tari?

CHAPTER 16

TARI: COMMISERATING WITH LORELAI

I *swish'd* Lorelai. She appeared in a hologram. "I need your help." Her eyes widened. "What's wrong, Tariana?"

Holding back tears, I answered, "Adam and I will soon celebrate our tenth anniversary. My 'gift?' My selfish husband just told me to pack up. He and Tezhouse are tossing me and the kids out of the home I've created – moving us to another moon – with no choice, no voice in the matter."

"Lorelai's brows knit with concern. "I'm sure your husband was not given a choice."

"What about me? I have to say goodbye to friends, neighbors, and coworkers." A hot tear rolled down my cheek. "He's telling me to rip my children from their schools and leave immediately. Tojo and Kaleeva are with friends for the day. Adam will be home late, as usual. Can you come over?"

"I can be there in an hour. Are you OK until then?"

"Yes. Thank you." As soon as we disconnected, the tears I'd managed to hold back burst free. Learning we would move to the Second Moon broke my heart. As I finished my second glass of wine it was only three in the afternoon. In my darkest moments, Lorelai was always there for me. I hoped she'd help me find some answers.

Why wasn't Adam there for Tojo's birth?

I might have been happier if I'd never surrendered my nursing career after our son's birth. All the child-rearing and homemaking responsibilities fell to me. And Adam no longer showed any passion for me. He cared more about Tezhouse and clubbing. But why? I had devoted my life to him.

Why wasn't I at least consulted about the new assignment?

Lorelai also had an ambitious husband; she might help me weather my feelings of abandonment. Apollo sighed softly as he jumped into my lap, spilling some of my third glass. I pushed him to the floor, unnecessarily harshly.

I love Adam. But this is too much. I want Adam to need me as much as I do him.

I longed for my husband to understand my unquenched desires. I ached for us to be two traveling through life as one. I hungered for Adam to share fully in both the joys and responsibilities of raising our children.

We are meant to dream dreams and fulfill them together.

Too often, Adam grimaced whenever I poured out my soul during private moments. We used to talk nonstop during our courtship. About everything. But lately he'd listen to me as if it was a burden. In those precious early days, we never wanted to stop kissing. We couldn't get enough of each other. But lately Adam had become only partially present, his mind always buried in work. His long hours, laboring over his inventions, left me lonely and unsatisfied. He's always abandoning me, just like my father did.

It's not fair. I can't take abandonment again.

When I assumed the lead raising our toddlers, Adam and I began leading different lives. Our conversations became scarce. Intimacy faded. We drifted apart. I began volunteering at TSU and at GVCA and gradually increased my hours. Adam either didn't know or didn't care. Then I began drowning my sorrows in booze.

My way to ease the pain.

I finished the bottle of wine. My head was swimming. I recalled our fifth wedding anniversary. We got a sitter and went out for what was supposed to be a celebratory dinner. Juiced on sparkling wine, I became my nastiest ever. I nagged about his faults: coming home late, missing family dinners, departing on trips without notice. At that dinner he shouted, red-faced, for the first of many times, "I'm doing this for you and the kids." He actually believed his own bullshit. Since then, everything has been sliding downhill.

I threw the empty bottle aside and opened another. The doorbell triggered another flood of tears. I threw myself into Lorelai's arms, slurring, "Thanks for coming. I'm having a breakdown."

"Let's go into the gardens, Tariana. No breakdowns allowed there." I carried the second bottle and a glass with me, despite her protestations. Bright yellow arches of flowering vines, their perfumes intoxicating, adorned our now mature backyard. Adam had planted them, but I did the feeding, watering, pruning, and weeding. Of course, others lauded his gardening skills – while I got zero recognition. No one ever praised me for being a great mother, let alone a skilled gardener.

I stammered, "I love it here, Lorelai."

Apollo danced ahead of us. He always enjoyed the gardens, chasing after squirrels, rabbits, and the mefra who flitted about our backyard collecting debris for their small homes. In a springy gait, Apollo raced into green woodlands – returning in a self-induced bliss, covered with the blue, sparkling dust of rafflowers.

"How can I leave this place? My kids – they love our small schlice of paradishe."

We sat on a bench built amongst butterfly bushes. "Tariana, tell me what's going on."

I refilled my glass and took a huge gulp. "He didn't even ask me. Like I don't even matter. Like I'm a piesh of meat. I'm devashtated. How could he do this to me?"

"Well, I've got a surprise for you." She laid a hand on mine. "My family will be moving with yours."

I forced a smile after hearing the first good news of the day. "I . . . didn't know."

"It's not Adam's fault. Or Randahl's. It's the conflict with Bogart. Tezhouse wants to separate our husbands from that monster."

"But I have friends here. I'm involved at TSU. What about me? Why not me-firshht for once? And the kids will be dishhrupted too."

"Tojo and Kaleeva are young and well adjusted. They'll make new friends easily. My children are older than yours, and they are really excited about the move. Our kids will be given free tuition at the best private schools. They'll be fine, Tariana."

Her positive outlook was usually contagious, but not this time. I filled my glass to the brim. "I'm mostly upshhet about being hit with this like a schh . . . schhledgehammer. Without warning. Without my say in the matter."

"Of course, sweetie." She squeezed my hand. Her validation of my feelings helped. "Listen, you and I will go forward with our husbands. It's not fair, but they are the breadwinners. If the roles were reversed, Adam would be excited for you, as Randahl would be for me."

"Ohhhhh, I doubt that. Adam has never cared about what I do at TSU, my GVCA work . . . or anything that makesh me happy."

Lorelai pulled me up. "Come. Let's gather some flowers."

I slogged down half my glass and refilled it. As we strolled I staggered a bit. Memories of the good times flashed through my mind. Picnics with neighbors by the rippling creek. Harvesting fruits from the trees now in full bloom. Pleasant aromas floating on the breeze. The kids playing with Apollo, who now trailed behind us. This place and the memories it held were beyond beautiful.

Lorelai locked her arm in mine. "We must show our husbands we are proud of them – and enthusiastic about what lies ahead."

She was right, of course. We paused and turned toward each other. I slurred, "Yessh . . . I will accept it . . . and I will adjust."

We embraced, tearing up. The support and love of my true friend mildly eased my pain. "Lorelai, Adam and I are drifting apart." I swigged some more wine. "This move will make things worsh. You know, when we met, it was love at first sight. Everything was perfect. The courtship and wedding. Our kids. This perfect home. Now I'm worried our fairytale will end badly."

"I've feared as much, but I'm saddened to hear it."

"Adam is great when he's focused like my husband and lover. I love him beyond words, and I know he loves me the same. But there's a dark side. Adam's other love affair – with Tezhouse."

"You're not alone. Lots of wives are abandoned by their husbands' other interests." She was trying to be supportive, but there was no way I would accept further emotional abuse.

"Am I being shhelfish to want more of his time . . . more of his attenshun?" I struggled to walk straight and leaned against a tree for support.

She glanced at me as she bent to pick flowers. "Is that all you want?"

I grabbed a stick and threw it for Apollo to retrieve. "Yessss . . . but I don't know how to make it happen."

"I can't give you the answers. You've got to find them."

"He's the perfect dad . . . when he's around . . . which he's usually not. That makes me the dish-dish-iplinarian. The 'bad guy.' I have to set the rules. He juss plays with them when inclined."

I inspected one of our newest vines, pinching off a few dead blooms. Butterflies wider than my hand swirled about, intensifying my headache. "The kids are getting older. Adam miss...missed Tojo's shheventh birthday last year and Kaleeva's sixth birthday party last month. But when he's with them, it's all smiles and giggles."

Lorelai leaned against a tree, twirling one of its pink blooms in her fingers, before a sassy mefra flew up and plucked it away. "Your kids adore him. Correct?"

"Yessss! They think Adam's the greatest. They make mud pie

handprints on a big dead tree across the stream, ride bikes, throw balls around, and draw funny faces with street chalk. Most mornings, before work, Adam jogs with Tojo around the circle out front."

"Nice – don't you think?"

We returned to our bench and I refilled my wine glass, sloshing some over the side. "No," I snapped angrily, "he's all play while I'm all work: preparing meals, laundry, shopping, and cleaning." I staggered to my feet to emphasize my complaints. "Oh but Adam . . . he gets to enjoy playing with Apollo . . . while I'm the one who takes cares of *his* dog, bathing and feeding him, walking him and picking up his sch-shit." I kicked at a stray stick and nearly face-planted. "I even take Apollo to the vet . . . not Adam. And it's his dog. It all sucks."

"I can't disagree, Tariana."

"If only he'd be more like Randahl."

She grimaced and shook her head. Her hands fisted. "Randahl and I have our problems. You wouldn't swap if you knew everything."

I blinked. "I always thought your marriage was pur...perfect."

A darkness settled over Lorelai's face. "Let's not go there. I bear the brunt of my husband's furious temper, his inner rage. Something he skillfully hides from others. The grass is rarely greener on the other side. You never know what goes on behind closed doors. Not in my house, nor anyone else's."

I slurred, "I'm schtunned."

"If we all took our problems to the village square, hoping to swap, and we learned the travails of the others, we'd gladly return home with our own sacks of shit. We are used to our own garbage, and we'd never swap it for something that might even smell worse."

"Nobody would take my isshues with Adam."

She glared at me sternly, "Look, Tariana. We both have successful husbands. I urge you to take the good along with the not-so-good – and be grateful for the former. Enjoy your amazing children. Create life and friendships separate from Adam. Develop your talents. Do your own things. Be selfish. Enjoy life."

"I am doing shomm . . . my own things." Taking my mind off of Adam and focusing on myself would never fill the void. *I need Adam.*

I changed the subject. "He always pisshes me off. He gets accolades, while I remain the faithful, ever-loving wife. Then he has the nerve to call me schelflishh when I want more intimacy. He thinks our rare less-than-juicy date nights should be enough." I took yet another big gulp of my booze. The second bottle was now near empty. "But on those dates, he always takes Tezzshouse *swishes*. It's like he's having an affair. I hate it."

I hate dumping on her, but I need to vent.

Lorelai took my hand, the one without the wine glass. "Tariana, a couple of months ago you told me you were trying to spruce up your love life. Any success?"

"Well, before this latest nightmare, we had a heart-to-heart, followed by some progress. I even shhtopped complaining. He showed more passion. He brought bouquets from our gardens and showered me with unexpected gifts. Then this."

She nodded. "Do you discuss each other's work lives?"

"He's opened up about his problems with Bogart. But whenever I try to share my paltry stories about GVCA or TSU, he half-listens . . . and never asks questions."

"Do you affirm Adam's successes at work?"

Why should I? "No. He gets all the acclaim he needs at Tezhouse."

She looked down. "Do you console him about Bogart?"

"No. I don't give a sh-shit about his problems with Bogart. And I don't really care if he shhucceeds at Tezzshouse. In fact . . . I pray he won't."

Lorelai changed the conversation. "How was your recent vacation?"

"Great, as always. It's been three weeks now since our vacation at Lake Lunar. We went with a dozen neighbors. We schwam in the lake, laid in the sun, and rode bikes on the boardwalk. We drank too much and laughed ourselves shhilly for a week." I giggled uncontrollably recalling those moments.

A smile parted Lorelai's lips, but she was clearly annoyed with me. "Sounds like great fun."

"Except when Adam dishhappeared for Tezzshouse things, without telling me. 'An important meeting' or 'a critical game of clubbing with customers,' he'd later say. To make things worshhh, I'm always humiliated when our friends look at me with pity. Today it's like our vacation never happened, because Adam resumed working late again as soon as we returned."

"Would you rather he was having an extramarital affair?"

I slurred my response. "Ohhh absolutely! I'd rather he was having passhonate sex every day with some floozy than ignoring me like I'm a slab of concrete." I squeezed my eyes to restrain tears threatening to spill. "At least I could understand a seshual affair. We'd probably get beyond it. Adam's love affair with Tezhouse has no solution."

I drank what was left in my glass and emptied the bottle before tossing it aside. Lorelai sighed and looked at me with saddened eyes, filled more with pity than understanding. "I have to leave my friend. No more wine."

The tears I'd barricaded overflowed. "I can't it anymore. I can't take any more rejection. I'm lonely. I'm being cheated by his love for his job. Now he 'orders' me to move to another moon. End of dishcusshon."

She gave my hand a reassuring squeeze. "I repeat. You've got to take the good with the bad."

No way I'll ever do that!

"The worsht of all is when Adam repeats, 'I work hard to earn more for you. I do what I do for the family.'" I deepened my voice to mock his.

My friend scoffed. "How do you respond to that lame argument?"

"That sets me over the edge. He's delushhional. I tell him he loves Tezhouse more than me, and that his priorities are all messh-hed up. Given the choice of family or Tezhouse, he'll always choose work. *Always*. I tell him he acts for himself . . . not for us. I even tell him we need couples' therapy.'"

Lorelai wrinkled her brow. "His response?"

"Outrage. He shhtomps out of the room. He's scared Bogart will find out if he sees a shhrink."

After I finished dumping my crap, Lorelai stood to leave, her smile less than sincere.

She'd likely had enough of my complaining.

"We'll talk again soon."

After she departed, I resumed sobbing. And drinking. My head was really pounding. The new assignment would be good for Adam. But it couldn't possibly help our marriage. It would likely destroy us. If Adam were eventually chosen as CEO, our family would pay a very dear price indeed. To spare Randahl, I didn't mention that Adam was now a CEO candidate.

CHAPTER 17

FAREWELL TO FIRST MOON

My meeting with Komourin motivated me to continue to put Tezhouse first. His offer to guide me to the finish line boosted my confidence. If I played my cards right I'd be CEO in fifteen years. The hideous truths about Bogart opened my eyes. The war with my nemesis would be long and relentless. Tari barely spoke to me as we packed up for our move. The kids also hung their heads, saddened and likely insecure about beginning their young lives anew.

They'll be fine.

My mind kept wandering to Komourin's harsh declaration that Bogart and his cohorts were evil – a word not to be used lightly – and that they would become even more relentless. I remembered Roshi was the first to tell me evil existed in Taoland. I'd promised myself and Komourin, "I'm ready, willing, and more than able to engage in the battles – no matter how ugly."

Moving from engineering would take me out of my comfort zone. Business development and customer relations were foreign to me. While fear of failure always followed me, I concluded that the fear was likely worse than failure itself. The thorny conflict between my work and family lives exacerbated my inner struggles.

For Komourin, it was a given that I'd always favor Tezhouse over Tari and the kids. He saw this not as problematic but typical when competing for power and position.

Easy for him to dismiss my problems at home.

Tari would certainly prefer me to step away from the CEO competition and live a simpler life – more focused on her, the children, charity work, and personal friendships. She'd winced, as if in bodily pain, when I'd informed her of the move. Her complaints about neglect and abandonment – her displeasure and resentment – would intensify with my huge promotion and the relocation.

Admitting my actions were selfish while trying to explain that it had to be done did nothing to calm her fury. She was pissed about her lack of voice in the matter and rejected my point of view that my becoming CEO would be good for us. She was badly hungover from drinking the day before, and our discussion turned into a bitter argument – with her slinging insults and me storming out of the room before we headed to the farewell party at Roshi's.

We landed, with Tojo and Kaleeva in tow, on Roshi's front lawn, alongside a noli carrying Randahl, Lorelai, and their children. About three dozen Tezhouse and TSU coworkers and neighbors were gathered by the pond. It was time to say sad goodbyes to those who'd been part of our Taoland journey so far. Tari grabbed a glass of wine soon after we arrived.

Tendrils of smoke wafted from the feast Roshi was preparing on the grill. He stepped away and threw his huge arms around me. "I'll miss you, Adam. But I'm hopeful you'll find your purpose as you move on."

"It's a major step forward in my career."

"You've enjoyed an amazing first decade at Tezhouse. Going forward I urge you to take time to smell the flowers, get lost in the sunsets, and give your heart, all of it, to your family – unconditionally."

I frowned. Everyone thought they understood my situation better than me. "I know you're trying to help. But I love what I'm doing at Tezhouse and cherish the respect I'm given."

"That doesn't give you the right to make your wife miserable and abandon your children. I'm disappointed and have been for a while. You must look beyond your own selfish wants."

I was taken aback. "Leave me alone. I'm doing fine." I crossed my arms and leaned against the pergola.

"Adam, you're not only selfish but you remain insecure. You constantly seek praise from those at Tezhouse. But it's far more critical to win approval from those who love you for who you really are."

He'd never spoken to me so harshly. "Roshi, I don't need your advice anymore. I've discovered my purpose. I wish you and everyone else could accept this."

Roshi turned his face away. "You don't have a clue what your purpose is. But please know you remain an important part of my purpose. I want you in my life."

Dealing with his and everyone else's constant badgering had pushed me to a breaking point. I lost it and pounced. "I never asked you into my life, Roshi. You and I were thrown together through no choosing of mine. Of course, I'm indebted to you for getting me started here. But it's time for you to get out of my way. I've had enough of your philosophy and lecturing. Let's just agree to disagree about my purpose."

I immediately regretted my outburst. He didn't deserve that.

Roshi was visibly shaken. "Adam . . . how could you?" His massive body quaked like a feeble twig. He lowered his head and lumbered away to one of the tables – where he slumped over, head in hands, tears trailing down his beard. Not knowing what to say, I slinked away down to the water, like a coward.

Something is wrong with me. I've become some sort of beast.

Abraham clambered out of the pond. I'd met with him at least monthly since arriving on the Moon of New Beginnings a decade ago. He was my best friend and always kept me centered. Fortunately, he'd not observed my ugly exchange with Roshi. "Adam, I'll miss you more than you can know."

"You'll always remain my dearest friend, Abraham. I need you in my life. I'll visit you whenever I'm back on the First Moon – probably several times a year. We'll also have *swish*. Not a perfect substitute. But we'll connect often."

"Of course. You've been offered a terrific opportunity, and I know you'll make the most of it. As you move on, I want what's best for you, my friend. But you don't know what that is yet. I urge you to remain open to a higher calling, which I know will surface, when you're ready."

Even Abraham? Enough! Everyone brings up a higher calling but ignores what is a tangible reward – staring me in the face.

I changed the subject and soon left my friend to meander back up the lawn. The party continued for several hours. Dulcet scents from grilled meats and roasted mazzor pods filled the air. A large fowl simmered in a smoker, beckoning. Randahl coaxed a crackling fire in the firepit at the center of the patio and a group of fire sprites danced in a circle above, the flames licking at the embers of their tiny feet.

I sulked wishing I hadn't spoken to Roshi that way.

The guests began dancing to the pleasant music which floated on the breeze. As the party ended, fond memories flooded my conversations. The many kind words and well-wishes blew me away, as I'm sure they did Tari. The Taoset, one of the most breathtaking we'd experienced, was followed by the entrance of the reddish moon. I held Tari's and the children's hands as we witnessed it rise, its colors brushing the clouds. We gasped at one of Taoland's eternal miracles – as if for the first time.

Then I ruined the moment. "We'll be there tomorrow, kids. I can hardly wait to see our new home." Their smiles vanished.

I'd avoided Roshi out of utter shame since I'd attacked him mercilessly. My treatment toward him had been vile, and the thought of it made me want to vomit. Before departing I tapped his shoulder and invited him down to the pond. I could barely squeeze out an embarrassed whisper, "Please forgive me, Roshi."

He smiled and embraced me, accepting my apology, without words.

The next day, I awoke to our quiet house in Green Valleys with Tari and the kids still sleeping. Neighbors and friends had already moved our belongings to the field where *Wanderer* would soon descend. I grabbed a mug of coffee and a warm bread and headed excitedly for the site, hoping for a few moments alone with Malaika. I hadn't seen her in ten years. So much had happened.

CHAPTER 18

REUNITING

D*eja vu* overwhelmed me. *Wanderer*, a part of the Fifth Dimension, appeared in the morning sky, just as it had a decade earlier above the plateau in Novana. My heart pounded. The warmth of the rising Tao vaporized the morning mist. A full rainbow encircled the cloud as it came to rest. Mellifluous music filled the space.

Malaika appeared and floated down. She smiled warmly – her golden glow more beautiful than I'd remembered. Her wide-opened eyes hinted at an exciting new adventure. Her presence brought a burst of life to the area. Small animals and birds in full-throated song greeted us from the woodlands. Flowers sprouted, and a soft breeze brushed my cheeks.

Ahh . . . Malaika's magic.

Her neck-to-ankle emerald-green tulle lace gown featured elegant beading, with white flowers interlaced. Long white sleeves, below her gossamer wings, reached down to her soft hands, which I accepted into my own. Atop her pulled-back golden hair she wore a tiara, with green stones, possibly emeralds, embedded in clusters of diamonds. She fluttered her wings.

We embraced with a connection beyond words. After some

silence, her lovely voice floated over me. "You look marvelous, Adam."

"You as well, Malaika."

"I am proud of much of what you have accomplished here on the Moon of New Beginnings."

"Only much of what I've done?"

"Looking back, I cannot say all."

Her intoxicating scent buckled my knees. "Well, I've never looked back. I've been looking ahead, ever since we headed into the heavens above Novana. You rescued me from oblivion. From death. I am forever grateful."

She lifted her hands to hold my cheek. "The best is yet to come, my dear friend, if you continue to trust me. I left you a note back then. Did you find it helpful?"

"Yes. I've revisited your words a dozen times."

"And?"

"I've dreamt of happy tomorrows, as you said, but at times uncertainties crept in."

Her touch on my cheek was like the loving nonjudgmental embrace of a child – yet motherly at the same time. Her head tilted as she gazed into my soul. "Has the journey been what you expected?"

"You suggested I travel with no expectations. I could never have anticipated all that has occurred."

She blinked her emerald-green eyes, a graceful sweep of eyelashes that took my breath. "Have you created loving relationships?"

Of course, she knew the answers, but I played along. "Yes. Tariana is the love of my life. It's not a perfect union, but we love each other deeply. We have two amazing children. I have several dear friends, Guru Roshi, Abraham, and Randahl. I have a great teacher – my mentor, Komourin."

"I told you that mutual trust and respect are rare and fragile gifts – once lost, irretrievable. Have you earned and returned the trust and respect of others?"

I looked aside, unable to meet her eyes. "There are some here who are untrustworthy – not worthy of respect. There is one I will never honor nor esteem – my nemesis, Bogart."

She paused. I returned my eyes to hers. "Evil exists as the absence of good. You must overcome the bad to embrace the good. You must forgive evildoers and show them compassion. Even Bogart."

What?

"That's an impossible ask. I hate him."

"You must come to love him."

I frowned. "Can we change the subject?"

"Perhaps the most important thing I asked of you was to be selfless. Have you been so?"

I bowed my head in shame. "I'm sure you know I often place my career ahead of Tariana and our children. This creates unbearable stress."

She raised my chin. "You must solve this. It is key to self-discovery – to finding true purpose and inner peace."

"I've found my purpose." Surprisingly she did not ask what that was. "I'm successful. No one my age has accomplished more than I have."

Her eyes glazed over. "In the corporate world of powerful people, the more one achieves, the further one is from success."

"That makes no sense. How can my achievements put me further from success?"

"You must place Tariana, Tojo, and Kaleeva above your self-interests. To reach selflessness, you must first come to know yourself. Not your rewards, promotions, and perks – certainly not power – but the real Adam. Only then will you discover how to fully love and serve others, including the least of these, as the path to inner joy."

Here was Malaika, joining the crowd, pushing me to serve others, while I only wanted to focus on achieving my career goals. "I don't understand. But I do want you to continue believing in me."

She smiled mildly, but it did not reach her eyes. "I will never stop believing in you. Never. You said you've discovered your purpose. Tell me. Why are you here? What is the meaning of your life?"

I can answer her now.

"Komourin has chosen me to replace him as Tezhouse CEO. This is my mission – my purpose."

Malaika's smile faded. "That is a job you are seeking. Not a purpose. I was expecting that answer, while hoping for another. It is sad but common for someone your age to lust for power and position."

"My plan is to be named Chairperson as well. Hopefully in about fifteen years. End of story."

"You don't have a clue what your life will be in five years, never mind fifteen. Don't try to plan it all out. Go with the flow. Let life surprise you a little."

Flying insects were lighting all around us, distracting me from her words. "I've no time to relax. I want to become richer than Komourin. I want to decimate Bogart and send him into oblivion. I'll do what's necessary to make these things happen."

The disappointment on her face nearly stopped my heart. "Someday you will discover your higher calling, Adam."

I tried to ignore the burning in my soul that told me she was right. "Please stop. I know what my mission is."

"To become wealthier than Komourin, you will need lots of lunis. To experience inner joy, you don't need any. The person who is richest is the one who values things which cost nothing. One who feels love is loved in return. Those with the greatest material goods and worldly powers are often the saddest of all."

What nonsense. But then she isn't human.

I countered. "Richness isn't a feeling. It's a physical reality."

"You mean things like your house? Your nolis? Extravagant purchases you really don't need?"

I sneered, "Now you're getting it."

"What percentage of your days do you spend seeking power and position?"

Without a blink, I admitted, "Most of my time."

"Have you ever spent any time thinking about yourself and what gives you inner joy?"

I understood her question but didn't respond. By choice I focused fully on career success. I had no time for seeking inner joy. That would come later.

She shifted slightly, the conversation clearly making her uncomfortable. "Do you consider yourself to be wealthy?"

I perked up. "All the time. Including right now. Tariana and I are headed off to a spectacular new house and great new nolis. We can buy anything we desire, including services from others. Our children will receive the best schooling – free."

Malaika opened her wings fully and looked to the skies. "Adam, inner joy comes not from those things, but from helping others. Tranquility comes from simply slowing down and becoming aware of all that is beautiful in nature, within oneself, and in others. Peace comes with the discovery of what makes one wealthy inside."

My face burned. What did she know? She spent half of her life flying around in *Wanderer* telling others how to live their lives. "Malaika, can we please stop talking? Can you just let me be? I know exactly what I want and what I need."

Her eyes opened wide and all the movement around us ground to a halt. "Oh my. Are we about to have our first argument?"

I raised my voice. "I don't want to fight. I just want you to accept me and my focus."

Her eyes grew more concerned – then softened as a smile appeared. "Your focus is misplaced on a false purpose. You know something is not right, so you are lashing out at me, as I know you have assailed others. You are going backwards momentarily, but that's often a precursor to moving forward. You will discover your true purpose in the years ahead."

At this I really snapped and shouted at the top of my voice, "Will you please stop?"

My outburst didn't faze her. "No, I will not. I must fulfill my purpose in guiding you. You just admitted you frequently choose self-interest over selflessness. That is never part of a purposeful life. It never brings joy. But I believe in you. I always will. I will never abandon you."

I was about to continue the debate when footsteps interrupted us.

"Hi." Tari approached with Tojo and Kaleeva. "You must be Malaika."

"How delightful to finally meet you, Tariana."

Malaika embraced each of them.

Tari whispered to me, "She's more beautiful than you described."

"Can we take Apollo?" Tojo asked, as he squeezed our dog to his heart.

"Of course," she responded, bringing joy to Tojo's face – and a smile to Apollo's as well.

When Randahl and his family appeared at the woodland's edge, Malaika beckoned to them. After brief greetings, she announced, "It's time to depart."

When we entered *Wanderer,* all eyes filled with tears. Our children and Randahl's family floated to virtual seats in an area below the center of the cloud. Malaika magically conjured snacks and drinks for the kids. Tari and I sat next to her on a floating bench. She waved her hand to reveal a virtual screen and commanded, "Destination – Second Moon." The Fifth Dimension lifted and headed at lightning speed into the darkness.

Tari stared into the abyss. "I forgot how black outer space is."

Malaika responded, "It is only in darkness that we discover the light."

She turned to me. "Adam, what will you be seeking on the Second Moon?"

"I came to Taoland in despair, with nothing. Now I've got a family and a career. I have high hopes and dreams for both. Destiny is calling me."

"And Tariana, how do you feel about your move?"

Tari held back tears. She looked down at her wringing hands. "I'll miss our friends. The beautiful home we've created. Our gardens. Our community. The children's schools. My social life and volunteer activities."

Why couldn't she be positive? She's embarrassing me.

Malaika responded with a warm smile. "True friends will remain true friends. Reflect on priceless memories created on the Moon of New Beginnings. Falling in love. Marrying Adam. Bearing children and raising them as the amazing youngsters they have become. Finding your own path. Cherish these memories, Tariana, always. Build upon them."

Tari looked up and smiled, seemingly finding comfort in Malaika's words. Malaika's magic affected everyone. I hoped for Tari it would last.

I'd traveled to the Second Moon a dozen times, but this was a first for Tari and the kids. As we approached the Second Moon, the reddish moon grew larger and the green moon faded from sight. Other colors on the Second Moon became evident. The landmasses, fields, hills, and deserts were splashes of yellow and orange. Red-orange bodies of water, lakes, and rivers filled much of the surface. Malaika informed us that the reddish algae that covered much of the waters provided nourishment for the animals and medications for humans.

"Look," shrieked Tari, pointing to the left. A crescent of the silver moon was waning over the horizon. Countless stars completed the spectacular panorama. *Wanderer* descended and came to hover above a field of orange grasses. While the others disembarked, Malaika floated me upward and spoke to me privately. "Welcome to the Moon of Abundant Harvest. Once again, it is time for us to separate. Time for you to take a bold next step on your journey."

"Malaika, forgive me for our little argument. You know you're important to me."

She leaned toward me, gently touching our foreheads together. "As you are to me."

Her magical vibes soothed parts of my soul where it ached. "It's been a bumpy ride so far, Malaika. But the positives have far outweighed the negatives. You promised life in Taoland would be better than my life in Novana. Your promise has been exceeded, many times over. Thank you."

She squeezed my hands. "I assure you, life on this Second Moon will be more interesting and more challenging. But I must warn you, there will be additional pitfalls, more dangers on the road ahead. Keep your eyes wide open for fierce animals and poisonous snakes on every path. Guard against Bogart – but love him at the same time."

"Oh, come on, Malaika," I jested, with a broad smile, "I was hoping everything would be easy and painless on this moon."

"By the end of your stay here, you will be closer to finding your purpose."

Here we go again.

Malaika led me to the edge of the Fifth Dimension. She kissed my cheek and once again inserted a folded note into my shirt pocket. "You will find Ambrosia below. Go with her to her home. She will be your guru here, as Roshi was on the First Moon."

I joined the others on the lunar surface. The midday temperature was considerably warmer than on the First Moon. We all looked up to watch *Wanderer* rise then disappear into the summer sky.

Malaika's words left me alarmed. I loved her, but she could be annoying. I wanted her to be proud of me. Instead, she insisted I was focused on the wrong goals. And she forecasted gloom and doom ahead instead of success. I frowned, hanging on her dour admonition to 'keep your eyes wide open for perils on every path.'

Bogart was now out of sight. Why should I still fear him? Malaika's suggestion that I love Bogart when he was doing all he could to destroy me was ridiculous. My momentary tension was interrupted by a growing warmth in my chest. A tender prod on my heart signaled Adriella's presence. She was always with me during life's transitional moments – always the comforting and reassuring touch I needed. I felt her glow as she approached. I met her glowing eyes. They sparkled with nonverbal love and affirmation. "Welcome, Adam," she messaged in a voice that resonated throughout my being.

CHAPTER 19

SECOND MOON, SECOND CHANCE

The first steps of the Moon of Abundant Harvest were also the first steps toward Tari and I putting the past behind and opening ourselves to new discoveries. Though Malaika had warned of dangers all I could see was opportunity – the new moon offered a chance for me to shine more brilliantly in my quest for corporate position and power.

"Welcome. I'm Ambrosia."

Her radiant appearance struck me. On her smooth, bronze face hazel eyes rested below gingerbread-brown lashes and brows – above a perfectly formed nose. "Hi. This is my wife, Tariana, and my children, Tojo and Kaleeva."

Tari gazed upon her countenance, seemingly as captivated by her beauty as I was. I next introduced Randahl and his family. Ambrosia's pink lips parted in a soothing smile. "Nice to meet you all. But we can chat later. Adam, we need to scurry to my home. I've arranged a 'Meet and Greet' with some of your neighbors-to-be from the Four Woods, where you will reside."

Randahl asked, "Shall we come as well?"

"No, there's a separate gathering planned at your new home with your new neighbors." She pointed them to a bright red noli parked on an adjacent field.

Ambrosia's crimson dress sat just off the shoulders, exposing her graceful sculpted collarbone. The dress sloped down to a hip gathering tied with a bright yellow sash that accentuated her figure. Her smallish bare feet displayed sparkling crimson toenails.

Tari teased, again in a soft whisper, "Malaika wasn't enough, Adam? What am I going to do about you and your luscious girlfriends?" Her joshing and playful reaction encouraged and delighted me. Her banter reminded me of the Tari I'd met a decade ago.

Ambrosia led us to her large nolivan painted a crimson that matched her gown. We flew off to her home not ten minutes away. Arrays of reds, oranges, and yellows, in the waters, fields, and orchards below created a bedazzling panorama. Mazzor and dozens of other vegetables were thriving in the warmer temperatures.

We hovered briefly before landing in front of her enchanting two-story summer cottage, a home considerably larger than Roshi's. Topped with a gorgeous thatched roof, her home was adorned in pink-gray bricks with red trim around the windows and front door. Picturesque tidy gardens of primarily red, magenta, yellow, and orange blooms added to the scene's grandeur.

As we left the noli, a beautiful, bronze-colored qilin trotted up to greet us. Its flaming orange mane and tail danced like fire. It bowed and greeted us in a deep voice. "Welcome, Adam and family."

The children's eyes grew wide in amazement as the qilin reared and dashed away. Tojo spoke gleefully. "It spoke to us." I was beyond thrilled that he could hear.

We entered the dwelling where Ambrosia offered soft drinks and sweets then invited us to wash up and change our clothes. She floated about gracefully, as if lifted by air, perhaps aided by the heavily feathered wings on her upper back. She first led the children to separate small but tastefully decorated bedrooms. Apollo darted inquisitively after them. She then guided Tari and me to her exquisite guest suite. It was adorned with flowers, both fresh and dried. Petals of red, pink, and yellow dotted the orange floor, on the carpets, and atop the bedspread of a handsome oversized bed.

Tari smiled. "This will do perfectly, Ambrosia."

Ambrosia gave Tari a knowing wink. "As soon as you and your kids are spruced up, come down and I'll introduce you to some new neighbors. They will soon be arriving."

We were back in the living space within fifteen minutes – greeted by maybe fifteen adult neighbors, humans of various species, and a group of children about Tojo's and Kaleeva's ages. I was polite – but held no excitement for meeting these folks. I was far more consumed with starting my new job the next day. Tari, on the other hand, was in her element. She beamed, smiled at everyone, mixed well, and thoroughly enjoyed the party.

Hmmm. This might work.

The 'Meet and Greet' lasted for three hours – way too long for my liking. The children departed for bed first, Tojo carrying a yawning Apollo with him. Ambrosia poured brandies and offered final sweets. I was genuinely thankful but wanted to get this over. "Thank you so much for everything."

Tari continued, "Moving to a new world can be challenging. I was apprehensive. But the way you've welcomed us is making it easy."

"I am here for you both, for whatever you might need. I am here to help. And to occasionally provide some magic for entertainment." She snapped her fingers, and a shower of twinkling red, orange, and yellow lights fell over Tari, causing her to light up in a smile.

I squinted in disbelief. "Well, your magic can't help me with my biggest problem. There are some bad folks at Tezhouse. And nothing can move them out of my path."

She wrung her hands, pondering my words. "Magic is a strength of dreamers, thinkers, and creators of new visions. You are such a person, Adam. You are a maker of music and a dreamer of dreams. Barriers will always exist; don't create additional ones in your own mind. With your honest efforts, magic will happen, and good will win over evil."

She doesn't understand. All the flowers and fairy dust in the Universe wouldn't take down someone like Bogart.

"We'll welcome your help." Tari responded in a much friendlier way. "We're in a far-off place, and it's always a bit frightening to start over. We didn't know anybody here a few hours ago, but you've got us off to a great start."

"There's nothing to be afraid of. Think of the Second Moon as the start of a new adventure. To help me help you, before you retire for the night, if you're not too tired, perhaps you can share with me – what do each of you hope to accomplish here. Adam?"

I stifled a sigh, annoyed once more by being queried about my purpose. "I arrived in Taoland a decade ago, with no clue what my life was all about. Now I do. I'm here on a mission to become CEO and eventually Chairperson of Tezhouse. That's my purpose." I raised my glass, but neither of them met it.

"Hmmm. Sounds like a job – not a purpose." Ambrosia ran a finger around the rim of her glass.

Not again.

"And you, Tariana? What are you looking forward to here?"

Tari adjusted her burgundy hair. "Ten years ago I met and fell in love with Adam. Today he and our children are the reasons for my existence. I want nothing more. But I do plan on volunteering at TSU here – picking up where I left off on the First Moon."

Ambrosia squeezed Tari's hand. "I'm delighted you are motivated to serve others." She then glanced at me. "Adam, your goals seem more self-serving."

I stiffened. Pissed off. I'd just met this lady, and here she was judging me, like everyone else.

How dare she?

"You've got me wrong, Ambrosia. I'm all about service, too. I want to serve my corporation, its shareholders, the employees, and my family members. They all benefit from my talents and hard work."

She continued, "No selfish motives? Don't you relish the acclaim – the salary increases, perks, promotions, and all the rest?"

I recoiled. "My primary goal is to apply my talents in serving others. I'm succeeding at that."

Ambrosia rolled her beautiful eyes. "Hmmm. Tariana, Adam's success does make life easier for you and your children – correct?"

Tari lowered her eyes. "I'd prefer Adam focused more on our family."

Why did she have to say that? She's always embarrassing me.

"I hope you both can find higher callings here on this moon."

Give me a break! They are all in cahoots to force me to surrender my goals.

Ambrosia sipped her brandy, her eyes peering over the rim directly at me. "My mission is to help, even if that calls for some tough love. Now, let's head off to bed." Once in our room Tari and I were too wound up to sleep. We settled into a sofa with carved armrests and together read Malaika's letter.

My dearest Adam,
You've discovered love, created a beautiful family, and launched your career.
You've achieved much in the face of discord and evil.
Now, it's time to discover yourself.
You will find life on the Moon of Abundant Harvest more intense, often with unfamiliar challenges, conflicts, risks, and disappointments.
Delete the need to control. The more you try to control, the more turbulent things will become.
Learn from the different points of view of others.
Neither judge nor become angered by those who seek to harm you.

Focus on common goals that unite, not on differences that divide.
Continue to dream dreams that never were.
Know that what you search for is only impossible until the moment you discover it.
Try always to choose selflessness over selfish endeavors.
As always, know I am here with you, even when unseen.
Love, Malaika

Tari folded the paper. "Sound advice, Adam."

"She means well." I put an arm around Tari, but her chilly demeanor turned me away.

We awoke to the Taorise, amazed to see our green moon high in the sky above. I anxiously awaited the time when I could head to the office. We held cups of hot tea as we meandered through Ambrosia's gardens. They were not as elaborate as Roshi's, but plusher, benefiting from this moon's warmer climate.

"Yip! Yip! Yip!" Apollo, who'd left Tojo still sleeping, led our way, barking as he scampered about. We laughed when he energetically flew into a small pond to play with a pair of shimmery, pink fish, who looked up and smiled directly at me and Tari.

"I do soooo love my little dog," I exclaimed joyfully.

"More than me?" Tari teased with a grin and a nudge. I was relieved she jested.

Colorful flowers, unlike those on the First Moon, lined our path. An amazing variety of bushes adorned with eight-inch round red and orange blooms, some in oakleaf forms, others in mophead shape, took my breath away. Blossoms everywhere complimented a closely manicured bright yellow lawn. We turned to the sound of footsteps to discover Ambrosia approaching with a basket of biscuits with berry jam. "Good morning. Sleep well?"

Tari grinned. "You may have difficulty throwing us out of your lovely home. The bed is amazing."

"Sorry, but this is only a one-night stopover. We'll head to your new home as soon as the children finish breakfast. I know you'll love it."

A muscular qilin with huge bright blue eyes and red skin and mane appeared at the gardens' edge. Its reddish-and-orange striped horn, at least two feet long, bobbed as it called out, "Welcome, Adam and Tariana," before prancing toward a rust-colored woodland.

"Did you hear that qilin speak?"

Ambrosia smiled. "No. They speak only to those who need to hear them. Sometimes the qilin's magic is only inside you."

"It had red hair. Is that unusual?"

"Those trimmed in red reflect the abundance of the spirit. They appear at times of change, good or bad. I hope you are prepared for what lies ahead."

Tari and I understood we had to settle into our new home quickly and get Tojo and Kaleeva situated in their new schools. Tari would then be free to spend time at the Second Moon's TSU – and hopefully stop focusing on me. When it was time to depart for our new home, we hopped into Ambrosia's nolivan. We'd only viewed the home Tezhouse provided by *swish*. Set in quaint woodlands, displaying a stunning array of colors, it exceeded our expectations.

"The leaves are all different colors."

"Yes. Trees exist in their own seasonal renewal cycles here. Some drop leaves in summer while others do it in spring or fall. They can even choose to change their schedules," Ambrosia announced.

"How is that possible?"

"Just another example of Taoland's magic. Some parts of this moon coexist in different seasons. Some gardens and trees and farmland experience all three simultaneously. Please don't ask me to explain because I cannot. Each of Taoland's moons has a mind of its own."

Outside the front of our new home a large, manicured botanical garden brought all varieties of magical birds and insects. The back lawn, double in size, featured a gracefully sloping lawn with gradients of yellow and green grasses meeting up with landscaped floral displays.

The children squealed at the sight of a swing set with slides and a trampoline. They took off running toward it. While they laughed and played, Ambrosia introduced us to our gardens. I blinked in amazement. I pointed at masses of three-foot-high orange and yellow speckled flowers in the border. "Tari, these are my favorite."

"Yes, Adam, but look at those roses. At least that's what we call them in Baukis. So I'm going to call them roses here." She pointed to a variety of bold flowers, some standing tall, some bushing, and others trailing up lattice fencing. In the driveway sat two large shiny super-nolis – a black sporty one with orange interior for me and a red nolivan for Tari and the kids.

Ambrosia led us inside. "Five bedrooms, guys. Each with balconies and ensuite bathrooms."

Tari shrieked with glee, "One for you, Ambrosia, whenever you can stay over. I absolutely adore these covered porches and their shiny yellow railings."

"It's a beautiful home," offered Ambrosia, "but understand – it's only a temporary resting place on your journey."

What?

We wandered through the huge, brightly colored first-floor space. Tari bubbled in delight when she discovered our beautiful and spectacularly equipped kitchen. "Oh, Adam. Never saw orange appliances before. I love them."

I hope her newfound joy and happiness will end our problems.

Upstairs, we were blown away by our bedroom – luxurious to say the least. The kids' rooms looked out over a large, black-bottomed pool, with a diving board, spa, sun shelf, and deck furniture.

"I must leave now," said Ambrosia. "Come over to my place tomorrow, evening and I'll whip you up a special dinner. In the meantime, please don't get overly absorbed with all this luxury. These are hygiene factors."

Hygiene factors? She's gotta be kidding.

"You must always be ever wary of any who tempt you with meaningless trinkets, which can poison your souls. Inner joy, which is what you must seek, comes with helping others."

Oh no. I can't take any more of this garbage.

Tari hugged her as I stood aside. Ambrosia then departed.

"Adam, I fought coming here. But I must admit, I really like this place. I'll never ask you for anything else, at least not materially. Now, my husband, let's turn this house into a home."

Tari's happiness told me all I needed to know. *And Ambrosia wants me to consider these things hygiene factors. What a joke.*

"Hmmm. Maybe I'll slack off now and spend less time at Tezhouse." She blinked. Then I burst into laughter. "Just kidding. That's not gonna happen."

Tari froze. "You sure have a knack for destroying a nice moment. How can you joke like that?" She moaned, "Would it be so hard for you to look forward to quality time here with me and the kids?"

Whoops. Another blunder.

I tried to restore her smile. "Sorry. My mistake. You know you're number one with me. I'm thrilled you like our new home."

As I spoke, Tojo and Kaleeva rambled back inside. Happy. Laughing. Dancing. Apollo ran circles around them – restoring Tari's joy, and thus my own.

Then Tari darkened my spirit. "Adam, we must heed the cautions from Malaika and Ambrosia."

"Why can't you just relax and be grateful for all of this splendor?"

Surely, these warnings were just the unfounded concerns of overprotective gurus.

CHAPTER 20

DIRECTOR OF WINNING

A new job on a new moon – reporting directly to the CEO. My new title was a mouthful: President of Business Development and Customer Relations and Co-President of Tezhouse Second Moon. I'd have preferred a simpler moniker, like Director of Winning. Winning wouldn't be a 'sometimes thing' for me. I wasn't meant to succeed once in a while. The desire to win would consume me, all day every day, beginning today.

I showered and dressed for work without leaving time for breakfast with Tari and the kids. Tari angrily tossed a kitchen towel on the counter. "Can you at least sit with us, Adam? Better yet, could you *swish-in* and postpone your first Tezhouse meeting and take the kids to their new schools with me?"

"My schedule is set up." I grabbed coffee and a bagel Tari had loaded with a creamy cheese.

Tojo responded, "Dad. I'm nervous."

Kaleeva tugged my shirt. "Dad – all I've ever known is my old school. I'm scared."

Ignoring their pleas, I barked at Tari, "You know I'm meeting with the guy I'm replacing. I'll be swamped getting up to speed. Don't expect me for dinner."

Her frown said it all. Bright red crept across her face. The kids bowed their heads. Heck, even Apollo hid his head between his legs. Tari's eyes avoided mine as I brushed her cheek with a quick kiss. I blew kisses to the kids, stormed out the door, and headed to my shiny new executive noli.

On the bright orange brick pathway leading to Tezhouse Second Moon headquarters I shook with uncertainty. Inside the grand entrance, I waved my wrist over the electronic sign-in booth and headed to the office of my predecessor, Mr. Vester. His digs were more grandiose than Komourin's.

In a few days, this office will be mine.

This weird-looking skinny man, about five inches shorter than myself, bore two faces, one looking forward, the other to the rear.

Human? I think I'll stop asking this question.

His conservative dark suit and red tie somehow distracted from his strange appearance. "Welcome to my world – which today becomes your world."

He caught me staring at his head.

"I'm from Jiang-Hiang, where we have eyes in the front and back, so we can see where we're going and where we've been, at the same time."

We small-talked at his conference table about families, sports, and the weather. Then Vester switched gears and began discussing my new role. "You're young for such a senior management position. But Komourin has assured you're up to the task."

I puffed my chest and squared my shoulders. I was ready for any doubters. "I'm ready. But I'd be lying if I didn't admit to some trepidation."

He leaned back in his large, leather chair. "Any specific concerns?"

"For one, I'm younger and less experienced than those who'll be reporting to me. I'm wondering how they will receive me."

"I held similar self-doubts when I assumed this role. My predecessor said, 'Vester, you didn't ask for this role. You didn't stomp on anyone to get it.' I offer you the same advice. Don't worry about any who might consider themselves unfairly passed over. That's their problem, not yours."

I cleared my throat. "Thank you."

"After two decades at this job it's time for me to rest and for you to take the lead. This is the most important job in the corporation."

I pushed back, tugging on my shirt collar. "Most say the most important jobs are in engineering and manufacturing."

"When they speak such nonsense, remind them that if you fail to capture new business there would be zero work for anyone to do." His words hammered home the importance of my role.

"Mr. Vester, I've been in engineering for ten years. What do I need to be successful in marketing?"

He placed his elbows on the oak desk. "I could write a book answering that. In fact, I might. The most important of all is integrity. Sacrifice integrity and you'll be finished not only at Tezhouse, but as a human being."

I didn't expect this. But Roshi had offered similar advice. "Can you get me up to speed on the various customers and bids out there?"

He hopped from his chair. "Of course. That's our focus today." He went over and retrieved something hidden in a false-front of a bookcase. "This, Adam," – he held up a thin silver disc, about one inch in diameter – "is *Guidogram*. It contains all you need to know. It updates me daily on customers and competitors and the status of our proposals. This info is only available to me, and now you."

"And me!" The new voice startled me before I realized it was coming from Vester's rear-facing face, from which came, "Sorry, I just can't resist doing that sometimes." Vester held the sleek circle near his mouth and whispered in an unfamiliar language. A 3D image, a large blue book, appeared as a hologram. I was unable to read the language.

"Now, I'll now erase my *Guidogram* access and set it up for you. Choose a password you'll remember. It will henceforth only recognize you – in your native language."

I rearranged the numbers of my Novanian ID and spoke as *Guidogram* pulsated in my palm. The heads-up display revealed the book's contents. This time in Novanian.

"Adam, nobody else knows *Guidogram* exists. It will allow you to understand the competitive landscape better than anyone. Update it frequently, based on conversations, facts, intuitions, interpretations of data, and opinions you gather. Add and edit info by voice command, in private."

"Will do. I'll begin burying myself in *Guidogram*'s info tonight."

"Now let's go meet the team, Adam." Vester led me to the main conference room where he introduced me; then he said, "I'm headed back to the office to gather a few remaining mementos."

"Can we meet up again for lunch, Mr. Vester?"

"Sure, Adam. Meet me in the gardens around noon," his rear-facing face said as he departed.

I found my teammates personable, professional, and reeking of confidence. Not one exhibited any jealousy. One of my vice-presidents suggested they brief me. "Plenty of time for that in the days ahead. Let's get to know each other a little. Beyond what's in our biographies."

I began, sharing my story from Novana to the First Moon and here. Each followed suit. We enjoyed a delightful two-hour chat. I met Vester at a picnic table for lunch. He'd brought sandwiches. At the edge of pleasant gardens, a qilin grazed, partially hidden in some hedges.

"Look, Mr. Vester – a qilin."

He looked up, but the magic horse was gone. "I don't see anything. What's a qilin?"

"Never mind. Just my imagination."

We small-talked as we ate our lunch then rose from the bench and strolled across the lawn. "Can we pick up where we left off, Mr. Vester. I know there's lots more not in *Guidogram*."

"Of course. A few tips. First, get to know our customers on a personal level. Always listen and understand before responding. In negotiations, create win-win conclusions. The trick? Ask for more than you need and then give up what's least important, allowing the other guy minor victories."

All made sense. Then I blundered. "Mr. Vester, I'm thinking I'll only deal top-down – gaining the trust of top decision makers. I'm good at this."

He flinched. "Be careful or risk pissing off those who like to introduce their bosses themselves."

"I've considered that. But, to beat Huggles, I'll need to play a different game, staying above the corruption, dealing only at the top, obeying the laws. If that bothers others, so be it."

Tears welled in Vester's eyes – all four. "You've got it all figured out."

"Did I say something wrong, Mr. Vester?"

"I'm just seeing myself as yesterday . . . and you as tomorrow."

Whoops! I've been preaching rather than listening. I hung my head, aware I'd made him feel useless. "Please forgive me. I'm here to learn. I'm so sorry."

"You are who you are. I need to find a new purpose, but I have no clue what to do next." He spun his head an impossible 180 degrees to use his rear face while he dried tears from the front one.

Abruptly he asked, "What else can I help you with?"

His head stunt befuddled me, but I managed to continue. "How . . . how do I deal with the folks at Tezhouse First Moon, where the proposals originate?"

The new face spoke just like the earlier one, except more perturbed. "That's where you'll meet your toughest challenges. The engineers hate others selling their designs for them. You must show them respect. And you need to placate the bean counters, who always worry about prices and risks. But never let Tezhouse lawyers bury your customers in their restrictive terms and conditions."

"But the Ts & Cs are important, yes?"

He turned to toss a tissue toward a waste bin but missed. He bent to retrieve it, his rear-facing face continuing the conversation.

"A good contract is one where your customer never looks at the legal bullshit after the ink dries on the contract. Best to let mutual trust and fairness rule – not the Ts & Cs."

"Thanks. Again, I uh . . . I'm sorry for how I spoke."

"Don't worry, Adam – mostly my fault. My insecurities. Whenever I meet someone new, and something uncomfortable is spoken, I tend to respond from both mouths. And I say too much. You should see how it annoys my wife." We both laughed. "I'll stick to one face going forward." We sat at a table. "Finally, there's Bogart. We'll discuss him tomorrow. I must go now. See you in the morning."

He stood, no longer smiling, gazing back at the building from his rear head. I shook his hand, and asked, "Can I sleep in your office tonight? I want to spend some time with *Guidogram*."

"It's your office now."

Vester gathered his boxes and departed, his rear face observing me as he hurried away. *I really screwed this up.* I returned to my office – *my office* – and buried myself in *Guidogram*. It was well organized, easy to edit or adjust by voice command, a treasure trove. I worked through the night, not even stopping to *swish* my wife. I'd pay the consequences later.

This is more important than Tari at the moment.

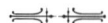

⇌⇋

After Taolight entered my office, I showered in my bathroom, called for coffee and buns, and beamed in delight when they arrived minutes later.

My own shower! Breakfast at my bidding!

I was raring to go when Vester arrived at 10:00 a.m. We settled on a couch. His demeanor was stiffer than the day before. His serious face meant it was time to get down to business. "Adam, I'd like to share an important guideline in securing new business. Both in proposals and in presentations. It's called the 'Rule of

Three.'" Vester crossed his legs and leaned back. "It's helped me enormously."

"I'm all ears."

A nonhuman servant with large, globe-like eyes and webbed hands delivered fruit drinks and sweet rolls.

"First, try to reduce your key message to three words if possible."

"Impossible." I knew I'd always have way to much to say to boil it all down to three words.

"You don't win bids with 500-page-long proposals filled with boring details. Hook the decision makers with a short theme. *Lowest Cost. Best Technical Solution. Smaller Size & Weight. Most Reliable.*"

I shifted in my seat, uncomfortable but anxious to learn more.

"Every decision maker has an overarching need – coupled with fears. You've gotta discover both – to understand his/her hot buttons." He leaned in, eager to make his point.

I scratched my head. "But it still takes way more than three words to win."

"Of course. But it begins with a simple thesis – an opening assertion you must prove going forward. Hook them with this. Reel them in with the details later to prove your claim. Then bring them totally onboard with a summary that drills everything home."

"Tell 'em what you're gonna tell them; tell 'em; then tell 'em what you just told 'em."

"Exactly!"

I straightened my tie. "Can you give an example?"

"You might open with a sentence or two asserting Tezhouse's offer represents *Best Value*."

"Then?"

"You ask: 'Why Best Value?' Then answer your own question by providing three reasons. You set the hook before offering any details."

"So, basically a theme with three supporting claims."

"You've got it! Then back up each of those claims with a few facts about each. Provide enough details but not too much. Use footnotes and load up details in appendixes for those inclined to dig deeper. Finally, summarize by restating the opening in a different way. All three – the opening, the body, and the close – reinforce each other."

I perched at the couch's edge. "So we hook the decision makers with the opening and the closing. In the body and appendices we reel in the more detailed proposal reviewers. Correct?"

Vester smacked the table in delight. "Yes! Decision makers never read the details."

"Can you give me examples of supporting arguments?"

Vester *swish'd* a holographic projection of Tezhouse technology. "Let's consider arguments to make under a 'Best Technology' claim. You start proving the claim by adding 'our solutions are patented' – and then provide a list of relevant patents." Vester rotated the hologram. "Then you say, 'While truly advanced, our designs are proven in the field,' and pile on specific test results, field data, and user commendations. Now Adam, you suggest a third proof here."

I gave this some thought. "We might include how today's solutions are easily upgradable in the future with technology we've planned and budgeted for years ahead."

He beamed. "You've got it, Adam. Your final argument is strong proof of lowest long-term risk, because Tezhouse solutions are not headed toward early obsolescence. Potential risks are what decision makers fear most."

He was compressing decades of marketing know-how into a single meeting. "I may not be fully ready for this job, but I'm far more so than two days ago. Thank you. Another question. How do we prove we're offering the best price, especially if our price is not the lowest?"

"State the fact that it's a flawed simplistic notion to consider the lowest bid price the best price. It rarely is. We've all made the mistake of buying the lowest price."

"I get that, Mr. Vester. I'd rather buy a 50,000-luni noli with great performance and a long-term guarantee than a vehicle half the price which would be worthless five years later."

"Exactly! Prove your price is 'best' because of X, Y, and Z considerations. And always include facts supporting your best service claim. Service after sales is where life cycle costs come into play. You've gotta differentiate Tezhouse service strengths by suggesting shortfalls and thus additional long-term costs in your competitors' proposals."

The moment we finished our breakfast, a humanoid server arrived to clear the dishes. I turned back to Vester, hands splayed. "But I wouldn't know what the competitor offered. How do I compare our proposal with the others?"

"If you don't know, make it up. 'Ghosting' is about creating fears about the other guy. Your competitors will be doing the same about Tezhouse. With experience, you'll get better about relating your competitors' past blunders. Expose their shaky reputations and weaknesses. Perception is reality. Plant doubts about your competitors without directly assailing them. It's tricky, but you can do it."

"I like the idea of making the customer concerned about the other guy. But it doesn't seem honest."

"All's fair in love and in the marketplace." Vester reached across and clapped me on the shoulder. "*Swish* me whenever you have questions in this arena."

"I value all you've taught me in a truly short time. I'm sorry if I suggested otherwise yesterday."

He shook his head, brushing it off. "Adam, you'll be dealing with individuals far more unethical and complex than you experienced as an engineer. Your challenges will be monumental."

"As I said, I'm more ready than yesterday, thanks to you. But actually my greatest challenge involves my wife and family. This job will raise tensions at home."

He looked away and to the floor, his other face becoming visible with a pained expression. "I can't help you here. I destroyed my own marriage with 'all work no play' twenty years ago. Have only rarely seen her or my three children since."

Am I headed there?

Vester abruptly switched subjects. "Adam, I still need to warn you about your greatest threat. It's not Huggles. Not the customer. It's Bogart."

"How can he hurt me out here anymore than when we were working in the same building?"

"The man is pure evil. He's been a constant pain in my ass, but I never posed the threat you do. I'm ten years older than Komourin, who has now announced that you, Bogart, and Randahl are the three candidates to replace him."

"Yes. That's the real reason Bogart hates me."

"He doesn't hate you. As for being evil, there might even be a decent guy hiding behind his bad behavior. Bogart fears you – ever since your early successes in engineering. You bring talents he lacks. His sole mission in life is becoming CEO, and you threaten that mission."

"But again, how can he hurt me in the marketplace?"

Vester leaned in. "Bogart is the ultimate corrupter. He has cronies and spies in every customer organization. He 'owns' some decision makers – by threatening to expose past sins. He bribes others. He might even disrupt any award to Tezhouse if a victory might add another jewel to your crown."

"But, if he kills a win to hurt me, he denies himself profits."

He sat back. "He would forgo profits to prevent your star from rising in victory."

"That's screwy."

"He'll never let up in his quest to prevent you from being chosen CEO. He'll strike from the darkness when least expected. Avoid him at all costs."

"I'm smarter and stronger than Bogart."

Vester's rear-facing face blurted out, "Humility is not one of your calling cards. I discovered that yesterday."

"I've never been accused of being humble. But I do apologize again for the way I declared my ideas yesterday. That was inconsiderate."

Without responding, Vester rose to leave. We said our goodbyes. I was left feeling motivated by his guidance but with a heavy dose of foreboding about Bogart's potential interference.

⇌

Over the next ten days, Vester set up two dozen *swish*'s with key customers and contacts. I discovered he was universally well-liked and highly-respected. I appreciated him assuring every one of my trustworthiness.

I'm off to a flying start at work. At home – a different story.

I set a personal goal to lead Tezhouse to victory in five important regional bids which would net over 5 billion lunies spread over six years. I directed my team to focus on twenty-plus other large revenue opportunities. I signed up for a combined bookings objective over that time span of 12 billion lunies, 2 billion above the ambitious goal suggested by the Board.

Jonnie, my executive assistant, arranged customer visits, and I hit the ground running. I would go 'all-in,' seeking victories in the marketplace along with victory over Bogart in the war he'd declared. There would be no option for runner-up positions.

Second place is for losers. But what about my relationship with Tari?

CHAPTER 21

CHALLENGES, AT WORK AND AT HOME

My first self-assigned target was in Thossia, a dark land where the citizens reside under the moon's surface. Despite their burrowing nature, Thossians were a human species who had created a highly advanced society. At the Lunaport I was stunned by the appearance of those assigned to guide visitors, including my nolivan driver. They were muscular, a bit taller than me, with chartreuse skin and sharp features. They wore no shoes. Their hands and feet were claw-like, three fingers or toes on each.

Humans? Yes. Strange looking? You bet.

Enroute to my apartment, in one of the few above-ground buildings to be seen, I discovered a desolate landscape that delivered a sinking feeling to my gut. After dropping my luggage off I headed to a tiny nearby archway declaring 'Thossian Government Headquarters' – where I met Pamplin, our local agent. We were ushered into a portal of sorts and transferred a mile underground. When the elevator door opened we found ourselves under a 1000-foot-high roof that enclosed the community 5000 feet under the moon's surface.

Kinda like Novana's Great Canopy, except solid in this case.

We stepped out to witness an impossible starry sky above – no doubt holographic projections on the glass-like ceiling. The twinkling lights gave the illusion of a dwelling place in open space. The entire 10 million Thossian population lived in a vast subterranean city lit with a beautiful array of colored lights of varying intensities – illuminations that were dimmed in the evenings then shut during sleep times.

Tao and its other moons were never visible except when residents went to the surface for vacations and special events. The ground beneath my feet lit up with each step, and a holographic projection identified me as Adam Novana of Tezhouse – before I was warmly received by local officials and led to a conference room.

Thossians were suffering cyberattacks amongst conflicting political factions within and from several outside nation states on the Second Moon. Government, businesses, and private systems were being compromised more every day. Thossia was leading a collaboration with three other above-ground neighboring nations in a request for proposal (RFP) for a highly-advanced shared security network. Our *X2* was a perfect fit. But three other bidders had better connected agents and attractive packages – and Tezhouse was not expected to win.

I'd never tackled a proposal in the marketing lead. Terrified by the challenge, I hid my fears. The first meeting was formal, and I felt cold. I was not at all encouraged.

Am I up to this task?

When we returned to the apartment above, I spoke to Pamplin, "A city-state below ground would seem impossible to sustain. What's the source of Thossia's wealth?"

"Reaching out fifty miles down below, beyond the occupied city limits, are fields of precious metals, diamonds, critical minerals, and uranium deposits used to fuel nuclear power plants here and elsewhere in Taoland. The city was created 5000 feet down to both access and protect these. Of course Thossia possesses infrastructure atop the moon's surface, but it's below ground where the action is."

I immediately liked Pamplin. He and all other Tezhouse agents were incorruptible, per our culture and rules. But each of our competitors' agents were corrupt, adding to our challenge. During the competition, Pamplin and I exposed two attempts at influence peddling and a scandal causing one of the decision makers to resign. I also successfully protested a last-minute spec change aimed at unfair advantage for Huggles.

For eight long months, we labored over the details of the bid. In the customer organization, I worked only with Gretta, the most-senior decision maker on the Selection Committee. I was able to answer all her questions quickly. With her, I employed Vester's Rule of Three with a message of *superior technology, comfortably within-budget,* and *a clever warranty* added with Randahl's help in the services portion of our proposal. In the end it was a close win for us. I stored lessons-learned in *Guidogram*.

It was an 800-million-luni win, with significant add-ons ahead. A dozen other lesser wins by my team during my first 250 days more than doubled this amount. We were well ahead of the goal. To my dismay, there was no celebration, no praise. No bonus. Not even a thank-you. All I got were complaints from Bogart that I'd left 50 million lunies on the table. A little praise from top management would have given my team a boost and confidence to go secure more wins. Komourin and the Board pissed me off with their silence.

What the heck do they expect of me?

I'd given every waking hour to the effort – leaving virtually zero time for my family. In return, Komourin ordered me from Thossia to Zermund, where once again Tezhouse was given no chance of winning. They didn't even offer a pause for me to spend time at home.

I *swish'd* Tari with the good news about the Thossia award, hoping she'd say, "Well done." Of course I also had to inform her of my Zermund assignment.

"Nice of you to connect," she grumbled sarcastically, looking at her fingernails. "I have no time to talk. I've got to get the children to their activities. That's my purpose – while yours is apparently to ignore them."

"Tari . . . please." I had enough stress to deal without her being difficult.

"Perhaps you can *swish* Tojo and Kaleeva once in a while if you can fit them into your schedule. You might actually be able to convince them you care about them."

"Tari . . . PLEASE." I'd given her everything she could possibly need and more. Any other woman would be grateful. All she did was complain.

"Adam, you have a pathetic need for acceptance from folks who don't matter. Fear of failure and rejection has you handcuffed. If this is the way it's going to be, with your oh-so-important new job, we might be over."

She disconnected.

I stared at the blank hologram.

Without returning home, I moved into the Zermund Grand Lunatel, my new temporary home away from home. The Zermund Medical Research Institute (ZMRI), which purchased systems for health-care providers throughout the region, was working closely with Canzon, a local company, and with Huggles, bidding against Tezhouse on an RFP for advanced medical devices, new multi-species care facilities and trauma centers, and pharmaceutical laboratories.

"It's going to be tough here," warned Randahl, who met me there. "We barely qualified as a bidder."

Huggles, long entrenched in Zermund, was considered clearly

in the lead. The other competitor, Canzon, was the hometown favorite – but they lacked certain needed software depth. We had the best technology, and I was easily the best one to lead here for Tezhouse, since I had invented the *X3*, the solution we were offering. But *X3* was still new to the marketplace and risk-averse Zermund officials were dubious.

I got an idea and maneuvered to meet with Ericson, Canzon's CEO. Once in his office, I got straight to the point. "Ericson, you cannot possibly beat Huggles. But together, we can win."

I proposed a joint bid, with half of the service business going to Canzon. Ericson loved the idea. After we'd refined to plan a bit he said, "I'd like for us to present this at headquarters immediately." The very next day we convinced the Canzon Board to approve the plan. We then flew together to the Third Moon, where two days later we presented to the Tezhouse Board where, after contentious discussion, our joint venture (JV) was approved by a 5–4 vote.

Ericson then secured us a meeting with Nigel, the ZMRI Director. Throughout our presentation, Nigel sat stoically while asking penetrating questions. In the end, he happily accepted our JV as a bidder. In the final days, I threw in several goodies beyond our initial quote. We squeezed by with a narrow victory – worth 750 million. More lessons learned for *Guidogram*.

Not a soul at Tezhouse had expected the win, which everyone attributed to my JV idea. This time, the Board offered a nice bonus, which I accepted on condition that Randahl, who helped me structure the JV, would likewise be rewarded. Bogart, as usual, asserted the extras I'd added would destroy his profits. Plus he cast aspersions about my cutting a corrupt deal with Nigel. Nobody at headquarters fell for his bullshit.

I was now two-for-two in major wins, and we continued to overachieve in all other bids. Midway into my second year on the job all was looking great. Once again, I *swish'd* Tari to boast about the good news, especially my sizable bonus. Her unappreciative reaction stunned me.

She turned her face away when she appeared in hologram. "I couldn't care less about your victories at Tezhouse, you jerk. You ignore me and don't even return my *swishes* for days on end, then boast to tell me how great you are? I won't seek a divorce right now. That would devastate the kids. But it's coming. Sooner than you'd think."

My heart slammed against my rib cage. "Tari, you're overreacting. I love you. I want to grow old with you."

She rolled her eyes. "The man I fell in love with is no longer here; perhaps never was. You are self-consumed. Tezhouse owns you, body and soul. You value your corporate pals far more than me and the children. I can't take it anymore. I need to live for myself, find out who I am."

"Please Tari, I need you to be less selfish and consider my plight. Please never again threaten to leave me."

She suddenly seemed unable to take a deep breath. "How dare you call me selfish? You're driving me to drink." Her fingers trembled and tears welled up in her eyes. She screamed, "I *swhish'd* you last week when I was deep in despair., but you didn't even respond, did you? More like you didn't want to respond. I bet you were out clubbing – or worse."

"Tari, I've told you repeatedly – everything I do is for you and the kids. My purpose is to provide for all your wants and needs. And I provide everything, including great schools, for our children."

Whoops. I know she hates this argument.

She glared at me, her eyes now totally ablaze. She raised her voice. Loud! "Oh please cut that crap, once and for all. We would happily make do with less materially in exchange for more of your time. You never think about our spiritual needs, which you as a husband and father should attend to. You, you, you – it's always about you. When have the children and I *ever* come first in your life? And schools? What schools? You don't even know what grade levels your kids are at now. You've never even been inside the walls of their schools. You never attend their school events. You are blind to the luxury of love that your family constantly swathes you with."

Is it too late for us?

Tari's eyes widened displaying ugliness I didn't know rested in her soul. The sharp thorns of her words spiked my skin everywhere. "You are such a sad case. Mr. Businessman of the Year. Maybe a good shrink might help you figure it all out. But I'm not waiting around. As soon as both kids are in university, I'm filing for divorce." She disconnected without a goodbye.

She has zero appreciation for my struggles to give her and the kids the best life.

I *swish'd* Ambrosia, hoping she'd help make Tari understand. "Tari has threatened divorce. I was attempting to share some great work news when she totally lost it. Can you talk some sense into her?"

She rolled her eyes. "Adam, you are trying to put everything you have into Tezhouse, while still finding something in reserve for Tariana and your family. That simply is not possible."

"If I make a few simple adjustments, I can achieve at Tezhouse and still be a good husband and father."

She leaned in, a stern look on her glowing face. "You are delusional. You have made the choice to go all-in toward becoming Tezhouse's next CEO. You leave only scraps for your family."

"I need both in my life."

"Some wants and the demands they place on us eliminate the possibility of other wants. You simply cannot have it all."

CHAPTER 22

FALSE PURPOSE

After Zermund, I stayed home for three days. It didn't go well. I was emotionally conflicted and drained. Tari and the kids avoided me. My renewed attempt to show I could be a good father and husband failed.

Just as I'd chosen Tezhouse over her, Tari threw herself into her TSU work. She was away from our home most of the time, as were Tojo and Kaleeva, who were happily engaged with friends and extracurricular activities. At least Apollo, now approaching thirteen, cuddled by my side. But he slept constantly.

I was alone in my own home – nobody to speak with. *Tari must feel like this most of the time.*

After those dreadful few days I moved to my next project, a nearly unwinnable bid in Smerland. It was a long shot, because in this desolate region bribes, big ones, were a way of life. Huggles had the most corrupt agent of all – a thug who 'owned' everybody at the Smerland Regional Homeland Security Agency (SRHSA).

"A win in Smerland is highly unlikely," acknowledged Komourin, "but I'm hopeful you'll pull off another of your miracles, even though not a single soul at Tezhouse thinks you've got a chance."

I jockeyed my way into a one-on-one with Wilfred, the SRHSA

Director. I suspected he agreed to meet me privately hoping I'd offer him a bribe bigger than that from Huggles. Wilfred didn't know who he was dealing with. Inviting me in alone was his blunder.

We sat face-to-face in his lavish office. He was shaped something like a bloated rhombus, only five foot tall. After over a dozen years in Taoland, I didn't ask or care if he was human. I ignored his ostentatious digs. His opening play after 'hello' was unexpected. "Huggles' price is 10 percent lower than yours, Adam. What would you do if you were us?"

I narrowed my eyes at the grotesque, mustached creature sitting back in his chair, arms crossed, failing to mask his discomfort with my being there.

"Same specs?"

"Yes."

"No caveats in the Huggles technical proposal?"

He looked away, mumbling, "None whatsoever."

"Same service-after-sale offering and guarantees as ours? Same terms and conditions?"

He spoke, avoiding eye contact, lying through his clenched teeth. "Yup. So, what would you do if you were us?"

Hearing no bribe offer, he likely wanted me out of his office. "Well, Wilfred, if that's true, I'd go with Huggles. But I must add a big fat warning."

That jerked his attention. "Such as?"

I invaded his space, glaring. "Such as – we will expose the truth if you select Huggles. We'll leak a dossier about your agency to the Taoland Bureau of Investigations. The media, throughout Taoland, will be given irrefutable evidence about what's going on here. It will be ugly. And there will be no Tezhouse fingerprints to be found."

Wilfred broke into a sweat. "I have no idea what you're talking about."

Disrespectfully jabbing my finger in his face, I continued, "We know the corrupt game SRHSA is playing with Huggles. At least a dozen on your proposal evaluation team have been bribed."

Wilfred wiped his now wet fat lips. I continued my relentless attack.

"In a fair, honest competition, Huggles' price to develop technology we already have would be at least 30 percent higher than our total price. And we both know their support package sucks."

He grimaced, his blubbery shoulders drooping. He remained silent.

I moved even closer to where he could feel my breath. "Huggles intends to sign a low-ball contract with you, and then 'get-well' with add-ons as soon as the ink dries on the contract. The bribed ones will get more incentives."

Was I bluffing? Absolutely. Would Tezhouse allow me to play out this scenario? No way. But this was my best and only shot.

"By the way, Wilfred, we'll never drop our price. Not one single luni. Our solution is perfect, and our price is fair. And we've got no illicit or illegal involvements."

"But . . . Bogart . . . the big shot in Tezhouse . . . is our friend."

When he opened that door I rammed a nolitruck through it. "I don't give a shit about Bogart. By the way, if we are not chosen, we will prove Bogart himself is taking Huggles' money as well. Bogart's a bad dude. I suggest you stay clear of him."

He stammered and lied. "I . . . I don't know the man . . . personally."

I laced my fingers behind my head and leaned back in the chair. "Maybe not, but you have some corrupt folks around you who do. You'll learn their names shortly if you select Huggles. Thanks for your time. I'll see you at the award announcement."

I stood and exited, leaving the door open, without a goodbye.

Trying to be a good father, I intended to go home that weekend to take Tojo to the stadium for his game and ceremonies after, but now I needed to stay in Smerland until the decision. I *swish'd* Tari to adjust plans and ask her to apologize to Tojo.

Tari glared at me. "Enough!" I couldn't recall her ever looking so furious. "You always place Tezhouse above me, but now you're choosing your work over your only son. Tell him yourself."

She shifted her virtual display to Tojo, who could not possibly miss her rage.

Why won't she cover for me?

"I'm sorry, Tojo. I hope you can forgive me."

Tojo was scheduled to start at forward for the first time. It was the league championship game. Of course, he longed for his dad to be there. Expressionless, he fibbed. "No problem. I don't care. Here's Mom again." I was jolted by his abruptness. He barely looked at me. And here I was, doing what was best for him. *Or am I just trying to convince myself of that?*

Tari's usually pretty face bordered on ugliness when I declared, "Stop bugging me. I'm living my life the best way I know how."

"You're not living your life. Your life is living you. Stay in Smerland forever for all I care. I can't do this anymore." She looked away and disconnected.

Smerland awarded us the contract. Another 950M. A bluff that worked; a new addition for *Guidogram*. Another victory for Tezhouse; another failure at home. I was learning lessons in business but learning nothing about how to be a good husband. I returned to my family and attempted to repair the damage there. Tari wouldn't look me in the eye during my entire stay. The kids hugged me but with tightened bodies. Their words bore no emotion. There were no family smiles. *I'm falling apart.*

One day I *swish'd* Abraham and Roshi and brought them up to speed. I needed shoulders to cry on – if only virtually. I longed to be there with them at that magical spot at the pagoda, away from my constant tensions with Tari.

"Guys, I just brought in my third major win, this one the most difficult so far. I got another huge bonus. The bad news? I'm exhausted and emotionally drained. And while I can't possibly overstate how ugly it is out here in the real world, it's even worse at home. I'm in deep trouble. I need your help."

With a saddened face, Abraham responded, "Sorry to learn you're at a breaking point."

I squirmed. "I'm under constant stress. Losing sleep. Except for you two, I have no real friends. Worst of all – and I hate to keep dumping on you – my home life nightmare is now beyond impossible. I'm losing Tari, and the kids too. I'm suffocating."

Roshi knitted his eyebrows with concern. "We've repeatedly warned you to find balance. Find time to work, to play, and to rest. It's essential, and doable, but totally up to you. All we can do is advise."

"I can't let up. I've gotta pass both Bogart and Randahl in the race to become CEO."

Roshi stiffened. "Why do you have to become CEO?"

"It's my purpose."

"No, it isn't."

I changed the subject. "I feel Bogart in every shadow. Whenever I bring in new business, he dumps turds on the table, complaining I signed a bad deal. When I head to another battle, he blames me for any schedule delays and cost overruns."

Abraham responded, "He wants to be CEO more than you do."

I pounded my desk. "He's got thugs in every arena constantly trying to undo my work."

Roshi's glare was matched by unusual harshness. "Bogart is pure evil. You can't expect anything different. And you enable him by fearing him. You are headed toward burnout, self-destruction, and loss of your family – simultaneously."

He waved his oversized fingers at me, something I'd never seen him do before. "You, not Bogart, will be the one to sink your ship, my friend. I love you. Abraham loves you. We both want what's best for you. And that is *not* becoming CEO."

Abraham leaned in. "You need to let go of what you are at

Tezhouse – so you might become who you are meant to be. Drop your false purpose before it's too late."

Oh, please, just shut up. The two of you.

"We'll always disagree there. Gotta go. Bye." I slapped the air mightily, ending the *swish*.

CHAPTER 23

SHOCKING NEWS

Three years into my job on the Second Moon, I was three-for-three on major bids, and our win ratio and bookings on all other bids were well above targets. I was headed toward being chosen CEO.

No one can stop me now.

But my marriage was on the rocks. Tari seemed unsympathetic about my past life – an existence void of emotions or goals. Now, as I was fulfilling my career dreams, she offered a chilly goodbye, but zero support, when I headed out to my next conquest.

The fourth of the competitions that I'd chosen to lead myself was in Bhadran – a cluster of 1400 islands hovering magically in the sky – about 8 miles above the surface of the Second Moon. As I approached my destination, the Capital City of Heldari on the Island of Zendabari, I was thrilled to fly under dozens of other islands and witness other nolicraft doing likewise. The larger islands featured enormous ranges of mountains, some 25,000 feet high, rising above the surfaces of these mile-deep archipelagos – feeding fresh waters throughout. I'd read that on rainy days the islands mysteriously floated to rest just above the clouds.

More Taoland magic.

In flight I read about the customer, the hi-tech Airborne Surveillance Institute (ASI), which had issued an RFP for a suite of advanced hardware and software to be housed aboard the *Noliex*, an airborne surveillance platform stationed there. It was designed for pilotless high-altitude monitoring and command control.

Komourin had informed me of the importance of the bid. "Adam, a win here would secure market dominance in an exciting field – and engage Bogart's engineers for three years. But we are the least favored bidder. A local entity, Amanibhar, has a huge edge because their winning would advance homegrown technology capabilities. And then there's Huggles, as always. We need yet another Adam Novana miracle."

The nearly 700-million-luni contract would be eclipsed fourfold when other users signed on to what would emerge as a Taoland-wide airborne surveillance network. The local engineering company, Amanibhar, had an overwhelming insider advantage. We had an enormous mountain to climb. Building on our success in Zermond, I decided to climb that hill with a partner. I had cleared my concept with Komourin before leaving for the amazing nation of islands in the sky.

After landing I grabbed a nolitaxi driven by a man named Rhamish. We chatted during the drive to my hotel. "Rhamish, how many of the islands here are inhabited?"

His dark brown eyes studied me in his rearview mirror. "You mean by humans?"

"Yes."

"About 95 percent of our population of 140 million reside on the 24 largest islands. Twelve million live here on Zendabari. A scattering of other humans live on smaller islands where they work in tourism, agriculture, ranches, fisheries, and mining – or reside in exclusive private retirement or vacation homes. More than a thousand of our islands are jungles, with an abundance of wildlife and spectacular flora. Others are barren deserts."

We drove through neighborhoods displaying an awful contrast

of decrepit slums interspersed with thriving businesses, restaurants presenting delightful aromas, blocks of flower-covered apartment buildings with impeccable landscaping, and beautiful public buildings. Remarkably it was in the slums where folks smiled, children played – some with naked distended bellies – and adults toiled carrying on various activities, including herding animals through the busy streets. Traffic crawled.

I was struck when a woman on the street met my gaze, her eyes full of hardship. She balanced a large pot, which Rhamish explained was full of water, on her head with ease. Her round face, skin blackened by the light of the Tao, was adorned with various piercings and brightly colored markings.

I found it all perplexing. "What a stark conflict in living conditions, Rhamish. Some obviously comfortable. Others absolutely horrific."

"Yes. But it's getting better. Our government has been quite successful in eliminating half of the extreme poverty of decades ago – with improved education, housing and food subsidies, and most importantly empowerment zones where better jobs and small business ownership are available. Still a long way to go, but here on Zendabari and throughout Bhadran our elected public servants are resolved to improve conditions and opportunities for all."

I hired Rhamish for the remainder of my stay and checked into the Mathah Lunatel. I *swish'd* to secure a meeting with Satella, the CEO of Narendra, an influential, local hardware producer with superb field engineering credentials. The next day I entered Satella's large, welcoming office.

"Good morning, Sir. Thank you for granting this meeting."

The tall, dark, and handsome individual, oval faced with a wide nose, was seated behind a blond wooden desk. He responded, "Drop the 'Sir.' You said you wanted to talk about the RFP from ASI. We're not involved. We don't have the software know-how for a prime bid. But, of course, we'd love some piece of the action downstream."

I smiled. "It doesn't have to be downstream. I'd like to partner with you – right now. I want to launch a Joint Venture – Teznar, Inc – and for us to bid as a team. Fifty-fifty in all decisions and as close as possible to fifty-fifty in revenues. Dual signatures on everything. But the clock is ticking. We'd need the JV in place in two weeks. And we'd have to keep it confidential until the final day for bid qualification."

His dark brown eyes opened wide. "Oh my. You don't waste time getting to your point. And I haven't even offered you coffee yet. This is an unexpected shocker."

I leaned forward. "I've brought an outline for our partnership. My CEO has blessed it. We are flexible and open to any and all ideas. Of course, we'd have to move forward at record speed."

"As you know, Adam, successful fifty-fifties are rare. They require mutual trust, and we've just met. Even if you were to convince me your idea makes sense, my Board would be reticent."

"I understand. Hear me out." I had him right where I wanted. His hesitation would soon fade. He sighed and brushed back his straight black hair with arched fingers. "OK. If I like your pitch, I might consider calling a special Board meeting. Let's talk over lunch."

We dined in his gardens, where his wife and children joined. A host of unfamiliar spicy treats were served buffet style – gloubbi, chasalah, placknir, bhark, ticcamas, harini, and dholaji. The various dishes had meats, fish, and/or incredible blends of vegetables in expertly spiced sauces and gravies. Everything was complemented with tasty thin pathroti flatbreads prepared fresh atop a dome-shaped oven and a savory starch called rasmoti. Platters of exotic fruits and a super sweet spongy dessert concluded the magnificent meal.

Satella didn't like my proposal. *He loved it.* He made a handful of immediate suggestions, which I incorporated on the spot. The next day, he and I briefed at an emergency meeting of the Narendra Board. After lengthy and spirited discussions, all Board members approved – overtly delighted with the possibility of upsetting Amanibhar.

Later that week Satella and I briefed the Tezhouse Board via *swish*. We received a mixed reaction, but once again the vote went 5–4 in my favor. Komourin *swish'd* after the decision. "I'm going to contact Bogart, who likely has already heard from his Board cronies. We've actually got a chance now, Adam. You speak with Randahl. We'll need him fully on board. I need you both there in Bhadran full time, for the duration."

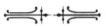

Back at my apartment, I swallowed hard and *swish'd* Tari to tell her I'd be in Bhadran for a while. She barked back at me, "How nice of you to think of us. Of course, as always, you're too late."

Baffled, I responded, "Too late? For what?"

"We buried Apollo this morning."

Oh no. No.

"I'm . . . s-s-sorry . . . I didn't know."

He was my first ever pet. I'd let my family down. I'd not been there to share the pain. I wept. Tari snapped. "You didn't know? Your dog has been failing for months. I had to make the decision, all alone I might add, to put him to sleep. I can't talk now – I'm still consoling our heartbroken children. You remember them, I assume."

"I said . . . I'm sorry." I barely choked the words out.

"How can you continue to ignore your family? From now on, don't bother coming back home. It's over, Adam. I said I'd stay for the kids. But I can't do this anymore." Abruptly, as had become routine, she broke the connection.

I am loveless, friendless, adrift, abandoned, forsaken. Even Apollo is gone.

But then, I'm not the victim here. Tari is.

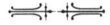

Although aware my wife and kids were suffering, I brushed thoughts of them aside. As usual I yielded to the demands of my company, like a repetition of a horrible nightmare. Once again, the offer of a generous reward for my victory was too alluring. I poured myself into our new JV. The folks at Amanibhar were thrown off message.

Two months later I received a *swish*, shocked to see Tari – disheveled, sobbing uncontrollably.

"Tojo's had an accident. I need you here, Adam."

"What? . . . How? . . . When?" My heart raced.

"He crashed a super-nolicycle. He's in surgery."

"No! Oh no! I'll be there as soon as I can."

"Please hurry. I'm falling apart." The urgency in her voice rattled me to the core.

"How bad is it?"

"He's got internal bleeding – and a concussion."

"Is someone with you?"

"Lorelai and Ambrosia. *But I need you.*"

I *swish'd* Randahl and told him of the crisis. "I need you to take the lead."

"No problem, Adam. I've got this. Keep us up to date on Tojo."

Komourin offered immediate assistance. "I'll have a high-speed transport across from your lunatel in twenty minutes." Soon the spacecraft was soaring through the sky. An otherwise six-hour trip took only ninety minutes. We landed on a pad atop the hospital two hours after Tari had given me the horrible news. She ran to me, threw herself into my arms, and fell apart. I held her, without words, as she buried her head in my chest.

I wiped tears from her cheeks. "How is he?"

"He's been in the operating room since we spoke. No word yet."

The surgery went well, perfectly the doctors said, but for two days there was no sign of recovery as Tojo remained asleep and motionless. Tari and I were in constant distress. On the third day, I felt Adriella's warming presence nearby. I ran into the hall searching for her.

"Adam." Hearing her telepathically brought overwhelming calm. "Lead me to your son." She entered Tojo's room and sent out a healing wave of brilliant light toward him. Tari and I were on either side of his bed when he suddenly awoke, acting as if nothing had happened.

"Mom. Dad. What's going on?"

Tears of joy burst from Tari's eyes. "You had an accident on Michael's super-nolicycle. You've had surgery and have been out for forty-eight hours."

Adriella had been with me through everything, always there at critical moments to bring relief. This time to Tojo. With a special telepathic message for me. I understood what she was telling me lovingly. I needed to focus way more on my wife and family.

Tojo's surgeon rushed in with an excited smile. "I was not expecting this. It's a miracle. We'll do a brainwave immediately." I smiled at Adriella, knowing she was the reason for Tojo's miraculous recovery. She pulsed with compassionate energy and faded from view.

The results came back quickly. The doctor was elated. "Tojo's brain waves appear as if nothing ever happened. His bruises will linger for a while. He'll wear a cast and use crutches for some time. Other than that, he's a lucky lad indeed."

I stayed home for two weeks as Tojo recovered. I never even checked in with Randahl in Bhadran. Tari and I took a pause in our differences. Tragedy has a way of temporarily healing a wounded relationship. In the gardens one evening I shared my new hopes with Ambrosia. "There are still tensions with Tariana, but it's promising."

"Tojo's accident created a crisis. Crisis is opportunity. Seize this moment, Adam. Let it be the start of a revival of a beautiful love affair that never really went away. And a reconnection with your children." She gave me a reassuring hug.

Tari and I walked the grounds almost every day, hand-in-hand, but our conversations were hesitant, and far from perfect. There was no real hint of a renewed love affair.

I drew closer to Tojo – enjoying more one-on-one time than I had in years. One day, over lunch, he began an apology, "Dad, I was speeding – I mean way above the speed limit. And I was not wearing a helmet. I'm so sorry I created such agony for you and Mom."

I pulled him to me. "Tojo, all that matters is your complete recovery. We all make mistakes. But the good news is we learn from them. Put this behind you and focus on the road ahead."

"But I was so reckless. I'm sorry." He looked up at me, tears welling in his eyes. The guilty look on his face struck a chord. He was growing up, able to process complex things and show emotions and feelings that I ran from at his age. My boy would soon be a man, and I was absent from too much of his early years.

"It's me who owes you an apology, son. My screwed-up priorities have left me missing out on quality time we should have spent together. You'll only be a teenager once. I still want to share with you what's left of those years. I've still got work commitments. But I'm going to ask, no I'm going to demand to spend more time at home. Please trust me."

"I do trust you, Dad."

I meandered down the hall to Kaleeva's bedroom and knocked softly. She smiled and invited me in. She hugged me when I began apologizing to her. "You are a great dad. Not perfect. But I wouldn't trade you for anyone else."

After some quality time at home, I returned to Bhadran for the final push. Randahl had filled in for me seamlessly. He and Satella had placed us in great shape for closing arguments and final pricing.

"Thanks so much, Randahl."

"Are you kidding? Thank you for allowing me the pleasure of dining here every day."

In the end our JV, Teznar, Inc was awarded the prime contract at 820M. Once again, our superior technology, services offerings, and fair price were critical. But it was our partnership with Narendra that sealed the deal. Another feather in my cap. This time with at least a ray of hope at home.

Komourin *swish'd* while the ink was drying on the contract.

"Congrats, Adam."

I didn't acknowledge his congratulations. Close to burnout, I made a request, which, if granted, could perhaps turn things around at home. "Komourin, I need a break. I need time, a month or two, with Tari and the kids. She's on the verge of leaving me, but we began patching wounds as Tojo recovered. I'm encouraged we might get it all back. But I need time away from the field."

"That's not possible. You're being transferred. To Kamyabi. With your family. For a year."

Now my marriage really will be over!

CHAPTER 24

EXILED TO KAMYABI

"How dare you ask me to drag my falling-apart family to a shithole like Kamyabi. That place is rampant with corruption. You can't do this to me. I won't go."

"We need you there."

Bogart must have convinced the four Board members he 'owns' plus one of the newcomers that I should be sent there. "I smell Bogart behind this."

"Well, he convinced the Board members that Kamyabi is important to Tezhouse and you alone might turn things around there. And I agree."

I shouted, with disrespect fully intended, "Fuck Bogart. He only wants to end my winning streak and have me blamed for wasting precious Tezhouse resources. Everyone will have short memories of Bogart's suggestion once we lose."

He frowned. "It's out of my hands. I'm CEO, but the Board rules."

"Why must Tari and the kids be disrupted?"

"Our only shot in countering Huggles' position is for you to become socially engaged with the Ruling Family there, and thereby get close to the top officials. Having Tariana there will make this possible. Her social skills can make a difference. Bringing your children will add an element of respect."

"I told you, I'm not going."

"This isn't a request; it's an order." Komourin's face showed unfamiliar rage.

"An order?"

"Get your ass home. Tell Tariana and your kids to pack their luggage. You depart in three days. The Board has spoken."

"She won't go along with this."

"If you can't convince her we'll be ending your quest to become CEO. Your choice."

His seething eyes convinced me he meant this – and that further argument was futile. I hesitated, head down, ready to vomit.

My life's purpose is to become CEO.

Komourin didn't give a shit about me or my family. He stared, and fumed, angrily forcing me to make my decision. He knew I wanted to become CEO more than anything else in my life. It was my purpose. After a brief moment of struggling with my choices I broke a long minute of silence. "I'll . . . we'll go." As soon as I spoke these words, I owned the decision.

Nobody in their right mind would want Tezhouse involved in Kamyabi. No sane husband and father would ever move his family there. Except for me, obsessed with my career. I *swish'd* Tari and gave her the bad news. It was a monologue. She didn't respond, but simply ended the connection.

Tari and I won't survive this.

Tension hung thick in the air when I got home. It was late and I was exhausted. Tari stood at the bedroom door. I stumbled around, trying to get undressed and into bed. She didn't budge, just staring with blank eyes. I opened with small talk to test the waters.

"It's been a couple of weeks. All OK at TSU? How are the kids doing at school?"

She snarled, "Like you care."

Her anger and icy demeanor was back – as bad as before Tojo's accident.

"Tari . . . please."

She kicked the clothes I'd dropped in disgust. "You are a miserable piece of garbage. I was hoping we'd build on the healing time we just spent together. Now this!" My gaze dropped to the ground as every word she spoke rang of truth. All I could do was listen to her rant. "We're not going to Kamyabi. I'm leaving you. The kids support my decision."

The ferocity of her words clobbered me. Then my shock turned to anger. "We are going to Kamyabi. End of story. Neither of us has a choice in the matter. It's an order from the top. If we refuse, my goal to become CEO is over."

Tari's eyes widened as she grasped my words. "And I should give a shit about that? Your arrogance and ugly ambitions are wrapped in your demand. I hate you."

Her fingers trembled as tears spilled. She screamed like never before, "How dare you ask this of me and the children. You've gone off repeatedly without us. Do it again. Except this time – don't return." Her callous words had me shaking uncontrollably. We'd never reached this depth before. I took a step back, pummeled by the venom in her voice.

"You left us a long time ago. Do it forever this time." She paced the room, pouring out her frustrations. "You spend most of your free time clubbing, rather than checking in with us. And now you want to isolate us in Kamyabi, which I've heard is a disgusting place. *How dare you* ask me to leave behind my friends and the life I've made . . . once again!"

I took a deep breath as the thorns on her words cut through me. She continued to dump her pent-up rage, built over years of neglect. "You claim you're working so hard that there's nothing left in your tank. Well, what about us? When will I and the children I *ever* to come first in your life?"

I turned away and fought off an urge to flee the room. This

was Komourin's fault. He allowed Bogart to derail hopes for us to get back on the right track. She continued her rampage, her arms folded tightly across her chest, rage growing by the instant on her reddened face.

"Adam, our children are teens now. They love their schools, friends, and extracurricular activities. They're looking forward to college years. They would hate moving to Kamyabi more that I would."

"Kamyabi would only be for a year. And we'd be living first class."

Now she shouted at the very top of her lungs. "FIRST CLASS! We don't want to live 'first class.' Why can't you understand this? We don't need nor have we ever asked for luxury."

I pleaded for her support, "Please, I beg of you. Let's give this a chance. I don't want to end us, even though I don't deserve you and the children. We are in desperate need of a family miracle. A year in Kamyabi will either save us or end us once and for all."

She sagged into a wingback chair near the doorway. I sat on the bed. Her voice collapsed to a whisper, as tears gushed down her cheeks. "You should have been with us all these years. But you chose Tezhouse. And now, you're wanting to disrupt our family as it's falling apart. Taoland is a place of magic. But I have *zero* confidence moving to Kamyabi would provide the miracle we need."

"Please . . . I'm begging you." She stared at the wall in silence, her eyes devoid of the life I always saw in them. "Tari, I know it's a huge ask – but it may be our last chance. But, if it's a firm no, I'll *swish* Komourin right now, even if that means the end for me at Tezhouse. I need you in my life way more than I need Tezhouse. They only want me if I'll do their will. Tari, it's your decision, which I'll accept willingly either way."

I went to the chair and knelt at her feet. Her body softened and she took my head into her lap. Our conversation had my nerves on edge, but I meant it – I'd comply with her decision. I wasn't ready to give up my family for anything. Then, through tears she said,

"I'll give it a chance, for three months, while the kids are out of school. Then we'll decide if we will stay for a full year, which I seriously doubt."

I gasped. I hoped for but dared not expect her answer. I raised my head and gazed into her swollen wet eyes. I felt her pain. I vowed to do whatever it took to make Kamyabi a positive game-changer for my family. "Thank you. I know it's a shitty place but making the best of it as a family might just save us. Maybe Kamyabi can be a place of miracles."

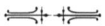

Kamyabi was indeed a backward region. Most inhabitants had arrived over a 500-year period from the planet of Fiendor in the Plagmus Galaxy. Over the past fifty years this long-impoverished land had found significant wealth with the discovery of energy reserves. Still, there was no assimilation into the Taoland culture. Kamyabians lived in isolation, apart from all others on the Second Moon.

Two days later, bags packed, we traveled to this distant place, barely speaking to each other. We landed in a scene of drab isolation at the Kamyabi Interlunar Airport – with orange sand blowing everywhere, including into our eyes. A driver, Shamar, arrived in a filthy nolivan and gathered our luggage as we piled in. She didn't bother to offer a greeting.

We headed off on a miserable trip, along congested, bumpy roads – obstructed by yelling hawkers with filthy carts – to our lunatel in the city center. Vast slum areas stretched beyond our sight as we traveled through the Capital City of Heteron.

This is worse than I'd imagined.

Kamyabi was rich in natural resources, but the elite hoarded the wealth. All we saw on our drive were miserable peasants living in abject poverty in depressing tents made of plastic scraps, discarded boxes, and sticks. The shanties slumped feebly against each other. Three-wheeled nolitaxis, broken-down vehicles, and public transports spewed out toxic smoke – made more noxious by fumes from filthy animals and the stench from open sewers. Humans with heads held low, including women shuffling barefoot in brilliant colors as if to ward off reality, added to the hopelessness of the scene.

Tears fell from Tari's eyes. The kids snuggled close to her as she held them in her arms, not looking at me. Fortunately, the lunatel turned out to be a pleasant surprise. A courteous staff escorted us to a massive 4,000-square-foot apartment Komourin booked to ease our settling in. As soon as I shut the door, Tari growled the first words she'd spoken since we left the airport, "We're not staying here in Kamyabi."

The tensions building up in me exploded. "Oh yes, we are."

"I don't want our children in this disgusting place. Not for a day, not for three months, certainly not for a year."

"I made a deal with Tezhouse – we are all staying for the duration."

Tojo and Kaleeva hid their faces as we argued, something we had always avoided in their presence. I growled more firmly than ever, "I'm the head of this family!"

So much for family harmony.

I stomped out of our suite to the dust-covered van in the parking lot and directed Shamar to take me to the Tezhouse Building. She parked in front of the facility, at the bottom of a steep hill in a grungy urban area. I found Soodi, our husky, dark-featured agent, and the rest of the team – gathered on a terrace, one floor above the ground, sullied by dust and the fact it overlooked the chaotic street. We introduced ourselves and sipped tea through sugar cubes while munching on warm flatbreads filled with goat cheese and wild greens.

We leapt from our seats when alarmed by a loud screech from below. A massive nolitruck careened through the street and crashed into a small boy riding a bike. The boy flew into the air;

then the vehicle swerved and slammed into my nolivan. "We've got to help!" Soodi led us down the stairs.

The boy was dead. As was Shamar. Her body was crushed. Lumber and bricks were strewn about. Two dark, wispy figures loomed over the bodies of the victims. I'd read of shadowy figures who come to escort the souls of the dead, but I'd never witnessed it before my eyes. Shouts and jeers drew my attention. Within minutes a crowd of perhaps fifty had gathered from nearby buildings. They dragged out the screaming nolitruck driver whose wild reptilian eyes were wide with horror. With bats, sticks, feet, and fists, they slaughtered the woman.

Stunned, I turned to Soodi. "How could they do that?"

"A life for a life."

"I don't understand."

"The boy died. Shamar as well. The driver was sacrificed in exchange."

Sacrificed?

"But the driver could not possibly have seen the boy."

"Doesn't matter. It's the law."

No judge. No jury. Mob rule.

Still in shock, I dismissed everyone and returned to the lunatel – in a new clean noli with my new driver, Herous. I instantly liked his caring nature but felt guilty about my zero compassion for the ill-fated Shamar. We flew rather than drove to avoid intense traffic. Multicolored animals, small and large, meandered aimlessly amongst nolis on the streets below.

Herous spoke. "It's always best we fly here, Mr. Adam." Flying suited the lithe and graceful man.

"You don't have to convince me."

Swish. It was Komourin, appearing in hologram in front of our noli.

"How are things so far, Adam?"

"Worse than you could ever imagine," I snapped disrespectfully. "Any chance I can return home tomorrow?"

Ignoring my plea he barked, "Before I arrive in a couple of weeks I need you to find a home and lease it for a year."

He disconnected. It was a quick, distant, cold conversation. Unlike Komourin.

Am I being set up?

CHAPTER 25

FAMILY BONDING

Crisis is opportunity. Both Roshi and Ambrosia taught me this. But for the life of me I couldn't make anything positive out of this mess. I entered our grand apartment but didn't mention the tragic deaths I'd just witnessed. But I did bring in Herous and introduced him as our family driver. His warm personality won my family over.

Tari and the kids had calmed down, or better said, Tari had calmed them down. Her reasons for staying were a mystery, but she must have come to understand this was one last chance to save our family. We agreed to select a residence as a family endeavor. With Soodi looking more like a bodyguard than a guide, we began our search the next morning. We visited eighteen large rental houses over the span of seven days, each with their own luxuries. Each came with servants of various kinds – some living in tents in the rear of sizable backyards.

"We don't need servants, Soodi."

"Not your choice. They come with the homes."

The search became a bonding experience. We'd never made a big decision as a family before. We agreed a unanimous vote was required. The kids and even Tari enjoyed exploring the beautiful properties of Kamyabi's wealthy. All came with swimming pools and other areas for entertainment. Some even had magical elements – like a team of tiny, flying servants at one of the most luxurious. They flitted about, constantly cleaning and catering to guests.

On the third day, we found the perfect place – until we went out to inspect the swimming pool. I almost vomited when we witnessed servants slitting the throat of a flailing, four-legged beast. Blood spurted and splattered everywhere – into the pool and on the concrete deck. Soodi saw our horrified expressions and explained, "This is our custom – whenever a new pool is built. It brings good luck." The four of us raced back to our nolivan – not looking back. If other pools had been so ritualized, it was best we didn't know.

We finally leased a nice home, at the northern tip of Heteron, with beautiful gardens, a swimming pool free from any evidence of blood, a game room, a tennis court, and even an automated AI system for all household functions. Oranges, reds, and yellows painted the landscape from the rear balcony view. Snow-capped mountains, rare on the Second Moon, tinged with these same colors, rose behind our property. In backyard tents lived two gracious servants, Niesha and Caspian, both human but smaller than the average size and with a third eye similar to Roshi's but sprouted at young ages.

"I know you don't want to be here, Tari. Nor do you, kids. But let's be open to this experience. I'll do my best to create adventures we can enjoy together."

This time I mean it.

After Komourin arrived two weeks later, we hosted a grand party. Soodi used the arrival of the CEO to convince high-level officials and several members of the Ruling Family to accept our invitation. Soodi also selected *swish* music, Kamyabian folk pieces, and taught us all how to perform native dances. Tari twirled and moved her hips to the music, quickly becoming an expert. The joy on her face was beyond anything I'd seen in some time.

Everyone fell in love with my wife's charming nature. She'd decorated our new home nicely with breathtaking floral displays and table settings. Soodi installed a dozen multicolored, intricate, silk-and-wool carpets throughout the house. "Keep them here throughout your stay, Adam. The more foot-traffic, the softer and more valuable they become."

The foods Tari selected with the caterer were perfect. Best of all, Tezhouse paid for everything. We'd only just arrived, but we were fast becoming members of Kamyabi's elite – an advantage I'd seize in addressing the challenge of winning the crucial contract.

Komourin stayed with us for his first night, having canceled the suite at the hotel. He joined me on my virgin visit to Tapah Doshan, customer headquarters. Chaos ruled the streets as Herous set us down, avoiding restricted airspace. There were no lane markings, no traffic lights. Domesticated animals, being herded to markets or slaughterhouses, further disrupted the maniacal traffic. The brightly painted creatures meandered noisily in unruly patterns. Herous left us across the road from Kamyabi Central Command, where we met up with Soodi. He stepped off the curb, ignoring oncoming nolis, and motioned for me and Komourin to follow.

I froze, shrieking, "Are you berserk?"

"Avoid eye contact with the noli drivers, and they won't hit you."

Komourin and I strode, anxiously clutching Soodi's cloak, as vehicles lurched to find openings, screeching to stops often within inches of our limbs. We made it across unscathed. Panting, I asked, "What if one of them had struck us dead, Soodi?"

"That would have marked our destinies."

Komourin and I stared at each other, unable to respond. After we signed into headquarters, two skinny seven-foot-tall uniformed guards, clearly not humans, led us up a white marble staircase to a suite of well-guarded rooms on the second floor. Pressa, the broad-shouldered Kaan of Kamyabi, was seated alone on a white throne, his dark skin glowing in the window light. Two of his aides, who were never introduced, sat in chairs on either side.

"Welcome." He personally poured tea and spoke in a soothing voice, his initial stern look transforming into a heartwarming smile. We sat on a comfortable cushioned-bench facing the king. A rectangular bejeweled table rested between us. After introductions and some small talk I nervously began talking, wanting to announce our purpose. Pressa raised his graceful hand to silence me.

"Let's enjoy our tea, Adam. Let's get to know each other."

Near the end of a delightful hour, I attempted to discuss our Tezhouse proposal, but Pressa raised his hand in mild protest. He was clearly far more interested in learning more about us. The Kaan's behavior reminded me of what Vester had said, "Customers do not purchase products from companies – they give contracts to those with whom they choose to work – folks they come to trust and respect."

As we stood to depart, Pressa spoke. "Adam, thank you for inviting my sister and my cousins to your party last week. They spoke mainly about your wife – how beautiful and gracious she is."

"She's my secret weapon." I winked at the ruler, then second-guessed my gesture.

A wide grin spread across his face. "Oh, they might have mentioned you briefly as well, Adam – but from their comments, I suspect you really married up."

He turned to Komourin and continued in a jovial mood, "I definitely can't recall them mentioning you at all, Mr. CEO."

We all laughed. Then, with outreached hands, Pressa concluded, "I'm looking forward to our next meeting. Perhaps we'll find a way to include Tariana then?"

As we searched for Herous out in the wild streets, Komourin bragged, "It was a brilliant move on my part to bring your wife here."

"I'll certainly tell her of the Kaan's kind words."

"As will I."

Komourin departed two days later, leaving operations in my

hands. I poured myself into our existing Kamyabian contract, by which we were launching Kamyabi Electronics Industries (KEI), a company we'd launched with local influential business leaders, and a keystone in our new bid. If we won, we planned to use KEI for some assembly and install work and services-after-sales as well. I invited my family to the KEI ribbon cutting event two months later.

Driving south of the capital on the way to the event, we passed black tents which served as schools for nomadic children. Herous pulled off the road and arranged a breakfast for us. Tojo and Kaleeva moaned in delight, taking second and third portions of tasty teas, yummy breads, cheeses, and spicy greens. Strange animals begging for scraps of food elicited giggles and rewards from my children, gladdening my heart.

The adventure, sights, and sounds of this place may just win them over.

The launch of KEI went flawlessly. I took an instant liking to Abol, the newly appointed CEO. Upon returning home, I gathered the family. "We've been here almost three months now. Let's share our thoughts on the place so far – and decide as a family if we're OK with staying the full year."

Tari began. "This is your life, Adam, not ours. But we support you. I'm happy with the changes in you since we arrived. I love Herous, Niesha, and Caspian. It's not perfect here, but it's bearable. I agreed we'd stay for a three-month trial period. But I'm OK with staying nine more, if the children agree."

"How about you, Kaleeva?"

"Dad, the best thing is you're more fun than ever. I like that we're doing so many things as a family, every weekend, and most evenings. I enjoy walking with you to the candy store. I'm crazy for those giant pixie sticks. And the colas and warm breads." She glanced at her brother who nodded eagerly. "Thanks for letting me take care of stray cats on the roof. And for treating me like a grown-up by allowing me to go to *Superpharket*, all by myself, though I was really scared at first." Her smile faded as she added,

"The people here are different, and it's difficult for me at times. But I am making a few friends. I'm OK with staying."

"Tojo?" I gripped his shoulder.

"I echo what Kaleeva said about our family bonding – being here has been super in that sense. For me, it's all about the diving board. I'm becoming an expert. I like bringing my friend Rabi over to swim. Thanks for hiring Manny for our tennis lessons. He's also teaching us indoor table games. One of my funnest times is spitting fruit pits from the roof and watching birds and squirrels scurrying after them." He looked up at me. "You said we should make the best of this. We are. I say let's stay the full year."

"How about the food here, guys?" I knew this we'd all agreed on.

"The kababs and grilled veggies are delish," said Tari, "and I love when the waiters cook egg yolks inside the hot rice."

Everyone nodded and voiced agreement.

"I know you kids are not thrilled with your schools."

"Yeah. Not so good," answered Tojo. "The schoolwork is OK, but I am mostly alone here. Rabi is my only friend because he's also an outsider. The locals ignore us. Sometimes I'm bored – like being isolated at home with a virus. But at least I've got *swish* for entertainment."

Kaleeva continued, "Dad, I agree with Tojo; they are unfriendly. They act so weird at times."

"You mean different from you?"

"Not exactly. Folks all over Taoland are different. But they are always friendly. Kamyabians don't accept us and only want their own ways."

"I don't understand what they are saying half the time," interjected Tojo. "All over the rest of Taoland, we understand each other. But these people use totally off-the-wall slang words. Still, I'm enjoying the new stuff that I think I'll miss after we leave."

"Dad," Kaleeva said, "don't you ever feel like you just don't belong?"

I lied. "When I do, I adapt. I feign interest. I ask dumb questions to make conversation. These are tricks you must learn."

"Seems phony," said Tojo.

"Maybe – but necessary."

Am I teaching them something I shouldn't?

Tari jumped in. "I disagree with your dad here. All humans are different – in appearances, skills, ambitions, and emotions. Some are rich, some are poor. We have different skin colors, different hair textures, different body types. Some of us are tall and skinny, others short and fat. And we come from different customs. We hold different beliefs about the Universe and its origin. Sadly, these differences can make us wary of each other at times. But if we accept and honor the differences, we will not only better get along, we will learn from each other. We are each on an individual journey, trying to find our ways home."

"We are all different, but we are all the same," Kaleeva responded.

"Exactly. We have different talents and different ways of showing the world who we are. But, my darling children, I want you to focus not on differences that can divide us, but on universal values and dreams we all share – on common truths that can unite us. Smile at your Kamyabian classmates, and you'll soon find them smiling back. Get to know each other's stories. Learn from each other. It's impossible not to love one another once you understand each other's stories."

"So we're all unique, and we should respect that, right?" Tojo concluded.

"Absolutely. And beyond respect – relish the differences. We are each created with individual purposes. Each of us is meant to do something only we can do. In the vast Universe, no two humans are identical, not even identical twins. When we realize that, there is no point in comparing or fearing one another."

I was awestruck. Her advice was so rich, so profound, yet so clear. She conveyed meaningful lessons to the kids without lecturing them.

She included them in the conversation, a key ingredient in any learning experience. I beamed, overwhelmingly proud of my wife. Her sage advice would mold my children into the adults we both desired them to be. Humbly and sincerely I said, "Thank you, Tari."

We'd never bonded quite like this. Our time in Kamyabi was bringing us closer. But as the days and weeks went on and on, our longing for home intensified. Mindful of our dependence on each other, I spent minimum time at work. We played. We explored the region on weekends. We had tons of fun together.

Something really good is happening.

As our initial Tezhouse-Kamyabi contract was nearing closure, an unexpected drama emerged. The customer failed to make one monthly payment, then missed another. I wrote a letter, demanding payment, and delivered it in person to Commander Swindmore, a Kamyabian official overseeing our contract. In his humongous office, I opened abruptly. "We will halt work until all back payment is made."

He barked as if it was we who owed him, "Do that, and we will declare Tezhouse ineligible in the current bid, which will be for over 1 billion lunies."

"We don't need further business from a customer who fails to meet their end of the bargain. We're in business to make money. Here we're lucky to break even, because of the pitfalls you create. Pay us what you owe, or Tezhouse is leaving Kamyabi. I don't make veiled threats."

Swindmore raised his voice, the whites of his eyes turning red. "Leave my office. Think about this. I'm sure you'll reconsider. We'll pay you fully – later."

"That's not how it works. Pay now, or we're out of here."

I stood up and stormed out of his office, without a goodbye, rudely leaving his door ajar. I returned to my office and booked three commercial nolicraft, launching plans to evacuate our entire team, two days hence. I directed everyone to halt whatever they were doing and pack.

First thing the next morning, Swindmore ordered me back to his office. He'd learned of my decision. This time he was crimson faced – his dark arms folded tightly across his chest. "You are not seriously thinking of leaving, are you?"

I stared at him. "I made that crystal clear yesterday."

"You're pretty terrible at customer relations."

"To the contrary, I excel there. I enjoy friendships and mutual respect with customers all across Taoland."

He shouted and slammed a fist on his desk, "I said we'd pay you later."

"And I responded we would leave unless paid immediately." I maintained my composure unlike this hotheaded man.

"I could have you thrown in jail, because Tezhouse paid a commission to an agent on your first contract. That was against our laws."

"Nice try. But we always obey the laws wherever we serve. Your Ruler knows that, and he trusts us. Ask him, if you're welcomed in the Palace, as I am. If you even suggest we broke your laws, which we did not, we will broadcast everywhere that you, your cronies, and your family members constantly receive a high share of bribes from our competitors – which carries the death penalty."

This momentarily silenced him. After a long pause, he said, "You have to request payment in writing."

"I did yesterday. I personally handed you my letter."

"Did you log that letter in at the Records Desk?"

"Nope."

"Then it doesn't exist." He smirked.

"Except at Supreme Command, where yesterday I delivered a second original, along with a recording of our conversation. Today I'll be dropping a personal copy off for Pressa at the Palace."

He was now ready to explode. "You recorded our conversation?! How could you? That's illegal." Then, head down, he murmured, "Go to Room 345. Your payment is there. But know that Tezhouse will not be chosen for the follow-on."

"The only thing worse than losing a 1-billion-luni contract is winning one with you around, where no profits are possible. But we have Pressa's support and confidence. You'll soon be gone – on the outside looking in, while Tezhouse celebrates winning the new contract."

Once again, not hiding the smirk on my face, I rudely turned my back and departed.

The next day, we were paid in full for all invoices in arrears. We finished the remaining tasks on our earlier contract and received complete final payment a week later. We submitted our proposal, and we were selected for a 1.2-billion-luni contract. Others' bids were higher, having to cover huge agent commissions and bribes.

But we never began the new work. In the weeks after signing the contract decades of corruption caught up with this strange place. Over the years billions had wound up in the pockets of corrupt officials, denying the people needed goods and services. Those who were expecting bribes on the new contract struck out publicly against Huggles and Swindmore with accusations of past corruption.

Insurrections erupted everywhere. Pressa called me to the Palace. "It's no longer safe for your family here."

"I know. I think we need to leave soon, at least until things quiet down."

Violence escalated every day. Underprivileged rioters demanded better pay, more food, and improved government services. Martial law was declared. Military vehicles roamed the streets. Armed noliplanes filled the skies. All electricity was cut off at Taoset every evening. No one was allowed on the streets after dark. A revolution, simmering for years, exploded into the streets. Magical attacks, despite the previous ban on the weaponization of magic, were launched from all sides.

With each passing hour, a growing number of military personnel began siding with the common people. Komourin reached Pressa to offer his condolences and to announce that all Tezhouse employees were leaving. Pressa readily agreed, "I too must depart my homeland." Komourin sent evacuation nolicraft not only to the main airport but to several remote locations where our folks were resident. We got everyone out safely – except our family who stayed on a bit longer.

The sounds of shouts, wailings, and military machines filled the air. So I gathered Tari and the kids. "It's time to go. It's all happening so fast. It's no longer safe for us to remain." We packed only our most essential belongings, deciding to leave all else behind. Komourin directed that we take a well-deserved vacation. Frightening wailings filled the skies over Heteron as we packed our things into a bright orange nolivan, a gift from the CEO. We said difficult goodbyes to Herous, Niesha, and Caspian, saddened we'd likely never see them again. We gave them money as we worried about their safety.

We took a long, slow route home, leaving Kamyabi behind in turmoil and flames. Our new nolilvan could fly, but once beyond the Kamyabi border, we traveled close to the ground, experiencing everything up close and personal. We traveled through several regions including Pelan, Kolkata, Lansha, and the Islands of Peenish. We stayed at the best hotels, dined in the streets and in markets along bustling waterways, learned local music and dances, and toured historical sites. We learned a great deal about the lives and worlds of different peoples. And about ourselves.

Once, in an extremely poor section of Porsing, small, barely clothed children with extended bellies, emerged from the shadows. They begged for scraps of food. We gave them everything we had. We drove away, overwhelmed by what we'd just experienced. After a lengthy uncomfortable silence, Kaleeva spoke, holding her heart, with tears welling in her eyes. "The next time they ask us at school to contribute a few lunies for the underprivileged, I will truly understand."

At that, I stopped the nolivan for a family hug. Through this experience, each of us learned about the not-so-fortunate in a profound way. And about the abundant blessings we enjoyed and would continue to enjoy back home. We would never take these for granted again. This experience would change us forever. Our stay in Kamyabi had been challenging – and especially torturous at the end. But our time there had brought Tari and I and the children closer. Our return trip was the best time of our lives. We arrived safely back home, more strongly bonded than ever.

Tari had experienced firsthand some of the ugliness in business life and tainted competitions. I'd shared the horrible details, as I'd never done before. "Adam, probably not fully, but for the first time, I understand how tough are the challenges and stresses you face when you're away from us. And how corrupt some of those you are forced to deal with are. I understand a lot that I didn't before."

Through our ordeal in Kamyabi, we'd taken time for conversations we'd avoided earlier. And I came to comprehend the precious moments of our lives I'd been missing out on. Tari and I drew closer, renewing our amazing love affair and deep friendship, a relationship on the ropes only a year ago. Life was good and continued once we settled back home. We had miraculously turned a page together. I was ready to face whatever trials lay ahead – with Tari by my side.

CHAPTER 26

LIFE IS LIKE CLUBBING

Whack!
I slammed another ball into a net I'd set up in our back yard. Today was my chance to impress the Chairman, who I'd never met, with my clubbing skills. I would not screw this up. When I spotted Komourin's noli landing, I jogged back into the house and gave Tari a kiss. She always hated when clubbing took me away from the family. But she knew this round with the Chairman could prove important.

I climbed into the CEO's noli. "Looking forward to today, Adam?"

"I've never not enjoyed a day clubbing."

"Today is not about clubbing, not about how we play. I want you and Randahl to become acquainted with Chairman Westin."

"Bummer," I jokingly responded, "I was hoping the purpose was for you all to marvel at my clubbing shots."

He didn't crack a smile. "In your dreams. Your ego is way too big already."

Hmmmm. He's uptight.

I'd become one of the top clubbers at Tezhouse. Randahl was still better, but neither of us had ever beaten Komourin. Westin's skills were unknown to me.

"I understand you've improved since we last played, Adam."

"Not yet as good as you." I toyed. "But every time I hit the ball on the sweet spot, it thrills me. An elation unlike any other."

"If every strike gave you exuberance, you'd lose interest."

"Part of what makes me passionate about clubbing are new challenges each time out. In a way it's a simple game. Then again, it's endlessly complicated. Rewarding one minute, maddening the next."

"Just like life," said Komourin as he landed his shiny black noli on a bright red lawn. Two orange long-legged birds, a foot taller than their pink-gray Novanian counterparts, splashed noisily out of a nearby pond and growled at us. "Adam, passion is essential to any success. With passion, every new chapter is special. Without passion, life is mired in failure and feelings of inadequacies."

Westin and Randahl greeted us as we signed in. We headed to the grill room for a quick breakfast. Komourin announced the venue. "We'll play thirty targets. Three times around the field of ten. Randahl and Adam will play the first ten together. Then it will be Randahl with Westin, and me with Adam. Finally, me with Randahl and Adam with the Chairman for the third trip around."

Before starting, we took a quick tour of the grounds, two to a nolidray. The approaches to manicured yellow carpets were covered in light orange closely cut grasses. Murky depressions, filled with various slimy stuff and rocks, threatened shots too far left or right. Red lakes and ponds featured enormous scaly creatures with mouths full of jagged teeth, dozing at the edges. I glanced at Randahl, who assured me they were not dangerous.

We reached the first starting box. My initial shot traveled further than those of the other three. After each of them had hit nice second shots onto the carpet where the target rested, I swung poorly and my ball wound up in some muck. I finished the target at two over norm. Westin brought laughs when he joked, "The longest first hit mattereth not if you fucketh up the second shot."

Westin's language surprised but relaxed me. Insults were a fun part of the game, and it was great he landed the first punch.

"You made a dumb mistake there, Adam." Komourin said, as we all stood at the second box. "As in life, being a good player requires strength not of body, but of mind. This game is 90 percent mental." He spoke not lightheartedly as had the Chairman.

"And the other 10 percent?"

"The other 10 percent? It's mental as well."

As we drove on, I said to Randahl, "Today is clearly not about clubbing. It's about you and me, and indirectly about Bogart. They hate that prick as much as we do. And they want one of us to replace Komourin. If you're chosen, Randahl, I'd be OK. You'd make a fantastic CEO."

"If it's you, Adam, I'd be more than OK as well. With one caveat. My only concern about you is your obsession with winning."

"What's wrong with that? We've had four big wins in a row. And dozens of smaller ones. And the improbable victory in Kamyabi, even if it's never realized. You and I teamed well on each. I half expected you to pull out a cold bottle of lunar bubbly by now, to celebrate as we play. Instead, you say you're worried about me?"

"Yup." He shot me a concerned glance.

"So, winning is somehow a bad thing?"

"No. I said it's your obsession that's bothersome."

"What the heck are you talking about?"

"Losing is part of life, but you never fail. Not even back when you were being awarded patents and escaping repercussions from that explosion years ago. We learn way more from our failures than from our successes. In the future, you'll lose bids. You may lose your quest to become CEO. You might even lose Tari. I don't think you'll survive defeats well. You'll crash and burn when those inevitable failures rear their ugly heads."

"Randahl, we haven't spoken much since Kamyabi. I'm a changed man. I'm actually listening to what you're saying – and taking it all in. Thank you."

"You're the best of all at business development and customer relations. You have a gift in bringing others on board – and inspiring teams to high performance. That gift is called leadership, and you're chock-full of it. I expect you'll be the next CEO. But prepare yourself for defeats along the way."

I grabbed his shoulders as he drove on. "I never say this, Randahl, but I'm really grateful for your friendship and counsel through the years." I really meant it. He'd been there with me through so many ups and downs.

We shifted nolidrays for the second ten targets. I broke the ice and asked Komourin for his opinion, "Randahl just told me he's concerned about me always winning. And concerned about how I would take any losses. What say you?"

"No concerns for Tezhouse. But I do worry about you personally. When your defeats come, as they most certainly will, I'm afraid you'll crumble. We learn far more with our feet stuck in muddy valleys than when we're atop the mountains. Defeats bring more valuable lessons than victories. But I share Randahl's concern that you're not prepared to lose."

I never thought about the possibility of losing. *Maybe they are right.*

"Additionally, I'm worried about your battle with Bogart. Each time you win, he becomes more obsessed with destroying you."

"I've proven myself stronger than Bogart. He's failed miserably trying to defeat me."

"He and his cronies look forward to the day I'll step down. In the meantime, they'll do all they can to destroy us. You know Bogart has extortion materials on me, on the Board members he controls and on others throughout Tezhouse, and in customer communities. Your behavior has provided nothing he can use against you. That makes you doubly difficult to bring down. You must beware."

The topic of Bogart soured my mood. "I don't frighten easily."

"When you suffer defeats, Adam, Bogart and his goons will be the ones orchestrating and then pouncing."

We arrived at the box for the longest target. "I can't even see the carpet," I declared.

"It's the same length as every target – five inches – the distance between your ears – the same distance for every objective you set in life. Believe in yourself. The rest will take care of itself."

I swung confidently and hit the best first and second shots all day. I rolled the ball in for my first one under norm – on what was rated the toughest target.

On another target, my first shot dove left and finished behind a huge body of orange muck. I wailed, "That was just plain stupid! It's still a long way to the target, and slimy all the way,"

Komourin responded, "Don't fear obstacles in your path. If you can't go over them, go around. But, in this case, you're correct – you can't get there. Hit a safe shot out to the right, well short of the carpet."

I ignored his advice. I attempted a high-risk heroic shot over the junk. I swung wildly, though I knew the best shots, as in life, came with calm. Splash. Into the muck. I finished three over for that target, falling further behind the others in score.

Komourin shook his head. "A dumb mistake, Adam. But forget it. Mistakes are an integral part of any game. The only thing worse than the mistake itself is not learning from it. How one recovers from errors is critical."

I finished the second round far behind the others. As we headed back to the clubbing center for a pit stop, Komourin said, "Adam, you have more raw talent than the rest of us, and you'll improve with age. You'll better assess risks versus rewards. Westin and I, older and less flexible, score better. Someday you'll wise up and figure out why.

I hopped in the nolidray with the Chairman for the final ten, nervous because I'd never been alone with him. My anxiety increased when he didn't speak as we drove to our first target box. I again had the longest hit, dead center on the approach. Westin laughed loudly when we reached my ball. "Don't fucketh this up again." He made me laugh.

I want to jab back, but he never gives me an opening.

I hit my second shot perfectly, stopping the ball ten feet from the target. I was the last to roll. It was fast, downhill. I nervously decelerated my swing, and the ball wound up a foot short. Westin joked. "Quite weak for a CEO candidate." He got me again. A humongous reptile next to the carpet roared.

Westin and I settled into a comfortable chat about our families, Tezhouse, life in Taoland, sports, politics, and more. I enjoyed his company and valued his advice as we played. On one of the targets, I hit an errant second shot into a pond. Perhaps my worst mistake of the day.

"Another dumbass shot," I bemoaned, "I'm going to finish well behind all of you today."

"Adam, you're not competing against us. You're competing against yourself. Never worry about the scores of others. Not here, not in life. Just make sure you never beat yourself." He walked over to align his own shot.

"Komourin suggests I'll get better with age."

"Hopefully. Just like a fine wine that's started well and aged in a barrel, if you use your natural gifts, hone your talents, gather experience, in the end you'll be amazed by the person who emerges."

Pausing to let this sink in, I nodded in appreciation. "I hope someday I can play as well as you do. Your swing is effortless."

He put an arm around my shoulder. "Never quit, Adam. It took me decades before I had the first inkling of how to best play wise and stress free. Stop overreaching. Just deal with your limitations."

On another target, Westin dropped me out in the middle of the approach and headed to the left side where his ball rested. I found my ball to the right, lying inches behind a bright red tree trunk, with a fifteen-foot lizard snoozing too close for comfort. I swallowed my fear of the beast and stepped up to assess my dilemma. Suddenly the creature's eyes parted. It opened its wide jaws and hissed. Just as it launched toward me, I punched the ball backwards to where I had an unobstructed path, then leapt out of the way. It cost me a shot, but I had acted honestly while simultaneously escaping black saliva from the creature's mouth. I wound up one over norm for that target.

Driving to the next box I nodded to Westin. "Randahl said those lizards were no threat."

He slapped his leg and laughed. "No threat if you stay away from them. By the way, I didn't know you were stymied back there."

"It was only by a couple of inches, but I had to punch away in the wrong direction."

Westin stopped our nolidray and looked into my eyes. "You could have kicked the ball to get a clear opening. Nobody would've seen you. You showed integrity, which trumps performance every time. Challenges in life call for honesty – and respect for the rules, opponents, and the game itself. I'm proud of you."

Once again a teacher speaks about integrity.

"I'd have only cheated myself if I moved the ball, even if no one suspected. I could never be okay with achieving something dishonestly." Then I added with a wink, "Besides that beast woulda' had me for lunch if I didn't get out of his way immediately."

He grinned at my sorta joke. "Komourin informed me of your unflappable integrity. Sometimes, you get bad breaks or unfair bounces in life. You then have a choice. You can cheat. You can moan. You can complain about victimhood. Or you can take your medicine and move on. Shit happens, but don't ever dwell on it; focus always on what's ahead."

On the final target I again faced a choice – hit a safe short shot well left of the target or hit a riskier shot over some deep junk to the far-right where the target rested. I glanced at Westin.

"Go for it, Adam. This time the reward is worth the risk."

I calmly accepted his challenge, launched the ball high, and cried out proudly when it stopped six inches from the target.

"Congrats. You would've regretted it if you'd skipped that chance," said Westin, with a roaring laugh. "Now don't leave this next shot short."

When we finished, we drove in for drinks. "Wow, we've been out here for over six hours," I remarked.

"When you're having fun with good people, time is irrelevant."

"I blundered out there a few times; but in the end I'm proud of how I played."

"Everyday life brings a mix of successes and failures, opportunities taken and some missed, pitfalls, temptations, and self-doubts. A constant search for unachievable perfection. In the end of any pursuit joy comes from knowing you played with integrity and to the best of your abilities."

"I've really enjoyed the day, Mr. Westin. Maybe not the screw-ups so much. But I know what I did wrong, and I'll learn from those mistakes. I found everyone's advice valuable."

He lifted his fizzy drink. "Treat clubbing like life and treat life like clubbing. Be humbled by the game. Keep a sense of humor. Conquer fear with confidence. Always remain calm. Enjoy every moment. And of course, let the magic happen."

CHAPTER 27

WHO'S NEXT?

Now came the most important part of the day – discussions about our individual futures and playing as a team in Tezhouse corporate games. We sat for dinner in a quiet area of the restaurant. My goal was convincing Westin and Komourin I had what it takes to lead Tezhouse. Just as clubbing teaches, this would require focus, utilizing my talents, learning from others, constant improvement, and awareness that everything comes at a price. Recalling the experiences of Kamyabi, quality time with Tari and the kids, and the rekindling of my love life – I fidgeted with uncertainty.

Is becoming CEO worth the price?

I became distracted by the strange reptilian staff and a completely foreign menu. A server crept over to take our orders. Komourin ordered several unknown items as appetizers, cleared his throat, and commanded our attention.

"The Chairman and I want the four of us to leave here on the same page – with a game plan for the next seven years. That's when I'll retire. Westin will still be Chairperson. Randahl and Adam, one of you will replace me." Randahl and I exchanged supportive nods. We were in this together even if only one of us could win.

Westin spoke next, a serious expression replacing the easy smile he'd worn all day. "I'm delighted I got to know you a bit today. I'd be happy for either of you to take the reins, especially since I share Komourin's resolve that Bogart must never become CEO. But four Board members are committed to making his ascension happen – for all the wrong reasons. They've been getting filthy rich and whoring with Bogart since before I became Chairman – from about the same time you joined the company, Randahl." He shifted his glance to me. "And before you, Adam, even knew Taoland or Tezhouse existed."

Komourin continued, "They'll escalate their evil doings if Bogart takes the helm. Tezhouse as a company of integrity would end. The four of us must work as one to guarantee that prick never becomes CEO."

"Will the Board remain as is for seven more years?" asked Randahl.

Westin responded, "No certainty here. But Bogart's cronies and the other four are relatively young and healthy. I say we assume all eight will remain on the Board until Komourin retires."

Komourin continued, "Longuemare and Crennik are clearly not Bogart fans. Both are leaning toward Randahl. They're not acquainted with you, Adam, but they are impressed by your recent achievements. The final two newbies are uncommitted. We need all four to permit Westin to cast the tiebreaker vote when the time comes."

Westin leaned forward, his chin upon his right fist. "You've both told me you respect the other and would be happy with either choice. Randahl, why should we select your friend."

"Adam is a superstar, the strongest leader in Tezhouse, present company excluded," Randahl quipped. "His natural abilities in befriending and negotiating with top customers are beyond my own. He places Tezhouse success above all else. He takes calculated risks, followed by well-considered actions that usually bring success. He is a man of integrity and is completely trustworthy. He really wants to be CEO. You couldn't find a better candidate."

So generous. I shifted in my seat, uncomfortable with such open praise from Randahl. A scute-ladened server sat a purple swirling drink in front of me. I hesitated when something in the liquid moved. Komourin chuckled, "Don't worry, Adam. Your drink is safe. Enjoy." He tipped and drank from his own glass of bubbling liquid. I declined.

Westin went on, "And Adam, why should we choose Randahl?"

"Randahl was the first friend I made in Taoland. I know and love him like a brother. He has shown great leadership in heading Engineering and now Service-After-Sales. He's well-liked and respected – by peers and employees alike. He is the most family-oriented person I know, and his tension-free homelife brings calmness at work. He is a more in-the-box thinker than I, but he's not risk averse. He's the safer choice."

Westin smiled knowingly. "I think I detected a few hidden meanings from each of you. What did you mean, Randahl, when you suggested Adam puts Tezhouse success above all other matters? Does he put his family second?"

Randahl shifted in his seat. "You should be asking Adam."

"I'm asking you – for your opinion."

He glanced at me, then looked down at his drink. "I've shared with Adam my concern that he needs to find a better balance between work and family. I'd like to leave it there."

I jumped in. "Far too often, I do place Tezhouse above family when priorities conflict. So yeah, I've suffered difficulties at home."

"Do you want to change? Can you? Can you start saying no to Komourin and yes to your wife and children more often?"

"I have no other choice if I want to save my marriage. We are working as a couple, and as a family, to heal and bond. We did well in Kamyabi and enjoyed a great trip back. Today, we're stronger than ever. Our love for each other is unyielding. I'm gonna find that elusive balance."

"Might you emulate and learn from Randahl?"

I searched for the right words. "I admire but don't emulate

others. I'm my own man. But I know I can learn from others, including you, Randahl, and Komourin. I can't fix my behavior by myself."

Westin beamed, seeming more confident in my abilities to turn things around than I was. "Randahl, you said Adam really wants the job. Why did you include that?"

My friend finished his drink and shrugged. "He wants it more than I do. If I'm not chosen, I'd be proud I'd been considered. I think Adam would take it harder the other way around."

"Adam?" Westin's questions were uncomfortable – a test for both of us.

"As I said, Randahl would make a great CEO. But I do hope you select me. If it's Randahl, I would be disappointed. But I'd work my butt off under his leadership. If Bogart is selected, I'd leave Tezhouse." All nodded in agreement. Bogart as CEO was the worst possible scenario. It would completely destroy a great company from within.

"You both commented on the other about risk-taking. Care to expand, Randahl?"

"Adam is way more of a risk-taker than I. That's one of his strengths – but an area for concern. I very cautiously take risks, but never those as dangerous as those Adam would consider."

"Adam?"

"I don't share Randahl's apprehensions about the risks I take. Yes, he's more careful, which many would consider a strength. But some don't understand that the chances I take are informed by my intuitions. Whenever I don't see a way forward, I create one. My instincts guide my decisions. I make quick decisions, because standing still is always sliding backwards."

Westin raised his brow. "And if your haste leads to error?"

"I always have a Plan B. If I find I've wandered in the wrong direction, I promptly alter or reverse course."

He looked back and forth at Randahl and me, then nodded in Komourin's direction. "It's amazing to witness such introspection, mutual respect, and candor. Bottom line, I agree with your earlier private comments, Komourin. Randahl is the more cautious and Adam borders on audacity." I groaned. "I'm convinced Tezhouse would be well served with either as CEO, seven years or so downstream. Now let's discuss Bogart."

Randahl raised his hand. "I want to say something up front about that prick. Bogart will do and say anything to damage, no, to destroy, anyone in his way. He knows Adam and I are straight arrows. So, he'll have to resort to falsehoods to deal with us."

Westin paused, then responded, "If Bogart's accusations were false, surely you could and would expose his lies."

Randahl shook his head and signaled the weird server for another round. "Many deem the accused guilty until proven innocent. Irreversible damage can be done with false aspersions. I love my family far more than I thirst to become CEO. Bogart believes I'd withdraw from the CEO race if my family were invaded with scandalous untruths. He's correct. I'd never put them through unfair humiliation or embarrassment, even if based on lies. If that means I'm too soft for the top spot, so be it."

Westin spoke again. "So why do you think he fears Adam more?"

"I suspect Bogart has concluded, rightly or wrongly, that Adam would not yield to threats involving his wife, his children, or their private lives. That makes Adam the far more dangerous candidate in Bogart's eyes."

"Adam?"

I spoke boldly, but with respect. "It's true I'd never cave to threats. I'm prepared to stand firm and counterpunch against whatever Bogart throws my way. But that doesn't mean I'd place my family at undue risk. Regardless of his attacks, Tariana will stand with me. We've done nothing to be ashamed of. I hope that keeps Bogart up at night. He's evil. I've never said that about another human being."

"You speak from experience, yes?"

I knew he probably knew the details but I elaborated. "Since the day we met, he's treated me like shit. Ten years ago, he tried to destroy me with a devastating explosion he wanted to blame on me. He almost cost Tezhouse a critical contract in the process. And he tried unsuccessfully to concoct a scandal to destroy my marriage. Several other times, while I was leading proposal efforts, he tried to turn Tezhouse victories into defeats, trying to make me look bad."

Westin nodded. "We know the stories. It's clear Bogart is willing to lose Tezhouse business to deny you praise. He's sick."

"Yeah – and it's appalling he cares more about hurting me than about Tezhouse jobs and profits. He never leaves fingerprints. Still, it's beyond pathetic that his crimes are ignored. All because of bad stuff he has on four Board members."

Komourin bowed his head, interjecting, "Not only those four. You all know he's got the goods on me as well."

The Chairman brushed off Komourin's remark. "Adam, do you worry Bogart will escalate efforts to bring you down?"

"Oh, I'm certain the worst is yet to come. But I'm ready for it. I'm smarter than him. In a perverted sense, I relish the confrontations 'cause I take joy in upending him."

"And Tariana?"

"She hates it all, of course. But she's my rock, except when we get lost in personal problems. When I share Bogart's evildoings she stands by and comforts me. She's completely selfless and loyal. I don't deserve that, but I treasure her." I needed another drink. Confronting the facts was hard at times. "She wishes I'd choose a lesser role, giving up my quest to become CEO. But she accepts who I am."

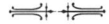

We moved to the dining area, a bit looser after drinks, and ordered meals, or rather Komourin did so for us. "You guys won't recognize anything on the menu. I'll order my favorites for you."

Several curious appetizers graced our table. Komourin forked and bit into the leg of a small, strange, whole, fried creature. With a steely expression, he continued speaking.

"I hate Bogart more than any of you. I'm ashamed that his extortion threats render me impotent. He wouldn't hesitate to use what he has, even if it created a scandal devastating our stock price and throwing our shareholders into financial ruin. That's why there can never be an investigation."

Westin stopped eating and looked over at him. "Komourin, you've served Tezhouse like no other. Your leadership has been invaluable. I'm saddened you carry this burden."

Komourin shook Westin off. "My wife holds me as her hero. She's oblivious to my past mistakes. I've cleaned up my act, but Bogart retains the evidence. He'd destroy me, my marriage, my reputation, and Tezhouse in an instant if I dared expose him. Fortunately, the dirt I have on him would send him to prison. So, he avoids crossing certain lines. We coexist in a stalemate. I hope you all can someday forgive me."

Westin waved his hand and laid it on Komourin's shoulder. "We hold nothing against you. We've all made personal mistakes. Spare us yours as we bury our own. It's difficult for good folks like us to accept that any human can be as evil as Bogart. I'd like to pity him, and his cronies, but I can't. They live in darkness, sucked into black holes, shrouding any possibility of reason or goodness. It will all backfire someday."

A green-gilled server crept over to deliver our main courses that shimmered into existence on a hovering service tray alongside her. Her golden eyes met mine as she placed my peculiar meal in front of me. It was like looking into a million eyes all at once as my reflection was multiplied endlessly in the facets. With her blink my attention turned to my aromatic delight. It tasted way better than it looked.

A still somber Komourin took a bite of his and continued, "Bogart and his Board cronies are five pieces of crap. And we're stuck with them. We must rise above. Going forward, the keys for us as a team must be solid performance, continued successes, and personal integrity. We must never give Bogart any more ammunition, beyond what he has."

Westin spoke. "Team Bogart will not only continue working to take the two of you down – they'll try to seduce either of the two Board newcomers to provide the fifth vote. They've long ago given up on my vote, and the votes of Longuemare and Crennik. Komourin and I will provide the two of you rug time with the newbies, Figaro and Rigsby. You must seize the day when we do." Randahl and I nodded in agreement.

"Bogart and his cronies also work the bureaucrats," Komourin continued, "at headquarters and at Tezhouse First Moon. Bureaucrats can hurt you. Like amoeba that kill off giant beasts. Bogart makes bogus claims about the two of you causing undue risks and hurting profits. He says you, Randahl, are incompetent, and that you, Adam, are corrupt and always overpromising. Unfortunately, some listen to this crap."

I fought the urge to pound the table. "He's so full of shit! But bureaucrats are frequently afraid of their own shadows and ready to believe the worst."

Komourin interjected, "Don't ever underestimate the mindless plodders. They may appear to be brainless, but they use their claws to grab, entwine, and bring you down."

Westin wrung his hands. "The bean counters and lawyers feed off his aspersions. As you suggest, Adam, it's in their DNA to be fearful, negative, and suspicious."

"So, the answer here?" I asked.

"Komourin and I will increase contact with the bureaucrats at headquarters, correcting falsehoods, hopefully planting suspicions about Bogart and his friends in the process. The two of you must spend more time, by *swish* at least, with the bureaucrats at Tezhouse First Moon. Ferret out and address their concerns. Make them think your fears mirror their own."

Komourin continued to advise, "Always be polite with them. Appear respectful, even if you're not. Never bait them into arguments or aggression. Remember, they have no love for Bogart. But if they don't hear from you regularly, he'll declare you reckless and cement misgivings about you. You must ease if not erase their trepidations."

Westin then concluded, "We've gotta meet more frequently. By *swish* and in person. We need to get out in front of Bogart's plans and put out fires while they're only simmering. Let's agree to connect at lunchtime the first day after financial reports, every month. Okay?"

We agreed and enjoyed the rest of what turned out to be a superb meal. Our camaraderie would help our teamwork forward, hopefully warding off new conflicts that were certainly coming.

Flying back with Komourin, I made an urgent plea. "We agreed one of my shortcomings is failure to better balance work and home responsibilities. I told you I've made progress in this area recently. I need to build on this. I want to spend more time at home going forward. I need a break from field assignments."

"Timing is everything, Adam. In this instance, your timing sucks. We've decided to move you to Aboodin, for the next three months."

It was like a sledgehammer slammed down on me. I was unable to speak.

"This time, Adam, it will be without Tariana and the kids – Aboodin is no place for children, nor for women."

Oh – and Kamyabi was? Give me a break!

"You've got to be there in five days. Sorry to drop this on you, but our bid there represents the largest opportunity in Tezhouse history in terms of revenues, technology breakthroughs, jobs, and follow-on potential. We're wrapping up our Aboodin proposal, and we're headed for a loss. We're asking you for one final miracle, before we cut you some slack. Last time, I promise."

Not again. How can he do this to me?

I resisted. "Westin said I had to learn to say no to you. So, I say hell no."

"The Chairman wasn't referring to Aboodin. Sorry, my friend. Once again, this is not a request. It's a demand. It'll be over before you know it. Just three months."

This good and productive day has suddenly turned into a pile of dung.

CHAPTER 28

ABOODIN AND DIAZAMEL

Once again Tezhouse was sending me away, this time just when things in my marriage were looking up. After the Chairman advised me to say 'no' when asked to place Tezhouse over family, I learned it meant nothing. Total obedience is a requirement for reaching the top slot.

Dread hung over me like a dark cloud as I informed Tari. "I'll only be there for three months. I'll do my best to be home every weekend. We'll be pausing the family bonding we've been building since leaving Kamyabi."

Her reply stunned me. "We'll be OK, Adam. We're not going to slip back. I'm extremely hopeful about our future, for the first time in years. Just promise me one thing," she winked jokingly, "no clubbing when you're home with us."

I laughed aloud at her welcomed banter. This gem of a woman had been through so much with me and still hung on. "I give you my solemn pledge. I love you and the kids to the other two moons and back. You're totally correct – taking a step backwards can't happen. You are my blessing, Tariana Novana."

Days later a company nolicraft descended into a sparkling city surrounded by swirling orange desert sands. Although furious I'd been sent without my input, I was beyond grateful Tari had been amazingly understanding in accepting my fate – our fate. The value over the life of the new Aboodinian contract would be over 20 billion lunies. A win would nearly double the size of the corporation. But nobody gave us an ounce of a chance.

The ultimate decision maker was Lifason, the eldest son of the Ruler, Zalifhar. Those in Lifason's inner circle, including his three sons, were literally in the pocket of Huggles and their Aboodinian agent. Huggles had held a dominant position in this nation since their first contract. Tezhouse had zero presence.

We had invested half of Tezhouse's annual proposal budget on this long-shot opportunity. But I had strategically kept my distance. Now I was in with both feet. I'd make our final offer in ninety days, and there was no obvious way to alter our chances.

My first meeting was with Caojolie, a purple-skinned, dark-haired, bearded agent personally brought on board by our Chairman. We began with a cup of afternoon tea at his luxurious villa where I'd be staying my first night. "Westin tells me you're a miracle worker, Adam. He says you love pulling huge victories out of tiny empty purses. Ready to create some magic in Aboodin?"

Praise from my superiors never made me uncomfortable – but I wasn't about to boast. "My talents have limits. I'm told I'll not even be granted an introductory meeting with Lifason. No access to the decision maker, no magic possible."

A knowing smile tugged at the corner of Caojolie's mouth, revealing pointed green teeth. "I'll be introducing you to his younger brother, Diazamel. You and he will make the magic that seizes victory from the jaws of defeat."

"Right! How about giving me some of whatever you're smoking. Aside from our CEO, there's not a soul who imagines a Tezhouse win here."

"My friend, never allow yourself to be limited by the imagination, or lack of, in others. We'll meet with Diazamel tomorrow. He and I have been close since childhood. Like you, he's one who loves to make the impossible possible." He gestured to his view of the city skyline where the tallest towers reached into pink afternoon clouds. "He made all this happen."

"Will the miracle require bribery?" I asked. "If it does, count me out."

"Oh, what little faith. Diazamel would never be involved in corruption."

In Caojule's gardens we enjoyed pit-grilled unknown fish, fine wine, and great conversation – followed by a Taoset that revealed both the green and silver moons far off in the heavens. I tried to focus on the moment and securing the deal – but Tari dominated my thoughts.

⇌ ⇋

At Taorise, we departed for Diazamel's estate. We flew low, Caojolie serving as tour guide. The desert landscape was breathtakingly beautiful, unlike the dirt and dust of nearby Smerland and Kamyabi. Golden flowers and shrubs blanketed brilliantly painted orange sands and dunes. Countless flowering trees, farmlands, vineyards, and sparkling ponds of red created a spectacular panorama. Vast herds of deer-like animals crept like ants across the lands below. The desert grew greener as we approached the city.

"Adam, with carefully designed infrastructure projects, led by Diazamel, the Ruler has brought water and life to the desert. Our towns, villages, and Aboodin City, the Capital below, are ultramodern."

"Astonishing. I've learned Aboodin is the richest region on the Second Moon – in fact in all Taoland. I understand valuable mineral deposits made this possible. But I don't know the details."

"Fifty years ago, we discovered massive reserves of a previously unknown rare metal, valithion, beneath the deserts at the foothills of the Aboodinian Mountains. The good thing for us is it's only found here. It possesses unmatched energy characteristics, with an estimated half-life of 700 million years."

"I doubt I'll be around that long," I quipped.

"Today valithion has revolutionized power generation and transportation. Fully automated mining and refining will generate hundreds of billions of revenues annually, for decades to come."

"So, Aboodin's future is secure."

He tilted his head, a concerned look crossing his face. "Not exactly. We lack the human capital and innovation needed to secure our future. The wealth created from the valithion industries could transform everything in this once-impoverished land – except for one critical factor – our culture holds us back."

"I don't understand."

"Aboodin remains primitive in many ways. Insular. Except for our servants, we're mostly from the same planet, Meneah, where patriarchal tribal rules dominate and restrict progress. We need new blood and new ideas to create real change. Our new contracts will continue our modernization materially. But we need to unleash the power of our people."

"How can that be done?"

"We need young leaders to replace the elders. We must attract foreigners to assume residence here and intermarry. They can introduce alternative thinking, out-of-the-box innovations, new laws, and new ways of governance. That's the only way Aboodin will ever become a diverse, prosperous, and sustainable society."

What he was saying was nearly impossible. "A lofty goal. But historically cultural transformation is only achieved after bloody wars or revolution."

"Diazamel will lead this transformation, without bloodshed. He will release our women and children from paternalistic isolation in tribal compounds. He is an amazing visionary. He will succeed. With your help."

With my help?

We landed at Diazamel's massive manor house that stood tall on a hilltop at the outskirts of the city. We entered the massive greeting area where elegant red couches and brilliant orange carved tables defined the perimeter. At the center of the room gorgeous, multicolored carpets spread across a white marble floor. Two men sat far off in a corner to the right of the entrance.

"The taller man is Diazamel," Caojule whispered as we approached, ". . . the other is Paladin, his protector, who will remain silent."

We took seats at the corner facing the two. Like Caojolie, they had heads twice as large as their bodies would suggest. Diazamel's skin was deep purple, Paladin's a few shades lighter, more of a bluish pink. Servants arranged tea, without any eye contact – still not a word spoken. To say I was intimidated would be an understatement. Caojule nudged me to begin.

I broke the silence. "Your Majesty, I —"

Thunderous roars of laughter erupted. Tears burst onto Diazamel's handsome oversized face. Caojule joined in the merriment. Even the stern-faced Paladin cracked a smile across his sharp jawline, displaying his green teeth.

Diazamel's voice was a deep and commanding bass, but the utter joy across his face softened his appearance. "Caojule, you told me I'd like this guy. But I didn't expect this. Your friend just promoted me to King!"

The white-robed Diazamel roared again. He turned his kind countenance to me. Something about him didn't look human, but then I'd doubted Roshi was human when I first met him. Diazamel displayed elevated, thick, arched eyebrows, long flowing black hair, and a neatly trimmed black royal beard.

His brilliant oval green eyes danced in merriment, as he spoke through full lips. "Thank you kindly, Adam, for the promotion. Now would you please contact my father and my older brother and order them to step aside."

Yet another burst of boisterous belly laughs, along with a few more whoops. A three-inch gold earring jingled from his elongated right ear. I was the butt of the joke, but Diazamel's response won me over. Not the slightest bit embarrassed, I joined in the merriment.

"Most folks address me as Your Highness. But since you've brought happy tears to my eyes, how about you just call me Diazamel."

I held out my hand, which he embraced in both of his own. "I'm Adam."

Paladin cringed and began to lunge toward me as his boss and I touched, a no-no I supposed. Diazamel waved him off. We did not speak of business throughout the hour we sat together. It was small talk with more tea and delish finger-sandwiches, finished off with cups of sweet ice cream.

"Can you return soon, Adam? I'd like to discuss my thoughts about possibly working together."

I answered, "I'll have to check my calendar."

The loudest laughter yet rumbled through the room. "I genuinely like this guy. Let's all meet tomorrow here at noon, for lunch."

The following day, I arrived with Cajole at the Palace to be swept away for a personal tour. Diazamel pridefully showed his grounds and boasted about the well-cared-for exotic animals from various planets he held in massive naturally landscaped cages. Several of his children dashed around the grounds, playing with various pets and toys. After the tour, we returned to a private lounge to be seated at low sofas and elaborate lounging cushions. This time Diazamel spoke seriously, but the twinkle in his eyes and his engaging smile remained.

"This contract will transform Aboodin. But only materially. All infrastructure, even some very new, will be replaced over the next decade. Every aspect of public services and transportation will be updated, applying the most advanced technology in all of Taoland. Telecommunications, power plants, schools, hospitals, buildings, smart airports, highways, streets, bridges, water, and sewerage resources – and more."

Several men entered the room carrying a massive steaming pot. They covered the pot with a single large silver tray and, to my surprise, flipped the whole thing onto the floor in front of us. Steaming riccia and roasted vegetables spread out on the tray with a whole charred animal in the center. A most pleasant aroma filled the space.

Diazamel scooted toward the platter. "Now we dig in." Literally. He first plopped a scoop of riccia and veggies on my plate and then with two fingers forked a luscious piece of meat and offered it to me. I quickly adjusted to the tradition and joined in, as we shared the delish offerings.

What a magnificent way to bring folks together.

As we enjoyed the meal Diazamel continued between mouthfuls, "Hundreds of thousands of new jobs will be created. We are prepared to pay more than any region of Taoland has ever spent per capita. Only Huggles and Tezhouse possess the expertise needed to lead the effort."

"Tezhouse would be honored to take the lead. But we cannot win here. Huggles is too entrenched."

He paused to look into my eyes. "Don't hedge your words. If we are to become partners we need to be brutally blunt. Explain 'entrenched.'"

"Diazamel, what's going on here is bribery and rampant corruption."

"Most outsiders would agree with you. But here it's simply a cultural norm – the only way to redistribute wealth from contractors' profits to the masses is via commissioned agents. A more efficient way, I might add, than tossing golden lunies to the citizens from an overhead noli."

I plowed ahead. "It's corruption. The agents involved, and their friends, are enriched. There is no free media to expose it all. Tezhouse cannot possibly win here."

"I will change your assessment."

"We know Huggles is close to your brother." I'd interrupted him, making Paladin flinch. "Over the years, they've made impossible any fair competition. Huggles always increases their price by whatever it takes to cover the costs of their bribes."

Diazamel raised his hand to stop me. "Through these agents we control and buy the allegiance of countless officials here, and others who might otherwise disrupt society or threaten our rule."

I looked into his eyes, a darker green than his teeth, and spoke firmly. "Those on the take determine who gets the scraps. That spells corruption – there is no other word for what wins here."

He looked away and wiped his face with a cloth. "My brother is not a bad person. The Huggles' approach to business is the only one he knows. I intend to open Lifason's eyes to a better way. With your help, we will reform business here, beginning with the new contract."

Again – with my help?

"I'm at a loss as to how I might assist."

His striking glare penetrated my psyche. "Adam, I want all Aboodinians, especially those yet to be born, to contribute to our society. Our females today are protected by the males – and reduced to the sole mission of having sex and childbearing. By unleashing women we will double our numbers contributing to a new way of life, as corruption and dependence on the state give way to opportunity, individual purpose, ambition, and self-achievement."

Dream dreams that never were.

"Again – how?"

"Partnering with you, I will convince Lifason there is a better way – a path for Aboodin to become a respected member of the greater Taoland community once we end the payouts currently necessary to win business here."

I chuckled, "Good luck with that." Again Paladin grimaced.

"Adam, my goal, while ambitious, is to give *all* Aboodinians a purpose for living, an opportunity to cease being 'takers' and become producers and wealth creators 'takers.'"

"I applaud your objective, but I'm still clueless about my potential role."

Diazamel stood and led us into the gardens, where ice cream was served. "We must end condemning our citizens to purposeless lives. We must end dependency and enslavement to the state."

"Diazamel, I come from a society where technology and advanced robots rule, where folks suffer a different form of slavery – dependence on AI and machines – a place where human life is purposeless. I totally get what you are saying. But still, you refuse to answer my question. Why me?"

"I want you to ponder that question by yourself."

"I said I have no clue." There was no way I could affect a foreign culture. "Why not just better educate your people?"

"Adam, some would think the answer rests in education. Well, we do educate our youth. But after schooling, they find no meaningful employment. So, we risk discontent and social unrest. An overeducated underutilized mind is a terribly dangerous thing."

"So – meaningful jobs must be created."

"Exactly. For that we need time. And we need outsiders to help us unleash the talents of our people. We must transition Aboodin from clan rule to a land where individual rights and achievements are celebrated, for men and women alike. You and I will make this happen."

Getting more frustrated by the minute, I raised my voice. "H-h-how?"

"You will help me answer the 'how.' Enough for today. I've planted a few seeds. Let's meet again seven days from today – a special celebration I've arranged."

"More ice cream?"

"If you're lucky," he roared. "Until then, consider possible answers to 'how.' I want your unencumbered ideas. Then I'll offer my own. After that, we'll concoct a plan that will change the world."

CHAPTER 29

AWAKENINGS

For the next week I worked feverishly on concepts for Diazamel, but with no real clarity. On the appointed evening, Caojule landed us in a remote area of the desert under a moonless sky. Diazamel met us at the entrance to a large tent where several hundred men were seated. As we made our way, Aboodinian music and tantalizing aromas filled the space. Diazamel warmly greeted many of the guests.

The roasted body of a massive bovine, head still attached, lay in the center of our massive first table. Diazamel spoke. "The carcass has been wrapped and slowly roasted for ten hours in a paqanaqalah – a coal-fueled stone oven buried under the desert sands. It's a treat you'll never forget."

Additional charred animals rested atop mounds of savory starchy white seeds at buffet tables around the tent's perimeter – accompanied by a delish gravy. Pungent grilled vegetables and warm breads around the circumference of the platters completed the feast.

Still standing, Diazamel plucked out the right eyeball of our animal with his fingers and placed it in my mouth. I'd read about this custom. I compressed the large squishy blob, forced it past my teeth, and swallowed it whole.

"Being offered the eye is a great honor," Caojule whispered. "You did well."

The sounds of music, small talk, and laughter filled the tent. Men danced around on the center carpets, each swirling individually. Before dessert, certain to be ice cream, Diazamel took my left hand in his right. We led the others a hundred yards to a foothill of the Aboodinian Mountains. Diazamel ordered the generators turned off.

"Look down, Adam."

The night was so pitch black that I couldn't see my sandals.

"Now gaze up."

I was startled by a hologram, at least fifty feet high, rising against the mountainous backdrop. It was Zalifhar, Diazamel's father, waving gently, the smile on his purple face matching that of his youngest son. He spoke a single word: "Peace."

"It's my father's 75th birthday. I ordered this show to honor him."

After prayers, songs, and speeches praising the Ruler, servants restarted the generators to restore the lighting. As the others returned to the tent, Diazamel held me back. I sat to his left on the cool sand. Paladin crouched to his boss's right.

"Does this mean I'll miss the ice cream, Diazamel?"

He roared. "They'll save some for us." He immediately turned serious. "Have you thought about how we might transform Aboodin?"

I met his gaze. "More than one thousand years ago, a man came to Taoland and offered inspirational words: *'Some see things that are wrong and ask why? Others dream dreams that never were and ask why not?* You and I are dreamers, Diazamel. You know better than me what's wrong here. I'd be honored to help with the why nots."

A wide smile spread across his face, his teeth gleaming in the tent light. "Adam, I look forward to dreaming new dreams with you." He continued, "I believe it's impossible to imagine things that are not possible."

"I agree. And the 'how to make it better' begins with the dreams."

I rose as Diazamel stood with his hands resting upon my shoulders. "We will unleash the imaginations of millions. Imagination is what distinguishes humans from other life-forms. Imagination, dreaming our own dreams, makes us human."

"I'd be proud to serve the people of Aboodin in making your dreams become my dreams – and then making them come true."

We walked slowly, hand in hand, toward the tent. "Adam, my vision goes far beyond the contract. It involves something way beyond that scope. I want a long-term partnership, a fifty-fifty JV with Tezhouse, by which we will transform not only Aboodin's physical and cyber infrastructures, but the very future of generations to come."

His every word excites me.

"We will call our JV *Awakenings*. I want a handshake with you on this, to be approved by your Board, of course. I am asking for a Tezhouse commitment to invest in Aboodin. I will serve as JV Chairman. You will be CEO. You can manage from afar, *swishing* daily with Paladin, who will serve as your deputy."

"How does this relate to the current competition?"

We paused our walk and sat down again in the sand, still some fifty yards from the tent. "*Awakenings* will be formed by a contract addendum, to be revealed at the signing ceremony."

"So, investment in the JV will replace bribes. Correct?"

"You'll be offsetting part of your profits by investing in Aboodin's future, in our people, and in the profitable businesses to be launched under *Awakenings*."

"As for staffing, I assume we will bring the outsiders, correct?"

"Exactly. You guys will bring the needed scientists, engineers, and other high-level workers of all kinds."

"We'll have to offer good incentives."

"Of course. Vet and select those willing to become long-term residents – to assimilate here, with their families, or by creating new families by marriages with our locals. They'll provide new blood needed to modernize our culture."

I added some levity. "Am I allowed to tell them all the marriage candidates are purple?" Diazamel roared.

I continued, "And the packages we'll use to entice them?"

"Signing bonuses and high financial compensation – with free housing, nolis, great schools, and a promise of the marvelous lifestyle they and the Aboodinians in their charge will create."

"You say the *Awakening*s offer is to be made as an addendum?"

"Yes. Kept top secret until signing. Only I, you, Paladin, your CEO and your Chairman can be part of this. I don't even want Caojolie to know, even though I trust him completely. This proposal is to be made separately – and on word of honor."

"That will keep Huggles in the dark 'til the end."

"Yes. Along with those at Tezhouse who might try to upend this. And some Aboodinians, mainly in my brother's camp, who live on bribe money. They'd love to destroy this vision." He looked down at a desert twig he twirled in his hands.

"What about the details? And the price?"

"You'll take the lead. Paladin will advise. I want this to be risk-free to Tezhouse. While *Awakenings* will be fifty-fifty, I will take full risk on the launch price. I will subsidize small business start-ups, betting that reinvested profits will make the JV self-funding within three years."

I blinked, hoping he wasn't being overconfident.

Diazamel continued, "You and Paladin will formulate the details. We'll then share these, in secret, with your two superiors."

I dug my feet into the cool sand. "How will it affect the final decision?"

"I'll share everything, once agreed upon, with Lifason, before he makes his decision."

"Will they buy in?"

"That part is up to me. I'll urge them to select Tezhouse, because of *Awakenings*. I'll promise to bring Smerland and Kamyabi into the deal, securing significant funding to supplement the launch monies and help their reformations as well."

We discussed the possibility of the Tezhouse price coming in higher than what Huggles would bid. Diazamel directed me to include two years' start-up funds approximating what he estimated would be the amount of the Huggles' bribes. The start-up funds would carry *Awakenings* for two years until other nations came on board with additional funds. Diazamel was confident in his ability to win over Zalifhar and Lifason by convincing them *Awakenings* would open opportunities for all Aboodinians.

I can easily sell this to Komourin and Westin. "This just might work."

"We'll launch and subsidize new businesses as incubators, locally owned and managed in Aboodin, Smerland, and Kamyabi. We'll train future business leaders in the process."

His eyes lit up with love for his people. He jumped up from his reclining position and pointed. "Adam, look! Good luck is shining upon us." It was a golden desert qilin, smiling down at us from a dune. "Do it!" the horse urged, in a voice more booming than Diazamel's. Adriella flittered by with a matching smile. We returned to the tent and parted after ice cream.

The very next day Westin and Komourin gave their blessings to *Awakenings* via a secure *swish* conference. Paladin, who had barely spoken with me before, worked long hours with me for the next month, as we fleshed out a plan. Paladin would share progress with Diazamel every few days, as I did with Westin and Komourin.

It was fun, energizing, and – most importantly – more meaningful than anything I'd ever done. Every weekend I returned home to Tari, who marveled at the newly alive person I'd become.

"Adam, I'm thrilled to see you motivated by something other than Tezhouse profits. I can feel the positive energy in your bones. I love you, my husband."

For the very first time, my bride respects what I'm doing!

As Paladin and I neared completion of our *Awakenings* proposal, it was time for us to bring Westin and Komourin to Aboodin for a face-to-face meeting. They flew in secretly and stayed at my modest apartment. The next morning, we gathered in the Palace, in that same humongous room beyond the entrance. Westin, Komourin, and I sat to Diazamel's left while Paladin settled to his right. A lengthy silence reigned at the onset, without any eye contact. By their fidgeting, I could tell my bosses were uncomfortable. I hid a smile, knowing the game Diazamel liked to play.

Nervously breaking the stillness, Westin opened, "Adam has spoken about you with profound respect, Your Highness."

In a booming voice and furrowed brows, Diazamel bellowed, "Who?" Appearing confused, almost angry, he turned to the perplexed Chairman. "Adam who?"

Westin stumbled, pointing at me. "Errr . . . Adam . . . Adam Novana . . . t-t-to my left."

The roars this time were deafening. Now it was I who had tears rolling down my face. Diazamel had broken the ice with a sledgehammer. His contagious laughter was infectious. My bosses caught on and joined in the frolicking. The meeting went brilliantly. We agreed on every *Awakenings* detail – the price tag, the investments to be sought from Smerland and Kamyabi, the incubator and self-funding schemes, and the ultimate privatization. The five of us shook hands.

After sandwiches and more ice cream, Diazamel stood, appreciation obvious across his face. "There is nothing more we can do until Lifason makes his decision and my father blesses it. This should be within the week. Let's hope for the best."

Westin, Komourin, and I could not contain our smiles as we approached the Tezhouse nolicraft. Returning to my apartment we shared our hopes that something quite special was right there on the horizon. A huge win-win-win – for Tezhouse, for Aboodin, and for the region. A major loss for Huggles. A dream that never was about to become a reality.

For the first time, we had a chance. No – we had a great chance. We were going to win this thing! And for the first time in my life, I was doing something that would have profound meaning for millions of folks for generations to come.

CHAPTER 30

A LUNCH MEETING TO FORGET

A *swish* alert via a secure device Diazamel provided awakened me. I was not expecting to hear anything for several more days. He looked stern. My heart thundered in my chest.

It's over. His brother rejected our idea.

I squirmed when he refused to make eye contact. And remained silent. Suddenly his grim expression exploded into a huge grin, followed by uproarious laughter. "Got you again, Adam. I'll take you out of your agony. Last night, I met with my father and brother – to discuss the addendum. I couldn't resist telling you myself, my dear friend, in advance. They love *Awakenings*. We'll announce Tezhouse as the winner in five days."

I darn near fell off the bed. With the exception of meeting and falling in love with Tari, and the birth of our children, this was the most exciting moment in my life. I hesitated, gathering my words. "I don't know what to say, Diazamel. All I can think of is a simple 'thank you' – for your trust in Tezhouse. You will not be disappointed."

"What? You don't get it, do you. We're *not* selecting Tezhouse. We'd never trust our future to any company. *We've chosen you*, Adam of Novana, to deliver what is promised in both Tezhouse proposals. Partner, I highly value our relationship, one that we've only begun to build. Far more important than your talents, you are a man of integrity. I trust you. Now let's together make our impossible dream happen."

Tears of pride and joy fell on my face. "I will. You are too kind."

"We'll never look at the ridiculous number of Ts & Cs attached to your company's offering. They are meaningless to us, meant only to protect Tezhouse. I know in the years ahead I can contact you, wherever you might be, and together we can solve any problem – be it technical, financial, legal, or about services."

I gathered my composure. "Of course. You honor me, my friend." The level of confidence and trust he had in me and my decisions was something I'd never experienced.

"Adam, it is you who honor us with your friendship and respect. Were you expecting good news? Or were you concerned after you departed my place?"

"Knowing Lifason would make the selection, most at Tezhouse had our chances at below zero. But Westin, Komourin, and I floated away when we left your Palace on a cloud of hope. I think we might have left our noli on your grounds." We both laughed. "Tell me, Diazamel. How did you bring Lifason around?"

"It was surprisingly easy. My brother is a good man but mired in a long-standing corrupt business culture. I shared your proposal and promises with him and Zalifhar. I told them how it could transform our culture, that it was an honor agreement, and that I trusted you completely."

"But still, how was the decision made so quickly?"

"When I finished my words, my father turned to Lifason and asked if he was prepared to make his decision. My brother's response was immediate and one-word: *Tezhouse*. Like you moments ago, I was speechless. Zalifhar was noticeably delighted. Gotta go now. Tell nobody. See you at the press conference."

Euphoria didn't begin to describe my emotions. I headed to

our local office to prepare for final questions from the Aboodin bureaucrats, even though I knew the competition was over. I *swish'd* Tari but did not share the news, per Diazamel's admonition. "Just calling to say I love you."

A pleasant and satisfied smile crossed her face. "I love you more, Adam. Please don't forget – Tojo's game begins at 1:00 p.m. He's more nervous than usual. He knows you're away in Aboodin. But if you can *swish* him and encourage him before the big match begins, it will really surely help."

"Will do."

As I headed to my noli, my feet never touched the ground. Soon after I arrived at the office, Bogart *swish'd* and threw a damper on my exuberance.

"Hey, Asshole. Connichar, Director of Taoland's Airspace Management Authority, wants to meet you for lunch, at the Aboodin Capital Inn, twelve thirty sharp. He's preparing TAMA's final report on our proposal for the Aboodin Review Board. Don't be late. And don't screw this up."

Bogart, nasty as ever, disconnected before I could reply. As always, I was offended by his cruddy demeanor. But I was unconcerned, knowing secretly we'd been selected for the most important contract in Tezhouse history. I headed to the luncheon happy to meet Connichar for the first time.

I arrived early at the Inn and was ushered to a rear table. I *swish'd* Tojo as I waited. I smiled broadly when he appeared in hologram.

"How are things going, buddy?"

"Great, Dad." He beamed with enthusiasm. "I'm surprisingly confident."

"I'm so proud of you, Tojo. I'll be recording the entire game. Just do your best – that's more important than the outcome."

"I know, Dad. I know you're swamped. Thanks for connecting. It means a lot. I don't tell you often enough, but you're the best. Talk later."

"I love you, Tojo.
"Back at you."
I'm so happy I made this swish.

Waiting for Connichar, I pondered the significance of our victory here. It would mean huge sales and profits for years to come. Then there was *Awakenings,* where we would make a long-term difference for all Aboodinians!

I knew Bogart would not give me any credit. Period. Heck, my friends back on the First Moon told me he was spreading rumors I'd been secretly meeting with Huggles counterparts. He was asserting that I was taking bribes and making errors in the Tezhouse bid to steer the award to Huggles. My *swish* with Diazamel told me all of Bogart's maneuvers were in vain.

Two men approached my table. The short well-dressed man with a triangular head, pale face, pimply skin, and blackened teeth introduced himself as Commander Connichar. I fought off a cringe as he shook my hand. The other even more grotesque man towered over both of us but remained silent. He had an odd, egg-shaped face, pinpoint ears, and a distorted nose above oversized red lips.

Connichar informed me they'd finished reviewing 'The Plan.' His choice of that term perplexed me. Throughout the lengthy luncheon, there was only small talk. Nothing personal. And strangely, no talk of the Tezhouse proposal.

Hmmm.

Connichar's buddy silently focused on me the entire time, mumbling words to himself.

Strange.

My glass was constantly filled with the most delish wine I'd ever tasted. I kept drinking and it never emptied, while the sidekick continued weird chanting. I should have stopped, should have questioned the never-empty glass, but I didn't. The drink was smooth and luscious. I'd never had problems with booze, but my head began spinning soon after my first glass.

I kept wondering when Connichar would get around to discussing business. He interspersed leading comments like 'nicely done, Adam' and 'we're going to take care of you, Adam.' Out of context, not tied to the rest of the conversation. Didn't make any sense.

Why?

Soon quite tipsy, I found myself slurring and worrying if I could coherently answer any eventual questions related to our proposal. Fortunately, instead of a review, this whole thing seemed like a celebration. "We appreciate all you've done, Adam."

He must already know Tezhouse has been selected.

I turned my throbbing head to detect Connichar's partner conjuring some sort of spell over my drink as it refilled magically before my eyes while he murmured: "Hmmm . . . Dizi . . . Rivi . . . Toxi . . . Hmmm . . . Dizi . . ." Over and over. I met his glaring eyes and confronted him as best I could with a thickened tongue, forcing words through paralyzed lips. "W-w-what . . . was . . . that?" He ignored my protest.

Is he poisoning me with some sort of magic potion?

Ignoring my concern, Connichar blurted out, "This luncheon has been a courtesy. We're going to be working with the other guy."

I knew this wasn't true.

My head spinning, his shocking pronouncement added to my state of confusion. I tried to respond but couldn't get any words from my brain to my swollen lips. Connichar's buddy then tossed a full glass of red wine all over my white shirt. He spoke, for the first time and loudly, as he placed an envelope in my right jacket pocket. "Here's what we agreed to." I was too dizzy and nauseous to respond with anything, except a feeble, "W-w-what? . . ."

Connichar barked for all around to hear, "We've got your back, Adam." The two stood up and turned toward the front. "Thank you for all you've done to make this possible. Don't worry. We've compensated you generously." As drunk as I was, as they rushed away I finally realized Connichar and his buddy were not from TAMA.

I've been drugged!

To add insult to injury, Connichar (if that was his name) stiffed me with the bill. I rose from my chair and fell over. After staggering to my feet, I stumbled to the front, trying my best to disguise my condition. I swallowed deeply as I paid the check, 445 lunies – plus tip – for lunch!

I somehow made it to the sidewalk where two men bumped me from different directions, grabbing and shoving me. I thought one might have rummaged in my left coat pocket, but I barely comprehended the invasion. Far too drunk to drive myself, and barely able to stand, I decided to *swish* for a charge-a-noli.

A woman standing across the street aside a shiny vehicle called in a loud voice, "Over here, Adam. I'll take you." It was too convenient and made no sense, but it kind of fit the rest of what had happened. High on booze and likely drugs, I didn't even question her offer.

I fell at the curb, managed to right myself, and headed shakily to her vehicle, dragging my left foot. It was an Ettiore, the most expensive surface vehicle in Taoland. Brilliant gold, no top, with red leather interior and shiny black wheels. Hardly subtle. The stunning, sexy female driver bit her ruby lips, tucked a strand of hair behind her pointed ears, threw her arms around me, and planted a lengthy kiss on my mouth.

W-w-what?

"I'm Vixen," she added in a raspy voice, her tongue dancing enticingly. "Hop in the front with me – best way to experience this beauty."

The Ettiore or the driver?

I crawled into the passenger seat – uncomfortably close to hers. She squeezed me and announced in a full voice easily heard by those in the street, "Let's party!"

Vixen waved to gaping onlookers as she sped away. I had no idea where we were headed. I found her astonishingly seductive, engaging, and charming. Though I didn't understand anything, her sultry voice put me in an incoherent stupor. I'm sure I heard the words 'sex,' 'booze,' 'mob, and 'drugs' several times. But none of it really registered as I only nodded in incomprehensible agreement.

Definitely improperly dressed as a driver, her long legs were fully exposed under a short red skirt that crept up her thighs. Long, flowing, soft blonde hair framed her ravishing pink face. Something about her lulled me into a stupor. I finally did my best to ask, slurring, "So . . . w-w-where . . . w-we going?"

She smiled and winked, a move that caused the world to fade around me. "To the orgy – as you requested. We're going to PARTY! As quickly as I can get you there."

She must have been going over 250 mph. She swerved off the highway, loudly, slowed down, and screeched the Ettiore to a halt in an abandoned strip mall in front of a boarded-up establishment. "We're here. It's orgy time. Now, how about my lunies?"

Plastered beyond any capacity to respond, I reached into my pockets to discover I'd lost my wallet. Those two thugs outside the restaurant must have taken it. My head pounding, I blurted, "S-s-sorry . . . n-n-no . . . m-money."

"No problem." She reached into my right-hand pocket, retrieved, and audibly counted five 1,000-luni notes. Then she returned the envelope to my jacket.

"W-w-where . . . is . . . w-w-wallet?," I slurred.

"Must be somewhere," she responded. "Let's search for it." She raised her tiny skirt above her slim waist, crawled out of her seat and onto me, and purred in an amorous voice as she planted a long passionate kiss on my lips – then another one – then a few more, letting her tongue slip into my mouth. Her breasts popped out of her blouse, and she placed my hands on them. She grappled everywhere in my pants, apparently looking for my wallet, but instead finding my privates. She was on my lap, facing me, wiggling and grinding on my paralyzed body for what seemed like forever – as my silent protestations failed.

I've never been unfaithful to Tari – not ever!

Several minutes later she exited the vehicle, exclaiming, "It's been great, Adam. You're quite the lover. Thanks for being so generous." Then she fled down an alley, never looking back.

I did my best to collect myself. I crawled out the open driver's door, falling to my knees, pants around my ankles – only to discover a massive police officer standing over my slumped body.

"Our drones reported you doing almost 300. And the vehicle markings tell me that this Ettiore is stolen. Care to explain?"

Grabbing his legs, I stumbled, raised myself to his chest, and vomited all over his uniform.

"You fucking slobbering pig." He punched me, hard, cracking my jaw, then kicked me violently in my ribs. He grabbed my shirt, pulled me up, and violently slammed me against the police-noli. "Hands on the vehicle."

Oh I ache so.

With help from his partner, he ripped my arms behind my back, handcuffed me, and made me take a breathalyzer test. With a rough hand on my pounding head, he pushed me into the back seat and hauled me away.

The next two hours were beyond dreadful. I had no wallet, no ID, and couldn't recall my *swish* password. My body was racked in pain, mostly from a broken jaw and cracked rib cage. All I had on my person were two envelopes, each stuffed with 1,000 luni notes and packets of white powder. They also retrieved what looked like an info-storage device. I pissed myself, adding to the vomit stench. A DNA test yielded my identification. A blood test proved I was really high, not only on wine, but on several illegal narcotics.

Bang! Bam! Boom! My head pounded in agony, my vision blurred, my speech remained unintelligent as I tried unsuccessfully to answer questions – about driving recklessly, without a license or registration. Driving a stolen Ettiore while intoxicated. Pushing and imbibing illegal drugs. Bribery. Prostitution. Assaulting a police officer. Being involved with a criminal mob.

I attempted to explain that the girl, not I, was the driver. Still drunk and high, I said my wine must have been spiked, that I would never take illegal substances willingly. I don't think they understood a word I slurred out. I was booked and thrown into a jail-cell. The next morning, seriously hungover, a guard dragged me to the front desk, where Bogart stood, tight-fisted, sporting an expression more angry than usual.

What is Bogart doing here?

Outrage wafted from him when he shouted, "You've really fucked up this time, Asshole." He paid my bail, and we exited without my saying a word. With my head throbbing after spending a night on a concrete floor, the last person I wanted to speak with was Bogart. I stumbled to the parking area.

"Get in my noli," he growled. "I'm taking you home."

I was out of options and barely able to stand, so I entered his nolicraft. Bogart attacked. "You cost us a victory in Aboodin, Asshole. You're finished. Bribes from gangsters. Even worse, bribes from Huggles. Drugs. Having sex with a whore tied to the mob! Stealing an Ettiore and driving recklessly while intoxicated. Accosting a police officer. Possession of child porn. Anything I've missed?"

Child porn?

"Everything has been recorded. Your entire escapade. Tariana has much of it already on video. It will all be made public tomorrow, without my fingerprints."

Without his fingerprints? What is he saying?

He handed me a coffee, which I welcomed as we lifted into the skies. I threw it down my dry burning throat into my grumbling belly. I immediately felt sickness wash over me. This time quicker and more severely.

Oh shit. He's spiked my coffee.

My vision went black, and ringing swelled in my ears. Then I passed out.

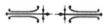

Ouch. I woke up to Bogart shaking me violently. We were hovering a few feet above my driveway. How was that possible? I gazed at the clock. I'd been out for hours. Bogart thrust open the right side of the noli. With an evil grin stretching ear to ear, he brutally kicked me out of his vehicle. I fell, face first onto the sharp driveway gravel. He yelled from the open door, "Your time at Tezhouse is over, Novana." He drew his fingers across his throat, in a slitting motion. "Victory is mine, you loser. Have a nice day." The noli door shut and he lifted off.

I dragged my unsteady, badly bruised body to a kneeling position. My hips buckled, and I fell again onto the trenchant surface, opening new wounds on my face, arms, hands, and elbows. My torn skin screamed in pain. Blood wept everywhere. My throat tasted like a once-fresh egg that had rotted for a week in midday heat. My physical agonies were exceeded by unimaginable torments in my brain – the awareness that all I'd worked for was no longer possible.

I turned to look toward my front door. Tari was standing there.

CHAPTER 31

COMFORT

My head was spinning out of control from the latest dosage of drugs, courtesy of Bogart. I struggled once again to stand, but I couldn't. My own stench forced me to vomit again before Tari and Tojo picked me up off the gravel and dragged me inside the front door. Tojo had the strength of a grown man. I looked up at him. Up. He was taller than me. *When did that happen?*

I attempted to speak, but my thickened tongue would have none of that. "Shhhhhh . . ." advised Tari. "We'll talk later." She and Tojo managed to carry me upstairs to our bed, which was blanketed in soft red towels. My jaw and ribs wailed in tune with my pounding head. They stripped me naked, tended to my wounds, then carefully lifted me into our delightfully warm bathtub filled with soothing oils.

"T-t-tari . . ."

"Shhhhhh. Plenty of time to chat when you're a bit stronger."

I tried but failed to explain all that had happened. I simply couldn't gather my words. ". . . Videos . . . recordings . . . set-up . . . drugged . . . Bogart . . ."

Tari put her finger to her lips. "I know and trust you, my husband. I smell Bogart all over those trashy recordings left at our front door this morning. I love you unconditionally. You've made many mistakes over the years, but infidelity has never been one of them."

I felt beyond blessed and assured almost beyond belief. Our love affair had been filled with my many broken promises and missteps. At times I'd felt unworthy of her forgiveness and unadulterated love. But Tari was correct. Neither of us had ever been unfaithful.

Our love affair is special.

Tari dressed me in loose clothes and helped me back into the bed. Kaleeva came in. She and Tari alternated ice for the swellings and sweats followed by heat when I got the shivers. They lovingly applied poultices and healing liniments everywhere, before tucking me in. I zonked out. I awoke sometime later to find Ambrosia by my side, holding my hand. She told me I had slept for twenty hours. I began pondering the disaster of Aboodin. I knew my dreams of becoming CEO were gone – forever.

"Don't try to speak yet, Adam. It will take a few days for the drugs to be fully flushed out of your system. It's going to be OK. Wipe those worry lines from your forehead."

She poured me a glass of warm tea, which I gladly swallowed through a straw. I enjoyed a few small bites of a biscuit as well. "Where . . . Tari?"

"She sat with you and tended your wounds throughout the night. I arrived a couple of hours ago to give her some relief – and time to sleep."

"T-t-thank . . . you."

"Adam, what's happened is a harbinger of good fortunes ahead. Your time of discovery is fast approaching. You learn not at the summit but down in the gutter. Don't be frightened. Find solace in your family. Reflect on the good you've experienced over the years – as you step toward new joy."

I tried to sit up but was thrown back to the pillow. I'd never experienced such extreme vertigo.

"You're a couple of days away from getting up. Be patient."

"I've n-n-never been so out of it b-b-before." The room was spinning wildly.

"Take this time to recharge, reflect, refuel, and regroup. This is an opportunity – a chance to ponder your future. And your priorities. The moons of Taoland won't stop rotating around the planet if you disengage for a while. Let's get you patched up and recalibrated."

She pushed open the windows to let in the Taolight. Birds were singing away in a boisterous cacophony, offering a cheerful chorus of morning songs, as if to encourage me – in this time of defeat. A brilliantly colored dragonfly hovered, then perched on Ambrosia's fingers. Two tiny multicolored birds landed on the sill, duetting melodious chirrups.

"I wish you could rise to see my beautiful qilin below. I hope you don't mind; she's chomping away at some sweet apples up in your trees." Fabbo, her teacup puppy, barked happily at the birds.

"Go to Adam," The little burnt orange fur ball scampered from below the window and hopped into my bed. She licked my face before cuddling against my chest and sending waves of healing energy through me. I smiled through my pains. *I miss Apollo.*

"Adam, did you ever notice how the animals find ways to boost our spirits and make us happy in the depths of our darkest hours?"

Fabbo's kisses eased the anxiety weighing down my heart. I didn't want the happenings of the past two days to destroy the confidence that had long buoyed me. I needed to somehow release the self-doubts created by the recent saga. But I knew Lifason would now reverse the choice of Tezhouse.

Ambrosia spoke in uncommon wisdom. "Your outlook and mindset can alter any situation. You can cultivate love and joy in the face of hatred, evil, and defeat. You can dream dreams that never were, to replace older dreams that are no more."

"T-t-thank you."

She stood in all her radiant beauty. "Adam, old ways will never open new doors. I urge you to leave the comfort zone that has long been blocking you from inner joy. Seize this opportunity to take a leap forward – and find what you really want. I'll return tomorrow." She faded before my eyes.

Tojo entered, taking her place. "It's horrible what they did to you, Dad. But it's going to be OK."

"Tojo . . ."

"Dad, we won the championship game. I shot the winning goal! Can you believe it? My teammates carried me off the field on their shoulders." I tried to smile, but it hurt. "Thanks for the *swish* before the game, Dad. It gave me a much-needed boost. We won! The championship! I was still on a cloud until I saw you in the driveway. We'll watch the game together when you're better."

"T-t-tojo . . ."

"Shhhhhh, Dad. Throughout my life you've been paying it forward. Now it's time for payback from your kids. We'll get you better."

My beautiful Kaleeva entered carrying a basket brimming with my favorite flowers, freshly picked fruits, and warm cookies. She sat next to me on the bed. "Oh, Dad, I can't stand seeing you like this. I can't fathom the pain you're in. I'd take it all away from you, *all of it*, if I could." She bent and gently kissed my bruised forehead, which was still smarting from the gravel.

I forced myself to say a few words. "T-t-thank you . . . b-b-both . . . I love you so much."

"Not as much as we love you," Kaleeva continued, beaming. "We love you to the Tao and back – more than chocolate-covered nobble cookies."

Just sixteen years old – and as beautiful as her mom.

Through the years, I'd loved my children the best way I knew how. I'd provided for them materially, and helped raise them, although Tari had borne the bulk of the weight. I'd guided them as they grew from toddlers to teenagers. Most importantly, I shared values and tried to serve as a positive role model. Of course, I'd never get back the hours lost when I'd chosen Tezhouse over them. But here they were nurturing me, showing that they loved their dad, despite my failings. *I'm so blessed.*

The kids departed when Tari came in, wearing that same smile I fell in love with two decades ago. "Hi, my love. Hope you're feeling at least a bit better." She'd seen the despicable recordings, yet she showed only unconditional love.

I found my weakened voice. "Honey . . . all that stuff they sent . . . it's all a lie."

"I know. We may have had our troubles along the way, but I've never doubted your fidelity or moral character – not for an instant."

"Tari, I'm finished . . . at T-t-tezhouse."

"I've told you countless times – that doesn't matter. We'll be fine. Besides, Komourin wants to *swish* us later. He says he'd like to chat. I have no idea what he wants, but who knows? It might be good news. Now, I'll leave you to take a nap." She kissed my cheek and left the room.

Then I felt yet another comforting presence – before I even saw her. Adriella.

CHAPTER 32

BOGART: DEAL OR NO DEAL

Throughout the return trip to the First Moon I was salivating in ecstasy. The vision of Asshole Adam writhing in pain and puking in his driveway replayed in my mind. During the flight I'd packaged all the 'evidence' in the worst conceivable context. Upon landing on my lawn, I *swish'd* my assistant.

"Jezabel, I won't be in tomorrow until after lunchtime."

"Get some sleep, Mr. Bogart. I'll be in early and will manage any incoming."

As I approached my house a huge snorting black qilin appeared in my path. A good sign. The stench from its sweating skin and atrocious breath filled the air. Fire leapt from his mouth. Its two-foot-long horn, disheveled mane, rippling muscles, and long mangy tail were jet black. With ears pinned back, nostrils flaring, and frothing at its mouth through several dozen sharp yellowing teeth, the beast spoke. "Welcome home, Mr. Bogart."

The qilin's front legs reared furiously as it leapt into the air, jacking up dust with its filthy hooves. When it returned to the surface, it roared garishly, a sick smile on its ugly face, before galloping into the darkness. I curved my lips in a grin as I pushed open my front door.

"Shaitan, I'm home."

She shouted back from the kitchen, "I couldn't give a shit, Bogart. Every day I hope it's the last I'll ever see of your ugly face."

Bitch. She always pisses me off – even now on the heels of defeating Novana.

"Just wanted to give you a heads-up so you can boot whoever is fucking you out the back door."

"He left half an hour ago. I miss him so much already."

I entered the kitchen to find her slumped over, her fat naked ass pressed to the floor. I looked her over with a grimace. "You sure know how to sour a good day, you worthless piece of shit."

She slurred, "Quit whining like a baby, which you are in comparison to any of my lovers."

My face reddened. She conjured up memories of my father, who launched insults every time he saw me. Not sure who I hated more: my lowlife wife – the worst bitch I'd even known – or the monster of a father who destroyed my life before Taoland. I stepped over Shaitan, then headed for my office. She had ticked me off, like an annoying insect. But it was time to get to work and hammer the final nails into Novana's coffin. *Let's finish this off!*

I needed sleep, but I worked a few hours first, taking another pass through the materials. After tweaking the compilation of the story, videos, audios, and documentation, the package was devastating. Hannibal and his goons and Vixen – my fav hooker – had performed excellently.

How brilliant of me – getting Novana assigned in Aboodin where I could set him up. And my prick father thought I was useless. I fell asleep at my desk.

I bolted out of bed, awakened by swarming sounds outside my office window. Countless bees, hornets, and locusts blackened the morning sky. Hundreds of them smashed to their deaths against the glass. Vultures screeched above. I was surprised to see spring flowers laying over – dead. A freak storm must have passed through. The gloomy scene didn't dampen my joy, nor did it wipe the smile from my face. I got a further boost when I spotted that sweaty black qilin through the mass of insects.

I began a final review of everything and planned to forward all to Hannibal around noon when I would direct him to hit the 'send' button from a fake location midafternoon. He would 'leak' everything anonymously, to everybody, including to the Royal Family in Aboodin. I knew Adam was incapable of being reached and interviewed. I knew both the media and police would want to speak with the restaurant staff at the inn and folks in the street for added details, so I included contact info.

This would be sweeter than when I'd murdered my own father back in my homeland, with Hannibal's help. He'd always been my 'right arm.' He worked at the Cabbadonia Crematorium, a key assignment from the mob there. After I put a bullet in my father's head, Hannibal turned the body, including the teeth, into dust. Then he and I spread the cremains in a woodland – and pissed on them.

I assumed Hannibal had paid his cohorts and they'd all returned separately to the First Moon. In any case, each had been heavily disguised, unrecognizable by any at the scenes of the crimes. Today would be the final day of Adam Novana's career. His life going forward would match the ugliness outside my office window. This was clearly the dawn of the best day ever in my quest to become CEO.

A brilliant plan perfectly executed!

An unexpected *swish* jolted me. It was Komourin, his face filled with rage, his voice howling. "Hey, prickface, I'm sending you a secure link – audio and video records of your most evildoings over decades – materials I began filing soon after we met, when I first saw the blackness of your soul."

I flinched but did not budge. "Hold on, big fella. Calm down."

He continued, "I've had eyes and ears on you all this time, you scumbag. I've employed dozens of moles, including a few of your closest advisors. Today, I'll strip you naked, for all of Taoland to witness."

I bolted up in my chair. "What the fuck are you talking about?"

"Your recklessness and vile behavior in Aboodin has ended you. You risked destroying the best opportunity in Tezhouse history – in your sick, perverted obsession to terminate Adam Novana. But you failed. And now you'll pay the price."

Could he have learned about the events of the past two days? Even if he did, and suspected I was behind it all, my fingerprints were nowhere to be found. I alone have the damming irrefutable evidence needed to end Novana's career.

"And what exactly do you suspect I've done?"

"Not suspect," he shouted, "I know what you did in Aboodin."

He's bluffing.

"I have complete recordings of your meeting at the Club Diablo last month – the silver bullet you could never have imagined. I also have recordings of everything from the past two days. I have eyes and ears everywhere."

What the fuck? I began to panic. He didn't even pause for a breath. "I employ spies, Bogart. And recording devices everywhere you are. I've got invisible drones all about. If you spent more time in the Advanced Engineering Labs you supposedly oversee as President, you'd be well aware of the tiny virtually invisible electronic birds we provide to the Taoland Intelligence Services."

"Drones?"

"I have my own personal drone air force. They proved handy at Club Diablo, in and outside the Capital Inn, in Vixen's Ettiore, at Aboodin police headquarters, and in your own noli yesterday when you brutally beat up on Adam."

I leaned in, knowing he was lying. "Bullshit. If you were watching, why didn't you stop it?"

"If I was watching what? You just admitted to your crimes, you dumbass. You've crossed a line with your latest escapades. It's time to end you, for good. I'm sorry Adam had to go through what he did, but the cost to you will now be far greater."

Sweat bloomed on my palms, but I couldn't show him the pressure I was experiencing. "You're so full of crap, Komourin. If you have any of what you assert, you'd keep it to yourself, knowing I can destroy you in an instant."

Komourin didn't miss a beat. "I can't bear the weight of my sins any longer. I'm gonna reveal all the ugly truths of my past to my wife and accept the consequences before your own crimes hit the media. I'm gonna confess my misconduct, my infidelities, and beg for forgiveness. Regardless of what you do."

Maybe he's not bluffing? I wiped away the sweat from my mustache.

Komourin continued, face redder than ever. "Two key players in your diabolical plot, Fiendor and Vixen the prostitute, are both my moles. And rather good actors. I paid them generously for their double-agent spying. Twice what you gave them, with bonuses for the extra data-drives they gave me, and for their sworn affidavits, taken in official court settings. It was easy to secure their help."

"F-f-fiendor . . . and V-v-vixen?"

"The only thing greater than Vixen's lust for money is her hatred for you. Oh, and thanks for assigning media relations to Fiendor. He set up nothing for you there, you dirtbag. He despises you. We've whisked the two of them away to a remote area of another moon. With new identities. They are starting new lives with generous monthly payouts for as long as they remain 'disappeared.' Nobody will recognize their altered appearances a few months from now. As for your sidekick Hannibal, he's on his way to a remote prison as we speak."

Holy shit! He's not bluffing!

Tremors racked my body. My head pounded, but I was not ready to surrender. "Let neither of us do anything rash, Komourin. Let's discuss this."

He chuckled; an evil laugh. "I'm gonna offer you a deal. If you reject it, I'm ready to hit the 'send' button to all media with proof of all your prior crimes, including in Aboodin. After that, they'll not report a word of the story you've fabricated."

While listening to his rant, I opened the link he'd sent. It was devastating. He'd doctored the evidence to make me appear even more of a monster than I was. I cowered but tried to maintain composure. "What happens to Adam?"

"To begin, the Aboodinian police have agreed to drop all charges against Adam and expunge his arrest record. Adam and Tariana will relocate to the Third Moon as soon as he's recovered. He'll serve at headquarters as Westin's Executive Assistant."

"So there's some good news. The Asshole will be demoted to a staff job."

"Promoted, you shithead. With an enormous raise. Adam will become corporate liaison to the Tezhouse Supreme Command, freeing Westin of this role. He'll also enter politics and run for high public office."

"But as a staffer he'll be removed from CEO consideration. Yes?"

"In your dreams, Bogart. To the contrary, Adam will be receiving final preparations to replace me. And there's nothing you can do to stop it."

NO! NO! NO!

Komourin went on, "The offer I'll now make to you is predicated on your destroying the garbage you gathered in Aboodin and eradicating everything you have on me. You'll also end your illicit contacts with Huggles. We have a mole there as well, and tons of evidence."

I could hardly register all of what he was saying. Everything I'd worked so hard for was slipping from my grasp.

He went on, "If you reject the deal, there will be serious ramifications. You'll be fired. You'll receive no pension. And you will be prosecuted on three counts of first-degree murder for the three separate occasions your thugs killed men who stood in your way. We even secured your goons' confessions and depositions about those murders after granting them immunity. The evidence I'll share with prosecutors is irrefutable."

How could he possibly know this? I slipped up by asserting, "They were not murders."

"You are really unbelievably dumb. You just admitted to your crimes. Of course these were murders. And by the way I'm recording this conversation."

I had to take a last shot at him. "I'm not surrendering the goods I have on you, Komourin. If you try any of this, I will release everything I have on you. Even if you confess in advance to your wife, she and everybody you know will find the sordid details, that I've doctored a bit. Truly disgusting. And the media will destroy Tezhouse as they take you down."

Komourin rubbed his forehead, clearly on the edge of a violent outburst. "You jerk. Haven't you been listening? I already told you I'm taking that card away from you. If you pass on my deal, after I confess to my wife, I'll get you started on your way to prison or worse, resign from Tezhouse, and publicly apologize for my past behavior – negating any scandal you might hope to unleash."

I tried, probably without success, to mask my trepidation. "How about we compromise?"

"I'll try again to get this into your thick skull. If you refuse my deal, I'll reveal all the evidence I have on you. Today! You would soon be prosecuted, found guilty, and either be put to death or rot in prison for the rest of your miserable life. I'd vote for the latter."

Komourin continued to bark. "One more thing I'm happy to report, shit-for-brains. You've failed completely in trying to deny Tezhouse a victory in Aboodin."

What? Not possible.

"Now I know you're bullshitin' Komourin. Victory in Aboodin is impossible. We both know Huggles will win. My plan was only to take Asshole Novana down with the Tezhouse loss."

"Wrong. Westin and I traveled to Aboodin last week when Adam and Diazamel presented a brilliant side offer – a second contract creating a fifty-fifty JV between Tezhouse and the Ruling Family. It's been well received, accepted, and the leaders have chosen Tezhouse."

"An addendum for what?" I couldn't believe they'd done this without my knowing. "An addendum for what?"

"None of your fucking business."

"Do they know about what happened with Novana here?"

"I contacted Diazamel this morning to reveal your misdeeds. This actually solidified our victory."

My entire body was shaking. "N-n-no way."

"Westin and I will meet with the royals tomorrow morning in Aboodin. We'll agree to make Adam available to the JV CEO, operating remotely from Tezhouse headquarters, for the contract duration. We'll stay for the signing, news conference, and celebration – now set for tomorrow afternoon."

This can't be happening. I wiped a cold sweat and struggled unsuccessfully to stop quivering.

"Bogart, if you accept my offer and downstream ever violate the conditions of the deal, even to the slightest, you'd be in breach and I'd push the 'send' button, distributing everything I have on you. You'd not only be rendered luniless, but you'd then face prosecution. So I'll be giving you one chance."

"So exactly *what is* your deal? What happens to me if I accept it?"

"My offer, reluctantly made, is I'll withhold but not destroy the evidence on you to avoid even the remote possibility of any corporate scandal. We'll allow you to continue, in a limited fashion, in your current position. But to be paid, and retain your pension, you'll have to sign and honor nondisclosures."

Bile rose up in my throat. "That's it?"

"Dragoon, Schmohun, Rimoltz, and Swaltman will resign from the Board. Westin will choose their replacements."

Vomit threatened to burst from my mouth. I swallowed, pushing it and a possible mental breakdown down. "Are you done?"

"In addition to never contacting Adam again, nor any Board members, you are grounded. With a fifty percent salary reduction. No more travel. Not ever. And no more perks. Now – end of discussion – final chance. Yes or no?"

CHAPTER 33

A STUNNING ANNOUNCEMENT

Tari gently shook my shoulders. "Adam, wake up. Wake up. Westin and Komourin want us to *swish* right now. They are in Aboodin."

I awoke feeling more alive and less drugged than since that first sip of spiked wine at the Aboodin Capital Inn. Adriella's healing magic eased my pain – speeding my recovery. Her comforting touches had already healed my broken spirit. But I'd still not spoken to my bosses since the 'incident.' Facing them was a hurdle I'd now have to overcome.

"They are in Aboodin? Tari, did they say want to talk about Aboodin? Are they meeting with the police?"

"I don't know. They connected with me ten minutes ago. I told them you were napping. Komourin said, 'Wake him up – we've got good news.'"

She put a cup of coffee on the bedside table and sat alongside my aching body.

Good news? "OK. Let's do it."

We *swish'd*. They appeared in hologram, standing at the foot of our bed. Komourin began, a warm smile across his face. "I'd like to say it's great to see you, Adam. But you look like shit."

"You shoulda' seen me a few days ago," I quipped.

Westin interjected, "Greetings, Tariana. We've not met."

Komourin's pleasant smile put me at ease. "Sorry to wake you, Adam – but unlike you, we busy executives don't have the luxury of napping midday." He and Westin roared.

Westin adjusted the lapels on his suit-jacket and puffed out his chest. "It's early evening here, and we're headed to a celebration. Two hours ago, we signed both the contract and the addendum with Lifason and Diazamel – at a formal press conference announcing the Tezhouse victory – the most important in our history."

What?

Tari threw her arms around me. Her quick motion jarred my broken jaw and aching ribs. But the pain didn't matter – elation took over. If I could have lifted my arms I'd have pinched my cheeks. I was expecting the worst. I didn't know what to say, so I joked. "I wish I could be there with you, but I've got a minor chest cold."

Westin laughed. "Looks more like you were run over by a nolitruck."

"I haven't spoken with you guys. But you know I had a pretty nasty final couple of days in Aboodin. Today, for the first time, I've got a half-clear head. I was certain the Aboodin leaders would reverse their decision, because of me, and award it to Huggles – and that my career was over."

Westin responded, "Adam, we know way more about what happened than you do. Aboodin leadership knows the truth as well. As do the police. Bogart fabricated every last bit. But rest assured, none if it will ever be reported."

My eyes nearly popped out of my head. "What?"

Komourin propped his hands on his hips. "It was all a plot to destroy you. I told you years ago, I've always got eyes on Bogart. Well, this time he went way too far, and now it's him who's finished."

Westin leaned in and nudged Komourin with his elbow. "Bogart set you up and had you drugged and arrested. But we've cut a deal with him. He'll never distribute nor speak of his phony 'evidence.' And his Board cronies have submitted their resignations."

A bit of disappointment pricked me. "You guys were aware of it all as it happened?"

Komourin rubbed his neck and broke eye contact. "Yeah. Sorry you had to suffer through this, but we had to end Bogart once and for all. Now there's only smooth sailing ahead."

"I have so many questions." I let my head fall back onto my pillow.

"Later. Right now, let's discuss the immediate future. We want you and Tariana to depart for the Moon of Blissful Snow as soon as you feel up to it. Sometime in the next week or two would be perfect."

"What? How could you do this to us again?"

An equally perplexed Tari repeated, "Wait . . . what?"

Westin raised his hand. "Adam, you're being reassigned as my Executive Assistant. You'll replace me as Tezhouse liaison to the governance body at Tao Central Command."

"But . . . another move? To yet another moon?"

"You'll also chair an important government committee. You'll get involved in politics. All of this will prepare you to replace Komourin, and perhaps myself."

"Chairperson as well?"

"We've never had a Chairman-CEO. But then, we've never had an Adam of Novana before."

My mouth wide open, I asked, "What about my current duties?"

"Randahl will assume the sole role of President of Tezhouse Second Moon and continue as Director of Services. He'll promote a new VP to lead Business Development and Customer Relations."

Tari asked, "Will this put an end to Adam's constant travel?"

"Yes. Except he'll be spending a few days each month in Aboodin, serving as *Awakenings* CEO, which we're setting up as an off-book, nonprofit business. We are proud to be part of this initiative."

I turned back to Westin. "Being part of Diazamel's vision inspires me, fills me with new purpose. But, what about Bogart?"

"He's signed a deal that leaves him impotent. As long as he behaves and honors the agreement, he'll remain President of Tezhouse First Moon. But he'll be 'handcuffed' in a variety of ways. If we fired him, we'd risk him doing irreparable damage to Tezhouse, our shareholders, and dozens of good people. You'll never see him again. He's history."

Tari trailed her fingers over the edge of her chair, nervously, "What about me? And our children? I have friends here. And a significant role with TSU."

She'd been so supportive every time Tezhouse dragged us place to place – but I worried this move might be the final straw.

"Tariana, if you accept, we've arranged for you to become CEO at TSU," said Westin.

A stunned Tari rubbed her eyes, as if in disbelief. "CEO? Why me? I've never served in an executive role, not anywhere."

"You know TSU is the most important charitable organization in all of Taoland. What you may not know, Tezhouse is the largest donor in the critical work they perform. And we believed you are best qualified to replace Cristinez, the outgoing CEO who thinks the world of you."

Tari's next words were mired in suspicion. "Is this just a convenient way to placate me?"

Westin continued, "Please Tariana! We do not make such assignments lightly nor for any reason other than to select the most qualified candidate. Your volunteer work over the past two decades has not gone unnoticed. You are respected by all involved. Cristinez is actually the one who put your name forward, naming you her perfect successor. Everyone at TSU has agreed – unanimously."

"But TSU is headquartered in Tao City, on the Third Moon. So again – what about our children?" Tears of confusion flowed.

Our children were her priority – but this was the opportunity of a lifetime.

Komourin rubbed his chin. "Tojo will soon begin his sophomore year at Tao Institute of Technologies. Kaleeva is buried in schoolwork and extracurricular activities in her final year at high school. If you agree, she'll begin studies at Tao Medical University on the First Moon, next year, with a full scholarship. We'll arrange for your family to be together frequently."

Tari hesitated, rolling her damp eyes. "But, still, you're asking us to move away from Tojo and Kaleeva. I don't think we can do that."

Westin spoke. "They've already moved away – you just don't see it. We can't make the decision for you, but maybe it's time to cut their umbilical cords and begin new lives as empty nesters. You're most of the way there already."

Tari gasped as if this were beyond comprehension. What he was saying was true, but her motherly instincts created doubts.

Komourin continued, "We've dumped a lot on you." He paused, likely reflecting on the weight he'd placed on our shoulders. For years, our family had sacrificed for Tezhouse. I only hoped he appreciated everything Tari and I had done.

"Take your time thinking about our offer. Discuss with your kids. We're headed to the celebration – there's a bottle of bubbly staring us in the face. Adam, well done with humongous win here. Congrats to you as well, Tariana – future TSU CEO. Please know we love you both."

Westin added a final sweetener, "When you speak with your children, tell them they'll have two fully paid trips every year, during school breaks, to the Third Moon. And tell them that you two will have a one-month annual vacation, all paid-for, between school terms, when you can gather as a family."

The *swish* ended. We stared at each other, speechless, trying to gather our thoughts. Empty nesters? Our life had come full circle. I smiled recalling those early years when it was just Tari and me.

I broke the silence. "If the kids like it, and you like the notion of leading TSU, I'm all-in."

"Let's call them, Adam. Their opinion is critical."

We *swish'd*. Both appeared instantly, and we shared all the details. Tojo's face lit up excitedly. "I love it, Mom and Dad. I'm so proud of you."

Kaleeva began bouncing up and down. "Wow. Two trips a year to visit you on the Third Moon, during breaks. I can't wait to take up skiing."

"Me too," injected Tojo, "and I know we can come up with exciting adventures for our annual vacations."

The bubbling Kaleeva spoke again. "Mom, Dad, most students see little of their parents during university years. This is an amazing gift."

They were fully on board. They made our decision easy. We gave virtual hugs and ended the *swish*. Our concerns about separation yielded to excitement for the future.

"Tari, this means no more heading out into the hinterlands to hunt new contracts. No more Bogart. And lots of quality time for us and as a family."

"I'm overwhelmed by the children's positive response. I guess all parents hesitate in cutting those final umbilical cords. Kaleeva is not yet in college." She took a deep breath. "It will be difficult saying goodbye to Lorelai. But I'm totally thrilled about the idea of leading TSU. I can't believe they chose me."

"I'm proud of you Tari. And, if we say yes, I'll have a certain path to CEO, and maybe Chairman simultaneously."

Tari sighed and took my hands in hers. "That's the part I don't like about the package. But I still say 'yes' – with the warning I'm going to continually urge you to consider a more important future. I love you, my husband. I'll not nag, but I hold a deep belief there is a higher calling ahead for you."

"Honey, lately I have more questions than answers about my true purpose. I too have mixed emotions about spending the rest of my life at Tezhouse. But I'm thinking of something Malaika said to me twenty years ago in Novana – 'When a door is opened, push through it. And never look back.'"

We sent a one-word message to Westin and Komourin. "Yes."

We walked, hand in hand, into our gardens. Birds sang as colorful aromatic flowers opened to celebrate us. Small animals scurried about. *Everything feels right.*

A rustle in the forest drew our attention. Bright light enveloped the scene – then a brilliant white qilin leapt into the sky, a coveted sign of new adventure. It bore heavily feathered wings, something I never thought possible. The qilin's silhouette covered most of the half-risen silver moon as it majestically crossed the blue sky.

As soon as the qilin disappeared, a dark cloud erupted on the horizon – forewarning new dangers ahead.

CHAPTER 34

BLISSFUL SNOW

Travel isn't always pretty – or easy. Sometimes it can break one's heart, especially when it means leaving loved ones behind. But in this case, taking residence on yet another moon felt good. We'd likely see Tojo and Kaleeva more often than if we stayed on the Second Moon.

This will change me – for the better. I know it. I'm ready.

Of course, as always, there was that fear of the unknown – concern I wasn't prepared for uncharted waters of the silver moon. I was also becoming anxious about my health. Strange sharp pains shot through my gut area ever since the beatings. Keeping that secret from Tari added stress.

Wanderer descended from the heavens before resting gently on the surface –as Tao rose from the darkness. Malaika appeared from the cloud some thirty feet above, wearing that bountiful smile I hadn't seen in a decade. Her shimmering silver slacks and matching long-sleeved blouse glittered in the morning light. She beckoned to us. At the entrance to the Fifth Dimension we embraced – then waved goodbye to Tojo and Kaleeva below.

We chatted constantly with Malaika throughout our trip to the Third Moon – a silvery ball that grew in size as the Second

Moon faded from our view. Malaika settled next to us. "It's been ten years. Tell me everything."

Tari and I spoke of all that had happened during our decade-long journey on the Second Moon. My success in winning contracts for Tezhouse – only to be hauled back into new unknown thorny bushes after each victory. Tari's passion for her TSU work. The family separations and marriage struggles. Our children growing into their teenage years. All the ugliness with Bogart. The most recent nightmare in Aboodin. The new roles we'd accepted.

"Quite a complicated ten years. You must be emotionally exhausted."

I sighed and leaned forward, elbows on my knees. "I am. Yes. We both are. But today we're filled with hope as we begin a new adventure."

"Remember, from my first note to you, 'Have no expectations, but abundant expectancy.' You know there will always be bumps in the road. Life would be boring otherwise. Traversing them is how you learn and grow."

We spoke on and off for ten hours before beginning our descent to the Moon of Blissful Snow. *Wanderer* hovered above a blanket of fresh snow glistening in the midday light – the first Tari had ever seen. Her eyes grew wide. "How gorgeous. It's amazing . . . more beautiful than I'd imagined."

Malaika led us to the edge where we embraced silently, for a long time. "Adam, do you think you're closer now to discovering your true purpose?"

"If confusion is part of discovery, then perhaps I am."

"Doubts arise when we struggle to convince our heads of something our hearts already know."

When we prepared to depart the Fifth Dimension, she slipped a note into my shirt pocket. "I love you, Adam. I love you, Tariana. This Moon of Blissful Snow is a land of many blessings, open for all ready to receive them. Illeana will be your guru here. I will see you again when you are ready for another journey."

Another journey?

We drifted to the surface from *Wanderer* and hopped into the shallow snow. Malaika waved her hand, and our belongings floated down alongside. After a decade of reds, oranges, and yellows, we were somewhat blinded by white everywhere. Tari giggled and kicked the fluffy stuff about like a small child. I was delighted as she danced and explored our new environment. Before we could blink, the huge amorphous mass that was *Wanderer* rose into an azure-blue sky sprinkled with white puffy clouds.

A glorious creature stood facing the horizon some thirty feet from where we'd set foot on this Third Moon. She wore a gown that flowed from her neck to the ground like a silvery river. Sparkling jeweled sandals glittered on her feet. We approached in silence. Her long silver locks of hair fluttered in the breeze and fell slightly below her waist. Her exotic slanted eyes blended beautifully with her lightly tanned golden skin. Three pairs of small crystalline wings flexed then folded against her torso – a dyad at her shoulders, another at her breast line, and a third at her waist.

Dazzling.

Tari locked her arm in mine. "Oh, Adam, your gurus are each more astonishing than the other."

"Well," I joked, "the last two are clearly better-looking than Roshi."

A great white steed stood by her side, drinking icy blue waters that flowed through the snow. She reached down and raised and cupped the animal's winsome face with one hand, while plucking and feeding it red fruit from an overhead tree with the other. Their silhouettes covered half of the full red moon.

Fruit growing in frigid temperatures?

She turned her radiant face toward us, apparently aware of my question. "Hello. I'm Illeana. This tree is one of the many miracles here. May you never cease to be amazed by our magic."

I thought her equine was possibly a qilin, but it was two feet taller and sported great wings, at least ten feet across, attached to its back behind a long white flowing mane. The air shimmered, giving the creature an ethereal presence. Its silver eyes seemed to stare into my soul. A spiraling silver horn projected from its forehead. Its long silver tail swished behind.

"Is your horse a qilin?"

"No. It's a pegacorn – predecessor to the qilins."

"I've never heard of a pegacorn."

The animal wore a silver chain of armor that held dozens of large sparkling gemstones. Upon its head, above its eyes, sat a halo of silver links holding clear, sparkling jewels.

"This is CloudChaser. With powerful wings it can fly anywhere – into the far reaches of the Universe."

Hmmmm. Quite an assertion.

"Your pegacorn is magnificent," marveled Tari. "Such a beautiful creature."

Illeana gently stroked its head. "CloudChaser is always near to me, my faithful friend, my constant inspiration, my only source of transportation. You'll find it a good-hearted, gentle creature, always eager to help."

"Is it male or female?" I asked.

"Actually, it's both. But I often say 'her' because she lays inseminated eggs by herself to create offspring."

I chuckled and glanced at Tari, who looked equally confused. "A self-impregnating egg-laying horse? Come on."

"Absolutely. Several eggs every year."

"Can we touch her?" Tari queried, already reaching forward.

"First let's get to my home. I'll ride on CloudChaser." She pointed to our left. "There's a noli over there for you – a gift from Westin. Your things will be taken to my house later."

CloudChaser bowed and knelt to accept her. Illeana raised up adroitly to take a seat sideways, aided by one of CloudChaser's feathered wings. Our new guru reached forward and fed her pilot a final fruit, which the pegacorn devoured in a single bite. "Thank you, my lady."

Once again, a talking animal.

As we stepped through the snow toward our noli, I had to restrain Tari's frolicking. When we entered our shiny silver vehicle, Illeana took hold of CloudChaser's mane and they took flight. We followed close behind.

Illeana's home rested on a snowy hilltop, looking out over a large lake toward an ice-capped mountain range. Two enormous peaks formed a 'V' through which river waters flowed. Our guru floated down from CloudChaser and gestured across a snow-blanketed area. "Your new home is a mile away in that direction."

As we entered her house we were awestruck by the beauty of her home. A glass façade yielded breathtaking views, in all directions, from throughout the living area. "You must be tired after your long trip. Your room is up in the loft, the first door on the left. Perhaps you might freshen up. I've invited several of your new neighbors for dinner tonight." When we got to our room, we read Malaika's note.

"My dearest Adam,
Sometimes you have to travel a long way to find what has long been nearby.
Your days on the 1st and 2nd Moons have paved the way for this moment.
Go forth with enthusiasm on this Moon of Blissful Snow.
Love generously and unconditionally.
Speak kindly and care deeply – especially for the least of these.
Understand that this destination is not a place, but a new way of seeing.
Move beyond the past to a more meaningful future.
Have you made mistakes? Of course, as has every human. Forgive yourself.
Love yourself, so that you might genuinely love others.
May every word that passes your lips mirror emotions within your soul.

May self-interests yield to selfless service.
Here you will discover yourself, your true purpose, and inner joy.
Go where there is no path and leave a trail.
As always, know that I am here for you, even when I am not seen.
Love, Malaika."

We reread and embraced every word. Her message struck deep chords.

I cradled my wife's hand in mine. "I love you, Tari."

"I love you more, my husband."

My wife appeared more beautiful than ever as she gazed into my eyes. We freshened up and headed downstairs – ten minutes before the guests were to arrive. Illeana greeted us and waved her hand. A flurry of snow dust swirled around as two flute glasses magically appeared – filled with sparkling wine. Tari displayed a joyous smile as her wine glass floated to meet her hand.

"Are your accommodations to your liking?"

"Absolutely," answered Tari. "We might move in."

"Well, the views could be better," I joked.

Illeana's dark brown eyes twinkled below gray brows and lashes. "You'll be staying with me for just this one night. Your belongings have been sent to your new home, where you'll be settling in tomorrow."

Tari beamed. "I can hardly wait. We haven't seen our new home yet. Not even via *swish*. Westin wants it to be a complete surprise. As you must know, our move happened quite unexpectedly."

"You'll find your new home beautiful, with views at least the equal of mine. Westin has sent a crew to do some of the unpacking ahead of your arrival." Her muted pink lips added to her rare beauty. "There will still be lots of decorating to do, and I'd love to help, Tariana."

"Wow. I'll happily accept your offer."

"I know you might not like this question, Adam, but folks here will ask you why you've come to reside on the Third Moon."

"Pretty simple. I've got a new assignment, as does Tariana. We're both excited to start here." I squeezed Tari closer to my side.

"May I ask about more personal goals?"

I spoke boldly, holding my head high. "I plan to become Tezhouse CEO and possibly Chairman."

"No. I mean more personal."

More personal?

I paused, lowering my eyes in reflection. "Well, I know I want inner peace, which I never find in my work. I want to share with others what I've learned. I've been greatly rewarded materially, and I'd like to begin giving back. I'm not certain what that entails. Or whether it best be done as head of Tezhouse or in some other role."

"However and wherever you give selflessly, you will receive far more in return." Her eyes lingered on me a moment – then she turned to my wife. "And you, Tariana?"

"I have a clear path to giving back. I'll be leading TSU, a dream that never was. I'm hoping for an end to the interpersonal conflicts Adam and I experienced in the past. I'm looking for our fairy-tale love affair, richer today than ever, to further mature. My top priority – I want to be a good wife – and of course a good mom."

Illeana smiled and cocked her head as if she understood something we didn't. "A suitable place to pause our conversation. The guests are arriving. Let's go greet them."

We met two dozen warm and welcoming neighbors at Illeana's lovely dinner party. The foods and wines were scrumptious – the conversation even better. This time, unlike the welcoming dinner Ambrosia hosted for us on the Second Moon, I was delighted to meet new folks. The party ended with a glorious Taoset smiling on us in silent delight. Illeana led us down to the lake where she sat with CloudChaser. The magnificent ice-capped mountains in the distance remained lit by the evening glow.

"You are both in a special time – in a beautiful place. Feel the soft breeze and smell the crisp winter air. May this scene fill you with hope as you release the past. Take this opportunity to evaluate your lives, explore your purpose, think about what might lie ahead, and make needed changes. Surround yourselves with people and chores that bring you inner peace."

We chatted for a while, returned to the house, and said goodnight before taking the winding staircase to our room. While getting ready for bed, a sharp abdominal pain doubled me over. I maintained my composure – not wanting to alert Tari.

Worry kept me tossing and turning all night.

CHAPTER 35

TARI: A DAY WITH ILLEANA

After Adam left early for headquarters, I enjoyed a relaxing breakfast with Illeana. We sat on her rear patio, gazing at the grandiose mountains. While the temperature was lower than on the Second Moon, I felt surprising comfort as Tao welcomed us with morning warmth. I wanted Illeana to better understand me, and Adam as well. I wanted her to help us through this next phase of our journey.

"Thanks for everything, Illeana. You've filled our first steps here with hope."

Her smile glistened in the morning light. She got serious right away. "Happy to do so. Tariana, I want to continue yesterday's conversation. You referred to your love affair as a fairy-tale adventure. Have there been rough spots amidst the positives?"

I pulled my warm coffee mug closer. "Fairy tales are never without adversity."

"Yes. Otherwise, they'd be boring. There'd be nothing to learn. Princes slay dragons and trolls. Wicked stepmoms enslave innocent maidens. Cauldrons of witches spread fear. Heroes suffer for years in horrible prisons. It's the fairy-tale ending that we dream of and live for."

"Adam and I have struggled. But I wouldn't trade a minute of the ride. Today I'm optimistic as we begin a golden stage of our life."

She lifted her brows. "Are you certain your troubles are behind you and Adam now?"

"I'm hopeful they are." I traced my finger around the rim of the mug, searching for the right words. "We've fallen into deep, dark valleys, but our love has survived. I'm certain we'll experience a few more bumps in the road, but I'm optimistic we'll be able to address any new challenges early to prevent them devolving into serious conflicts."

"I'd love it if you'd share lessons learned during your marriage, so I might pass on to others."

"Sure. When we wed, Adam and I committed for better or worse. When faced with 'worse,' we stumbled . . . badly. For years. I was actually talking divorce."

"So, you and Adam argued?"

"Oh, my, yes. Of course. He often lost his temper. I overreacted at times. We've each placed self-interests over our marriage. Even worse was when we stopped arguing and didn't speak with each other."

"Your intimacy must have suffered." Her question didn't feel intrusive.

"There was a two-year period without any intimacy. Oh, we might have had sex a few times. But without intimacy. That was worse than no sex at all."

Illeana stood and opened her six wings as she gazed off to the mountains. "Did you ever worry it would all end in failure?"

"Yes. When I threatened divorce, I meant it. I shut him out at times, as he did me. We each said horrible things. But through the worst of times, I cherished Adam as my life's greatest blessing."

She turned back to me "What saved your marriage?"

"We were virtually done. Our love in the beginning had been unconditional, but over the years we each placed conditions on it.

Then a miracle happened. In an awful place called Kamyabi we rediscovered each other and our love affair. It was in hiding but not dead."

I brushed some snow off the table as I continued, "We forgave our grievances and placed them where they belong – in the past. A successful marriage requires forgiveness."

"I hesitate to get too personal, but were there . . . infidelities along the way?"

"No. We remained faithful to each other even through the darkest of times."

"I'm sure that helped with your healing."

"Since the day we headed out of our dark tunnel together we've focused on the light ahead, instead of the blackness in the rear-view mirror."

Snow danced through the air. I would never grow tired of the crisp wintery environment. I delighted in the flakes brushing my face, the taste upon my lips, the smell in the air.

"Illeana, they say no two flakes are alike."

She beamed at her chance to marvel at the beauty of nature. "Ahh yes. All different shapes and sizes." She held out a finger to catch one flake, then another. A wave of her hand had dozens of them spinning magically. "Just like humans – each is unique. Each human brings different talents, passions, dreams, and purpose. They make choices and achieve much, in accord with their abilities."

"Adam says back in his homeland all people look and act pretty much the same – and nobody has any purpose or dreams."

She sat back down as she released the flakes. "How terrible."

"Our children are quite different, like two dissimilar snowflakes." I couldn't control my smile at the thought of them.

"Speaking of your children, were they ever impacted when you and Adam stumbled?"

"We always kept our differences from them, as best we could. When he was home, Adam remained a terrific dad, albeit far from perfect – because work demands and clubbing dates often kept him from Tojo and Kaleeva."

"It's wonderful that your children cherish the good times they spent with their dad."

"The three of them, Adam, Tojo, and Kaleeva, are pals. They love each other to death. I helped. I've always told my children when their father returns from a trip or a tough day at work they should run to greet him, because he thrives on their hugs and kisses."

"Is he their hero?"

"Absolutely." A warm feeling swelled in my chest. "He's my hero as well."

Illeana stood and motioned me back into the kitchen. "I believe the two of you are on a path to a rewarding life, one beyond Tezhouse and TSU. I'd like to help guide you there. Now let's head over to your place. I want to see your face when you discover your new home." We packed some snacks and wine knowing we'd find none there.

Illeana climbed on CloudChaser and patted her back. I was nervous about hoping aboard, but her pegacorn turned to me with a look in his eyes that oozed of friendship. My heart fluttered like a child's when we lifted off the ground and glided through a wispy snowfall. CloudChaser landed as light as a feather on another hilltop – where I fell instantly in love with views of our new home and the ice-capped mountains. It was like a real winter wonderland – with sweeping snow-blanketed lawns, a glorious icy lake, and rolling white hills in every direction.

Adam will be amazed when he sees this.

With tears in my eyes, I hugged Illeana as we danced through the white stuff. "It's all beyond my wildest dream. Adam and I are soooo blessed."

When we moved into the living area I ran my hand across a luxurious fur blanket draped over one of the soft leather sofas facing a stone fireplace. Illeana snapped her fingers and a pleasant fire sprang to life.

As we settled in for snacks, Illeana spoke. "Tariana, I've never married. We gurus never do. But most of those I help are married. So, I'll appreciate any further tips you might share so I might better help others who find difficulties in their marriages."

"Wow. A guru asking me to be a guru." We both smiled and chuckled. "Illeana, couples need to communicate – openly and often. Each partner needs to use their ears, twice as often as their lips. Spouses must never let tiny wounds become infected with cancerous animosity. Advise those in your charge to never go to bed angry."

"Great advice, Guru Tariana." We laughed again.

I took a sip of crisp white wine. "Selfless love is the goal. It doesn't bloom overnight. It takes time, patience, and forgiveness. It must not wither as life becomes more complex. Rather, it must deepen with shared challenges and experiences."

Illeana joked, "If you've still got more advice in your quiver, I'll help you apply for a guru license."

I smiled and went on, "Before we married, we didn't have sex. We became best friends. Throughout our married life, we've remained sexually faithful, through the worst, and remained honest, even when arguing. Date nights, whenever possible, have helped us focus on how blessed we feel to have each other."

"Have you always been totally open with each other?"

"No. We hold some secrets from each other."

"Even now?' She tilted her head.

"Yes."

She knitted her brows as if processing the information. "Well, having secrets is a bit out of sync with what you've been saying."

"I think it's okay to have a few secrets, as long as both mates remain humble and selfless. Some secrets, if shared, would only do harm. I call it compassionate fibbing to hide them."

Illeana nibbled on the snacks and nodded. "I get that."

"Also, couples must avoid judging each other. They should explore common interests and do things together. And always celebrate anniversaries and special moments, relishing fond memories."

Illeana paused and stared at me, her eyes glowing. "You are special, Tariana. I am blessed to have you as my new friend . . . and as my guru." She took my hands in hers. "Anything else?"

"One final thought. A good marriage is one where two people complement and complete each other – a union where two become one. One where the sum of one plus one becomes greater than two."

We finished our light meal and did a bit of decorating in each room. Illeana helped me bring our belongings to life, as we transformed the house into a home. We placed memorabilia on shelves, hung artwork, and framed photographs. Carpets that Adam and I had collected rested perfectly on marble floors. Our mostly white dwelling came alive in brilliant colors.

When Illeana rose to leave, I gave her a hug. "Thank you for your help. Nobody needs or deserves such opulence. This only inspires me to give back more – to have Adam by my side as I do."

Before stepping outside, Illeana whispered unknown words and waved her hands toward all areas of the house. A fresh breeze brushed my hair back, bringing with it a sense of peace and belonging. "What was that Illeana?"

"It was my blessing for you, your family, and your space." With that she winked and floated out the door toward CloudChaser.

Not long after she departed, Adam arrived from work, eyes wide in amazement. "Wow. I love everything, Tari. You've found perfect spots for all our things."

I wrapped my arms around his neck. "Couldn't have done it without Illeana's help."

We swished Westin – to express our gratitude. "Thank you. Thank you. Thank you."

"You are most welcome. Enjoy. We've asked a great deal of you, and over the years we've disrupted your lives several times. We appreciate you, even though at times it must have seemed otherwise."

I was sworn in as TSU Chairwoman the very next day. Illeana joined as a volunteer. Her goodness impressed everyone, as she graciously opened her heart to the physically and spiritually hungry.

That evening, I shared my joys about my new job with Adam. "My lover, there is nothing that touches my soul like serving those in need."

"I want to find that someday myself. I'm going to volunteer more." He winked. "And you can be my boss."

I joked and pinched his cheek, "You'll have to work your way up the ladder before reporting directly to me."

The silver moon had become a new home for me. Adam said the same. We would no longer have to show up at phony parties, spend time on yachts with business types we barely knew, or wine and dine at fancy restaurants. I'd be spared making nice to folks I neither liked nor respected. But I worried Adam would find the political parts of his new assignment unpleasant. He hated politics. When I broached this, he responded, "If I'm to take the next step at Tezhouse, politics has to be part of my life."

"Adam, as you get more involved with government officials here, and enter the political theater, or better yet the jungle, I hope you can manage the negatives, and spare me the phony social life we struggled with earlier."

He squeezed my knee and promised, "That life is in the past."

I stared into his eyes. "There's a good man in you, Adam of Novana."

He smiled. "Perhaps, but at times I've had to dig deep to find him."

Adam groaned, and bent over, holding his stomach.

"What's wrong?"

"Nothing. Just stomach acid."

He's hiding something from me.

CHAPTER 36

POLITICAL FLAMES AND SICKNESS

Pain intensified in my swollen belly. My concern was growing by the minute. Something was wrong. But I had to hide this from Westin. *I need to get this checked out. But I never see doctors.*

We met in Westin's office – an office I'd someday inherit. "So, Adam, do you like my Tezhouse dwelling?"

"It's intimidating yet inviting at the same time." The smell from a leather chair was not to my liking, but it greeted my ailing body with a warm embrace. "Extremely neat and orderly."

"Hopefully, it will be yours someday. For now, your digs are next door."

I'd never served in a staff role before. And I had misgivings about this one. But I began positively. "I'm indebted for all you've done for me."

"Thank me a couple of years from now when you're buried in new challenges – making your past struggles look like walks in a park."

I was not anticipating a bed of flowers, and I appreciated his frankness, but I joked in return. "Oh. I came to the Third Moon to perfect my clubbing."

He chuckled, "That's a hopeless cause. Seriously, this morning is an opportunity for you to ask questions and voice any concerns."

A sharp pain pierced my gut. "Well, you've told me I'm going to get involved in politics. I hate the stench of that word."

"That's 'cause you're misunderstanding the word. You're persuaded by the corruption in politics. The good things done get buried by the bad. Any system of governance involves power over others – be it across Taoland, in our corporation, or in a community. It's only as good as the people involved."

I shook my head. "But I have no political skills."

"You argued you had zero business skills when we sent you to the Second Moon." He held his hands, palms up, out at his sides. "And you exceeded expectations. What you don't realize is you're already an accomplished politician. You've been great at the game throughout your career."

Me . . . a politician?

I grimaced. "Kindly explain."

"Politics involves applying your skills to influence others. You've been an influencer since your first day at Tezhouse – with fellow workers, bosses, members of your teams, customers, suppliers, and the like."

"An influencer?"

"You constantly win others over with your words, charisma, good humor, honesty, and sincerity. Most importantly, with your vision and ideas. That's exactly what politicians do."

"I've long been concerned about how I bend the wills of others to my own. Cunning always feels dishonest, even sickening. Manipulation never brings me joy."

Hand on his chin, Westin pondered his response. "Manipulation is a harsh word. In your case, I prefer the term 'leadership.' You guide and inspire. You come up with out-of-the-box concepts others then internalize. You have the essential skills of a good politician – and those needed in an effective CEO."

"I've never considered what I do to be politics. I do what I do in my own self-interests – not to help others."

Once again, he offered a measured response, "All humans act out of self-interest to varying degrees. In advancing your career, you've secured new business – preserving jobs and creating new ones in the process. Your personal ambitions match well with those of your employer – that's a good thing."

I thought about the truth of his words. *I do help others.*

My thoughts turned to darker things. "What about Bogart? Do you consider him a politician?"

"Heavens no! To call him a politician would do gross disservice to even the worst of politicians out there – although many politicians do sadly get things done his way. Bogart's a bully. An intimidator. A blackmailer. Instead of inspiring others with ideas, he extorts and acts with vengeance. Instead of leading by example, he threatens – and creates fear in others. But he's outta your life now."

"He sure frightened me for years."

"It's normal to fear evil. Facing one's fears is the first step toward conquering them. Bogart is a lowlife insecure piece of shit. Forget he ever existed. Focus on the recognition coming your way. Receive this not out of pride, but to promote a healthy sense of self-worth and confidence."

We further discussed how I would use my talents to woo the Tezhouse Board. I wasn't as confident in my skills as Westin was – but his words encouraged me – and gave me a needed boost.

Randahl was a viable alternative as the next CEO, but I was the better choice, and I was resolved to convince the majority of the Board members of that.

"Adam, you'll be entering politics starting with replacing me as a corporate advisor to the Taoland General Assembly." He turned to grab a folder on this.

Another sharp pain struck inside my abdomen. I let out an audible groan.

He whirled around and looked at me anxiously. "What's wrong?"

"Just a few lingering issues from the beatings I absorbed in Aboodin. My wounds have taken longer than expected to heal."

"Then take more time off."

"No," I lied, "I'm OK."

"See a doctor. That's an order."

I squirmed in my seat and lied again, "I will. I promise." I changed the subject. "But please, tell me more about my role with the General Assembly."

He handed me the folder. "I lobby the members on behalf of Tezhouse, promoting policies and programs we endorse. You'll go with me the next few times, and then assume that role fully, as I step away."

Sweat gathered down my back from the pain, but I maintained my composure. "I'm good with that, as long as it doesn't involve bending the rules."

With the flick of his fingers, Westin brought up information on a holographic screen. "I've also had you assigned to chair the Taoland Human Rights Commission." The organization's animated logo played out on the screen. "It's one of the most important task forces in the land. This role will feed your desire to make a positive difference, as you're doing in Aboodin."

I leapt from my chair, unable to contain my delight, or possibly to get away from the pain. "Thank you. I love this. So will Tariana. I'm really honored. I will give this my all."

"If you do well in your assignments, and I know you will, you'll shortly be serving in public office, without the need to start at the bottom. Within a year, you'll be selected for the position of Governor of the Third Moon."

His lofty plans had me pining for the future he envisioned for me. "Can I do this while serving as your Executive Assistant?"

"Yes. It's a nonpaying part-time role, intended to bring private sector expertise to the public sector. It only involves a day-long monthly meeting."

"Will I have help?"

"You'll have a great assistant, Vickely, the woman who serves as chief of staff to the outgoing Governor. She'll schedule, organize, deal with daily issues, draft speeches, ferret through junk, and simplify tasks for you."

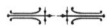

<hr />

I returned to Tari with the news. She was thrilled about the role I would have with the Human Rights Commission.

"What about you being named CEO?"

"All of this will groom me for that role."

She frowned, not hiding her feelings. "Something screams at me every day about that. I know your becoming CEO is wrong for us. Do we really want to spend the rest of our years with Tezhouse?"

I pulled her in for a hug and pressed her head against my chest. "I like what I heard from Westin. But I've told you – every day I'm becoming increasingly conflicted. I'll never make the decision about the CEO role unless you come fully on board. It's a decision not for me, but for us to make."

The yearning to become CEO had been consistent throughout the years, and I still felt it in me, but I was growing increasingly unsure that was my true purpose.

<hr />

Over the next year, my pains waxed and waned. While they never disappeared, I convinced myself the worst was behind me. My transition as Westin's Executive Assistant went smoothly. Board members, well, four of them at least, welcomed me. As did most in the General Assembly. I performed well leading the Human Rights Commission. Tari and I spoke frequently about a future different from the one promised at Tezhouse. We grew ever closer over our common desire to help others.

The only secret I kept from my soulmate was about my lingering pains. I kept hoping they'd go away for good on their own, but I knew underestimating my health problems was just plain dumb.

I was appointed Governor of the Third Moon soon after I began my second year with Westin. I was grateful for the incredible help Vickely provided. The next three-plus years proved challenging, productive, and quite enjoyable. Tari and I committed to our new responsibilities. She thrived as Chairwoman at TSU, where I frequently volunteered. I accepted my pains, now mild, as the new norm. I continued kicking that can down the road and never scheduled any doctor's appointments.

We enjoyed quality times with the kids during their visits with us. They both became expert skiers. We all loved our month-long annual vacations to the First and Second Moons. We s*wish'd* all the time. We attended Kaleeva's High School Graduation, and later Tojo's University Graduation. We met and fell in love with Tojo's girlfriend, who then became his fiancée. Tojo began to share my love of clubbing, and my bond with my son grew. I often thought back to those lonely times in Novana and how I would have missed all of this had I not made the decision to leave with Malaika.

My internal physical pains kept coming and going. I learned to live with them because I was totally healthy otherwise. I did my best to brush them off as an anomaly. Good days and bad days. Through good months and not-so-good months, I continued to keep my health issues secret.

Something is wrong. I've ignored this far too long.

I shared my activities daily with Tari – and frequently with Westin, Komourin, Roshi, Abraham, Ambrosia, Illeana, and even with Diazamel, who was experiencing political challenges of his own. I was blessed by each of my advisors. I continued to thrive in my political roles. I loved providing voice for the many who felt they had none. I applied balanced centrist views and advocated for limited governance. I would argue with fellow politicians, "The people must self-govern. Our role is simply to keep them safe."

I only endorsed centralization and Taoland-wide programs

where synergies provided cost efficiencies. For all else, I urged decentralization – leaving most authority locally with the voters. Others in the General Assembly strongly disagreed, suggesting 'common folks' were incapable of making wise decisions. I held my own. Advocating for the people became my purpose in politics.

I traveled quarterly for Board meetings in Aboodin, where supporting Diazamel added meaning to my life. During one visit there I brought up the topic of governance. "Diazamel, some in Tao City constantly argue for bigger government. My years in Novana taught me the perils of centralized authority."

"Of course I agree with you, Adam."

"I always worry about keeping technology in check here. I pray Taoland never repeats the mistakes made in my homeland."

We were walking through the gardens at his Palace hand in hand. "Adam, what you and I are implementing with *Awakenings* will enable self-governance. For centuries, our centralized command in Aboodin never allowed robots to control, but the results were similar. We unconsciously destroyed human creativity and ambition by providing everything, making the people dependent on us – just as those in your homeland became enslaved to the Plakerols."

"I hadn't thought of that comparison."

I winced and doubled over in pain.

"Something wrong?" Diazamel panicked and pulled me up.

"Just some stomach gas. I hate it."

He roared playfully, "I'll bet others around you hate your emissions."

Glad for his humor, I changed the subject. "The belief that people can be happy if relieved of responsibilities and challenging work . . . let's hope we send that idea to the dustbins of history."

He nodded in thought. "We both know those enslaved to dictators or machines can never be happy. Everyone needs to be free to make their choices about how to live a healthy, free, purposeful, and enjoyable life. We must allow them to take risks, make mistakes, and yes – fail."

"Diazamel, I never say this – but I always treasure our talks. I've been coached by bright minds in Taoland. But none smarter than you. I'm gonna start calling you 'My Guru' – instead of 'Your Majesty.'"

He howled. "A huge demotion, my friend."

As I laughed I let out a scream and grabbed my stomach. "Adam," he shouted angrily, "enough is enough. Something is very wrong. You're not being honest with me. You've not seen any doctor."

I waved him off. "It's just an intestinal issue, easily managed with meds."

"See a doctor. That's a royal order! Do not return here without a diagnosis."

I promised I would and headed back home soon thereafter.

A week later I'd forgotten his admonition as I again buried myself in work. I wanted to be a team player, but my core values were often challenged – especially when others in politics invited me to 'go along to get along' or risk being marginalized. "Adam, you've gotta vote with us, at least this time," they would implore.

For most of them, politics was a career. They made valuable connections and enriched themselves, caring little about their constituents. Most, I suspected, entered public life hoping to influence positive change. But constant adulation and power easily corrupted them, as did money and the promise of higher office. I had no wish to climb any political ladder. I entered politics only because Westin insisted.

Late one day I *swish'd* Abraham to cry on his shoulder about my disgust with the corrosive atmosphere in the General Assembly. "Abraham, there are way too many perks, especially with lobbyists making life comfortable for politicians, expecting favors in return.

They sign onto legislation with a few good things included, keeping their heads in the sand about the really horrible parts."

He dipped his head in the water; then he resurfaced. "Power corrupts. Integrity suffers."

"Yes. Their lust for power finds them sacrificing core principles to the 'special interests.' They accept horse-trading as the norm."

"Avoid them, Adam. Never allow their behaviors to poison the good man you are."

"It is they who are avoiding me. I am not one of them."

I poured out my thoughts and feelings on the one person I always sought out for counsel. "For years I've struggled. At social gatherings, I find myself alone in crowded rooms. There is no worse feeling. I left a frying pan heated by Bogart to enter a cauldron ablaze in political swill. I'm in smellier shit than ever."

"Then get out, my friend."

After disconnecting from Abraham, I *swish'd* Tari. I told her I couldn't take it anymore. She understood and gave her full support. Then I s*wish'd* Westin. "I've done all you've asked. But I really hate the ugliness of politics. The evils. The bad far outweighs the good. I want out."

He squirmed in his chair. "Come to my office, tomorrow, and we'll discuss."

That meeting never happened.

Before I reached home I was in excruciating pain. My head pounded mercilessly. My body was burning up. I vomited.

I'm dying.

CHAPTER 37

I'M DEAD, I'M ALIVE

I returned home with a high fever. Tari helped me to bed and iced me, head to groin. She was seated by my side, shaking, when she *swish'd* Komourin. "I need your help. Adam is seriously ill. His temp is 103. I'm frightened. Please bring him somewhere for tests first thing in the morning."

"I'll pick him up at 8:00 a.m." He disconnected.

Near dawn, I awoke – screaming in pain, burning up and soaking wet. "T-t-tari. T-t-tari." I discovered Komourin, not Tari, seated by my bed, one hand over his mouth in concern.

"Relax, Adam. Tariana's fine. I found her in the kitchen, sobbing, when I arrived an hour ago. I tried to calm her by saying you've likely caught a 'bug' – easily remedied."

I tried to raise up and failed. "Did she believe you?"

"I insisted on coming up to your room without her. As soon as I saw your condition, I knew what I said was a lie."

My sweats gave way to chills; my entire body shook violently.

"I returned to the kitchen to continue the deception. I forced a broad smile and told her your symptoms match those of others suffering from what's going around. I told her, 'No problem. I'm taking Adam to the best doc in town as soon as he wakes up. It's nothing.'"

Still shaking, I asked, "So did she believe this?"

"Hardly. But somehow I convinced her to head to TSU where she is scheduled to chair an important Board meeting this morning. I told her I'd pick her up if there was any new issue. She fought me. I literally had to push her out the door to a driver I had waiting for her."

My head spun as I maneuvered around in the bed. I was bloated, constipated, and nauseous. Komourin barked sternly. "You don't have the flu. I think you know that. Your temp is almost 104. We've got an appointment at the Silver Medical Center in half an hour. There's something very wrong."

I am dying.

Komourin helped me, virtually lifted me, to his noli. In spite of my pains, all I could think of was the party scheduled for that evening – an important gathering that Westin had asked us to host in our home. I pulled him to a halt. "Komourin, tonight's party is important to Tezhouse."

My priorities are really screwed up.

"My staff will take care of everything." He urged me forward.

"So, the show will go on?"

"Yes. You'll certainly not be there. But Tariana doesn't know that. Assuming the doctor admits you, I'll tell her you're fine but sedated and on IV antibiotics. I'll tell her you'll be staying overnight at SMC for observation. No visitors allowed, as a precaution against spreading whatever you have."

"She won't believe you." It would be near impossible to keep her away.

"I'll tell her they won't let anyone in the hospital. I'll pinch-hit as host at the party. Hopefully, the gathering will distract her. If she protests, I'll come up with a Plan B."

I could barely stand when we arrived at SMC and was transported by wheelchair. After an initial exam, Dr. Springman ordered blood work and a full body MRI with contrast. I managed a question between my groans, "What's wrong, Doctor?"

"Be calm, Mr. Novana. Let me review the test results. I'll be back soon."

I'm dying. He knows it.

I dozed off. Springman was there when I woke up. "Mr. Novana, you've been sedated, and you're now in our Critical Care Unit. Your condition is life-threatening."

I began to protest, but Komourin shushed me. "Doc, what exactly is Adam suffering from?"

"He's ruptured his colon. His intestines are severely torn. There's infection everywhere – the colon, the bladder, throughout his abdomen."

I don't want to die.

"The pictures indicate his illness has been progressing for some time. I'm certain the initial tearing began years ago. His immune system and self-healing abilities over that time have been patching things up, to a degree."

All the pain I'd been ignoring had finally caught up with me. I put my body through hell, but it still held on. But now I was at the end of the rope.

Komourin questioned, "What is his situation, right now?"

"Critical. His body temperature is hovering around 104 in spite of all we're doing to lower it. His heart rate is dangerously high and fluctuating dangerously. This can be fatal or lead to a severe stroke."

"What can we do?"

"The diagnosis is advanced toxic megacolon – a rare disease. It emerged from prolonged lack of treatment for his intestinal problems. I propose we operate tomorrow morning."

I'd done this to myself. Refusing medical care in fear of disrupting my career had led to this crisis. *How stupid!*

Komourin stood up. "Let's do it."

"We'll need authorization from next of kin."

I'm not ready to die.

"I'll bring his wife. So, this has been going on for a while?" His quick side-glance told me he'd suspected as much for some time.

"My guess, based on the pictures, is that the initial perforations started as long as five or six years ago. If he were otherwise unhealthy, with a high BMI, he'd be dead by now."

This likely started when my ribs were splintered in Aboodin. Bogart may have killed me after all.

"Deadly bacteria have invaded his entire abdomen. Hopefully, the cocktail of antibiotics we've started will reduce the infection and lower his temperature overnight. We'll know more in the morning."

"The survival rate?"

"Assuming we can operate, 10 percent, at best."

Good bedside manner? Not so much. This is the end for me.

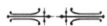

Beep. Beep. Beep. Something was stuffed around my mouth and nose. Tubes? I tried to speak, but no sound came out. I tried to reach toward Tari's tearful, panicked voice – but I couldn't move. Dr. Springman spoke. "No, Ms. Novana, you cannot hold Adam's hands. Or come any closer. Please understand."

She raised her trembling voice. "Adam . . . Adam."

"He's deeply medicated. He can't hear you. He's resting peacefully."

I can hear her.

"When will you operate?"

"We rarely operate on a feverish patient until we get their temperature down to 100. Maybe 101 in drastic cases. Adam arrived yesterday at 104. After 24 hours of icing and antibiotics, we've only lowered him to just below 103. If we don't start surgery now, he'll die later today. But it's risky. I need your authorization."

Tari did not hesitate. "Please, operate. Immediately."

I don't wanna die.

My silent panic went unheard and unseen. Just like my first twenty years in Novana. Even though Tari was there, she remained beyond my conscious grasp.

Tari pleaded, "Tell me he will survive."

"We will do our best."

She sobbed, now violently.

This day is my last.

"We'll start putting him into a deep sleep. You'll have to leave immediately. Surgery will probably take around seven hours. I'll send progress reports."

An overwhelming urge to say the things I'd never said overcame me. There was so much more to live for, so much more I wanted to do with Tari. I wouldn't even get to tell her goodbye. What little awareness I had faded. I floated in darkness.

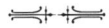

HMMM. BEEP. HMMM. BEEP. HMMM . . . . . .

The pulsing sounds from the machine ceased. The stillness within told me my heart had stopped. The doctor's voice broke through the muffled silence. "He's flat-lined."

I am dead.

My spirit rose toward the ceiling, watching the doctors and nurses frantically trying to revive my body below.

Why are they wasting their time? I'm dead.

I rose to the roof, through a virtual opening. I could still observe the frenzied scene far below where they labored feverishly in vain.

I am dead.

My spirit lifted into the sky. I could no longer see the clinic. I floated like a feather – calmly, peacefully. New scenes came and went at high speed, in waves.

I should have been a better husband. And a better dad.

Beautiful white mountains came into view ahead and blue waters rushed below. All of it was so vivid, brilliantly distinct. I marveled at unfamiliar melodic music. It was as if my senses had been dulled through all my years, and they had now come alive. I felt exhilarated – but saddened at the same time. I'd left the shell of my body and my wife behind and was present in only my spirit. I had no sense of any physical form. I held up my hands to inspect myself but couldn't interpret what I saw.

I am dead. I want to live. I want to be with Tari.

Once over the mountains, I dropped down and found myself flying just above a radiant snowy valley. Every tree and plant shimmered. The soil and rocks glowed. I slowed to discover cloud-like figures, human in shape but faceless, waving slowly in a brilliant white sky. "Come home." They beckoned to me. "Come home, Adam."

A tugging startled my spirit.

"It's not your time yet, Adam."

It was Abraham's spirit, holding my right hand as he joined me. "Turn around, Adam."

"I can't turn back, Abraham. I'm dead."

We were communicating, but not in spoken words. "Turn around. There is more for you to do."

"I do want to do more. I want to live."

"Imagine yourself in a breeze that is soft with the air smelling sweet. Experience the warmth of the Tao. Encounter inner peace."

I visualized myself on a beach, in the early morning, darkness lifting and warmth entering at Taorise. I envisioned Tari and I strolling hand in hand in soothing sand. I replayed the most important moments of my life. They were but few that really mattered. A beautiful white pegacorn rose from the waters and danced into the heavens. I could have stayed in this space forever.

Abraham's spirit broke my trance. "You're flying on the precipice of death. You're at a time and in a place where you can now discover your purpose. But first you must return to physical life, accept who you are, and begin making needed changes."

Abraham offered me a chance to revert to human existence – so I reversed course. I soon lost touch with Abraham's spiritual hand, and he disappeared. I drifted back across the meadows, back over the snowcapped mountains, back to the clinic where the virtual opening remained on the roof. I dropped down to the ceiling of the operating room where my dead body rested aside the flatlined machines. The doctors and staff stood silently – having ceased attempts to resuscitate me.

My spirit entered my body like a feather floating to the ground. The monitors came alive with sounds of life. *Beep. Hmmm. Beep. Hmmm. Beep. Hmmm. Beep. Hmmm.*

Somebody shrieked, "He's back."

"That's not possible." A flurry of movement surrounded me.

"Look. He's alive!"

"This can't be." Hands tugged at the tubes still attached to me.

I'm alive. I'm alive. There is more for me to do.

"It's a miracle."

There's more I must accomplish.

My spirit embraced my body.

My body accepted my spirit.

All went black.

CHAPTER 38

TARI ON ADAM'S NEAR-DEATH EXPERIENCE

I sat at Adam's bedside in silent torture, not knowing if he'd ever wake, weeping most of the time. For three weeks I stayed by his side – yearning for my lover's return. I spoke to my motionless husband frequently – confident he would return to me.

I know he hears me.

Machine noises filled the room, beeping and whirring, controlling his breathing and monitoring his vitals. They never changed. It was the same every trying day. I held his limp hands and gazed into his stolid face. He had always been the most alive, most handsome man I'd known. It was heart-wrenching to see him so waxen, looking like death itself. I longed for his smile.

Adam was in a medically induced coma – a deep state of unconsciousness. After his death and extensive loss of oxygen, Dr. Springman ordered this to achieve a deep state of brain inactivity, alternating with short bursts of energy, to hopefully avoid permanent brain damage and spur the restoration of brain function.

Illeana arrived and gave me a big, comforting hug. "Relief is here, Tariana. Time for you to head to the apartment and get some sleep."

"Thank you, my Angel."

As I was leaving, handing the reins to her, Dr. Springman entered on his morning rounds.

"Good news, Ms. Novana. Great news in fact. All indicators are finally positive. We will start bringing Adam back tomorrow."

"Oh my." My heart leapt from its cavity. "How wonderful."

He is returning to me!

"He's going to do great . . . the process will involve . . ."

I tuned the doctor out. I was sure he was beginning a long-winded explanation. All I wanted to hear was I'd soon be holding my Adam in my arms.

"Thank you, Doctor." I turned to Illeana. "I'll be back for dinner."

Buoyed by Springman's glorious announcement, I walked gingerly through a light snow to the gorgeous apartment Diazamel had generously provided for me and Illeana – just a short distance from SMC. After *swishing* for some soothing music, I enjoyed a cup of michamile tea and fell into a relaxed sleep, dreaming of the man I loved.

<hr />

After a much-needed nap, I returned to the hospital to dine with Illeana, a routine I looked forward to daily. SMC was not your typical health-care facility – but a medical oasis for the wealthy and 'important' folks. The amenities rivaled those at five-star lunatels. Soon after I reentered Adam's room the chef arrived, yes . . . Chef Wes . . . bedecked in a tall white hat, a white double-breasted jacket, and an apron worn over black-and-white houndstooth pants.

"What shall I prepare for you ladies today?"

We explored the dozen choices on the day's menu. Illeana, ever the foodie and full of her usual glee, began. "I'll start with pomodro caprese – then the grilled fish with karooton puree." I selected a crustacean salad and safroni sorooza with forest fungi-mussario.

"I took the liberty of decanting one of my favorite wines for you."

He beckoned us to taste. His selections always blew us away. This one was beyond exceptional – a complex full-bodied red with an oaky vanilla character.

"It'll have to do," I joked.

The three of us chuckled, a respite from the reality of our situation. As he moved to depart Chef Wes exclaimed, "I'll surprise you with a special dessert."

After he'd gone Illeana said, "We must keep these feasts our secret. Everybody thinks we're suffering through dreadful hospital meals every day." We both laughed.

Our first and then our second courses arrived, as always exceeding expectations. We sighed in delight. Mealtime and our accompanying chats always lit up my otherwise dreary days.

"Tariana, we've still not spoken about the day Adam was taken here."

"I've been avoiding speaking about that. Adam arrived home from work the night before with a high fever. 104. He was burning up. I got Komourin to promise to take him to a specialist the next morning – to make sure it was nothing serious."

Illeana rolled her eyes. "Serious? You might have called it that."

"Early the next morning I was in the kitchen when Komourin arrived. He visited privately with Adam. Then he informed me my husband was suffering from a 'bug' going around. He assured me it wasn't a big deal. I was mildly relieved. At Komourin's urging, and over my strong objections, I left for a TSU Board Meeting I was scheduled to chair."

Illeana spoke assuredly. "I suspect what Komourin did was for the best."

I sneered at her suggestion. "He did what was best for Tezhouse. They wanted me to be calm so I could host a party at our home that evening."

"That evening?!"

I grimaced. "Yes. Anyway, while I was at the Board Meeting, Komourin *swish'd* with another lie. He told me the test results indicated Adam only needed antibiotics for a stomach flu and would be staying overnight at the clinic until his fever subsided."

"Did you ask to be with Adam?"

I stiffened, the memory of that pain like a jab in the gut. "When I asked where Adam was, Komourin fibbed again, saying no visitors were allowed. He assured me Adam would be home the following morning."

"I don't know Komourin, but I'll bet he's mighty persuasive."

"Yes. Especially when he wants his way, which is always. He wanted the party to happen. I asked to cancel it, but he insisted it go on, saying it would serve as a distraction. Obediently, I went out shopping for special treats and decorations, knowing Tezhouse would take care of all else."

Illeana raised her eyebrows. "Don't tell me you actually hosted the party!"

I closed my eyes, recalling that night. "Yes. But little did I know Adam was near death. Throughout the evening Komourin propped me up, kept my glass filled with wine, and remained by my side as cohost. I struggled but acted cheerfully, doing my Tezhouse duties."

Illeana's eyes darkened. "Komourin and Westin should have canceled that party."

"No way, Illeana. There was royalty in attendance. And members of the Taoland General Assembly. It was important to them that the party go forward. That's all they cared about – not Adam."

Chef Wes returned with an exquisite dark chocolate cylinder with a smoked nutty praline, accompanied by a stunning milk mousse, pandon curd, and caramelized puffed riccio. We teased in unison. "Is that the best you can do, Chef?" The dessert's presentation was exceeded by the tastes. After he left, we preserved this memory with a *swishpic*, as we'd done a dozen previous times.

"Tariana, do you believe Adam actually died on the operating table?"

"Absolutely. His heart stopped beating for ten minutes. Then he returned."

Illeana placed her hands on her heart. "A miracle!"

"It must have been a message. There's more for Adam to accomplish."

Illeana smiled knowingly. "A message? From whom? From where?"

"I have no idea." With Adam's heart stopped for so long, some force from beyond Taoland must have pulled him back. Something more than just his love for me.

"You must be elated that they'll start bringing him out of the coma tomorrow."

"Elated doesn't begin to describe what I'm feeling. I can't even find the right word."

"Are you worried about how he'll respond? Will he be cognitive?"

I sighed. "I expect to hold my lover in my arms again. Nothing else matters."

"This whole horrible crisis may serve as a life-changer, Tariana."

"Yes. A change for the better – for both Adam and me."

Illeana placed her hands on her chin, pondering her next question. "Do you think Tezhouse will eventually select Adam as CEO?"

"I have no idea. I guess it depends on his recovery." I didn't want Adam to become CEO. In fact, I wished he would never return to work again. I want him released from the Tezhouse chains.

Illeana responded, "I'm certain you hope he will be passed over."

She could read my mind. "Yes. But it's Adam's decision in the end. He says it's our decision. I don't see it that way. He alone must decide. He knows my view and that I will accept his decision."

In the end, I would never prevent Adam from taking the steps he felt were best. But once he recovered, I would continue to gently prod him to a more purposeful course than Tezhouse offered.

CHAPTER 39

CONFUSED AND CONFLICTED

"Adam. Adam. Can you hear me?"

Tari's voice was like the sweetest of all music. But I was neither able to open my eyes to the light threatening to enter – nor could I speak.

"Dr. Springman. I saw a quivering in his eyes."

Illeana shrieked, "I saw it also."

"Yes. The process is beginning."

"It's a good sign, yes?"

I could hear Tari's voice filled with hope.

Springman's exuberance was evident in his voice. "Absolutely. We'll continue tomorrow."

As they hovered over me, a shroud of darkness returned. All sensation faded. After floating in nothingness for a moment my attention focused on a single speck of light seen through my closed lids. The glow was from Adriella. Her healing energy, almost humming aloud, was stronger than ever. Without words she touched my soul, encouraging me to return to consciousness. Before I was even aware of Adriella's departure, a loving hand gripped mine.

"Oh my. He moved his fingers. Adam . . . Adam . . . It's me. It's Tari."

I pried my eyes open to an assault of light. Tari's beautiful face was the first thing I saw.

"Oh, Adam. Oh, my Adam." She hovered over my face, kissing me gently, her warm wet tears falling to my cheeks. "Adam. My dear sweet Adam. You're back."

"Tari . . . my Tariana."

I'm alive. It is not my time to leave this world.

She rested her head softly upon my chest. Overcome with fatigue I slipped back into a deep sleep. With each new day, I spent more time awake, growing stronger. Life is full of catastrophes – none more devastating than death itself. But I'd been granted a second chance. I kept remembering the figures in the white light calling me from the heavens before Abraham turned me around. My death, while unwanted, had been indescribably beautiful. If it was not my time to go, perhaps some greater power was calling me to a higher purpose. I had to seize this day and each of the days ahead.

One day I next awoke with Tari by my side, beaming. I held her face in my hands and wept, "Tari . . . I was dead."

Tears poured from her eyes. "I know. I'm so blessed you've returned. You are the love of my life. You make my life complete."

I managed a smile. "I love you so much." We embraced each other in a hug that felt like forever.

Dr. Springman entered, smiling from ear to ear. "Mr. Novana, you are a miracle. My first ever miracle patient. You died on the operating table. You died! You were gone for over ten minutes. Then you returned. It's impossible. No one can explain it."

I whispered, "Not my time . . ."

"What?"

Still a bit foggy, I turned to try to explain. "I was dead. I left my physical body. It was all beautiful. Then Abraham . . . appeared."

Tari leaned forward. "Abraham? Where? How? Did he speak to you?"

"He said . . . it was not my time." I was probably not making sense.

Dr. Springman reached for my shoulder. "Adam, take it easy. You're confused. You've been in a coma for three weeks. Your wife or Illeana have been with you constantly. Now you must begin your way back – slowly."

Every day I became less dependent on the machines and soon took my first shaky steps with a walker. Dr. Springman coached me while an orderly lifted me to the bathroom. I was finally able to urinate on my own.

The doctor bellowed, "Music to my ears, Adam." Mild applause erupted from those gathered. Hardly a private moment.

"You've had a colonoscopy. The internal rips you suffered were extensive. You're wearing a 'bag' that you'll have to bear with for about five months."

"Darn. I guess no clubbing for a while." My sense of humor had survived.

I knew I'd be sidelined from more than just sports – but that was OK. I would use this time to reflect and consider future options.

"After that we'll do a second surgery to reverse the colonoscopy."

I took his hand. "You saved my life, Doctor. I can never adequately thank you."

His cheeks flushed. "Thank me by getting well."

Although in a deep sleep for three weeks, I'd never been alone. Tari had been there by my side, with Illeana offering relief as needed.

I'm so blessed.

Floods of flowers and messages had poured in every day while I was in coma. These gestures had comforted Tari and now the notes she'd saved comforted me. As personal visits began, I learned over and over about Tari's grace and strength through my extended stay.

I sat on the edge of the bed and held her close. "Tari, I'm certain you were terrified and feeling helpless every day. I don't know how you did it."

She laid her head on my shoulder. "I will never leave you. I've only fallen in love maybe four or five times in my adult life, and it's always been with the same amazing man." She giggled.

"Tari, everything I want, all I need, is right here right now. I will love you forever and a day."

Her warm embrace was pure ecstasy, something more than physical. "Adam, all I prayed for over these weeks was your return. We are soulmates, best friends, lovers. There is so much more we will accomplish now."

I recovered at SMC for another three weeks, putting back on half the fifteen pounds I'd lost. Every morning I'd awake to Tari smiling, holding my hand, showering me with kisses. She massaged my feet, rubbed my neck, gently stroked my cheeks. In the evenings, we enjoyed the facility's amazing dinners. The foods and wines were crazy good, though my diet was restricted.

"I've removed all gas-producing foods from the menu," Chef Wes revealed.

"Bummer. They are my favorites. What kind of chef are you anyway?"

He laughed. Then he left. I asked, "Tari, was the food this delish while I was in a coma?"

"Yup. Only better – because there were no restrictions. I could fib and say me and Illeana suffered through typical hospital meals. But every evening we dined like royalty." She grinned. "Actually Chef Wes was the only reason I visited." She too had retained her sense of humor.

Most nights our meals were topped off with creamy white ice cream, courtesy of Diazamel from afar, with exquisite sauces added by the chef.

I toyed with my lover. "Do we have to leave this place, Tari? The meals here are way better than what you feed me at home." She pouted, feigning insult. She knew I loved her cooking.

Tari's constant presence and encouragement got me back on my feet – eventually without a walker. We walked hand-in-hand out in the bright white hallways. Or Tari walked while I shuffled, taking tiny steps like an old man. One morning before breakfast she announced, "Today, we're going to venture outside. Doctor's orders."

I donned a heavy coat to protect against the cold winds. We strolled into the hospital gardens. Tao was rising, adding sparkle to the snow-covered ground. White winter vegetation graced every space. I breathed in the chilly dry air and came fully alive for the first time since dying. Wintry weather all-stars and other cheery winter blooming bedding plants brightened the scene.

In a bed cleared of snow, with freshly turned soil, the hospital gardener knelt scraping the earth and planting seeds in the frosty winter soil with gloveless hands. "Good morning, sir," I exclaimed. "Beautiful flowers and shrubs. You must indeed be proud."

He looked up and puffed his chest. "We are indeed proud of our frost-hardy plants. These silver ones might look a bit ragged after last night's deep frost. But they will come roaring back when Tao rises a bit more."

I reminisced about Roshi in his gardens. "Sir, the seeds you are planting are tiny."

"Don't be fooled by their size. Never underestimate the power of newly planted seeds, in gardens or anywhere else in life, even in messages to loved ones."

We thanked him for creating such splendor. He waved and returned to his work. As we continued our walk Tari squeezed my gloved hand. "I have something special for you today."

We swept away the snow and sat on a wooden bench. She handed me a shiny device. "With this, you can call up any music, by any artist. I've started by programming the greatest and most electrifying tenor ever."

When I powered on the device the great Pavori stood virtually in front of us. He tossed off every note in the human range – exquisitely and without effort. Each brilliant tone struck deep inside my soul, healing my body. His clear penetrating timbre and outpourings of pure vocal beauty radiated gorgeous warm textures. His voice was the most spectacular of all instruments.

". . . Oh mia aloso . . ."

As soon as the song ended, Pavori bowed to us, generously, and faded from view. I sobbed – tears of utter joy. *I will never forget this moment. I am truly alive – perhaps the very first time.*

We signed out of SMC and returned home to four difficult months of recovery. Wearing and dealing with 'the bag' was unpleasant and smelly. Sharp surgical pains plagued me. There were days when I became grumpy and unpleasant when I should have been grateful. The bowel resection could not have come soon enough. The best part of the whole ordeal was that I grew healthier than at any time since I'd first set foot on the Third Moon. Some higher power had renewed my lease on life. And Adriella was with me frequently, always cheering me up.

My 'death' had provided new insight into who I was and what really mattered. One day, as Tari buzzed around the kitchen, I pulled her to me. "Honey, once again, I could never have made it through this without you. I want this to be a full, permanent recovery. More than a physical one. Tari, grow old with me – the best is yet to be."

She looked deep into my eyes. "It's you and me, Adam, forever."

When my health was largely restored, I resumed my duties as Westin's Executive Assistant, including representing Tezhouse at meetings of the Taoland General Assembly. I also resumed my role of Governor of the Third Moon. I had a new bounce to my every step, and a far greater appreciation for life. My work life was less stressful – I was no longer burdened with business travels. Diazamel directed me to conduct Board meetings in Aboodin via *swish*, for at least six months. I took Tari to lunch almost daily. We had a date night every week where we mulled over future options.

If Tezhouse still wanted me after my near-death experience, I was no longer sure I would accept the top spot if offered. While my destiny was to make important contributions to Tezhouse, our employees, and customers we served, I sensed the seeds of a higher calling, one I could not yet identify.

I want to give back.

Serving others in my role as Chairman of the Tao Commission on Human Rights filled me with pride and purpose. The same was true for my role in Aboodin, where generations would be impacted by our work. I volunteered at TSU – visiting the sick and the elderly – doing what I could to motivate and inspire the depressed – feeding the hungry. I launched a mentorship program there, *Star Searchers*, for young people struggling to find purpose. I began giving back, receiving far more in return, as Illeana had promised.

On one date, Tari and I huddled close on a restaurant balcony hanging over an icy river. Glowing fish looking like orbs of light danced just under the thin ice. I pulled Tari close. "It's amazing. As I lose concerns for all things material, I discover greater self-esteem and a heightened sense of meaning."

"You make my heart sing, my lover."

My increasing involvement in selfless endeavors drew Tari and me closer. I knew she would reluctantly accept me in the CEO role if that was to be. But throughout my recovery she had done her best to pull me in another direction – toward service to the underserved. Illeana supported Tari's views – as did Roshi, Abraham, and Ambrosia from afar. Diazamel wanted me as his forever-partner in reforming Aboodin. My Chairmen and CEO were grooming me to lead Tezhouse. Regardless of my decision, I'd never please everyone. Of course, catering to the wishes of others was a recipe for failure.

Confusion and conflicting options tugged my heart and mind. I grappled with my choices.

Is becoming CEO my purpose – or do I have a higher calling? If yes, what is it?

CHAPTER 40

NEW ASSIGNMENT; CORRUPT OFFER

Westin and Komourin *swish'd*. "We need you to take a meeting in Gradelin – on the other side of this moon, about 4,000 miles from here. The request comes from the government."

I jumped up, spilling my coffee. "Oh, get real. You've got to be kidding or sadistic. I've returned from the dead. My doctor says travel is out of the question."

"We've cleared it with Dr. Springman. It will only be for a couple of days."

How dare they? I'm sure they've pressured Springman to agree.

I bristled and raised my voice. "No way."

Komourin nervously pinched the bridge of his nose. "Adam, we've not made this decision lightly. Your presence has been requested, or should I say demanded, by Adonia, Director of Tao Airspace Incorporated."

Westin spoke, avoiding eye contact. "Adonia governs all the airspace of Tao and its moons. She and her counterparts on the First and Second Moons are negotiating an insurance deal to open up travel and tariff-free trade everywhere."

"I've never heard of Adonia, and I don't give a shit about her. Besides, I know nothing about insurance."

"Adam, she's put the entire deal on hold. She demands your involvement. That's all we know," Komourin said.

"Why me?"

Westin looked directly at me this time. "We suspect your reputation as a deal-closer is her reason. You leave in two days."

They ended the *swish* abruptly. My blood boiled over the summons. When I told Tari, she clenched her fists and shouted—something I couldn't recall her doing before.

"This is outrageous – beyond the pale. You should refuse."

I held her hands in mine. "Last time, Tari. Last time. I promise."

She stormed away – her first angry moment since I'd come back to life.

Several days later I arrived in Gradelin, having no idea what to expect. When I approached the entrance to Adonia's building a sweaty black pegacorn, grazing on a bundle of dried grasses, glared at me, baring its teeth. Fire shot from its frothing mouth. Its stench turned my stomach.

I was immediately escorted to her offices, which were over-the-top grandiose. Gaudy actually. Adonia was about my age. Her mildly plump body, an inch taller than mine, had curves in all the right places, which she openly flaunted with her every movement. A vampish smile gleamed on her round pink face. Her head was far too small for the rest of her body.

A new species for me.

Sparkling pink eyeglasses sat on her smallish nose revealing pinpoint hazel eyes. She rose from her oversized desk when I entered and walked to greet me. She promptly invaded my space and spoke in a sultry voice. "So, you're the famous Adam Novana. I'm delighted to meet you. I've got a proposition I think you'll find to your liking."

She breathed heavily through full red lips. I resisted her allure and rejected any temptation to turn on my own charm. "Well, I didn't come here to listen to any proposal. I'm here to request you reverse your decision to halt the tri-lunar insurance program for air and space travel."

She leaned in. Way too close. Her perfume, which I found noxious, stung my nostrils. "Wow, no small talk from you. Right to your point. And why would I reverse myself?"

"Because that would be the right thing to do – for all Taolanders."

She smirked, mockingly. "Your reputation is one of persuasiveness. So far, I'm not the least bit impressed."

"You know full well free and open trade throughout Tao's airspace would reduce consumer prices and greatly diminishes opportunities for corruption."

She rolled her beady eyes. "I don't give a flying crap about other Taolanders. I thrive on all forms of corruption – it's the most important weapon in my toolbox toward enhancing my self-interests."

My jaw dropped at her blunt admission.

Get me outta here.

"So why have you asked for me?"

"I know of your talents. And of your impeccable reputation of integrity. These will help us pull off something extremely profitable. I want you to leave Tezhouse and become CEO of a new private venture, Tao-Wide Insurance. I'll serve as Chair. We'll each own 30 percent. My two counterparts on the First and Second Moons will hold 20 percent each."

"Sounds mighty dirty. And the three of you could make my vote useless." I wanted to run out of her office and exit her life.

She continued, "We'll 'tax' every mile of personal and business space travel and every export-import deal – requiring insurance against damages, including loss of life. We'll set the rates by travel distances and cargo weights. We'll start with low prices, gain acceptance, then increase rates every year."

She leaned over the table, exposing way too much of her ample breasts as she handed me an amber-colored drink. The smell told me it wasn't coffee.

"Thanks, but no thanks. Not interested. Not in the coffee. Not in your deal."

She shrugged, took a swig, and continued, "Purchasing insurance from us will be mandatory. TWI will be the only provider. We'll set terms to make any payouts difficult. We'll make a killing. You'll be compensated threefold over what you would earn as Tezhouse CEO."

I curled my upper lip and stared harshly. I wanted to say 'fuck you' but, instead, responded with a firm, "I'm leaving."

She fidgeted, playing with the buttons on her silk blouse. "Not so quick, Adam. There will be additional money for you and me to make on the side."

She reached for my hand. I jerked it away. "Goodbye, Adonia. I'm out of here. Have a nice life."

I headed for the door, then turned back to discover her mouth wide open. She wasn't used to being refused. I left her door wide open in defiance. For the first time in my career I walked away from a deal and felt proud for doing so. Losing was winning in this case.

I didn't *swish* headquarters – I wanted to get in Westin's and Komourin's faces. Back at headquarters I barged in unannounced and explained, in the harshest of tones, what had happened. "I met and rejected the most corrupt person I've ever encountered."

Westin bowed his head, avoiding my eyes. "I was worried we were throwing you into something untoward, but hoping it was something legit. Deeply sorry. Of course, you made the right decision."

"I'm pissed. And I'm hurting physically after this worthless trek."

Komourin crossed his arms. "Please forgive us, Adam. We had promised you no more travel, and then we dumped this pile of shit on you. So sorry."

I narrowed my eyes. His half-hearted reply set off something within me, and I suddenly lost control. "You two don't give a crap about me. To Tezhouse, I'm a piece of meat. A slave to go out and capture the victories and profits for Tezhouse." As soon as the words left my mouth, I realized the attack was overly vicious. *What's wrong with me?*

Komourin's mouth dropped. He jumped up from his chair and bellowed, "How dare you speak that way? I only want what's best for you." His eyes saddened with the birth of tears.

I moved quickly to undo the aspersion I'd cast. "I'm terribly sorry, Komourin. I have no excuse for my outburst. Adonia disgusted me, and I took it out on you. Please forgive me."

An uncomfortable silence settled over the room. Then, an obviously shaken Westin spoke. "Forgiven, but not forgotten. I warn you – take more time thinking before opening your yap disrespectfully in the future."

He stomped away, ending the meeting. My outburst had certainly ruined my chances at ever being named CEO.

That evening, Abraham *swish'd*. He did this frequently – whenever he somehow heard my silent cries for help. He'd been my wisest friend since my first days in Taoland. The friend who'd turned me around when I headed into the heavens.

"Abraham, I've come back from the dead, but now I find myself more confused than ever. I don't know what I want or what to do."

I trusted Abraham. He had no skin in the game, other than unconditional love for me. Whenever he appeared, it was always to help me, to inspire me to make something positive happen. I explained my struggles, my growing joy in service-oriented work, my episode with Adonia, and my absurd attack against my bosses. His calm response was unexpected.

"Adam, Taoland and Tezhouse are but fragmentary chapters on your journey. You'll soon enter another unfamiliar abyss. Be brave. Others will remember you not for the safe steps you took but for the courage you showed in risking everything. Alter your behavior and pursue what you now know is your purpose."

"My behavior?"

"Yes. We change our behavior when the pain of staying in the same place becomes greater than the presumed pain of changing. It's time, Adam."

CHAPTER 41

DAWNING OF A NEW DAY

Several weeks later, Tari and I were enjoying breakfast on the patio when Tao's early light peeked over the horizon. The distant mountains reflected in the lake, glistening as if sprayed in silver.

My *swish* buzzed. It was Westin and Komourin. To my surprise Komourin wore a broad smile. "Are you sitting down?"

"We usually are when we're eating breakfast," I joked.

Westin spoke. "The Board met last night, in a special session. We've selected you as CEO. I'll stay on as Chairman for another year to ease you into the job."

What?

I'd not spoken with them about the CEO role since my near-death experience. I half-thought they'd decided it would be too much for me. And I suspected my outburst after the Gradelin incident had tightly shut the door. Although I was not expecting it, their announcement surprisingly left me flat. I felt oddly perplexed and sullen when I should have been overjoyed. This was what I'd wanted all along. Instead of unveiling my confusion, I smiled. "Wow. Thank you both so much."

Komourin spoke with no real obvious emotion. "We need to keep this conversation brief. A follow-up Board meeting will start in a few minutes to formalize some documents. We are delighted – for the two of you and for Tezhouse."

Westin added, "We're planning a press conference in three days."

"The vote was 7–2," added Komourin, ". . . two long-standing Randahl supporters who registered concerns about your health kept it from being unanimous."

Tari's blank expression said it all. I turned back to the hologram. "Can we keep this quiet for a day or two? We'd need to tell the kids."

"Of course. Congratulations, Mr. CEO. Talk to you soon."

After they disconnected, Tari and I sat in momentary silence, holding hands. "Tari, the CEO role has been my quest across three moons – for over two decades. But if I say yes, something huge would still be missing."

Her eyes opened widely. "What would be missing, my love?"

"Everything that matters. And so . . . I'm going to say no."

There. I said it. I literally had to hold Tari up. She shook and sobbed uncontrollably and buried her face in my chest. Her tears dampened my shirt.

"Oh, Adam. I love you so much. Truly, I was not expecting you to say 'no' if and when this moment arrived."

"Being CEO is not what I want. I think I had to hear them finally offer it to realize that. My head wanted to be chosen. Vanity, I guess. My heart kept saying no. I've been constantly confused and wavering. But at the very moment they made the offer *I knew*. I choose you – and my true calling, whatever that proves to be."

Tari raised her head and gazed into my eyes. "Of course, I've felt your inner struggle, my love. Still, I expected your answer would be an unqualified yes."

"When Westin spoke, in an instant, without any doubt, I knew I no longer wanted it. It's like a heavy weight has been lifted. I don't want to be CEO. I want much more – and I want it with you by my side."

The expression on her face was the most beautiful I'd seen since the day we fell in love. "I love you, Adam of Novana, with all of my being." We hugged and kissed gently. Tao breached the horizon as we sat in a silent embrace.

After a long pause, she spoke. "So, what will we do now, former executive Adam – now that you're on the verge of unemployment."

"Hmm. I'm thinking I might go clubbing every day."

We giggled like two young lovebirds. She snickered and poked my side. "You wouldn't dare."

"I want more, Tari. I need to feed my soul. I know if I assumed the CEO role I could make a positive impact at Tezhouse. But I want more of that bliss I've tasted when serving others, regardless of their positions in life. I want inner joy. And I want it every day."

My bride wept.

"Tari, we've been enormously blessed. Now I want to give back – for the rest of my life. I don't know exactly how or where. I'm going to ask if I can stay on for a while on the Tao Commission for Human Rights. And I'd like to continue helping the people of Aboodin with Diazamel. I'd love to become more involved with you at TSU and get *Searching Stars* up and fully running."

"Well, if you fill in an application, and pass an aptitude test, I might consider you for a TSU job, my lover. No favoritism. No nepotism. Of course, your compensation will be miniscule."

We were giddy and continued laughing. I dampened the mood. "After a while, Tari, we'll need to depart Taoland."

"I know, Adam. That's been unspoken, but I'm ready to take that terrifying plunge with you, when the time arrives. I want nothing more and nothing less than to be by your side as we fulfill our promise."

"You know, my ordeals in Aboodin and my dying on the operating table were wake-up calls – opportunities for self-discovery, disguised as catastrophes."

Before contacting the kids, we *swish'd* Roshi and Abraham, separately. Then Diazamel, followed with *swish* connections with

Ambrosia and finally with Illeana. Our message to each was the same. Clear-eyed, we announced our decision, "We're rejecting the CEO offer. We'll be pursuing a far greater reward. We're choosing liberation and true purpose. Thank you for guiding me through my struggles. Thank you especially for putting up with me all those times I rejected your advice."

Each of them showed boundlessly generous support. They offered congratulations for my being selected as CEO and for the decision to turn it down. Our faithful friends proved they cared about us. That was what really mattered. After these welcomed conversations Tari asked, "Adam, is it OK if I *swish* Lorelai with the news?"

"Not yet, my love. I need to speak with Randahl first. Let's tell the kids."

Tojo and Kaleeva were surprised, stunned, overwhelmed, and lovingly understanding – all at the same time. "I'm going to work for your mom, kids. She's gonna be my new boss. I'm fearful she'll crack the whip worse than anything I've experienced at Tezhouse."

"What will you do there?" asked Kaleeva.

"I've started a mentorship program at TSU – *Searching Stars*. I'm mentoring others. It feeds my soul. And I've got a few other things up my sleeve – in time."

A proud smile spread on Tojo's face. "We're all-in. See you soon, Mom and Dad. Can hardly wait for our vacation. Madijen, too, awaits her Grampa and Gramma."

Kaleeva added, "And you'll finally get to spend some quality time with Jeritom. To add to this wonderful moment, we have a nice surprise for you – your first grandson is on his way."

Life doesn't get any better than this.

I swished Randahl and told him the news, advising it was secret until I got back to Westin and Komourin at headquarters. He was stunned.

"I am certain this is right for you, Adam."

"This means you'll be the next CEO."

He squeezed his forehead. "Yes, though I'd long given up on that."

Tari then swished her dearest friend, Lorelai, who was visibly startled, probably thinking immediately about what that meant for herself and Randahl, as she said, "I'm happy for you both."

The next morning, first thing, we swished Westin and Komourin.

"This isn't easy for me to say – but I'm declining your offer. It's a firm no."

They were speechless, but only for a moment.

"You know, Adam, I was half expecting that." Westin's face showed some disappointment, yet he seemed satisfied. "Though, we never spoke about your doubts."

I shared my reasons, as I'd done with family and friends the day before. Komourin surprised me with a smile and thoughtful response. "Adam, I fully understand and completely support your decision. I've never told anyone, but I myself have often been conflicted about service to Tezhouse versus perhaps a deeper purpose. I recall, as if it were yesterday, how I wished for a more meaningful path some twenty years ago, when I assumed the CEO role."

Westin folded his hands, adding, "Our loss at Tezhouse is a plus for the countless individuals you will help. I'm overjoyed you've found a higher calling. But you've caught us off guard. We must quickly move to Plan B."

I smiled. "Randahl will be an excellent CEO."

That evening, the Board confirmed Randahl as the next CEO by a 9–0 vote. I was surprised by an invitation to the press conference, something I learned Randahl had insisted on. Westin made three announcements – Randahl's ascent, the retirement of Komourin, and my departure from the company.

Randahl took to the podium. Lorelai and Westin to his right, Komourin and me to his left. Watching my friend assume the role I coveted for so long filled me with happiness. Randahl spoke: "I thank the Tezhouse Board of Directors for this great honor. I am truly humbled. I stand here fully aware of the responsibilities I will now assume. I commit to serve Tezhouse employees, customers, shareholders, and the Board to the best of my abilities, in the days and years ahead." Applause erupted.

Randahl held his hand up to pause the clapping. "I've asked to stand by my side today, Lorelai, my bride of thirty-two years. She has long been my rock. I would not be here today were it not for her love, support, and counsel." More applause, as Lorelai smiled warmly.

"Before I take questions, I must add I've been much blessed by two brilliant Tezhouse executives who have served as my teachers, role models, and most importantly, as trusted friends throughout my journey. Komourin is retiring for greener pastures after a long and bountiful career. Thank you, sir. You are the epitome of the word 'leader.' You have set an example for all to follow."

Komourin smiled broadly and took a bow.

"Finally, last but certainly not least, I want to thank my dear friend, Adam Novana, who is leaving early to pursue other dreams – lofty goals I admire. Adam, you are the most brilliant, most charismatic, most visionary leader I've ever met. Your genius has touched every one of our current Tezhouse products. Your can-do attitude and integrity have inspired countless employees and the many customers you've brought into our family. Thank you." I followed Komourin's example and bowed.

Tari and I hosted a private gathering at our home afterward. When Randahl arrived, I invited him to join me in my home office. "Thank you much, Randahl, for your kind words. They are etched into my soul. I wish you the best. You'll serve Tezhouse well."

Randahl grabbed my shoulders, firmly. "Adam, I'm thrilled with the decision you and Tariana have made. I'm certain it's the right one. I know you both will continue to impact others in the long life you have ahead." We embraced. The moment was the perfect ending to a wonderful day.

I was called before the Board one last time. Westin, Komourin, and Randahl were present. Only Westin spoke. "Adam, each of us says goodbye with sadness to see you go, filled with remorse because Tezhouse will no longer benefit from your talents, but with overriding joy in knowing you are called to a higher purpose."

The Board rewarded my years of service with an extremely generous bonus. They also presented a *plaque* reading:

> *'In recognition of Adam Novana's important and unprecedented contributions to Tezhouse over three decades. May he be blessed in all future endeavors.'*

A new day had begun.

CHAPTER 42

SERVANT-LEADER

Talents are perhaps the greatest of gifts bestowed on any individual. I was now free to apply mine in service to others. Tezhouse was in my rearview mirror. I'd been liberated to lift others toward the ultimate mountaintop – and bring myself a little closer in the process.

The next few years were my best ever. I proudly sported a new identity. Instead of Adam Novana, Senior Executive at Tezhouse, I was now Adam – a humble servant of those in need, especially those struggling to discover purpose. I reveled in taking *Searching Stars* forward and helping many young men and women turn the lives they once found worthless. As I was doing in Aboodin with Diazamel.

I was blessed to work with Tari and her team in homeless shelters, in hospitals, and in food kitchens. We traveled to be with our family whenever we could, Komourin always generously providing his *Chieftain*. We loved special times with Tojo, his lovely bride, Victoria, and their sweet little girl, our first grandchild, the pretty, bubbling Madijen. We were in the hospital when Kaleeva and Jeritom presented us with our first grandson, Eridru.

During these years, I fully discovered who I was and why I was here. My new life made me a more complete, more purposeful, happier human being. I reveled in the glow of my newfound purpose. Some mornings, Tari would start the day by asking me if I would join her at TSU that day. I would always joke. "Hmm. I was thinking of clubbing today, but maybe it's a bit too cold." Then I usually departed with her.

One day, I met Caleb, a man who taught me what service is really all about. In a few brief exchanges, he touched my soul. He was next in the food line when I, as his server, shifted from one pan of food to another. He was unshaven, disheveled and smelled like he hadn't bathed in a month.

He glared at me and shouted in a rage, "You gave the last guy meat and riccia. Then you give me noodles and cheese. That's not fair, you prick." He threw his plate violently into the air, its contents scattering all about. He stormed out.

What an ingrate! I was taken aback and wanted to storm out myself.

"Why do you do this, Tari? Some come in here feeling entitled. I'd rather teach someone to fish than give that person a free fish every day – especially folks like this last guy."

She wiped her hands on a towel. "I do this, my dear husband, because it makes me appreciate how blessed we are. With a little kindness, a simple smile, or a gentle touch, I might improve a life or two every day. I do my best to tell those far less fortunate, 'You are not invisible. I see you. And you matter.'"

This woman was a special blessing for me as well as so many others. I ran out into the snow after the man. I found him digging in his bag near a bench. His shirt was torn and tattered; his coat threadbare and frayed.

"Sorry. All we had left was noodles and cheese. I wouldn't eat that either. Can I buy you a meal?"

"Why?"

"Just because, my friend."

He smirked. "I'm not your friend."

I ignored his remark. "I'm heading to a restaurant and I could use some company. I'm paying. What do you have to lose?"

He dropped his hands from his hips and relented. At the restaurant, he ordered a steak. I had coffee and some fish. His fingers trembled, his fork wavering, as he took a bite. "First steak I've had in I can't remember when."

"Where are you from?"

"Loozarra."

"Do you have family there?"

"They're all dead."

"Friends?"

He lowered his eyes. "No. I ain't got none."

"Are you having trouble finding work here?"

"Can't find work."

"You've tried?"

He struggled to answer and lowered his head. "I have a prison record. Nobody will hire me."

"Why did you go to jail?"

"When I arrived in Taoland, I was hungry. Homeless. Desperate. I stole a gun, tried to rob a store. Got caught and spent ten years in prison."

Ten years?

I saw him not as a beggar, nor a criminal, but as a fellow human. I saw him not on the outside, but instead I looked within. He had not been blessed like I'd been. "Would you like a job? I can find work for you at Tezhouse, where I used to work. I've got friends there."

He stared at me in confusion. "Why would you do that?"

"I think maybe I should. No other reason."

He paused, then said, "Sure."

"What's your name?"

"Caleb."

I brought him to our home where he took a long shower and shaved. Caleb and I were about the same size, so I gave him some clothing and shoes I no longer wore. Tari made us a nice supper. He slept in one of our guest rooms, then joined us downstairs. "You clean up pretty good," I said over breakfast.

"Thank you, sir, for the clothes – and everything else."

"It's Adam, not sir."

I drove him to Tezhouse where I called in a favor and had Caleb hired into the Shipping Department. He was extremely appreciative and shed a few tears when I left him there. It was a simple, random act of kindness, but helping Caleb filled my soul more than winning a billion-luni contract for Tezhouse. I headed to TSU to meet Tari.

"Why are you smiling ear to ear, my husband?"

"Nothing special. I simply can't remember when I've felt this good."

"Some of that inner joy you've been searching for?"

Yes. And I want lots more of it!

I discovered once again the more I gave, expecting nothing in return, the more I received. Ambrosia's words came to mind. "One only experiences inner joy when helping others." I pondered the misguided path I'd long been on – when my ego and blind ambition led the way. Whenever I volunteered at TSU, I checked my ego at the front door.

Passion for winning had given way to devotion to service. Instead of tossing out money for some charitable cause, partially in guilt, I now wore boots on the ground, giving back to others – listening, teaching, coaching, helping them discover self-esteem – belief in themselves.

One day, I headed off to a roundtable luncheon with my group at *Searching Stars*. I'd been blessed with a handful of special teachers – now it was payback time.

A young guy in my group spoke. "Some of us are stuck, Adam."

"Well, if you stand still, you'll remain where you are."

Another queried, "So, what do we do?"

I stood up from my chair. "Each of us has a life to lead. His or her own journey. Yours will involve a constant search for the answers. We all run into roadblocks. I've been there. I've faced adversities and countless crises. With the support of others, I overcame. You will too."

A small pale-faced man at the end of the table offered his viewpoint. "Adam, we don't know who to turn to, other than you."

I sat on the edge of the table and replied, "Each of us receives blessings from others on our voyages – sometimes when least expected. We have to be open when angels appear. It might be a friend, family member, tutor, mentor, fellow worker, neighbor, therapist – or perhaps a stranger."

One guy grinned and leaned forward. "Maybe a wizard will appear out of the darkness."

"Sure. Why not? And maybe the wizard will tell you the answers rest within. Anything is possible, especially in Taoland. I guarantee, when you are ready, others will always come forward to help you reject self-doubts. Never give up."

Those in the *Searching Stars* program were blessings to me. Everyone, an individual I could assist. Another spoke. "Adam, at every session, you give us hope. But then you leave, and we get slammed by ugly realities. And we come up empty."

"My friends, it won't be easy. You will face frequent rejections, as I have. Just pick yourself off the mat when that happens. When you see your shadow lengthening, be open to new light that will drive it away – new light that can guide you to the truth."

Several members nodded without much confidence. "We will try."

"Trying is a word for losers. Don't try – do it. And don't ever think the world owes you a living. The world owes you nothing. It was here long before you. You must discover and then write your own story, 'cause nobody else will."

Here I was advising them to write their own stories. Heck, I was still working on my own. I continued, "Every road is filled with potholes and barricades. It can be easy to despair. Never let your problems paralyze you. Find courage and ways to crash through every roadblock."

"We don't have your wisdom, Adam. That's why we get stuck."

"Look outside." I led the group to the window. It was snowing fiercely. A small mouse-like creature was struggling, stuck in the snow below, unable to right itself. "It's easy to get stuck like that. That animal needs to relax to free itself." Just as I spoke those words, the tiny being stood up, as if hearing my suggestion. It smiled at us and took bounding jumps toward a forest, disappearing momentarily under the snow each time it landed.

"When facing tough decisions, use your instincts, like that animal just did. Pick a path and take it. If it turns out to be the wrong path, turn around, or otherwise alter course. Standing still is always the wrong choice. It gets you nowhere. Enough for now. I have to leave." I was scheduled to serve at a TSU fund-raising event Tari was hosting.

"Please, Adam. A few more words before you depart for the day. Something for us to ponder until we meet again."

I put my arm around a couple of the guys' shoulders. "Okay. Here are four simple gems taught me by my gurus. First, focus not on what you want, but on what you truly need. Second, never be afraid to make a mistake. Third, always exceed expectations. And finally, never allow the evils of others to become your own wickedness. I'll see you all in a few days." I fed off my students' hunger for knowledge. This new life of service and helping others was the most thrilling of all my adventures.

I left to pick Tari up for the evening event.

Saradev was the Guest Speaker at our charity dinner. She chose Servant-Leader as her topic. I'd read about this concept, but on this night it was like hearing the principles for the first time.

"Leadership is a special skill in service," she advised. "A

servant-leader does not coerce but is an empathetic listener – always ready to hear and understand the words of those who feel they have no voice. For those with leadership talents, you must create vision whereby others might buy-in. You've got to unleash the potential of those in your care – and help them discover their own unique abilities. A servant-leader inspires others to dream dreams that never were. As you acknowledge and reward others you'll be helping them believe in themselves."

Tari and I enjoyed evenings like this. While returning home, we talked about all that was going on. "Tari, I'm loving what is only a start of my new life in service. I get it that my leadership skills are part of that. And I especially feel blessed working closely with you every day."

She put her hand over mine on the seat armrest. "Likewise, my husband. And the children are thrilled for us as well." We knew our calling would soon take us elsewhere – to a place where we would make a greater impact. "I'm agonizing about how we'll tell our children and our friends we must soon leave Taoland. It's going to be heart-wrenching saying our goodbyes."

"It certainly will not be easy."

"If it's okay, honey, I'd like to speak briefly with Roshi." She understood and headed up to bed.

I swished my giant guru and spoke about recent happenings.

"Adam, why did you help Caleb?" Roshi asked.

"He was in need. I was meant to help him."

"Caleb was invisible and you saw him. He was hungry and you fed him. He was thirsty and you gave him to drink. He felt he had no voice and you listened. He was homeless and you provided him dwelling. He was unemployed and you found him work. Caleb was in despair and you touched his soul."

I couldn't stop feeling justifiably proud. "Yes. It all felt glorious. But Caleb is only one person."

"In Aboodin, with your friend Diazamel, you are opening new doors for millions. You will do the same elsewhere. Leadership is your greatest talent. Service is now your mission. Both will become your legacy."

"My legacy?"

"Your story completed. You will become a role model, inspiring countless others long after you are gone. Continue to serve in Taoland during your remaining days here as you prepare for service elsewhere."

I live again. I breathe again. I serve others – now and into the future.

CHAPTER 43

ROSHI AND ZALIFHAR PASS

Coooooo. Coo-coo. Coooooo. Coo-coo. Coooooo. Coo-coo. A pair of mourning doves shook snow from frozen grasses in search of seeds for their daybreak meal. I crumbled a slice of toast and tossed pieces in their direction. They smiled as they scurried to scoop them up. Tari and I brushed fresh snow from our patio table as we enjoyed hot java and warm biscuits. We huddled our mugs close, warming our chilled hands.

Tao was rising in that V-shaped gap between two distant ice-capped mountains. Just above, the Moon of New Beginnings, in its green glory, appeared larger than I'd ever seen. Tao-glitter across the rippling lake waters happily brushed our shoreline. "This scene is my favorite in all of Taoland. I will miss it greatly."

"As will I, Adam."

"When do we tell the kids? We can't keep kicking the can down the road."

Her face fell. "It's going to devastate them. We'll do it face-to-face while on vacation."

Our annual family break was fast approaching. Tears fell from

Tari's eyes, and we hugged. Unexpectedly, Abraham *swish'd*, sadness evident across his usually bubbly countenance.

He spoke somberly. "Hello, my friend. Good morning, Tariana." Without any small talk he continued, "Is there any way you could visit us as soon as possible?"

I answered, "Actually, we'll be headed to Green Fountains in two weeks – our first stop on vacation."

"I'm asking if you can come immediately. Roshi is on his deathbed. He wants to say goodbye to you. The doctor says he will pass within a few days. If you can't get here by tomorrow, perhaps we can schedule a *swish*."

The news shook me to the core. Trembling, I said, "Oh no. I'll get back to you within the hour."

We disconnected, and Tari took my shaking hands in hers. "We must go."

At our request, Komourin immediately offered his *Chieftain*. Fortunately, the First Moon was relatively close at this particular time, reachable in six hours. We arrived as Tao was setting, and checked into the Green Fountains Inn, a short distance away from where we'd met almost thirty years earlier.

We noli'd to Roshi's early the next morning and embraced Abraham, who met us just outside the front door. Our children and grandchildren arrived moments later, and we rushed to greet them. It was a mixed moment – joy in seeing the kids combined with sadness about Roshi's condition.

Abraham spoke. "I'm so happy you could get here. He may not live through this day."

Roshi's gardens were more splendid than the images embedded in my brain. I had failed to keep my promise to visit often after we left for the Second Moon. In fact, I had not returned to my giant guru's place, other than by *swish*, for nearly two decades. Everything was so much more plush, more colorful, and more aromatic than I remembered. Still standing outside the door I pointed to the left. "Tari, look over there. Roshi and I created that section with seeds and cuttings I brought from Novana."

"Adam, is that an apple tree blossoming in your garden?"

I couldn't believe it. The tree stood now at least twenty-five feet high. "Roshi dubbed it the Adam Tree. He told me, all those years ago, the tiny seedling we planted would give birth to a tree that would someday provide food for friends and shade for plants needing it." I brushed away a tear.

Entering Roshi's cottage, the nostalgia, real this time, overwhelmed me. As Abraham headed upstairs, the smell of java thrilled my nostrils, as it had every morning I stayed with Roshi after arriving in Taoland. Cut flowers in vases brought tears to my eyes, knowing they'd been nurtured by the loving hands of the man dying upstairs. My eyes welled up. "I've such fond memories, Tari."

Touching the furniture brought back memories of sitting in the living room and listening to Roshi's stories. More tears flowed as sweet chirping sounds of songbirds blended with the creak of the wooden floorboards upstairs.

"Come up alone, Adam," Abraham called, as he headed downstairs. Roshi's head was propped on his pillow. Deep wrinkles and sallow color revealed his failing state. His gentle smile belied the pain he was suffering. When I sat on the bed to hold him, his once-strong arms felt like feathers. His feeble fingers trembled in mine.

"I love you, Roshi." I winked. "In case you don't know it, you're my favorite guru."

He whispered, his voice barely audible, "I love you too, Adam. You are my favorite pupil." The usual red blossoms in his cheeks had turned chalk-like.

I moved closer. "I'm so sorry."

"For what?"

"For the times I rejected your advice and treated you with disrespect."

"All I'm experiencing today is exuberance. My spirit is soon to be released to begin a new adventure, an eternal one this time."

I knew of the spirit. I'd discovered my own when I died. "You're amazing. I know you're in pain, but you hide it well. I wish I could take it all from you, if only for a moment."

"The pain I bear is slight compared to others. I accept it in gratitude for the many blessings I've been granted over the years, and for all the amazing people in my life – not the least of whom is Adam of Novana."

Tears wet my cheeks. "It is you who have gifted me, Roshi. It is you who taught me so much and served me so generously and so selflessly."

"I tried to prove the best classrooms are found at the feet of the elderly."

"I remember." I stroked his large, weak hand.

"I taught you to plant seeds in the earth. As I depart Taoland, I want to encourage you to go forth and let your heart crumble into countless seeds of love. I want you to capture those seeds in the psalms of your hands and plant them in the hearts of everyone you meet, wherever you may travel."

"I will. You are my blessing, Roshi."

He spoke slowly. "And you are my treasure. I've received no gift in life more precious than the rewards I've received in helping others."

He coughed and winced in pain. I found some water and helped him drink.

"As my ancient body declines, Adam, my mind remains clear. I find myself eternally thankful for the talents given me, the life with which I've been blessed, and for the many opportunities I've had to do good throughout my years."

"I'm finally discovering what that all means, Roshi."

"Outstanding. Guess what, my friend? My bucket list was completed last month when I celebrated my 250th birthday. I was doubting I'd reach that milestone."

How could I have forgotten? "Forgive me, my guru. I'd not marked the date. I wish Abraham had given me a heads-up. Happy belated Birthday. If you can hang on for a few more days, I'll make you a delish chocolate cake – your favorite."

His eyes saddened, and he admitted what we both already knew. "That's not going to happen. I'll not last that long. Besides, you are a terrible chef."

I laughed, then realized it was likely the final joke I'd hear from his lips. He too managed a faint chuckle.

"Roshi, your teachings have altered my life. I cannot adequately thank you."

He whispered again, "Well, as a final thank-you, my dear student, tell me what you've learned. Share with me what you treasure most today so I'll know my lessons bore fruit."

I held his aging hands in mine. "Tari and my children top the list. And we now have two grandkids. Then there are friends, including you and Abraham. I treasure my eyesight by which I see you today. I value my hearing by which I welcome loving words. I have arms with which to hug, a heart with which to love, and a nose to smell your flowers and coffee. These, and the memories we've created, are my greatest treasures."

"Thank you," he whispered. "Each of us has limited space in our hearts. When we fill our lives with things of the world, we crowd out what fills our souls. I can now depart knowing you've discovered this."

"I want to add, Roshi, I even value the bumps in the road I've endured, because each has been a valuable learning experience."

Tears of joy welled up in his eyes, including the green one, which loomed larger but a bit dimmer than ever. "Adam, you cannot imagine how greatly my heart aches in joy as I hear you speak."

"Because of your example, I've welcomed the love of many and have loved many in return."

Rings of bone surrounded his eye sockets. His humongous ears protruded like jug handles, so thin they flopped inward. "In this, my final hour, Adam, my suffering is wiped away by your words – which I detect coming from deep within."

"As do your own words, always."

Another whisper. "Adam, would you grant me one final gift? Tell me – I've asked you many times – have you now discovered your true purpose? Who you are? And why you are here?"

"I am Adam. I'm here to serve others."

Roshi squinted, now sobbing. "Oh, thank you. I can now go to my reward. But understand, I will remain forever in your life." His head relaxed back as he nodded off.

I shook him gently to no avail. *This can't be the end.* I stayed on.

His consciousness resurfaced. "You've long been . . . part of my life as I've been part of yours." He took a ragged breath. Our friendship lives on in each other's memories. Wherever you go, know that I am there with you. Live well and selflessly . . . for all of your physical life that remains. That is all I ask."

Those were the final words I heard from this amazing man. As he sighed his last breath, a faint light hovered over him and then slowly floated out the opened window. It was Adriella. I sat in silence until Abraham cracked open the door. When our eyes met tears erupted.

The 'Celebration of Roshi's life' was conducted in the large pagoda down by the pond. Tojo and Kaleeva joined Tari and me. Abraham officiated and offered a touching eulogy. He engaged several water sprites in the pond to perform a farewell display for Roshi. They danced and twirled, sending water sprays above the surface where they reflected rainbows in the Tao light. He asked if others would like to say a few words. When it came my turn, I spoke through salty tears raining upon my lips.

"Roshi was the first person I met in Taoland. He taught me a lot. To laugh and to play. To consider one's life toils as managing a farm – to envision, plan, prepare, seed, feed, nurture, reap and harvest. To know you cannot do it alone. To respect all others. To be always honest and faithful. And when the day's chores are done – to lie in the grass in appreciation. His lessons were simple. His lessons were profound. His lessons will remain with me forever."

Roshi's frail remains, wrapped respectfully in emerald-green silk, were carried to a raft, built by Abraham's hands. A group of us poured a fragrant mixture of myrrh, cassia, and cinnamon gently on his clad body. Abraham lit the oils and coaxed the raft toward the center of the pond. The scents of burning incense filled the air. Perfumed pure white smoke reached into the skies.

All present were startled when a trumpet-like sound rose from the flames. A majestic eagle-like bird, adorned in bright red and golden feathers burst from the flames. It flew through the smoke and disappeared into the heavens.

In stunned amazement, I asked, "What was that?"

Abraham put his arm around me. "That, Adam, was a fenghuang – a symbol of hope, rebirth, and eternal grace."

Has Roshi's spirit been released? Where has it gone?

We remained in Green Fountains for another week and a half. We spent quality time with Tojo and his wife, Victoria; played endlessly with three-year old Madijen; and enjoyed walks and talks with Kaleeva and her husband, Jeritom – pushing Eridru in a stroller. Our sadness at Roshi's passing was softened when Victoria and Kaleeva happily announced at dinner one night they were both pregnant.

Two more on the way. Our little family is growing. How blessed are we?

We reunited with dozens of friends, neighbors, and coworkers we'd met during our decade on the First Moon. We shared both fond memories and dreams for the future. Tari and I openly revealed the discovery of our true purpose.

I visited Tezhouse, meeting with Hagan, who had replaced Bogart as President of Tezhouse First Moon. We hooked up with Dr. Garvens, still the Director of the Tezhouse Advanced Engineering Labs, where my career began. The three of us went to lunch in a revamped 'Tomorrow Today Café.' When a young man shyly approached our table, I broke the ice. "Hi. Join us."

"Thank you, sir. It's such a great honor to meet you."

"Same here. But call me Adam."

"Mr. Adam, I started at Tezhouse only a month ago. As I begin my career, I'd like to learn – what were the keys to your long and successful career here?"

My thoughts turned to how I might best serve this young man. *How can I bless him?*

I borrowed something Vester counseled some twenty years ago. "Integrity. Integrity. Integrity. Nothing more important. Also, hone and apply your talents. When given an assignment, exceed expectations. And never forget – you accomplish nothing by yourself."

A new spark lit behind his eyes. "Thank you."

"Be always grateful for and give credit to all who help and guide you, especially family members. Two final notes. Find what can be an elusive balance between work and homelife. And always heed any calling to service."

The next day, as I was reflecting on my early days at Tezhouse, Randahl *swish'd*. His tone was somber, his face saddened. "Adam. You should know – Bogart overdosed. He is close to death."

I uttered, "It's been a while since I thought about that bastard."

"After he left Tezhouse his wife divorced him. He's luniless, deep in debt to the mob he gambles with. Yesterday, he was found on his floor at the Green Valleys Center for Addictive Diseases."

Bogart was a scourge throughout my life. But having no remorse felt wrong. "Randahl, I'm not saddened. Should I feel guilty?"

"I'm struggling with the same dilemma. I'm actually void of emotion – and that feels horribly wrong. It's inhumane to care so little for another, no matter what."

After debating briefly in my head, I headed over to the Center. A nurse led me to Bogart's room, an appalling place. His frail body was propped up in a tiny bed. A dim lamp exposed his sad, sallow countenance. A disgusting stench filled the room. I sat and gazed into his expressionless face.

Nobody should end this way.

All I could think was this man is evil. He had constantly invaded my life, adding mountains of stress. He tried to destroy my marriage. He caused my death. Perhaps it was natural to be relieved he was dying. Yet I felt like vomiting in shame. When Bogart slowly reached out his hand, I accepted it, something I'd never done before. I felt not sadness or grief – but pity for the sad creature before me. Something or somebody must have led him to become the way he was.

After a period of silence, he beckoned me closer. I placed my ear to his mouth to hear his whispered plea. "Forgive me, Adam."

It was the first time he'd ever called me Adam. Astonished, but surprisingly without hesitation, I responded, "Of course, I forgive you, Bogart. Just get better. They saved you. You've been granted a new lease on life. You can do it. I know you can. You just have to find a reason to continue."

Holding onto one's past restricts one's future.

I detected a slight smile on Bogart's face but knew not what it meant. I departed, happy I'd visited. I recalled Ambrosia once saying that holding onto the past restricts one's future – that harboring bitterness forces happiness to dock elsewhere. When I arrived in the parking lot, a pure white qilin pawed at the earth near my noli, smiled, then charged away.

Before departing the First Moon, Tari and I took our kids and grandkids to lunch at the Tavern on the Green and then on to the small lake where Tari and I had gotten engaged. We embraced as a family at our favorite spot, then headed to the giant Green Fountain where we removed our shoes and frolicked in the waters.

On our final day on the First Moon, we rented out TowneHall and invited former friends, neighbors, Tezhouse folks, and members of the Green Fountains Civic Association to a picnic. We did our best to replicate that magical day almost thirty years earlier. We danced, sang, ate, and drank well into the bittersweet evening. We knew we'd never see any of them again.

The following day, as *Chieftain* lifted off from Omphalos Park, we smiled through tears. We lifted off for the Second Moon, some twenty-six hours away. As the First Moon disappeared from our sight, Diazamel *swish'd*.

"Adam, Zalifhar has passed. Can you possibly make it to a 'Celebration of Zalifhar's Life,' two days from now?"

"Of course we'll be there." I didn't tell him we were serendipitously up in space and could see the red-orange Moon of Abundant Harvest in the distance.

The 'Celebration of Zalifhar's Life' took place at the same desert location where Diazamel had taken me a decade earlier. Tens of thousands gathered to honor the great man who had long served as their leader. We were led to the main tent where Lifason sat on a throne-like chair, Diazamel by his side. Their words held sadness – but also joy in reminiscing over fond and funny stories. Diazamel's booming laughs filled the air as he led everyone in celebrating his father's life rather than mourning his passing.

We moved outside, below a myriad of twinkling stars in a moonless sky, where once again a fifty-foot Zalifhar hologram appeared. The deceased leader smiled generously and waved. He spoke only two words: "Thank you."

Tari met Diazamel at dinner for the first time – and they instantly connected. He couldn't resist an opening joke. "Tariana,

I have one concern about you – your terrible judgment in men." His familiar roar filled the room as Tari got to experience his audacious laughter up close and in person. The remainder of the evening featured various tributes of farewell for the great ruler. And an Aboodinian feast finished off with ice cream. Tari loved the experience.

We said goodbye to Diazamel the next morning. As we parted, he accepted my whispered invitation, which Tari couldn't hear, to come to our Thirtieth Wedding Anniversary Celebration two weeks hence in Ceswania.

From Aboodin, we traveled through parts of the Second Moon where Tari and the children had never been. Smerland, Zermund, Thossia, Bhadran, and Salema. Then a visit filled with memories in Kamyabi. My contacts in each area knew me as Adam Novana, Tezhouse President. Now they rediscovered me simply as Adam. It was an amazing, whirlwind two weeks – with heartwarming receptions at each stopover. Each celebration featured the best local foods, wines, song, and dance.

Tari, Tojo, Kaleeva, and I had the best times of our lives. Now it was time to travel to Ceswania, where, to Tari's surprise, we would celebrate our thirtieth wedding anniversary a bit early.

CHAPTER 44

RENEWAL OF VOWS

"Tari, I have a surprise. You've long wanted to visit Ceswania. That's where we're headed – to celebrate our thirtieth anniversary, a year ahead of time." Actually, it was closer to a date we considered even more important– thirty years since the day we'd met at that Picnic.

"Oh Adam, I've long dreamed of experiencing Ceswania, its indigenous people, and all its lore. One more thing to check off my bucket list."

I feigned mild upset and chided, "Well, it's not gonna be about your bucket list, honey. I'm talking about renewing our vows."

My bride beamed, wearing an impish smile ear to ear. "Hmmm. Oh, well. I guess I'll remarry you there – if you can find a way to get lucky again."

Marriage is about service – each spouse dedicated to the needs of the other. Our marriage had not been perfect. None can be. But we'd weathered every storm and arrived at this port deeper in love than ever. It was now time to recommit to our partnership, as we prepared for a monumental next step on our journey.

Our happiness at this stage did not 'just happen.' It was founded in unconditional love. It took listening, humility, mutual respect, forgiveness, and trusting each other. It definitely demanded a good sense of humor. It was wanting to spend the rest of our days sharing one umbrella to ward off any tempests.

We often referred to our marriage as a 'fairy tale.' This was made possible by marrying the right partner, which I certainly did. But it also called for me to be the right partner for Tari, which over the rocky roads of time, I became. When blessed with a happy marriage, it's the proper thing to treasure and celebrate. In Ceswania, we would demonstrate and share the deepest meaning of our love with those most important in our lives.

Tari and I had failed to celebrate our twenty-fifth anniversary. We were denied that by a 'minor' problem – I was in a coma. Four years later, with me fully recovered and our love affair on a new course, it was time to rededicate our union in the presence of our growing family and best friends. We knew we wouldn't be in Taoland when the actual anniversary date rolled around.

We headed off to Ceswania to take a panoramic survey of our life and rhapsodize three decades as husband and wife, soulmates, best friends, lovers, parents, and now grandparents. Upon arrival in this fascinating land we were met by Jen-Shing, a quiet, charming, unassuming, white-bearded man who Randahl knew well. As our host, he provided the children with a lovely three-bedroom chalet set in ten acres of kaleidoscopic summer gardens, on a bright red lake at the foothills of yellow-orange mountains.

Jen-Shing announced, "We'll celebrate the renewal of your vows here tomorrow."

We left the kids, their mates, and our grandkids there, and Jen-Shing led us to the Honeymoon Cottage, a half mile away. We found it smothered in roses, inside and out. Red petals blanketed the carpets and our bed coverings. Tari teared up. "Oh my. Thank you, Jen-Shing. This couldn't be more splendid and romantic."

We sat apart, writing our vows, keeping our words from each other until the ceremony. We fell asleep in each other's arms, as we had done 10,000 times before. As we prepared to close the arc of thirty years of marriage, I prayed for 10,000 more such moments ahead.

We are so blessed.

Jen-Shing arranged nearby accommodations for the few guests we'd invited to our ceremony – Abraham, Randahl and Lorelai, Ambrosia, Diazamel, and Illeana. Turns out Jen-Shing also invited two dozen locals to provide music, food, wines, games, and merriment. Regional dances, which Tari always delighted in learning, were to be part of the venue.

When we arrived in the gardens the following morning we discovered red hearts of assorted sizes suspended in the air by some local magic. Each heart would swell and burst into hundreds of tiny petals before floating away in the breeze. A local florist was putting finishing touches on a massive bouquet of thirty long-stem roses for Tari to carry. Several workers were preparing individual wrist-bracelets and boutonnieres, also red roses, for the wedding party: Tari and myself, Abraham as my 'Best Man,' Lorelai as the 'Maid of Honor,' and for Madijen, our flower girl.

"Tari. Look."

Our mouths dropped when Ambrosia and Illeana entered. Clearly, they had conspired. Each wore sparkling neck-to-toe gowns, with form fitting tops, flowing gracefully at the bottoms. Ambrosia's outfit was orange-and-white vertically striped at the top, bright red at the bottom, Illeana's was the reverse. To call their appearances stupendous would not do justice.

"You both look beautiful," Tari exclaimed.

Abraham was handsomely bedecked in a white tux. I could only imagine how he'd put it on. Lorelai wore a white-flowered ballroom gown. Madijen and Eridru entered the scene – our granddaughter prepared to spread red petals from a small basket, our grandson in a brilliantly decorated stroller.

Randahl and Diazamel approached, also in white tuxes. "Is this a wedding or a coronation?" roared Diazamel, loudly. "Am I finally to be dubbed, 'Your Majesty?'"

I returned the banter. "Wait your turn. You'll never let that go, will you?"

"Nope. Not a chance."

Local handmaidens led Tari and me separately over tiny bridges that rose gently above a trickling red stream – she to the bride's bungalow, and me to the groom's. They dressed us in golden regalia – resembling the wedding outfits worn by ancient Ceswanian settlers. Local musicians played frolicsome wedding songs on handcrafted wooden instruments when we returned to center stage, where we first discovered each other's attire.

I gasped as I beheld my bride. "You are beautiful beyond words, my Tariana."

"And you are my handsome 'prince charming,' Adam Novana."

Tari's natural beauty – she wore little makeup – was enhanced by a spectacular wedding dress, veil, and tiara – each golden and sprinkled with twinkling bits of yellows, oranges, and reds. The flowers throughout the gardens bowed and released an abundance of fragrances when she approached. I wore matching colors, but I faded into the scene.

Ambrosia initiated the ceremonies. "We are gathered to celebrate the thirtieth anniversary of the day Tariana and Adam wed. Today, we applaud the journey of two who have become one in every sense of that word. We salute all they have accomplished during their years, most notably their amazing family. On this occasion, they will renew their marriage vows – this time in accord with ancient Ceswanian traditions."

Illeana, sharing duties with Ambrosia, led us to the first of five tall marble stones, each standing in one of five small pagodas that encircled the gardens. "The wedding couple have written vows to each other, in accord with the traditional five elements and five seasons of Ceswania. Ambrosia and I will alternate in introducing each of the elements and seasons. Our couple will exchange vows in harmony with these traditions. Now we begin, with the first of the elements."

She then spoke words illuminated on the first bright green stone. "Wood symbolizes springtime, the time of new beginnings, the time for new growth. Wood can be flexed and extended. Spring is a time for childhood, green fields, first dreams, adventure, and a belief you can wander forever." Her words brought the nature around us to life as several woody vines stretched and wrapped green leaves around the pillars holding the first of the stones.

We now began to reveal our vows to each other. "Tari, I promise you the gift of my vision, as together we step into yet another future soon to begin. I promise to be always hopeful and flexible, to dream new dreams with you, just as new tree branches and shrubs awaken in springtime."

Tari followed. "Adam, I promise to share your vision, your hopes, and dreams – and encourage new growth in our marriage. I vow to stand by you in all things, as we create new boughs together."

A variety of large, showy, cup-shaped flowers, heralds of spring, swayed in a slight breeze, as did brilliant clumps of spoon-shaped flowers. Illeana spoke. "These buds emerging from the greens represent romantic devotion, making them a perfect selection for this milestone. They symbolize transformation."

Ambrosia led us to the second stone some thirty feet or so around the circle. It was a bright red stone representing the element of fire and the season of early summer. "Fire is the spark, the warmth, and the joy of a relationship. Early summer is a time of long hot days and bright starry nights. A time for seedlings to burst into young fruit. A time for travel and exploration. It's when one believes he/she can change the world by following one's dreams."

Her words blazed to life on the stone as flames leapt to several hanging lanterns. Cloudseeker, her mane and tail dyed red, and a ring of red roses around her neck, joined our group.

"Tari, I promise you the fire of my heart, the warmth of my soul. I vow to be always selfless in my love for you. I promise intimacy, tenderness, and laughter."

"Adam, I promise to love you without conditions. I vow to listen to your heart, to be compassionate, to manifest our love boldly for all to witness."

Dozens of bright, towering, large, cheerful flowers opened, filling the space. Ambrosia spoke. "These giant blossoms symbolize loyalty, adoration, and faithfulness. They call out, 'I believe in you.'"

We continued another thirty feet around the circle to the yellow marble stone marking the element of earth and the season of late summer. Illeana began, "Earth is the fullness – the ripened fruit of a relationship. Late summer is a time to refocus as crops grow and harvest approaches. It's a time to begin a transition to a slower, more introspective period in a marriage." On cue, fruits of multiple colors blossomed and magically ripened instantaneously on several trees around us. Several of our group reached up and enjoyed the juicy creations.

"Tari, I promise to love you abundantly, to taste your essence as a sweet, ripened fruit, as we travel to wherever the wind next carries us."

"Adam, I promise to treasure the fruits of our union, to nurture our love to a deeper level, and to always provide safe haven." Fully matured herbs popped up everywhere, along with flat multi-colored mounded flowers, shaped like quills.

Our fourth stop was at the silver marble stone representing the element of metal and the season of autumn. Ambrosia smiled warmly as she began. "We have arrived at the spot where our couple will solidify their bonds with rings made of metal, the element of quality, structure, worth, and spirituality in marriage. Metal can be melted and changed in form. Autumn is a time to reassess and release old beliefs as the leaves fall to the ground. It's a time to let go, to discover new passions, and to become aware of a more specific purpose."

"Tari, I promise to release the past as we await the future. I will always value our relationship more than the greatest of precious metals. I promise to be always open, and to breathe new life into our marriage."

As I spoke the words to her, I placed a silver ring on her finger; then a second ring emerged magically on my own. The metals gleamed brilliantly as we held up our hands in the light of the Tao. Tari choked back a tear. "Adam, I promise to value you above all others, to honor you, to recognize your worth, and to constantly remind you of the good within you. I promise renewed energy, renewed vitality, renewed strength – as we re-wed and as one honor our true purpose."

Flowers and bushes of pure white blossomed all about. Fragrant petals filled the air.

There remained one final stone on the Circle of Wedded Life – a stone of deep blue marble. Illeana spoke when we arrived. "This stone symbolizes the element of water and the season of winter, which always promises yet another spring to come – in arcs of life that repeat but never replicate." She poured us cups of crystal-clear water from a vessel that magically appeared. We drank.

She smiled and continued, "When winter arrives, married couples ask, 'Are we happy? Have we succeeded in life?' Winter is when the answers are provided, when the cold snow melts to provide fresh waters as a needed wake-up call. Water is the unseen container holding the embryo of future growth. In the case of Tariana and Adam, this coming winter will be a time for them to discover what they are called to do with the rest of their lives."

"Tari, I promise you my faith in the unforeseen future. I vow to journey with you to new places with new awareness – in service to others. I will love you forever."

"Adam, I promise to have faith in you and in myself. I vow to ever remain open to change. And to selflessly serve others with you. I promise to allow our union to assume new forms. I too will love you forever."

Tall trumpet-shaped flowers atop thick green stems burst into bloom. Triumphant music erupted as Illeana announced, "These symbolize purity and represent your renewed marriage."

We embraced. I held Tari close in the ecstasy of the moment.

Ambrosia then stepped in to conclude the ceremony. "I now pronounce you wife and husband – all over again."

Our surroundings now burst with excitement. White doves, tiny yellow hummingbirds, painted flying insects, rabbits, squirrels, and deer scurried about joyfully. Several alit happily on Cloudseeker's back. A beautiful swan-like bird appeared on one of the tiny bridges. A qilin at the garden's edge reared as it called out, "Congratulations."

Tari whispered, to me alone, "Thank you, Adam – for being you. You make my life complete. I am blessed to be your forever bride – blessed from all the moons of the Universe and back."

We kissed. Our friends and family applauded. Diazamel, always the loudest, ended the formalities, announcing, "Fasten your seat belts. It's party time."

We headed to a beautiful, large pagoda where musicians began playing. I took the mic and invited everyone onto the stone patio. "Come join us in dance – a shortcut to happiness."

Local villagers launched the 'shortcut,' swaying to the sounds and frolicking all about. They were joined in appalling attempts to imitate by Diazamel and Abraham. Soon everyone was dancing, my friends and family hysterically demonstrating newly made-up steps to the Ceswanians, who gleefully followed suit. Tojo and Kaleeva danced with their mates. Little Madijen wiggled to the music. Eridru smiled ear to ear in his stroller. The local children sang happy folk songs. Green, red, yellow, silver, and blue petals showered us from a splendid canopy of foliage.

"Tari, it doesn't get much more wonderful than this."

"I agree. Can't possibly get better."

Ambrosia filled and passed silver chalices brimming with bright, sparkling red wines. Illeana offered jeweled goblets, heaped with berries. The locals served other drinks and delish finger foods. The frivolity lasted until Taoset. Then, as the light dimmed, we slipped away in a chariot flown by two beautiful white-winged qilins who sped us into the night to the privacy of the Honeymoon Cottage.

We awoke in each other's arms and enjoyed coffee on a lovely patio. "Tari, what else can I say except yesterday was spectacular, start to finish."

"It was one of countless memories we will treasure and leave behind for our family and friends."

Our joy was tempered by utter anguish about what was to come next. It was time to say a final farewell to those we cherished the most. Tari and I had dreaded the arrival of this moment. How could we tell our children?

CHAPTER 45

FINAL FAREWELLS

Saying goodbye to those we never want to let go of is a difficult task, especially when it is likely to be a final farewell. Tari and I grappled over how to explain to those we love why we would create a never-ending heartache. We left the Honeymoon Cottage and arrived at the gardens where our family and friends were enjoying a lovely buffet breakfast, set among bundles of flowers gathered after yesterday's celebration.

After some frivolity and a few bad jokes, thanks to Diazamel, we excused ourselves. "There's something we want to share privately with our children. We'll be back shortly."

Our guests continued enjoying the morning, with Madijen and Eridru entertaining, as we headed with our children to their chalet. We gathered in a tight circle holding hands in the living room. The looks on our kids' faces signaled confusion and concern. I spoke as tears welled. "Dear Tojo and Kaleeva, today is the hardest day in your mother's and my life."

"What's wrong?"

I squeezed Tari's hand. "We'll be leaving Taoland soon. We'll no longer be by your sides. We'll no longer cuddle with our grandchildren. We've been called elsewhere."

Tari continued sharing with our wide-eyed kids. "We pray you'll someday come to understand. We've accepted a calling to a higher purpose that will take us away from Taoland. We know it's the right thing to do, even though it means letting go of you, Madijen, Eridru, and those yet to come. We ask for your blessings."

There was a long silence, none of us knowing what to say next. Then our handsome Tojo, soon to turn twenty-eight, spoke, stunning us. "I'd like to make this slightly less painful." He put an arm around Kaleeva, who looked at him and nodded. "Kaleeva and I have known in our hearts you might be leaving. Your hugs, tears, and the looks in your eyes lately have more than suggested this was coming."

Kaleeva continued with tenderness, "The words in your vows yesterday more than hinted something was about to change. We don't know what or why. But we do know every ending is a new beginning. Wherever you will now travel, we know you will serve selflessly. While our hearts are broken, please know you have our full blessings."

Over the next hour, as the others must have wondered what was going on, we told Tojo and Kaleeva of our plans, and that there was a possibility we'd never be together again. Then Kaleeva said, "You are the best parents any could ever wish for. You are gifted – and meant to make a positive difference in the Universe. We love you unconditionally. You will never be absent from our hearts."

As we shared more about the why, when, and where – our children continued to voice their support. Tojo, head bowed, spoke. "Our love for each other will endure forever."

I was shaking. "Not one of us will ever get over the loss to come. But we must find comfort in the fond memories we share."

We left the living room and strolled into the gardens around the chalet. Tojo broke the silence. "Our baby, a boy, is due in five months. We'll name him Charjak. We'll proudly and happily share with him and Madijen stories of and lessons from their grandparents."

Kaleeva continued, "Another surprise. We're having twin boys. We're naming them Riwes and Bendeen. We can hardly wait to tell them about the wonderful role models you are."

Tari teared up. "Oh my. Now my heart aches even more."

I shrieked, "How wonderful!"

After hugs, we held hands and again stood in a circle. Tari spoke. "My children, please share fond recollections of us with your children. And let those memories buoy each of us across lonely waters. Let us each find joy in the dances of the tomorrows."

The flowers all around us bowed silently as Tojo spoke again. "We will, Mom. We know your decision is made selflessly. We know your leaving will break your own hearts even more than our own."

As we shared a family hug, Tari spoke yet again. "Children, the two most important days in your life are the day you are born and the day you find out why. You father and I have finally made this discovery. We are meant to reach out to others far more in need of rescue than any here in Taoland. We are blessed that you support us, however reluctantly, in what we have decided."

We wiped our tears and headed back to our guests. "There are a few pieces of dried burnt toast left," Diazamel roared. Then his mood turned sullener. "I've gotta go now. Walk with me, Adam."

Somehow Diazamel knew. He and I sauntered through the gardens, heads hung low, to where his nolicraft rested. On the way I shared our specific plans and our reasons. He gave me a bear hug and thanked me for being in his life. He boarded and departed – void of the generous smile and roaring laughter I would sorely miss.

Then when Tari took Lorelai aside, I spoke with Randahl and shared our plans. "You've been a wonderful friend, Randahl. But we will now part, likely never to see one another again. Please take over for me in Aboodin."

"Adam, you've made an indelible mark across Tao's three moons. I know you'll touch countless others in the mission you've now accepted."

We gathered Ambrosia and Illeana to share our plans. They smiled knowingly. "We are so happy for you."

Finally, it was time for me to say farewell to Abraham. "I would not be standing here today, finally understanding my purpose, were it not for you, my dearest of friends. Without you calling me back when I headed into the heavens, I'd not be alive to venture forth."

"Adam, you will leave a huge hole in my heart, one that can never be filled. I love you. I will miss you greatly." We embraced.

It was time for us to depart the Moon of Abundant Harvest for the final time. We thanked Jen-Shing for his hospitality. Illeana boarded the *Chieftain* to return home with us. Tojo, Kaleeva, and their kids then entered. We would be spending one more week together before our final separation.

With tearful eyes, we waved to those remaining in the gardens and headed to the silver moon.

CHAPTER 46

A NEW BEGINNING

I arrived in Taoland at the age of twenty to restart my adult life. I was departing as a mature fifty-year-old. I'd arrived at this magic place never having been loved nor loving another. As I prepared to depart, I reflected on the boundless love in my life today. I'd arrived purposeless, clueless as to who I was or what I wanted. Now, I was departing on a mission of servitude, having discovered my strength rested not in how much I could lift but in how many I might lift.

I looked back over the years with gratitude. With Tari by my side and blessed by my teachers, I had traversed dark tunnels, conquered devils, and arrived at the light. Saddened to be leaving loved ones behind, I was filled with abundant expectancy for what lay ahead.

We gathered with our family on the patio for a final goodbye. Tao was setting in that 'V' shape formed by the two majestic mountain peaks – an image forever etched into our memories. Illeana had prepared a parting meal, complete with a birthday cake with a '50' on top, to celebrate Tari's fiftieth of six weeks ago, and mine just yesterday. I always joked that Tari had 'robbed the cradle.'

Tojo and Kaleeva led us in singing a boisterous 'Happy Birthday.' Tari and I successfully blew out all fifty candles. The children presented us with a gift we'd treasure for the rest of our lives – a framed family photo taken when we renewed our vows in Ceswania a week earlier. Illeana handed us a scroll, tied with a silver bow. "From Komourin," she announced.

Tojo wrapped his strong arms around us. "Mom and Dad, it hurts so bad. But we'll always find solace in wonderful memories and our indestructible family love."

Kaleeva joined the hug. "There are no words to describe my heartache. And no words to thank you for all you've taught us, especially about unconditional love, all you've given us, and all you will forever mean to us."

I too struggled to come up with words that I still needed to say as we parted. "For much of my life, I was too focused on a false purpose. With help mostly from your mother, I've finally discovered who I am, what I really want, why I was born. I've found my purpose – to serve others in need. I just wish our calling did not take us far away from you."

Kaleeva spoke again, through tears. "Mom and Dad, I want you to remember just one thing in the years ahead – you are leaving behind the proudest daughter in all of the Universe."

"And the proudest son," added Tojo.

We joined in a group hug. "Thank you, my dear children. Know we will remain with you in spirit forever. Find us always in the Taorises and Taosets. Discover our smiles in the soft rains, warm gentle breezes, and calming lake waters. Guide our grandchildren to aim high and speak out when change is needed. Teach them to dream dreams that never were – and then go make them happen."

Tari continued, "Feel our touches in the flower petals, in the leaves on the trees, in the soft sands, and on the snowflakes falling from the skies. Smell us in the evening breezes and fresh cut grasses. Listen to us in the music of the songbirds and insects."

Tao dipped to the horizon, and the skies began darkening to a deep cobalt blue. The velvet green and reddish-orange moons were full in the heavens, one atop each of our beloved two snowy peaks. A tiny intense white light made its initial appearance in the center of the moons – growing larger and more brilliant with each passing moment. The glow of the Fifth Dimension came above us. *Wanderer* slowly descended and hovered at the edge of the gardens atop a newly fallen snow. Our next adventure was upon us. We left the patio. Our children followed, carrying our grandchildren. Illeana was close behind.

Our bodies shook as we headed to the hovering cloud. Magically, we did not sink as we ambled across the foot-deep snow. Tari paused, turned to our children, and raised her hands to the sky. "Grief, which will soften, is the price of love. Grief is a passage, not a place to stay. We must never allow grief to define us; instead, we must permit grief to give way to a future filled with peace and joy."

When we arrived below the hovering *Wanderer*, Malaika appeared, frocked in a furry white jacket, opened to reveal a silver evening gown. She had not changed in all these years, aside from her beauty growing more astonishing. Heavenly music flowed from the otherwise silent, vibrating cloud.

Three silver pegacorns entered the snow-filled gardens from the left. Their long, spiraling horns glistened in *Wanderer's* pulsating light. Each bore soft cascading locks of alabaster hair above upright ears. Their long, flowing white tails fluttered above the ground as they trotted gracefully. Puffs of stringy hair partially hid brilliantly polished silver hoofs at the bottoms of their legs.

Illeana took our hands into her own. "These are my parting gifts. They are *Faith, Hope*, and *Love*. They will travel with you, bear young, and assist you in your next adventure." The three magnificent winged steeds approached, each in turn pausing, smiling, and speaking their names.

"I am *Faith*. I will provide light for you where others see darkness."

"I am *Hope*. I will help you conquer moments of fear, doubts, and anxiety. I will help you find peace amidst any chaos."

"I am *Love*. I will provide you with patience, humility, and kindness – to share with all others."

Malaika, floating above at the entrance to the Fifth Dimension, welcomed the pegacorns as they entered the cloud. Basking in *Wanderer's* pulsating light, she then beckoned to us. Tari and I rose, holding hands. Malaika embraced us before passing inside with the pegacorns – leaving us momentarily alone. Suddenly, Adriella appeared at the entrance, out of the view of those below. "Welcome, Adam. Welcome, Tariana," she whispered.

When Tari turned toward her voice I gazed in stunned confusion. "Did you hear her?"

Tari looked past me, her mouth widened in amazement. "Yes. And I see her. Who is she?"

"She is Adriella." My tiny helper had left her bubble and was now a full-size being, bathed in her own warm, glowing light. Her eyes shined like giant orbs, and she held out her thin arms to us. Her soothing presence assured us we'd made the right choice. She had been there for me through all the hardest moments in my life. And now Tari, with a look of pure bliss upon her face, hugged her. Adriella disappeared inside. Tari would now share my bond with her as well.

We looked down and watched as other items magically entered the cloud – nolis of several varieties, drones, animals strange to us before arriving in Taoland, pallets of valithion, plants, produce, and seeds for flowers, fruits, and vegetables we'd discovered over our years in this magical place.

We turned to those we were leaving behind, waving and blowing kisses – our final goodbyes. Then we entered *Wanderer* and floated, following Malaika to the center, where we perched on a cloud bench in front of the control panel hologram. Adriella stood alongside, like an angel.

Malaika smiled. "Adam, you may now direct *Wanderer*."

My voice quivered as I issued my command.

"Destination Novana."

It was strange to be departing the gorgeous and fantastical

Taoland – to return to a place most would be loath to call home, a land where human purpose was non-existent. I was willingly leaving a magical space flush with verdant fields of flowers, deep luscious forests filled with magical creatures, countless miles of healthy farmlands, Taorises to start every day, spectacular Taosets over sparkling waters at the close of the day, endless adventures, qilins and pegacorns, and for the most part cheerful, helpful, virtuous peoples from all over the Universe.

I was departing a land where I learned that while we are all different we are all the same. I was heading instead into a vast, empty, desolate, monochromatic abyss absent of color and beauty – where all humans were made to be nearly identical.

I had come to understand that neither Taoland nor Novana was 'home.' Because I learned in my years here that home is not the brick and mortar of any building, but that home is found within. Home is who we are, not where we reside. Home is wherever we dream dreams that never were and then make them happen. Home is about the people we love, past and in the future, the stories and memories we create, and the discovery of our true purpose – the service we provide selflessly to others.

We lifted into the heavens.

Those below faded to faceless figures like those I'd seen when I died on that operating table. When Malaika offered a gilded cup, I drank, as I had thirty years earlier, once again finding the deep-red elixir beyond delightful. When Tari did likewise the cup released a luscious aroma.

As *Wanderer* ascended slowly, the three moons, green, reddish-orange, and silver, formed a perfect triangle before vanishing against the brilliance of the golden Tao.

The skies exploded in a fireworks of spiraling colors.

Then everything went dark.

The End

Stay tuned!

Adam in Taoland is the first book in the trilogy *Dreaming Dreams.*

Book II, *Homeland Rescued,* is the story of Adam and Tariana's return to Novana to liberate the people from servitude to the AI State and the humanoid Plakerols who deny them any purpose. Our heroes bring with them some of the magic of Taoland and discover a hidden valley inhabited by millions of humans who have already escaped from Plakerol rule.

Adam, with Tari by his side, leads a bloodless 20 year revolution with the people throughout the land, rejecting dependence on the robots and securing individual liberties instead.

Book III, *Never Forgotten* – a decade long struggle with Adam as Caregiver to Tariana – who struggles with the scourges and indignities of Alzheimer's Disease. They are supported by angels, some human, some spiritual beings, who enter the scenes when most needed and least expected – and who bring joy to drive away despair. Adam leads a support group of two dozen other spouses who find themselves in the similar situations.

Unlike other books that stress depressing tales and hopelessness involved with Alzheimers Disease, *Never Forgotten* is uplifting and joyful – focusing on endearing love and the end of mortal life as the beginning of eternal life.

ABOUT THE AUTHOR

Jack Tymann shares in *Adam in Taoland* lessons learned through a much-blessed life-long adventure in the private sector, politics, marriage and family life.

Jack retired from the Westinghouse Electric Corporation as President/CEO of Westinghouse International where he led business development and government relations and $2B in annual revenues – in 75 countries.

He served under President Clinton and President Mubarak of Egypt as co-chair of the Presidents' Council for the Middle East North Africa – seeking peace through business collaborations.

In politics, Jack served as Senior Advisor and Consigliere in the U.S. House of Representatives – writing legislation and authoring speeches delivered on Capitol Hill.

His writing journey has included publications throughout his school years, the private and public sectors, and in community/church involvement. He's written countless proposals, presentations, and executive summaries. He's served as a talk show guest and lecturer – sharing on a belief a better world is possible if we focus not on our differences but on common goals that can unite.

Jack received his BSEE from Manhattan College, completed the Harvard Business School Advanced Management Program, and advanced studies at INSEAD in Paris and at the Brookings Institute.

Jack and his wife Lucille reside in Naples, Florida. They are most proud or their four children and twelve grandchildren.

Ayesha Abdul Ghaffar

Ayesha was born and raised in small town USA and has since traveled the world and lived in several countries in the Middle East and South Asia. She brings unique awareness of cultural differences and ubiquitous principles that unite the peoples of the world. She currently resides in Karachi Pakistan.

When she's not engaged in her passions of reading, writing, and editing – Ayesha can be found creating art, enjoying nature, and spending time with her two precious cats.

Ayesha is dedicated to making a positive difference in the lives of those most in need. Inspired by her personal life experiences, Ayesha strives to help authors bring their stories, scenes, and characters to life – and has done so brilliantly throughout the pages of *Adam in Taoland*.

Made in the USA
Columbia, SC
10 January 2023